FLAME TREADER

CRYSTAL BOUND BOOK THREE

DJ BOWMAN-SMITH

For Paul

CHAPTER ONE

From up here, on a clear turn, they said you could see forever and when she was a child, she had believed it. Maturity dispelled the myths of youth, now she knew the world stretched far beyond this horizon and a view of forever was only available to Mother God.

Here at the top, less than a stride in breadth, the rock had been smoothed by the wind and shone in the sunshine. Junas breathed deeply, turning a full circle as she did so, to take in the beautiful panorama of villages, forest and rivers and many other needles of rock, though none so high as this. She fixed her eyes on the farthest point, where she would have to go if she passed the trials, and wondered if the maps she had spent her whole life learning were correct.

Stone-fall brought her from her reverie and she stepped to the edge of the pinnacle and looked down. Clinging to the rock, her little face tight with concentration, was Arla. Junas knelt, and catching her skinny arm, hauled her over the edge. 'It's too high for you, little sister, you shouldn't have followed,' she said, yet it was hard to be cross with her on this morning.

'I'm alright. I did as you showed me and brushed my hands with chalkstone before the climb. Anyway, Mother says you could climb to the sky when you were eight and I am nine.'

Junas sat down and pulled her onto her lap, holding her close, and they watched an eagle making loops in the warm air pockets.

'Mother says if you pass the trials, I will be grown up by the time you return.'

Junas kissed the top of her head. Nothing she could say would reassure her and she was torn between the wish to succeed and love for her sister. Leaving her behind would be the hardest part.

Below, a root-horn sounded, the long deep note carrying across the valley, calling all those who would try to pass the tests. It was time to go. Junas got up, her mind already sifting through information she might need. Arla was crying now, although she was trying not to. Junas lifted her and looked into her face. 'Be brave,' she said, wiping the tears from her dusty cheeks. 'If you're not, then how can I be? And who will look after the goats while I'm gone? I want to see a nice healthy herd when I get back, they're yours to care for now.'

Arla hugged her neck; she was looking forward to the responsibility, as her sister knew.

'Are you tired, shall I carry you down?'

Arla nodded, her limbs ached, and it had been much higher than it looked – climbing down was always trickier than going up. Junas swung her onto her back where she clung, wrapping arms and legs around her with a good strong grip. Junas remembered when she had first carried her up the Sky-Pinnacle; she had been so little then. From a pouch at her waist, Junas took a pinch of chalk dust and after rubbing her hands with it, carefully lowered herself over the edge. She took the easy way down because the root-horn was calling and she needed to be quick; nevertheless, it was nearly midturn when she set her little sister back on the ground.

At the homestead, Junas quickly washed and dressed in the clothes her mother had laid out then joined her waiting family: four older brothers, her parents and Arla. Each trying their best to cope with the mix of emotions they felt; pride that she might succeed, sorrow that if she did she would be gone for many years, and anticipation of wealth to come. They were poor, and although they tried not to think about this part of the proceedings, nonetheless it would make a great difference to all their lives.

For them the walk was short. The trial tent was in their village because they had the Sky-Pinnacle. Other families stood about, Junas counted six; four of the girls she knew, and two were strangers.

The root-horn, which had been sounding so long no one noticed anymore, of a sudden, stopped. The waiting group were aware of their noise in the silence, the weeping of a mother, the tapping of a foot, a murmured prayer.

Junas stood aside. As a family they had already made their goodbyes, now she needed to concentrate, keep her mind clear, and not think about parting.

The trial tent was long, some hundred paces, and had been erected with such stealth in the night everyone was shocked to find it in the morning. It had been here three turns and although no ordinary shoken had been inside, it was busy with the comings and goings of Elders from the seventeen villages and even, there were rumours, some of the Faar. Children caught listening at the tent walls were none the wiser; the sacred language they spoke unintelligible.

When the skins across the opening parted, all looked there. One by one those who would take the trials entered as their name was called from within. Junas was the last. She

3

did not look back, knowing if she did the sight of her family, and especially Arla, would break her heart.

She stepped into the darkness.

Nothing would be the same after this.

The skin was re-tied across the opening and after the brightness of the summer turn, it was black inside until lamps were lit. They were in a cramped, sectioned off space. They stood shoulder to shoulder. First, there were words from one of the Elders, about how well they had done and prayers, then each went to a separate space, this filled with the maps they must sort.

Junas said a quick prayer to Mother God then gathered them into a pile and sat on the ground. She studied them carefully. Some were old, inked parchment, the colours browned from age; others were little more than a few sketches of settlements burnt onto boiled leather; one was a vast rolled scroll of painted silk. There were many, it took time. Methodically she began to lay them on the floor in groups; she had always a clear picture in her mind of the known world and found the task easy. Only the painted silk was a problem and she rolled it out again, and then smiled. It was a fake, little more than a piece of artwork – beautiful, but not a map of anywhere real. She placed all the maps on the ground, as far as space would allow, making one world. Two were less than accurate and she practised how she would explain.

One of the girls she did not recognise came in. 'Can you do it?' she asked.

Junas looked up from where she knelt. They were not supposed to speak.

'Swap. You go to my space and I'm staying here,' said the girl.

Junas stood up, enraged this stranger could even think

about cheating. The girl drew a knife, long and pointed, from where she had hidden it in her boot.

'Swap with me and I will win, refuse and you will win, and as you set off for the journey, know this – I will find your sister Arla, and kill her.'

Compliance had never been one of her traits. Far from being afraid of the other girl Junas was incensed that here, on such a turn, someone should threaten her, and the thought of this creature winning by unfair means filled her with anger. Well used to fighting with her brothers, she threw herself at the girl with a scream, knocking the knife from her hand with a well-aimed kick, and wrestling her to the ground where she punched her repeatedly in the face. The noise brought the Elders and in a moment, they were parted. The girl was smiling broadly even as she wiped the blood from a split lip. 'This one has the fire mother,' she said.

Junas, confused, was eager to tell her part. One of the Elders stepped forward.

'This is my daughter; she set you a test. You have passed. Come, Junas Pathfinder,' she said, leading her away. Others who had gathered followed. Junas looked back to where she had been sorting the maps. The Elder laughed. 'We already know you can navigate, or else why would any of you be here? What we needed to test was your fighting spirit.'

They stepped out of the tent and Junas was surprised to see it had grown dark. From the outside, the lit tent showed the shadows of those within.

'Yes,' said the Elder, 'they still believe they take the trials and will do so until morning. By that time you will be on your way.'

'Why make them carry on?'

'It will make the losing easier to bear if they feel they were tested on their knowledge and found wanting.'

'You have not tested my knowledge.'

'No. We already know what you can do.'

'Then the trials are not real?' Junas was filled with a sense of unfairness and pity for the others, who were being tricked, it seemed.

'Let's just say, they are a formality.'

Junas stopped. They all stopped and looked at her. 'This isn't right. It's not how it's meant to be,' she said.

The old woman smiled and frowned at the same time. 'Isn't it? Don't you believe you should be the one to make the journey? Don't you believe you are the best? Isn't this what you have thought about your whole life since you were a small child? Didn't you climb the Sky-Pinnacle at dawn and pray to Mother God for the safekeeping of your family while you were gone?'

Junas hung her head, the old woman lifted her chin with a gnarled hand so their eyes met. 'In your heart, you have always known it would be you.'

'Yes,' said Junas.

CHAPTER TWO

Orrld forced his webbed feet into the riding boots with a sigh and Pannitouli shook her head at the absurdity of it.

'Do they hurt?' she asked.

'No, not really, they just feel very odd, but then so does riding a horse.' He stood up, straightening his robes, and she came over and put her cool fingertips on the scar on his cheekbone where they had cut out the seeing metal. He could feel, even in her light touch, her remorse for hurting him, and he wrapped his arms about her and held her close, pressing healing and love into her one last time before they parted. There was too much to say, so they said nothing and went down the creaking stairs from the king's rooms to join the others in the hall. Outside on the cobbles, most of the Pack and an honour guard of Hush waited.

Sho came out of the dining room supported on the king's arm. Even after several turns of rest and food, she was frail. Orrld worried she was too ill for travel, but the king's need to be at Lak-Mur for the birth, or soon after, of his son was great. He stepped forward and placed a gentle hand on the back of her neck; unlike before, she did not move away or reject him, but accepted his healing with quiet grace, knowing he was her only chance of making a full recovery. Sho was difficult to heal. Soon, she nodded her thanks and moved away, and he could feel, if not hate, then certainly dislike, and understood she would never be able to forgive him for putting the king in danger. It would always be between them, a river that could never be bridged.

Outside Sten lifted her onto her horse. Normally she rode without any tack, but this turn the black horse, Swift, had saddle and bridle. Sten settled her feet in the stirrups, a look of concern on his face. Sho ignored him and pulled the hood of her cloak over her head.

Also hooded, in the manner of a novice Hush, was the Strick child, Math. He was, as the king had predicted, already as tall as a man, although less than a year old, that part of him which was Sturgar speeding his development beyond that of a shoken. He would not speak for some time yet was able to understand everything said to him, and Orrld, who had become his guardian, loved him like a son.

Math came over as soon as Orrld stepped outside and put his head on Orrld's shoulder. Orrld spoke to him in Ekressian, which he seemed to understand as much as any language. 'Don't forget to hide your tail away,' he said.

The Strick boy coiled his tail around his waist and tucked the tip into his belt lest it should escape, and pulled the hood well over his face to conceal his eyes, which were as the Sturgar: white with a single black elongated pupil. His were extraordinary as they had a fine red line demarking the black.

Reem came with a dark horse, the same as the Hush rode and Math mounted nimbly and took up the reins in gentle hands and Reem, checking the girth, nodded approval. He was teaching Math to ride horses and handle birds of prey.

The Strick boy had a surprising affinity with animals and he had grown fond of the boy, although he did not know what they would make of him at Lak-Mur.

Orrld mounted next, awkward as ever, making Reem smile, his scarred face more grotesque in mirth. 'You'll be a better rider by the time we return,' he said.

Orrld grimaced good-naturedly, patted the old warhorse Coup, took a handful of his mane and said a silent prayer to Ath not to let him fall, at least until they were clear of the city.

Ahead, the king swung into the saddle of the red mare he always rode, and the Pack and the honour guard of Hush fell into formation around him as they set off across the palace grounds to the front of Valkarah. Kren handed him the plain gold crown which he was carrying on his arm, and the king took it from him with a nod, placing it onto his head like an old hat as they passed through the gates, and into the city where the cavalry waited and the streets were crowded with onlookers come to see their king depart.

Orrld had ridden once before with the king's entourage when they had returned from Chete. It seemed like a lifetime ago, and as before the old horse Coup knew better than he what to do, keeping perfect step with those they rode alongside and Orrld began to relax in the spring sunshine.

In the tree-lined avenue in front of the gates of Valkarah, the crowds were thickest and all but silent in respect for a king leaving; there would be cheering on his return and then the bells of Valkarah would ring. A woman, whom Orrld recognised as one he had healed, ran into the road with an armful of sivernam leaves, which she threw into his horse's path. Coup, receiving no signal from his rider, paced on dutifully, unperturbed, and Orrld smiled his thanks, thinking it was an isolated incident. Then more came, men and women, young and old, each tossing the shining leaves ahead of the horse. Hush and cavalry made space to allow it to happen and soon Orrld was riding on a path of silver that shone in the morning sun like a river.

Sho rode with the Hush as if she was one of them, although she had no strength to fight and was even too weak to control the linegold blades, carrying them in a bag about her waist. Sleep clawed her constantly and through the daze she watched the people pay their respects to the Healer, and even as he kept her just this side of death, she resented him the accolade they bestowed; such glory, she believed, should only be shown to royalty.

Orrld was embarrassed, his face flushed red and hot, and had no understanding why he was honoured so. He wished he had chosen to wear the hooded cloak of the Hush like Sho and the Strick boy, and so pass unnoticed. When at last they went through the South Gate and travelled on the open road, and there were no more than a handful of peasants on the wayside, he let go the horse's mane and covered his face with his hands.

The king took off the gold crown and handed it back to Kren, who stashed it away in his saddlebag. Then he doubled back to ride alongside Orrld, and Arrant, the most powerful of the Crystal Bearers after Sho, followed and rode at Orrld's left.

'Why did they do that?'

Arrant spoke, 'They honour you for bringing their king back to life,' he said.

'He wasn't dead, and I only did what any Healer would do.'

'I was as good as dead,' said the king with a chuckle and squeezed Orrld's shoulder. Even through the thick robes he wore to stave off the spring chill, Orrld could feel the care in his touch and it warmed him.

The king was happy. He had long feared that the common

shoken might show animosity toward the Ekressian, in favour of his wife Sneela, but Orrld's work at the hospital had endeared him to many long before he had saved all their lives.

'When we return I will build a temple for Ath in the city,' said the king and Orrld smiled then. He had often wished for a place to practice his faith, and his lover had guessed as much.

They rode for a short while more, and then stopped so that the horses could rest and those soldiers in ceremonial dress could fit themselves more comfortably.

The king lifted Sho from her horse and Orrld gave her his healing once again. She was exhausted. Sten was waiting and he scooped her into a sling he had ready, looping it around his neck and shoulder to carry her like a woman might carry an infant. Sho was small, and he, one of the Lamash, standing four strides tall, was massive and powerful with skin black as a raven's wing, and his love for her made her light in his arms. He carried her to Oak, his horse, a huge wagon dragger, standing alongside animals so well-bred their lineage went back ten generations. Sten mounted carefully and once in the saddle pulled back the folds of the sling to ask if she was comfortable; Sho already slept.

Time was against them; they did not stop again and took some food in the saddle to ride well after dark. Then they made a quick camp, fires and bedrolls only as the weather was cold but fair. In this way, good speed was made on the road for five turns and when this became nothing more than a dirt track, they turned off for the open country, as without any carts to pull it would be the quickest way, and had the added benefit of providing the horses with some grazing each evening.

CHAPTER THREE

Mag'Sood sat on the bottom step of the dais near the fire and poked the embers with a metal rod. Above him, languishing on the throne, white scales contrasting the black reparda rock, lay the She-Aulex.

Mag'Sood glanced up; he found her beautiful and fascinating, and since she had eaten some of the Crystal and he wore a drop of the same about his neck in a bottle, they were inseparable. Her unquestioning devotion and protection gave him a sense of pride, and he liked to think it was not just the Crystal bond that kept her loyalty, but something more – what the softlings called love perhaps, for had they not been friends before?

Reaching forward he raked out the shoken head he had been warming and rolled it onto the hearth. He disliked eating frozen meat as was the norm here at Tarestone, yet found cooked food abhorrent. This was heated through nicely and as he picked it up, he vaguely registered that the face looking back from death was female. He pressed it between his powerful hands until the skull cracked and broke, then prised the two halves open to reveal the soft convolutions of the brain inside.

'Are you sure you don't want some of this?' he whispered to the She-Aulex. She did not reply; they both knew she disliked the taste of softling. Not so her pups who had gathered about the fire in anticipation. Each revealed themselves, changing their scales with a flutter from black, where they had matched the stone, to white. Mag'Sood pinched with finger and thumb a little for each of the fifteen before he had some himself.

The pups had been born in this room, and although still tiny had grown from helpless blind creatures to become little replicas of their mother; a broad chest supported by front legs longer than the back, and a wide, flat, earless head with teeth, long and sharp. Their intricate scales provided armour and camouflage. The Aulex could change colour at will, thus giving rise to the myth that they could make themselves invisible. Grown Aulex were huge, reaching the waist of any adult Sturgar stood on two legs. Double retractable talons on the front feet made them formidable fighters.

Mag'Sood ate greedily, scraping the last of the brains with his fingernails, then set the head down for the pups to finish. They came eagerly, fighting amongst themselves for the best bits, and picked it clean, then climbed up to their mother. Mag'Sood kicked the shoken skull onto a pile of others.

As footsteps approached, the She-Aulex concealed herself and the pups, settling to sleep around her, did the same. Now any who looked at the place where they were would only see the Black Throne.

The footsteps stopped outside his door and Mag'Sood let them wait before hissing quietly for them to enter. The Watcher came first, walking with one hand on her disciple's shoulder for guidance. Tall and elegant, he had always desired her, and he watched as the disciple carefully settled her on the bottom step of the dais and arranged her gown in folds about her feet before standing aside. The Curver Thist came next, crouching low even as he was small for a Sturgar, and knelt near the wall, eyes downcast.

Mag'Sood moved to sit next to the Watcher, hissing inwards: *speak*. Her disciple handed her a reflecting disk. It was small, fitting into her palm, slightly convex and to the uninitiated looked to be a mirror. The Watcher brought it to her face so she could see, and then began the delicate tilting of it until a moving image appeared upon its surface.

'Master, it would seem the softling king and his protectors have recovered. They make their way to Lak-Mur for the birth of the heir as planned. This image comes from a soldier.' She spoke in whispered breath and Mag'Sood leaned close the better to see.

The young archer who was marked with a speck of the reflective metal was unaware he committed treason simply by looking about him. He had no recollection of how, after a fight with a band of Sturgar four years ago, he had been knocked unconscious, and then awoken by the wayside later unharmed. The metal speck did not hurt, and being no bigger than a grain, did not trouble him.

From where he sat, almost at the back of the troop, he could see ahead glimpses of the king who rode at the centre, flanked by his Crystal Bearers and soldier monks known as the Hush. Cavalry from the Median army completed his protection at front and back. The king was easily visible even from this distance by his hair and beard, which were the colour of corn, but the others were too far away to identify.

Curver Thist eased his cloak under his knees to protect them from the cold reparda rock and listened for the Aulex. He knew they were here somewhere. Their smell permeated the room and he had learnt to distinguish the smell of fresh Aulex from a room that smelled of Aulex.

'Curver, how long will they stay at Lak-Mur before returning?' whispered Mag'Sood.

The Curver got up, keeping himself low. 'Last time they stayed only for one moon cycle.'

'Have we any seeing metal at Lak-Mur?' he asked of the Watcher who turned to face him. He looked into the unmoving black ovals of her eyes. So close, he knew she could see him. A lifetime watching the reflective disks had made her partially sighted like her predecessors.

'No, Master,' she breathed.

Mag'Sood tried to ignore the smoothness of her shapely head and how her grey skin glowed in the firelight. He flicked a finger: *leave*. A Watcher must always remain a virgin for her powers to work. The disciple came forward and led her away and Mag'Sood turned his attention to the Curver, making an inward hiss: *speak*.

The Curver drew closer the better to judge the Master's mood and chose his words with care. 'It would seem the softling king is busy expanding his army. He has recruited many. Across the Trilands, a campaign has begun to recruit more troops. He has issued a decree.'

'Just the Medians?'

'No, all the shoken, even lesser tribes are enlisted.'

'Do they go willingly?'

'Mostly, yet I have learnt the army will take by force the twenty in every hundred of shoken required if it is not given freely.'

Mag'Sood dismissed the Curver and he left quickly, relieved the bad news had not elicited the Master's temper.

When he had gone the She-Aulex revealed herself and, rising carefully so as not to disturb her sleeping pups, came over and rested her head in his lap, making her scales look like the fire. Mag'Sood smoothed his hands over her back and thought about the boy king who had never, as far as he knew, been in a fight himself, much less a battle. Yet he understood war was coming, and a fundamental rule was that the side with the biggest army would most likely win. It all came down to numbers in the end.

'You... be... happy,' the She-Aulex spoke, her speech stilted and difficult for her to make. 'He... grows... his... army... he is... afraid.'

CHAPTER FOUR

Arrivals were more important than departures, Saur had always thought. First impressions stayed longer in the mind, and as they had only been to Lak-Mur once before, when she had married, then this return – some twelve years later – was significant. Then she had been a mere girl, now she was a queen. A queen carrying an heir.

Saur had never been to Lak-Mur and had found out all he could. A temple carved from the red rock of the mountain-side dominated the citadel. Legend told that all the shoken tribes had stood beneath the roof to worship Nenimar. A ridiculous notion, of course. Peasants from the area populated the city and pilgrims from across the Trilands journeyed there to pay homage to Nenimar's birthplace. Simply touching the walls of Temple Lak-Mur guaranteed a place in the afterlife, the faithful believed. Walking around the walls was supposed to clarify the mind and enable Nenimar to reveal his true purpose for every shoken. Saur did not consider himself a religious man and doubted the sacred city would change him.

When they were no more than half a turn's ride away

Saur made camp, to allow the queen to rest and make herself ready, and sent a message of their imminent arrival.

Despite the searing heat, he planned to arrive in the middle of the turn when the sun was at its highest to avoid the afternoon rains. He ordered the Kassnets army put on the green ceremonial dress, polished breastplates and helms. The splendour would dazzle the peasants.

Queen Sneela would arrive on a gilded litter, as she was too heavily pregnant for horseback.

Throughout the arduous journey, the queen and her party travelled in twelve closed carriages, which protested greatly at the poor roads, throwing wheels, breaking axles, and because of their considerable weight, sticking in the mud when it rained. This did not help the queen's temper, making her either angry or tearful and sometimes both.

Sneela stepped out of her carriage. Saur had never seen her look more beautiful. The gown she wore flattered her pregnancy, her fair hair hung loose to her waist, and on her head was a simple diamond coronet. Four handmaids carried a canopy to protect her from the sun, whilst others fanned her as she reclined on the cushions of the litter.

Slowly they made their way, until Lak-Mur, shimmering in the heat haze on top of the mountain, came into view. It was a long walk, the track as rough as any on the journey, and incredibly steep. When they passed through the city gates the sun was high, and just as Saur had planned, the queen and her entourage shimmered like gods. They were met by a small group of soldiers, who walked ahead to show them the way through the huge, empty citadel.

The queen sat up, expecting crowds to appear at every corner, but apart from a few onlookers, the streets were deserted. They followed the soldiers to some fine buildings, fashioned, as were all, in the warm red stone. The queen alighted in a courtyard roofed with a vine to give dappled shade. After the heat of the climb, the breeze that came through carved mesh screens from the mountainside was cool and welcome.

Adernist monks and the king's council waited to greet her, but the cool air had done nothing to dissipate her anger.

'Did you get the messenger sent to inform you of my arrival?'

The leader of the king's council stepped forward, and made a bow. 'We did. He is safe,' he said.

'Where then is the king?'

'He is still unwell, and has not made the journey; our prayers are for his recovery, and his safe return to us.'

Sneela was unaware that the king was ill, and had assumed he would have been here already. Inside she bristled at the lack of information.

'And the shoken of Lak-Mur, they do not come to greet the arrival of their queen?'

'It is the middle of the turn, your grace; in the heat, it is more sensible to rest than risk the sun's vengeance. I suggest you do the same. Come, you must be tired,' he said, walking ahead, and indicating an open door.

Sneela remained where she was, keen to continue the argument. One of the four handmaids holding the canopy that shaded her fell. The canopy enveloped the queen, and when quick hands untangled her, she flew into a rage, kicking the unconscious girl violently in the face.

One of the monks stepped forward and took the girl into his arms, and received a few blows himself. Sneela was as angry as she had ever been, dishevelled and red in the face. Her crown still lay on the floor at her feet; no one dared to pick it up.

Beyond the screen a voice spoke, resonate and commanding. Sneela did not understand the words, yet recognised them to be the same strange language the king often spoke.

The speaker moved away, and she caught a glimpse of a large shadow behind the screen. The monks moved together, blocking her view.

Silence filled the courtyard and Sneela understood that she had been judged and found wanting, and cast a glance at Saur who was always on her side. Even he looked at his boots, embarrassed for her outburst.

Temper gave way to tears then, and she ran through the open door, slamming it behind her.

The Long Credola was cool inside. The mountain breeze wafting through the mesh screens was stronger here. Newly furnished in the style of the Kassnets, green silk fluttered on the walls. Sneela walked through the rooms and found the bedchamber. She closed and locked the door and walked about checking she was alone – lately, she felt watched.

She took off her dress and shoes and sat on the bed. There was water in a stone jug beside her and she poured herself some and drank deeply. It was surprisingly cold. She splashed her hot face and lay back on the cool, green silks.

The wasps, she had brought a pair, came out from the folds of her bodice, creeping softly. They drank droplets of water from her skin and she stroked their shimmering green bodies with a fingertip. These workers were not as large as the queen wasp, but she found them just as beautiful even without their wings, which she had pulled off, lest they fly away. When they had drunk enough the wasps climbed to the top of her pregnant belly and carefully groomed each other.

In the corner of the room, untroubled by the heat or weary from travel, stood the ghost of the murdered slave boy who had sired her child. He appeared as his last living memory of himself, as the newly dead often do; naked, his body riddled with the welts of the wasp larvae that had killed him. Silent and wretched, the sight of the wasps filled his soul with hate. His only resolution, to follow her everywhere, in some vain hope of protecting his unborn.

CHAPTER FIVE

E tter had seen it all before. The rabble brought before
her on this turn was no different from any other. She
walked past the ragged line, took her place behind her desk
and opened a ledger. Outside the tent, she could hear the
soldiers trying to get the reluctant recruits into some sort of
order and sighed. Of all the tasks she had carried out as an
officer of the Median army, this was by far the worst.

The king had decreed all the shoken of the Trilands
provide twenty in every one hundred of their population for
the army. This probably seemed like a good idea on some
war council at Valkarah. No doubt, those trained in warcraft
imagined that strong young men, filled with royalist fervour,
would flock to sign up when called. They were wrong.

The reality was that few believed there would be a war
and so each community gave their quota reluctantly, rather
than face army discipline. Those conscripted amounted to
the unwanted, namely, criminals, fools and vagrants, and as
the definition for those who could be enlisted was broad,
only excluding the very young or old, or those women either

pregnant or in the throes of early motherhood, then she had to accept all.

Etter adjusted the leather eye patch she wore over her left eye to make it more comfortable and beckoned in the first conscript. A short man, just this side of middle age, entered grudgingly and gave his name. Etter, resigned to her hopeless task, wished for the old times, when shoken had to be of a certain height and age, and show some aptitude for fighting, archery, or horsemanship. She doubted this old farmer had any such attributes.

The turn dragged on, army ranks swelled with ninety more recruits and Etter was glad to meet the last of them as the light faded. A woman, thin and forlorn, stood before her. She was filthy, her dress soiled and caked with mud about the hem. Her hair crawled visibly with lice.

'Name?'

The woman stared blankly ahead, and Etter had to ask her twice more to get her looking in her direction.

'What… is… your name?'

The woman, seemingly wrung from a dream, came to herself. 'Lorimore,' she said.

'And you're from this town of Patten?'

'Biscos.'

Etter reached for a different ledger and after consulting its pages found her memory had served her well. The Sturgar had erased Biscos, just under two years ago. Etter scrutinised her with a bright, dark eye, taking in the woman's features and the high-quality cloth of her dress beneath the dirt. Her feet were bare and cut to shreds and her hands were slim and fine. She was no farm labourer or petty thief; once, she had been gentry.

'Biscos is far away. Any idea how you got here?'

She said nothing; it was answer enough.

Etter poised her nib over the ledger and hated having to ask this wretch the next question.

'Do you have a next of kin?'

'Everybody is dead.'

Etter got up from her desk and came to the woman, held her by the shoulders and looked into her face.

'Lorimore, do you realise you are being conscripted into the army?'

Etter only ever let off the insane and weak, and after this woman's ordeal, she imagined she was probably both, yet the woman nodded. 'I want to die,' she said.

Etter patted her shoulder, moved back to her desk, and took up the nib pen. Unlike the shoken of these parts, she did believe the war was coming and had seen the aftermath of a Sturgar massacre – the rivers of blood still haunted her dreams even as she had lived a life of violence. She held the pen out. 'Make your mark.'

The woman came over and wrote, in a fancy looped script, her full name, *Lorimore Meshnore Con'Rinvayle*. Etter was impressed and carefully tipped sand over the ink before calling for her lieutenant. 'Take this conscript to the medic,' she said.

CHAPTER SIX

As they journeyed, the weather became warmer each turn and with the warmth came a change of landscape from the farmlands that bordered Valkarah, through ancient forests and thence to higher ground and the open plains. These gave way to mountainous surroundings with lush vegetation. It became hot and whilst many found the heat and humidity trying, Orrld did not. He rode in a fine silk robe and felt, for the first time since leaving Ekressia, truly warm. He was glad to be free of heavy clothing and feel again the kiss of the sun against his skin and would have been happy, if not for the burden of being unable to heal Sho.

Unlike the rest of the Pack, she had not fully recovered, but slept almost continually and, lacking any appetite, ate very little. The king, because of the closeness of the bond they shared, was, although not himself ill, melancholy.

The sun was almost at its highpoint, and soon they would stop to let men and horses rest until the greater heat of the turn had passed. Sten rode alongside with Sho, who slept, strapped to him in a sling like a child. Orrld automatically put out his hand to give her his healing and Sten leaned forward, allowing him to reach more easily. Orrld placed his hand on the back of her neck and let his healing flow into her as best he could. Sho's animosity toward him, and therefore her rejection of his healing, was hardly lessened even as she slept, and he knew far from healing her all he was managing to do was keep her from death.

The king's entourage made camp in the shade of a mountain and Orrld, never entirely at ease on horseback, dismounted with relief. Those soldiers who rode ahead had already put food and fresh water out for them. He sat down, ate, drank, and watched Sten as he carefully laid Sho down beside the king. She awoke and refused any food, taking only a few sips of water before returning to sleep. Orrld closed his eyes and said a silent prayer to Ath that he might find a way to cure her.

This turn followed the pattern of others; they rested, and when the heat lessened with the coming of the storm clouds and the afternoon rain, they moved off again, to travel on in the cool until well past nightfall. The next camp was by a river. Longing to be clean, Orrld handed the reins of his mare, Hoshkuur, to Math. The Strick boy had taken to horses and found a friend in Reem.

Jie came with him, as he always did. Like many inlanders he was unable to swim and sat on the riverbank, watchful for any danger. The river was quiet, and not for the first time Orrld wondered at the inlanders' lack of need for washing. The king's Pack kept themselves washed to some extent, but the common soldiers stank in the heat.

Orrld ducked under the water, pushed out his lung air, and felt his gills open along his ribcage. Unlike the muddy River Goot, where he had last swum, these waters were warm and clean. Shafts of moonlight cut through the surface, illuminating little fishes hiding among the waving plant-life. Enjoying the push of the water on the webbing of his hands and feet and feeling the ache of horse riding ease away, he swam on, until the riverbed deepened and the water became cooler and darker. Not wishing to go further, but enjoying the rare moment of solitude, he found some tree roots where he could secure himself and floated there with the current pressing him.

Most of the fish were hidden away, listless in their open-eyed sleep, but not all. As he hung there, he saw a ghost-fish swimming against the current to catch what morsels the river might bring past. No bigger than a hand's breadth and almost transparent, they were easy to miss. When a child he and his twin sister, Issolissi, had been afraid of ghost-fish with their clear skin revealing the strange, translucent organs beneath. As an adult, he watched with fascination and saw that there were two – swimming side by side in synchrony, it was difficult to see the one behind the other. As he looked through them, he saw a third, this one smaller and seemingly an illusion. Only when the three darted away could he be sure the smallest fish was not a trick of the moonlight. Smiling, he freed himself and let the current take him back.

Jie was waiting on the bank and they returned to the camp together. There the king sat and Orrld, his robe clinging to his wet body, joined him by the fire. He was glad to see Sho awake and making some effort to eat. Orrld ate and when he saw Sho curl herself to sleep again, he told the king how they might try to heal Sho together.

In the firelight when they were relatively alone, the other Crystal Bearers having gone to keep watch or rest, Orrld and the king knelt beside Sho's sleeping body.

'How do you know this will work?' asked Llund, stroking his beard thoughtfully.

'I don't,' said Orrld, shaking his head, 'it's just an idea I had when I was in the water. I thought if I put you between

27

me and her it might help. She pushes my healing away and I can't seem to give her what she needs to get better.'

'Why would she do that?'

'Because she still mistrusts me, I suppose,' said Orrld.

'No, she has forgiven you. None of it was your fault.'

Orrld said nothing more, what he felt through his healing touch told a different story. He leaned over and pulled back the blanket wrapping Sho. Lying there, she looked very tiny and frail. Orrld put aside his fear that she was dying, and nothing he could do would save her. He took one of Llund's hands and placed it at the small of his own back, and held it there; Llund's other hand he placed over Sho's heart and closed his eyes, saying a prayer to Ath for her life and felt his healing flow through Llund and into Sho. This time it met no resistance, and Llund felt the great warmth and power of it and remembered once before when they had done this. The sensation was no less strange than before.

Orrld lost track of time and remembered nothing of the passing of the night and when he awoke was surprised to see the sun in the sky and realised he had slept long and deeply.

There was a changed mood. He sensed it as soon as he sat up and looked about. All of the Pack were smiling. The king approached carrying food and sat beside him. He said nothing, only smoothed his hand over his freshly shaven face. It was enough; Sho always shaved him, it was their morning ritual. With her sickening, his beard had become an expression of his care.

Orrld chuckled and began to eat. He was even more hungry than normal.

'You should have woken me; we've missed a morning's travel.'

'Two, you've been asleep two turns.'

Sho came and the Pack touched the ground in respect as she walked by. She was dressed, her hair freshly braided at her nape and apart from thinness, looked well again. She knelt beside him and spoke Ekressian, reciting a prayer that thanked Ath for Orrld's gift of healing.

Touched and surprised she knew such a thing he made to hug her but she was already gone. The Pack followed.

'While you slept I had some news from Lak-Mur,' said Llund, smiling.

Orrld had already guessed and smiled back.

'I have a son, in good health. Sneela gave birth three turns ago.'

Orrld reached over and hugged him.

'How far now?'

'Not far now. If you're feeling strong enough, I would like to travel through the night. I think we could be there in two turns.'

Orrld looked at the sky, the sun was at its hottest and he could tell Llund was anxious to be on his way, yet he would not ask the men, or indeed the horses, to endure the discomfort of the heat.

'We should go to the river and pray,' he said, getting up and reaching out a hand to pull Llund up, 'give thanks for your son and heir and his mother's health.'

The riverbank was cool and Orrld led him to where a tree trailed a green curtain in the water. Underneath was cool and secluded, although he was not so innocent now and knew the king's protectors were always somewhere near. He put the thought aside and took off his Healer's sash and robes, and after taking a tablet of soap from the pocket, laid them beside his clogs and stepped into the water.

Llund stayed where he was, half-smiling, half-frowning. 'I thought you said we were going to pray.'

Orrld laughed. 'Get in the water, I'll show you a new way to pray,' he said, brown eyes full of mischief.

Llund stayed where he was, apologetic. 'I can't swim,' he said.

'Really?' Orrld tried not to laugh.

Llund pulled off his boots and unbuckled the sword, N'gar, propping it against the tree trunk. He sat on the riverbank.

'You don't need to swim,' said Orrld, washing his hair with the mint soap. 'Look, it's shallow here, I can stand,' he gestured, indicating how the water only reached his waist.

Llund considered a moment, then stripped off his clothes and got into the water tentatively. Orrld handed him the soap.

'So this is how you pray to Ath, by washing?' Llund asked, ducking his head under the water to rinse his hair.

Orrld came closer, took the soap off him, threw it aside, and embraced him. It had been so long since they had loved; the last time Orrld could recall was before Sho went missing. There had often been opportunity since but Orrld, sensing his lack of desire, left him. Now with Sho healed everything was better.

With their wet bodies pressed together, Orrld gave thanks to Ath for the gift of healing, his River talk lilting like a melody, dedicating this act of sex to the God. Llund guessed their meaning.

After, they lay together looking up at the blue sky through the tree branches, and for a while, life was simple.

CHAPTER SEVEN

Soldiers newly come to the ranks that guarded the king were tasked with hunting for the king's table when any journey was made. This was an old tradition that gave them the chance to meet their sovereign when they presented their kill to him in person.

This night a young archer had the privilege and Sho, who stood in the shadows, watched as he approached. The king and his Pack sat about a campfire. They had ridden past dark to allow them to reach Lak-Mur easily the following turn. Arrant escorted the archer into the king's presence.

The boy knelt. Unusually he had not endeavoured to catch a mighty stag or wild boar but brought three large river fish. Line-caught, they were perfect, and more importantly, they would be quick to cook. Something they would all be grateful for this late night.

Sho could see the boy smile as the king complimented him and knew that with a few words of encouragement he would elicit a lifetime's devotion in the young soldier. Arrant led the smiling boy away, and as they passed, she felt a faint wave of mistrust. It was nothing, a thing so slight she would have put it aside if she had not felt it before.

Sho walked alongside him as one of the Hush handed back the boy's weapons, a short sword and a bow recently made from yew. She saw it then, a small glint in the lamplight from a silver speck on his left temple. He was marked with the seeing metal. Just as Orrld had been.

Standing this close filled her with a hate so strong it took all her self-control not to kill the boy right there. Two things stopped her. Firstly, she knew a sudden act of violence would upset the Healer, and she was careful to avoid this, as upsetting Orrld troubled the king. Secondly, they had agreed that what they had learnt of the Sturgar ability to spy they would keep to themselves. The archer must die in a manner that did not belie the reason for his death.

Whether he was an unwitting spy or not mattered very little. The lord's safety required this boy's death. She took careful note of the insignia on his uniform so she could find him later, and joined the Pack by the fire.

Sho kept her own counsel. Later when the king and Orrld had settled to rest and Arrant, who had slept the first watch, came to take her place outside the king's tent, she slipped away into the night.

Sho had tried to reject Orrld's healing, yet he had found a way to bring her back to health, and now, seeing a threat that others had missed, she was grateful to be alive. She felt diminished yet she noticed subtle danger that the others missed. She could still do things that set her apart and knew she must put aside her death wish. Sho wandered through the camp, glad to be free from the constant need for sleep.

The young archer was not on watch as she had hoped. Sho found him sleeping in a line with others from his cohort. She walked on to those guards on duty as if her purpose was to check the watch on the camp's periphery. The men saluted smartly as she went by, and she nodded once to acknowledge their respect. Sho walked on as if returning to the king, but headed back when she knew herself to be out of sight and hid in some scrub bushes where she could see the boy sleeping. The bushes gave little cover but she was small with the ability to keep very still.

The night wore on – the second moon slid from view and the horizon showed a glimmer of light and she began to think she would have to kill the boy another time. The thought irritated her, as she did not want him to enter Lak-Mur.

The camp was on a wide plateau and the high ground had given a steady cool breeze and a welcome relief from the heat. In the morning, Lak-Mur would be visible in the middle distance. She could not remember when they had last stopped here, this close to Lak-Mur, and knew if it had not been for the Healer's fatigue, they would have ridden on to complete the journey.

Patient to the last, Sho's waiting was rewarded. The archer awoke before his fellows and left his bedroll with care so as not to disturb them. Sho followed as he made his way past the sleeping men and tethered horses. He was not going far as he had not bothered to pull on his boots. A sign of his immaturity; an experienced soldier would have slept in them and an experienced soldier would not wander off alone and unarmed even to urinate.

Sho wondered at men's fascination for pissing off high places as he relieved himself over the edge of the plateau. Dawn broke quickly in this part of Thanra, so she must act or leave the killing for another turn; already the sky was lightening. Sho weighed a large stone in her hand, then ran the twenty paces that separated them. He turned toward her when he heard the soft footfall, smiling, expecting to see a friend. The stone hit him square in the face, knocking his nasal bone into his brain and killing him instantly. As he fell, Sho caught him from tumbling over the edge and laid him down.

Since waking from the death sleep her linegold no longer obeyed her and she carried the blades in a pouch at her waist. The loss of this power was another reason why she lately wished to die. She took out one of the blades and cut from his temple a flap of skin along with the seeing metal. She put both away in the pouch and shoved his body over the edge.

Carefully, Sho stepped back the way she had come, brushing with her fingertips the marks her passing had made in the dust.

In the morning, they found the boy and it was deemed a sad accident for one so young and with such potential ahead. He had brought down one of the Sturgar when he was still a pacer. His cohort buried him on the plateau with haste. Many of the old soldiers considered the boy's death a bad omen and all refused to touch any of his belongings such was their superstition. His bedroll, kitbag, boots, and the newly made bow lay on the ground untouched as if the dead boy might rise from his shallow grave and make use of his things.

CHAPTER EIGHT

Saur, High Commander of the Kassnets army and twelfth cousin to the queen, looked at his reflection. He stood on his toes to see, as the mirror was too high for him. He examined his face and once again found his handsome features to be unmarked. He ran a finger down the centre of his face, from the forehead, between his eyes, along the left side of his nose and through his lips, tracing the cuts the line-gold blades had made. After the fight with Sho, he had thought to spend his life disfigured.

The Healer had mended the wound with his touch. No trace of injury remained, yet he felt the blades cut and the hot rush of blood that followed. He knew this was an illusion yet the feeling was so vivid he had to stop himself from grasping his head and crying aloud. Most times his face just hurt with a pain that peaked to agony and ebbed to a dull ache but never abated. He pressed his fingertips hard along the line of the unseen wound so they left white prints, and for a moment it helped. Saur moved away from the mirror with a sigh and dipped a linen cloth into a jug of water, then lay back on a couch with it over his face.

The Long Credola, high on the mountain edge, had carved mesh screens to let in the breeze. But in the middle of the turn, the draft was warm. He longed for the cooling rains that came in the late afternoon. Saur lay in the heat and worried about the queen. Motherhood did not sit easily with her. A wet-nurse was found for the baby and herbs given to ease Sneela's milk-filled breasts. She was in good health and the prince was the image of his father, yet none would acknowledge him as heir until the king had seen him with his own eyes. After which, Saur had no doubt, Sneela would be held in greater esteem and given the adulation that was her due. In the meantime, they had the interminable heat and boredom of this place to contend with until the king's arrival. Saur closed his eyes and slept fitfully.

Sneela woke to noise louder than the sound of the afternoon rains. Suddenly the whole city was on the move. She climbed the steps to the roof terrace where a black varuna vine shielded the sun and the rains, the blue fruits dangling beneath the carved black-wood frame. She leaned on the balustrade and looked at the streets below. The shoken of Lak-Mur had gathered as one, each waving a coloured streamer and unlike the crowds of Valkarah who cheered for their king, these shoken sang, their voices lifted in a rousing anthem.

After a time she saw the king, glimpsed their passing on some far off street and she thought from there he would enter the Summer Palace, but no, until nightfall he criss-crossed the streets ensuring all who had gathered would not be disappointed.

. . .

When he passed beneath, the only concession he had made to the occasion was his crown and this only a plain gold band. King and cavalry were half-dressed in deference to the heat and as the rain ceased, steam arose around them from the warm, red stones of Lak-Mur, enveloping the king and his entourage in an ethereal mist. Sneela turned away, irritated.

Somewhere the baby cried. The unnamed boy child that held so much promise and yet none would acknowledge until the king accepted him. Since his birth, she had seen him twice and with his blue eyes and flaxen curls, he looked the image of the king. Sneela felt assured of her position.

The baby was soothed and footsteps approached. She hoped they did not bring the child to her as feigning affection was always trying and she had never been able to endure not being the centre of attention.

Saur came onto the terrace and after bowing low, kissed the hem of her gown, as he always did. Since she had given birth he had been less playful, solicitous certainly, but his attentions lacked the sexual undertones of before and she missed that.

Sneela seated herself on a delicate, black-wood chair. 'How long until the king arrives?' she asked, looking up through the varuna vine.

Night fell quickly here and already the sky was nearly black. She was relieved she would be able to meet the king in the cool of the evening and present him with his son. The sooner the child was accepted and they could travel home and away from the interminable heat, the better.

Saur, still on bended knee, bowed his head. 'The king will not be here this night,' he said.

From where she sat, she could see Saur's honour guard waiting. Aware they were well within earshot she curbed her temper.

'He must be tired after the journey,' she said sweetly.

'I have been informed he has gone to speak with the Faar,' he said.

Sneela felt the wasps within her bodice begin to crawl toward the neckline of her gown. They sensed her agitation. She put her hand on her neck to stop them from getting out.

'I shall expect him at dawn then,' she said.

Saur, who was well used to the queen's anger, and not wishing to receive a kick in the face, slowly stood up and moved back a pace. 'Apparently speaking with the Faar may take several turns,' he said.

Sneela, pretending to smile, waved him away. When he had gone, she went into her sleeping chamber, curled up on the bed in the dark, and sobbed. Much better to cry than vent her rage at being put aside. The king would rather speak with a group of old fools than come and meet the son she had borne.

The two wasps, happy in the cool dark, crawled out onto her neck and she stroked each with a finger. They were all she had as a reminder of home and she comforted herself in the knowledge that she would find a way to bring them to the king's person. It was doubtful even the River Healer would have an antidote for such a rare poison.

CHAPTER NINE

Godwin looked up from his workbench toward the door on the far side of the room, someone in metal-tipped boots approached with a heavy tread up the tower steps. Only a foreign soldier would wear such attire in the heat. One linegold blade floated up and hovered beside his head as the door flung open. A Kassnets nobleman in doublet and cape strode in and looked about.

The small, circular tower had shelves that followed the curve of the walls, all overflowing. Books, phials, shells, decorated sword hilts, baskets full of arrow tips, coloured stones, bottles, preserved insects under glass domes, various animal skeletons, and a great many clocks. A ladder on rails allowed access to the highest shelves at the top of which sat a stuffed green monkey, staring down with orange, glass eyes. Dust motes floated in the light shafts from the narrow windows above.

Godwin glanced at the nobleman. He wore a bejewelled longsword that was too heavy. He carried a thin dagger concealed in his left boot and a needle blade up his right sleeve. None of the metal responded to his will; he was adept at nothing. Godwin bid his linegold to slip down the back of his cotton tunic out of sight.

'I am Saur, High Commander of the Kassnets army,' he said.

Godwin inclined his head and then continued sorting a pile of minute, intricate cogs and wheels with a long pair of tweezers.

'It is customary to stand in my presence,' he said, placing a hand on the hilt of his sword. Godwin doubted he could even unsheathe the weapon.

'I am,' he said quietly.

'What do you mean...?'

'I am standing,' he said and stepped from his stool onto the workbench. Now the two were eye-level.

'Fetch me the king's Blade-Master, dwarf,' he said.

'I am Godwin, Blade-Master to the king,' he said, making a bow. There was mockery in it.

Saur turned to leave. 'I am looking for a forger of rare metals and a linegold mover.'

Before he reached the door, eighty linegold blades of various lengths and size swirled around him, then floated, motionless, in the air. The sight of them made Saur wince. Hesitantly, he turned to face the dwarf and the blades glided back to their resting places about the room as the dwarf, grinning, made another bow.

'Why don't you pull up a seat, commander, and let us discuss what we may do for one another?' he said. His voice was rich and handsome.

'I should have you taken to the square and flogged for your impertinence,' said Saur.

The dwarf shrugged and sat cross-legged on the bench. 'I would enjoy a trip beyond these walls, but the lord has me bound to this place, and there is little room to swing a whip in here.'

Now Saur noticed a fine thread of silver tied about the dwarf's ankle. It snaked across the desk onto the floor in a large coil.

Saur sat on a stool. It was uncommonly low, and with the dwarf seated on the workbench, he had to look up at him.

'Well?' said the dwarf, picking up a handful of cogs and examining them.

Saur looked over his shoulder to reassure himself they were alone. 'I got into a fight with a linegold user and was cut, badly cut about the face. The wounds mended, but still, I feel the pain of them,' he said.

'That's unusual,' said Godwin, staring at him intently. He could see no trace of a scar.

'Normally linegold will mark you for life. Was it a small cut?'

Saur traced a finger down the centre of his face and Godwin could tell he felt the pain of it anew. 'I was cured after by a Healer from Ekressia,' he said.

'The king's companion?'

'The same.'

'It will make no difference that your flesh has been restored, linegold is a cruel metal. It marks more than skin. There are only three ways you may ease your pain. One, you could make peace with your attacker. Two, fight again and win.'

'I would not be able to win this fight.'

'Then peace it is.'

'You mean apologise?'

'If only it were that easy. You will have to truly believe that you were in the wrong.'

'I wish I had not done that which caused the fight. For that I am truly sorry,' said Commander Saur.

'Yet you still hate the one who cut you, even if you agree with the reason they...' Godwin made a play of examining a disembowelled pocket watch while he carefully chose his words.

Saur saved him the trouble. 'Punished me.'

'Yes, quite.' The dwarf set down the watch and folded his arms. He looked straight at the commander. His eyes were raven black.

'And the third?'

The dwarf smiled and his eyes glittered. 'The third is a little more complicated. And costly.'

'Tell me.'

'You could learn to be a linegold user yourself. I would be willing to teach you... for a price.'

The commander took a purse from his belt and tipped the contents onto the bench. Forty gold clowsters tumbled out. Godwin picked one up. Freshly minted, the king's likeness was pristine. 'What use have I for money in here?' he said, putting the coin back on the pile. Saur looked at the delicate, iridescent silver thread that imprisoned the dwarf.

'Believe me, I have tried everything. There is no metal or man strong enough to break this bond,' he said, guessing his mind.

'Whatever reason the king has for keeping you here, I would not interfere with the lord's wishes,' said Saur. 'Yet surely there is something that would... ease your burden?'

The dwarf raised an eyebrow.

'Anything.' There was desperation in the tone.

'I have one small desire.'

'Then speak it,' said Saur, taking out a silken square and wiping his sweaty face.

'No. It would not do to speak this aloud.' He cast a look about the room as if the very walls had ears. 'I will write it down for you,' he whispered. 'But I pray you will not read my words, commander, not until you are safe within your private chambers.'

He nodded. With that, the dwarf jumped down from the workbench and waddled over to a shelf where paper, ink, and quill were. When the note was finished, he dried the ink with powder and then folded it into a fat square before handing it over. Saur took the note and tucked it into his doublet.

Godwin hoped the man's sweat would not render it illegible before he had time to look at it.

'Until we meet again, Blade-Master,' he said courteously.

When he had gone, Godwin barred and locked the door. The orange-eyed monkey blinked, shook the dust from her silky green fur and came down the ladder, front feet first.

Smiling, Godwin tossed her a date.

Saur walked slowly in the increasing heat. His sweat trickled in rivulets and he prayed the passers-by did not notice the damp circles growing ever larger beneath his armpits. The clothes he wore were far too hot for the climate at Lak-Mur, but how else was he supposed to dress if he was going to show his proper rank and status? *He* could not go about half-naked with sandalled feet like a peasant. Appearances were everything.

By the time he reached the Long Credola, the streets were almost empty. Two lethargic soldiers stood to attention as he passed beneath the archway into the shade of the building. In his rooms, he carefully placed the dwarf's request on a table and wondered what it was he wanted. Whatever it was, he would find a way to provide it. He stripped and poured cooling water over himself, imagining how much more formidable he would be as a linegold user, and congratulated himself for discovering that, like any other weapon, their use could be taught.

Naked and wet, he leaned, arms above his head on the slatted wooden screens, allowing what little breeze there was to cool him. He closed his eyes. How sweet it would be to teach Sho a lesson. He was a high born Kassnets tricked into kissing a slave. Thoughts of her repulsed him. His face burned.

Picking up the paper, he unfolded it. No words were written, only a simple drawing; two men, one on all fours, obviously intended to be him, clad in boots and cape and the other, the dwarf, standing behind, thrusting an especially large cock into him.

CHAPTER TEN

Godwin opened a door cut for his height. Mirril the monkey, eager to be free, dashed ahead up the spiral steps. He took his time, there was no rush – she would not come until nightfall if she came at all. At the top of the tower, he sat between the crenelations and looked out across the city. The sun was setting, making everything red. Red stone, red sky; the reason the ancients called this place Blood City. He listened to the singing in the streets far below and watched the sky darken and the first moonrise.

The monkey returned from her raid. This time she had stolen a key and a peach. Chattering excitedly, she placed them in his lap. Godwin examined the key. Nothing remarkable; no doubt, someone was missing it. The peach was beautifully ripe and large enough to cut in half. They ate together, juice running down their chins. He waited until the need for sleep was too great then slept in a box-bed built along the curve of the wall in the uppermost room of the tower.

Mirril woke him. She was as good as any guard dog, only more intelligent. She patted his face with her little black hands, chittering softly and pointing. Sho stood on the window ledge.

Godwin, who did not share her night vision, lit a lamp, and set it on the table. As soon as he saw her, he knew something was wrong. He had not seen her so thin, not since childhood. She had linegold, yet it was not held to her body as it should be, and there was another metal, one he did not know and another weapon, not of metal. He hoped this last was not what he feared.

She knelt and hugged him and the monkey joined in, standing on Godwin's shoulder and stroking both their heads.

'Must be five years,' he said, holding her at arm's length and looking into her face.

'Six,' said Sho, smiling. From her doublet, she took a bag of cherries, which she handed to the green monkey. They both got into the bed then, one each end and wrapped themselves in the blankets. After the heat of the turn, the night was chill.

'How much do you know?' she asked.

'I'm not sure what is rumour and what truth. I heard the king has a lover at last. A Healer from the River Ekress and that he and the Pack nearly died. Tale is you ran away.' They both laughed at that, and then Sho told him the whole story. How she had mistrusted Orrld and tried to kill him. The way the king's anger made her weak, which enabled Lorimore the artist to trick and drug her. Sho told him how she was trapped in the box and about the seeing metal on Orrld's face and how they cut it from him after Sten rescued her. When she had finished they sat in silence for a while, then Godwin got up. 'Come on,' he said, 'you need to eat.'

The Tower had a kitchen of sorts, he found bread, cheese and watered wine, and they sat at a table by a window. Dawn was breaking.

When they had finished eating, Sho untied the purse at her waist and lifted out her linegold. She put the small, hiltless blades in a neat stack on the table.

'Do they cut you?' he asked.

'No,' said Sho, picking one up. 'I can handle them. Even throw them. They just no longer respond to my will. I thought once I was healed I would regain their control.' She shrugged and he could see how troubled she was. Godwin held a hand above the pile of linegold and closed his eyes to concentrate. Mirril sat on the table watching.

'Do you always carry them?'

'Doesn't seem to be any point. Sometimes I do and sometimes I don't.'

'You'd never be unarmed,' he said. There was accusation in the tone. Sho laid the glassknife on the table. Briefly, the shard was transparent and then swam with the faces of the dead. The monkey stared at it and then made off through the window. Sho returned the weapon to the small of her back.

'I need something to protect the lord,' she said.

'It's dangerous. It will turn on you in the end. Glass cannot be trusted like metal. You should lock it away. Better still, destroy it.'

Godwin saw her face become a mask again and he was annoyed with himself for being so harsh. If anyone could control a glassknife, then that person was probably Sho. He hoped so.

'I had a friend of yours visit me,' he said, in an attempt to lighten the mood. He fetched a block of paper and a piece of charcoal and sat again, resting it on his lap.

'A much overheated commander of the Kassnets army. Poor fellow was looking for some relief. He told me how he'd had his face sliced by a linegold carrier.'

'Did he say it was me?'

'Hardly. I am sure he is still nursing his injured pride from being bested by a little girl.'

'Did you give him the cure?'

Despite her blank face, he could sense she was annoyed.

'I told him learning to be a linegold user would be the cure.'

She smiled freely then and he fell in love with her all over again.

'No doubt you offered to teach him?'

'I did,' he said, adding a few more lines to his drawing.

'At what cost?'

He flicked the drawing over.

Sho laughed and he saw the good it did her.

When she regained her breath he asked, 'Why does he hate you?'

'We had been getting intimate. He saw my crystal bonds and called me slave.'

Godwin gave the silver thread that bound him a tug and the length that had been laying on the steps to his bedchamber came cascading down. He twirled it into a coil on the floor.

'What's the other metal you have?' he asked.

'You don't know?'

He shook his head. 'Something. Some metal with the power to hurt. Nothing I've encountered before.'

Sho's face was full of relief as she tipped a miniature closejar from her purse. The ornate sphere rolled across the table. Godwin opened it and held the speck in his palm, fascinated.

'It is the seeing metal. That which was cut from the Healer's face and from an archer I killed recently.'

'Do you think this was all of it?'

Again, the look of relief. 'I mistrust him still. Do you think you could tell if he still had some on him?'

'Now I've met and know it, yes. Bring him here. And the problem with your blades is that they have begun to change their allegiance. Perhaps the Riverman has other abilities.'

Sho picked up her linegold and stood. 'I must go. I feel the lord returning from the Faar. Once he is back no doubt the naming ceremony will shortly follow.' She smiled again at Godwin's drawing. 'If in desperation he returned and bent over for you, would you oblige?'

Godwin laughed. 'You're asking a man in the desert if he prefers wine or water.'

CHAPTER ELEVEN

Lak-Mur Temple, carved into the red rock of the mountainside, steamed from the dawn rains. During the night, the stone doors were levered back so that the crowds could see the naming ceremony within. Thousands had gathered and their joyful songs and cheers filled the air. Everyone was smiling, especially the king, who walked ahead with his Pack. Orrld followed behind with high-ranking soldiers, Hush, Adernists, and dignitaries of Lak-Mur.

Earlier, from a balcony, he had watched the queen arrive on a litter, gazing lovingly at the new babe sleeping in her arms, a perfect portrait of gentle motherhood. Remembering her cruelty, he prayed to Ath that she had softened.

At the temple steps, the king, smiling broadly, bowed to the crowds who gave one last cheer then fell silent.

The temple was long and low, the ceiling hung with hollowed bamboo of various length and thickness. As they clacked together in the breeze, they made a pleasant, peaceful sound.

Twenty paces from the entrance a high dais provided a better view for the onlookers. Men and women in red ceremonial robes waited there. Orrld wondered if they were the Faar. The king joined them and so the ritual began.

There were prayers and chanting then the Crystal Bearers came forward, each blessed by the priest as they made a circle around the lord, their faces reflecting his mood. Orrld had never seen them look so happy. Only Sho's face was impassive.

Now the Kassnets arrived through a side door. The queen's guard were led by High Commander Saur and they looked overheated in heavy green robes. Sneela wore a modest dress of thin white silk and looked a little cooler. Her fair hair hung loose and glinted with emeralds. They were her only ornament.

She took slow, measured steps, her face serene. At the foot of the dais, a plain-faced girl who had gone unnoticed handed her the baby. Sneela carried him up the steps and laid him at the king's feet. He awoke as she unwrapped his swaddling and kicked his chubby legs, happy to be naked and cool. He was a beautiful blue-eyed infant, his head wreathed in soft blond curls.

Orrld expected the king to pick up this longed-for son. Instead, he stood where he was, looking down, disappointed. The Pack no longer smiled. Every eye was on Sneela. She stepped back, glanced over her shoulder at her guards. Before she had the chance to speak, Arrant grabbed her, hauled her to the centre of the dais and made her kneel. Sneela was screaming and the baby cried. The king stood over her and the Pack came close enough to touch him as he placed a hand over her heart.

Orrld remembered how the hand of truth felt. How all that was asked must be spoken aloud and nothing could make it stop. He could not watch, yet he listened as Sneela answered in a high-pitched, terrified voice. She told how she had used a mute slave to give her a child. He made her confess many cruelties, including killing Alt, a young man he loved. The temple amplified the voices, every listener, within and without, heard her crimes.

Arrant dragged her to the top of the temple steps when it was over. Below, the crowd, recently so happy, demanded her death and shouted obscenities. Sneela wept, prostrated herself before the king, and pleaded for her life. He raised a hand. The noise ceased. In the quiet, the unwanted baby cried. Orrld picked him up and held him close, and immediately the boy calmed and settled.

'I am no killer of women or children,' spoke the king. 'But I will have a divorce from this Kassnets.' He looked at Sho then and she took a linegold blade in her hand. Arrant held her firm while Sho shaved off Sneela's hair. The golden locks tumbled down the temple steps and those shoken nearest scrabbled for the emeralds tied within them.

When Sneela was bald, Arrant wrenched her to her feet. The crowd jeered.

'You will walk every street in my city and display your shame. Then you will leave,' said the king.

Orrld stepped forward then and handed the baby back to her. His kindness uncomprehending of the cruelty of others, he could not believe a mother would not want her child, no matter how that life had come to be.

Sneela took the sleeping child from him and began to descend the steps. Some of her guards trailed hesitantly after. The crowds took up their chants again, louder than ever. She stopped halfway, looked briefly at the child in her arms, and threw him down. His soft head hit the stone and shattered, his little body bounced and broke more than any Healer could mend until he lay contorted and shattered on the last step. The crowd were shocked to silence. Sneela turned to the king. 'I leave now,' she said. 'Or your small-folk will be slaughtered.'

Now they saw the glint of steel as Kassnets soldiers revealed themselves. They were not dressed in the heavy green brocade, but cool cotton and silk as befitting their disguise, and carried various weapons, axes and short swords, daggers and skinning knives, anything easily concealed. The cavalry arrived, surrounding the area. The Kassnets were everywhere, holding ordinary shoken at knifepoint.

Outnumbered and outmanoeuvred, nobody moved. The queen turned to the king.

'Divorce!' she shrieked. 'This marriage was never consummated!'

She walked to the bottom of the steps where Saur helped her mount a horse. She rode through the crowds and her army followed – many more than had arrived with her.

Orrld felt sick and weak, his legs shook, and his bowel felt loose. All he could think of was the baby, so soft and warm and innocent sleeping in his arms, then, moments later, dead. He blamed himself. Why had he not taken the child away? No one would have stopped him.

The rooms he shared with the king were large, airy and simply furnished. Woven grass mats covered the floor, the furniture delicate bamboo, and the bedding cotton. On a table, there was a jug of cool water. Orrld poured himself a glass and drank. There was fruit, but he could not eat.

As was so often the way when trouble came Llund had gone to speak with his Pack, leaving him alone here. He knew Jie, who seemed to be his bodyguard now, was outside the door. Sometimes his constant presence made him feel safe, other times a prisoner. At this moment, he felt the latter.

Even if he had the energy to heal, he doubted Jie would let him leave.

All he could do was wait for Llund to return and decided sleep was what he needed most. He liked the bedroom with its huge pots of giant orchids. At midturn, their scent was particularly heady. He picked a white bloom all speckled with dark brown spots. A large glass bowl sat in front of Ath's image, this also made of glass. Orrld dropped the flower in and prayed. When he opened his eyes the sun had moved, slanting rays making rainbows around the room and reminding him that even on a turn like this, when he had witnessed such terrible cruelty, Ath's love was always there.

Orrld slipped off his clogs and went to the bed. On the cotton pillow was a small box tied with green silk. It could only be a gift from Llund. Orrld smiled and sat on the bed to open it.

Inside was a wasp.

The ghost of the mute slave stood over the body of his dead child and in the twilight where the souls of the departed floated was his keening. The mournful sound filled the Temple at Lak-Mur for those who could hear it. The ghost of Issolissi came to them in their pain. He looked up and into her, felt her love and understanding. She enveloped him with her compassion, healed him from the ghastly image of himself, and named him. He was complete, handsome and young with a voice of his own. He gathered up the soul of his baby and Issolissi lit the path so they could find their way to peace and light.

CHAPTER TWELVE

The wasp was large and green. It shimmered in the sunlight. Someone must have pulled its wings off. Orrld tipped it from the box onto his webbed hand where it quivered its sensitive feelers as the fine, transparent wings re-grew.

Orrld had no idea why a wingless wasp had been left here; he only knew all creatures should be free. 'We're both a long way from the River, my friend. I think one of us should go home,' he said quietly as he carried the wasp over to the window. 'Who shall stay and who go?' The wasp tried its new-grown wings a few times and then took flight. 'I thought so,' said Orrld, watching it fly.

He went back to the bed, picked up the box, and examined it. Perhaps there was a note. Inside the lid was an ink-stamp of a stylised wasp, the same as the Kassnets crest. Then Orrld realised this mutilated creature had been intended as a murder weapon. Untreated, this wasp's sting could be fatal, which was why every River baby was given some larva juice for the immunity it provided. If the lord had been stung, it would have been short work to cure him. No doubt, someone had tricked an unsuspecting servant into delivering it. Orrld tore the box into little bits and threw them from the window. These rooms were on the top floor, and he watched until the last had fluttered out of sight. No harm done. He could not face an inquest. Exhausted, he lay on the bed staring at the flowers painted on the ceiling, his mind too troubled for sleep.

Jie came in some time later. 'I think the lord would like me to take you to him,' he said, pouring water for them both.

Orrld drank and slipped on his clogs. 'Where are we going?'

'I don't know.'

Orrld followed the Crystal Bearer through the Summer Palace. Now and then Jie would stop, the better to feel the direction of where the king was, and then they would continue. They walked through many empty rooms until they came outside by way of a plain wooden door. High, stone walls stood either side of a narrow path. Vines criss-crossed the top of the walls making a canopy and providing shade. The path turned this way and that and Orrld had the notion they were in a maze. Rounding a corner, they found the king and Arrant. Jie touched the ground with his one hand as they approached.

'I'm sorry for leaving you alone again,' said the king.

Orrld shrugged. He understood he could not be a part of everything he did. They walked down the path together. Orrld glanced back over his shoulder. He liked to know how far or near any of the Pack were before he spoke, and was surprised to see Arrant and Jie walking away. He looked about for the others, fully expecting to see Sho atop the wall. Now Llund was smiling.

'This is the only place I am considered to be safe.'

They waited until Arrant and Jie disappeared around a corner. When they had gone, still, he had a watched feeling, although he never said. Llund held his hand as they walked. 'I'm sorry you saw that this morning,' he said, looking at the ground. 'I thought I was sharing with you a happy moment of my life.'

Orrld could feel his profound disappointment and sadness. 'No one could have anticipated such cruelty.'

'I might have guessed she would try to trick me…'

'There was nothing you could have done,' said Orrld, taking him into his arms and holding him.

'Some say I should have had her executed. That we should have taken up arms and fought at least. But what's the point, Orr? All that bloodshed. All the lives that would have been lost. All those innocent shoken just come to see a new prince.'

Llund broke free of the embrace and sat down by the wall, resting his head on his knees. Orrld sat beside him, an arm about his shoulders.

'You did the right thing.'

'They say I am a weak king. Truth is, I've never felt like any sort of king…'

'Compassion takes greater strength than giving in to violence. And shoken that seek power are probably the worst sort of rulers.'

Llund rubbed his face and stood, pulling Orrld up with him. They walked on for another hundred paces before Llund stopped by an archway.

'I want you to meet the Faar. But you must give me your word to never speak of what you see here. Few know their identity. Just the Crystal Bearers and some others.'

'Of course, you have my word. Does Sho know you're bringing me here?'

He did not answer and led him under the low arch. On the other side was a wild garden. They walked in long, tangled grasses beneath majestic trees. It was beautiful, the ground softly undulating into the distance. Plants and flowers grew in natural profusion and Orrld could hear running water.

'Don't be afraid,' said Llund, holding his hand. Ahead, an animal came loping toward them. As it came nearer, Orrld saw it to be some kind of tiger, only it was larger, much larger than any tiger he had seen in Ekressia. When it came to stand before him its eyes were level with his, and the eyes were the same bright sky-blue as Llund's.

'This is Lashka,' said Llund. 'She's one of the Faar.'

Orrld had not thought the Faar to be anything other than shoken; certainly, Llund had given no clue when he had spoken of their wisdom. He was speechless.

Lashka leaned forward and sniffed at him, her thick white whiskers flexing as she did so. Orrld did not know what to do. Being so close filled him with fear and elation. Her coat gleamed in the sunshine, black and gold and white. She was magnificent and dangerous. Her lips curled back, showing white teeth, terrifying to behold. Was it a smile or a snarl? It was hard to decide. She shook her head and then bent low and gave him a gentle nudge with her broad head. In that touch, so much came flooding forth. Her wisdom and her compassion and all of a sudden, he felt safe. Safer than he had ever felt in all his life. When she lifted her head there was another expression in her eyes – amusement.

'She's your sister!' Orrld blurted out. Lashka laughed then, a deep growl of a laugh but a laugh nonetheless. Then she spoke. Orrld recognised the language – it was the one Llund spoke with Sho and Arrant.

'She says how right you are,' said Llund. 'She can understand anything you say. But Faar are unable to make shoken speech. I'll translate.' Lashka and Llund spoke together as they walked along.

The sun was high, the hottest part of the turn and even

Orrld, who liked the heat, was beginning to feel overcome from tiredness and lack of food.

Lashka led them to an ancient tree whose branches dipped to the ground and where they met the earth, saplings sprang forth in tall profusion, reaching through the old tree's canopy and then branching out above. Lashka picked her way among the stems and branches to the thick trunk and a place on the ground worn smooth. With a grunt, she lay down in the dip, stretching out her legs. They sat beside her.

Orrld was relieved a basket of fruit and bread was there. He ate while Llund and Lashka talked. Under the tree, it was cool and their voices were soothing. Orrld lay back on the grass and slept.

CHAPTER THIRTEEN

J unas was tall even for one of the Mithe. She had to shorten her stride in deference to the Elder. All night they had walked, the other Elders returning to their villages as they had passed. Now they were alone. She marvelled that the old woman could keep going for so long without even a drink, let alone any food. Junas said nothing, concerned that this might still be some part of the trial. Certainly, it had all seemed too easy. She expected to fail at any moment. When the second moon had risen, they came to the last of the sky-pinnacles. After this, the land continued flat and barren for five horizons. This pinnacle was the smallest of all, and around the base were various objects. 'You may take three things,' said the Elder, handing her the lamp.

There was much from which to choose. A bag of coin, bread and fruit, a coat of coloured silks, a thick necklace of twisted gold, and clothes, far better than any she was wearing. Weapons, some worn, others new and ornate. There was even some meat roasting on a spit. Junas ignored her hunger pangs. She knew nothing about the task before her. Nobody did. Always she had felt it must involve a solitary journey – why else teach map-law and survival?

A single walk around the pinnacle and Junas knew what she needed. She brought the objects to the Elder. A pair of striking flints, an old, medium-sized knife, and a waterskin. This last she had chosen with care. Two were hanging in offering; she had sniffed them both, rejecting the one filled with wine.

They walked on; dawn broke early, the sun rising rapidly in the clear sky ahead of them, bright rays across the flat ground. 'Do you know where you are?' asked the Elder.

Junas did, although she glanced about briefly to make sure this was not a trick. 'We are south of Konset. Three hundred and fifty paces to the left flows the river and ahead, the Flatlands...'

'Yes, yes, child, you have a sound memory,' the Elder cut her short. 'Yet here is a place not marked on any map you have ever seen.' Abruptly she bent down and Junas thought she had stumbled until she saw how she searched with her hands, feeling and prodding in the scrub-grass. The sun was fully up when she found that for which she searched... a slab of rough stone partly concealed by plants. Taking a small round pebble from her pocket, she tapped a simple rhythm upon it, one-two-three... pause... one-two-three.

'This is where I take my leave,' she said, standing. Then, unexpectedly, hugged her and walked away. Junas watched her go back the way they had come until she disappeared from view.

Junas pulled her hood over her head to protect her from the sun and shield her eyes so she could see more easily. Turning slowly, she scanned all of the surrounding Flatlands. Empty of shoken and beast, all she could do was wait. Thirst and hunger gnawed but she was afraid to move lest she should not be able to find this spot again. Junas sat, wondering if she should tap the stone again. It was hot; she allowed herself a sip of water. A locust hopped near, which she caught and ate alive. They were nicer cooked with honey but she was too hungry to care. Several more came within reach and she gave thanks to Mother God for feeding her.

Junas was soon bored. Inactivity and patience had never been her strength. Whilst the locusts had taken the edge off her hunger, she knew she would surely die of thirst if she did not seek water and refill the waterskin. She scraped her hands over the rough rock, pulling away the grass and plants, hoping to find a clue as to what she should do next. The flat rock was an uneven shape and entirely unremarkable. Upon its surface, she could see no mark. Tapping the rhythm with her knife brought no response. All she could think of was lifting it. Perhaps there was a tunnel beneath and the stone was, in fact, a door. Moving it was no easy task as the rock was a broad stride across and when she dug with her blade into the dry ground to free it, it was thicker than she had anticipated. Eventually, she managed to get her fingers under the edge and with a great act of will, stood the stone on its side. There was nothing but the dry ground beneath. With a heave, she pushed it over. At last, she had an answer, for on this side was a crudely etched map.

At the top, a rising sun and then the Flatlands she knew with, importantly, the positions of streams. Struck across the top were four parallel horizontal lines – a traditional way of providing directions. This then was the first part of her journey, to walk four horizons in the direction of the rising sun.

At the bottom in the centre, in the home place, was a circle. It was gouged deeper than all else. This was what she must find although what the circle represented was unclear.

Junas traced each line on the map with her fingers, closing her eyes occasionally to check that the picture in her mind matched the one in front of her. When she was satisfied that she had committed every detail to memory she rolled up the memory-map and set it atop the sky-pinnacle in her imagination. With difficulty, she flipped the stone back over and did her best to hide it as before.

Now she knew she must cross the Flatlands, she rolled in the dust, patting handfuls into her hair and face for camouflage and as a shield from the sun.

Then, facing the way the sun had risen, she scanned that horizon to find a way-mark. The Flatlands were aptly named. There was no feature she could discern. Junas took fifty even strides out from the stone and looked again. A barely discernible speck poked up from the land into the sky. She watched it to be sure it was solid, not some trick of cloud. When she was satisfied, she began walking.

Junas walked without rest, drinking sparingly and thwarting her hunger with any edible insects she could easily catch without straying from her path. The way-mark looked to be a bare tree the nearer she came. It was dusk when she stood beneath it. Using her knife, she prised off some of the dry bark looking for grubs. The tree was dead, the wood brittle and crumbling. With care, she stepped fifty paces, to re-align herself with the stone map and the setting sun behind her.

Darkness came quickly to this part of Opherion. Not wishing to lose her way she made a hollow in the ground where she stood, the knife her only tool. This was an effort after the turn's walk, yet necessary. When it was deep enough, she curled inside, covering herself with the dry, dusty soil as best she could. It would protect her from the night's chill and more importantly keep her smell from predators that might prowl the Flatlands at night.

Hunger awoke her before the light did. After taking a few sips of water, she filled in the hollow, setting any stones to one side. Then she prayed to Mother God as the sun rose.

All who entered the trials did so without weapon or provision. Once again, she wished she had her things. Even a bag would have been useful.

She sorted the stones, setting aside six that were heavy, small and round, and two others, one broad and flat and the other similar but rough, these palm-sized. Junas honed her blade, first with the rough stone and then with the smooth, returning the edge to sharpness.

Her cape was made of soft, thin goat-skin, light and strong. With the now sharp knife, she cut a hand's breadth off the bottom and from this, one thin strip. She cut the strip into three and platted them together, creating a good strong cord. The larger piece she sliced in half and used one part to fashion a simple knotted sling, which she tucked into her belt. With the last, she bound the round stones, flints and the sharpening stones and tied them with the cord, leaving a small opening at the top; it was makeshift but better than nothing. She fastened this to her belt, tucked the knife at the small of her back, and slung the half-empty waterskin over her shoulder.

Now it was fully light she could see the horizon against the cloudless sky. Directly ahead, there was a bulge in the otherwise straight horizon line. From this distance, it could be anything, a small hill, a clump of trees, even some dwellings. Throwing her cape on, she set off. With perseverance, she could reach this next way-mark before the sun was hottest. Food and water were becoming an urgency; she kept a lookout for rabbits. The Flatlands were barren as ever.

The sun was halfway to midturn when she saw a flurry of crows gathered around some carrion. When she approached, they flew off squawking. She expected to find a dead animal. What she saw shocked her.

A girl, recently dead, lay sprawled on her back. The crows had pecked out her eyes and some of her face. Junas turned away, retching, her empty stomach not even managing to bring forth a mouthful of bile. She took a sip of water to steady herself and thought how the Elder had tapped the stone. At the time, she had thought it to be a signal for another to meet her. When no one came, she wondered what the tapping had been for – now it was obvious. She was the third.

Afraid and alone Junas thought back to the vow she had taken all those years ago. Then, little more than a child, the words had no meaning. Now she understood. *Succeed and live or die trying.*

Junas did not intend on dying.

She stood up, shooing away those crows bold enough to resume their feast with her near. When they were circling overhead, she went to the body. This is what she knew – map-law and survival. How to look. How to see. How to find the useful, in every situation. And how to remember.

Junas took a deep breath and made herself look at the dead girl's face, reminding herself that if she let her concentration lapse, if she failed to bring together all her knowledge, she would be the crows' feast.

Apart from the crow damage, it appeared she had simply died of thirst. Her waterskin was empty. Junas gratefully took it. Two would be useful.

Judging from her clothes and braided hair she had come from a wealthy family. Evidently, wealth was what she valued as she found no weapon or knife but she had a bag of coins at her waist and about her throat, she wore a gold rope similar to the one she had seen in the choosing objects. Junas put the necklace and the girl's finger rings into the coin bag. She took her belt and pulled off her boots. She could see they were too small for her own feet; a shame, they were better leather than her own. Perhaps she could sell them. She was curious why this girl, who had the sense to pick a waterskin had not picked a knife. Sure enough, in her boot, she found one hidden. It was a long thin blade in a boiled leather sheath decorated with her name, Adarna. Junas tucked it into her own boot. Weapons at the trial were forbidden. Somehow, knowing the girl had cheated made her death easier.

There was one more thing the girl could provide. Above, the crows were circling. Loading her newly made sling with a stone, she crouched near. It was not long until the crows forgot about her and settled once again to their feast. Junas was a practised shot and patient enough to wait for them to return between each killing. When she had six, she put the stone back in her pouch, cut the girl's braids and used them to tie the crows by their feet onto the belt.

The way-mark was clear now, a small cluster of trees. They promised shade and a fire to cook the birds on. Junas said a prayer over Adarna before she left.

CHAPTER FOURTEEN

Mag'Sood awoke with the first thud. Light seeped into the chamber, making him feel groggy. The thud came again. He got up and opened the shutters, wincing from the sudden brightness. Across the courtyard, a working party was busy freeing the walls of the thick ice that amassed on every surface of Tarestone. Hordes of Sturgar were occupied on the light and dark of every turn freeing the black reparda rock lest the castle became buried in the Ice Wastes. Mag'Sood watched as those on the ramparts swung an immense spiked ball from a chain, causing the ice encrusted on the wall to shatter and fall. Another party on the ground gathered it up and took it away. Lately, he had them use this ice to build a wall around Tarestone, like the stone ones he had seen encircling shoken castles. Many complained about the futility of such a task. They would praise his foresight in the end. War would bring the shoken here. When they came, they would be ready.

The She-Aulex was not here. Occasionally she took her pups out onto the ice-plain to hunt. Without her, he felt strangely alone.

Another thud. Tarestone shuddered; ice split and fell, crashing to the ground. The noise would only get louder the nearer they came. He decided to go to the other side of the castle to rest. Before he could close the shutters, the door to his chambers burst open. Six of his Primary Warriors stood in the wide hallway, and one of them walked into the room.

He was young and bold, and Mag'Sood had felt his animosity grow. As they circled each other he realised he should have challenged him, kept him in his place. Complacency and death were companions.

'I see you are alone,' breathed the warrior. 'You have no Aulex to protect you now. We must return to the old ways, where the strongest among us rules.' The warriors in the corridor hissed their assent.

Mag'Sood stood tall. Although bigger than the young warrior, he had fought too often to judge a rival on size and waited, attuning his fight prescience.

When the warrior made his first move, he was ready, blocking the double-fisted blow to his face. Still, he reeled back. Knowing where a strike would come was useless if an opponent was stronger and quicker. The attack was vicious and relentless. Repeatedly the warrior flew at him, snarling and biting. Defence took all of his energy. In comparison, he was old. Soon he would tire. Once he was injured, the rest of the Primary Warriors would join in. When it was beyond doubt that he had lost, they would drive him out onto the snow so that the nation could witness the killing blows delivered by their new Master.

Mag'Sood cried out in the hope the pious would rescue him. 'I am your God!' His song resounded unanswered. 'Without my wisdom, you will never gain supremacy over the softlings!'

In the courtyard below Sturgar, roused from sleep, stood

in silence, listening to the fight, not knowing who was winning.

The body blows continued and the warrior was smiling. Mag'Sood saw his teeth were already filed to points... the mark of a leader.

'Crotus has spoken,' he sang, quieter now.

On the ice flow, the She-Aulex heard Mag'Sood's cry. The words meant nothing to her. She did not understand this other speech the Sturgar made when they issued the high-pitched sounds. Yet she heard something in the calling that let her know he was afraid. She ran then, her pups following behind. Going through the castle would take too long. Every cry filled her with longing for him. Crowds of Sturgar parted as she hurtled into the courtyard. Thick ice still covered the walls beneath the opening where he liked to sleep. Digging in her long claws, she climbed the wall with ease. Inside he was losing a fight with one of his kind.

Her scales turned red as she lashed out. The Sturgar stood where he was, shocked by the sight of his intestines spilling onto the floor in a wriggling mass. Another slash, this to the throat, and his lifeblood poured as he sank to the floor.

Some other warriors cowered nearby. She had no interest in them. Outside she could hear her young calling. They were hungry. On the ice, they had just been about to make a kill. No longer angry now he was safe, the She-Aulex returned her scales to black and began eating.

When she had eaten all she could she walked slowly through the castle to find her pups where she had left them. Sturgar were awake, even though it was the light side of the turn. Ignoring the onlookers she regurgitated lumps of chewed flesh for them to feed on then lay down nearby, watching them quarrel over the best bits. He had followed her and now spoke to his kind. They kneeled before him and chanted his name. She had no interest in their words. He was safe. When he was safe, they were safe. That was all she understood.

Growing fast, the pups' squabbles were becoming ever more dangerous. Sometimes, for their safety, it was necessary to intervene, especially when, as now, a few of them ganged up on another. The She-Aulex went over and with gentle jaws plucked the runt of the litter from the fight. She carried the scrawny creature to where she lay, hawking up part-digested food just for her.

The runt ate greedily of the soft, bloody lumps. There were many in the litter, all strong and lively. This little one was not needed. Such a pitiful creature should have been left behind on the ice to die. She had an empathy with the runt's plight. After all, this was how she had made a beginning. Abandoned because she was too small to keep up with the rest of the litter. If he had not found her, fed and cared for her, then she would have died a nothing.

Exhausted from the fight, although he hid this well, Mag'-Sood went to the throne room to sleep and wrapped himself in the furs and softling skins that draped the Black Throne. At the bottom of the dais, the She-Aulex licked her pups. Her closeness was a comfort, that and the sounds of the sung prayers that resonated throughout Tarestone, praising him, praising the Aulex. Giving thanks for his safety.

Troubled thoughts kept him from the sleep he craved. It had been a near miss. If the young warrior had prevailed a few moments longer then he would have died, he was certain. Now he considered each of his Primary Warriors and wondered who would make the next bid for supremacy. They had seen how he had struggled. Soon another would wait for the Aulex to leave. Next time he may not be so lucky. Total devotion was what he needed.

Devotion like the shoken king had from his protectors. Holding up the tiny glass vial he kept around his neck, he looked at the glowing drop of gold liquid. This was the shoken king's secret. It was what bound his Pack to him. He needed to know more. Two questions worried him throughout the light side of the turn as sleep eluded him. Just before the darkness came, the nation ceased their singing; in the sudden quiet he had slept out of sheer exhaustion. On waking, he had the answers.

CHAPTER FIFTEEN

B oth moons had risen when Mag'Sood strode across the ice. Curver Thist scuttled beside him trying to suppress his shivering; even the full-length whale fur was little protection from the bitter cold. A few paces ahead the She-Aulex loped softly along, her scales alternating between grey and black, giving her a half-seen, shimmering appearance. To the Sturgar that they passed, she was truly a mythical creature. Behind marched five Drith Primary Warriors. Now none of them posed any threat – all suffered tail rings like those he had inflicted on the Tethlic Primary Warriors who became his after he killed their leader, Mag'Goro. It was a good solution. Killing them would have made him look weak. This way he had control. Each turn he would release and move their rings, up or down, depending on the warrior's loyalty. A ring left unattended caused the tail to fall off below the metal ring. A short tail was a disgrace. Each turn Mag'Sood liked to administer the key with his hand and the only key dangled from the She-Aulex's neck.

Mag'Sood was once again supreme. There was just one he feared – a Raider who was seldom at Tarestone. His renown had spread. Songs about his courage and strength regularly drifted across the ice. He had become a leader in his own right.

They went to the ice holes where the sea kreggs bobbed in the water and lines of Tethlic Sturgar loaded and unloaded the vessels, passing bundles from one to the other. When the workers noticed the Master, they knelt, and soon the activity stopped, all waiting in silence. The ice creaked and groaned.

'I seek the Shoken-Slayer,' whispered Mag'Sood. They passed his words from one to another like a ripple. They waited and far back, from behind the kneeling crowds, a figure approached. Tall and lean, he ran across the ice, his long tail raised. Many had heard the rumours of how the Master would have died if not for the protection of the She-Aulex. Those who could not quite believe his divinity wished for a fight between these two knowing the younger male would win.

The Shoken-Slayer stood before the Master, looking directly at him. His slit pupils were demarked with a fine red line, a warning to any he possessed fight prescience. At first, it seemed like an act of defiance. Then he prostrated himself at Mag'Sood's feet, quietly repeating one word, 'Redeemer.'

Mag'Sood glanced down at the Curver, for he had the gift of telling whether another spoke truth or lie.

'He loves you, Master,' said the Curver. It was true. The Shoken-Slayer was full of religious fervour. The Curver felt a wave of relief – he did not think the masses would tolerate the She-Aulex eating the Shoken-Slayer, and he feared to have a new Mag. Better a known devil than a new one, he thought.

'Stand,' whispered Mag'Sood.

The Shoken-Slayer stood, head bowed, knees bent in supplication. Even so, it was still clear he was bigger than the Mag.

73

'I would ask of you a task,' said Mag'Sood and waited for the kneelers to pass on his words for all to hear.

'Let me be your strong arm, a force in the darkness, a bringer of the truth,' whispered the Shoken-Slayer. It was from the scriptures, although the Curver fancied the quote was lost on most of those present, including the Master.

They walked back to Tarestone, everyone kneeling and calling out words of devotion as they passed. Once again, the Curver wondered if the Master truly believed he was a God or was it just a way to rule effectively? Certainly, he appeared a God now. Striding through the castle, his head and arms bare despite the bitter cold, trotting, devoted at his side, one of the greatest Drith warriors the Sturgar race had ever known. Ahead loped the She-Aulex, terrifying and powerful, her scales mirrored gold.

The Curver had counselled that they should summon the Shoken-Slayer. Going out onto the ice was too dangerous. The Master had been adamant. Scurrying behind, the Curver was not sure whether the Mag was stupid or brave.

On the ground floor of Tarestone was an audience hall. Like much of the castle, it was closed off, disused, and neglected. Recently the Mag had opened and repurposed the immense space to become a kind of temple. A high dais, fashioned from reparda rock was at the centre, on top a simple slab of ice that served as both altar and throne. The space was harshly cold for the preservation of ice-sculptures that stood around the perimeter. Every life-sized image was a likeness of Mag'Sood, carved by the devoted.

Mag'Sood and the She-Aulex walked around the dais once before mounting the steps. The Shoken-Slayer followed. High-ranking Sturgar, mostly Drith, filed in and when the room was full, the doors closed and a new hush dawned as the North Priest raised his arms to the vaulted ceiling invoking the God, Crotus. Beside him, smoke from a small brazier rose in a line. He passed his hands within it, making the smoke snake back and forth.

'Crotus, we beseech you,' hissed the Priest. 'Crotus, we beseech you. Crotus, we beseech you – send us Wolash.' The Priests South, West, and East now stood from where they crouched at the corners of the ice slab and raised their arms. From them came a sibilant whispered chant, one word repeated: Wolash. When the North Priest deemed the Messenger God was present, he lowered his hands and the hall was silent.

A door opened and the onlookers parted, making a path to the altar. The disciple led in the Watcher in a silver gown trimmed with seal-fur. They mounted the dais steps and the She-Aulex changed her scales from gold to red.

The North Priest beckoned the Shoken-Slayer forward and he came to kneel before him, head back, throat exposed and arms extended behind, making of himself a sacrifice. A ripple of whispers shushed among the crowd. The disciple twirled a piece of metal with long tongs in the fire.

'Mag'Sood is the will of Crotus made flesh,' said the North Priest. 'You have impressed him and God.' The Shoken-Slayer did not move. 'Will you become a mark of your devotion?' asked the Priest. The congregation repeated his words.

The Shoken-Slayer hissed his assent and the disciple lifted the white-hot metal from the fire, twisting the tongs between her palms. The Watcher grasped the Shoken-Slayer's face. The disciple held the tongs still so the molten metal gathered into a globule and dripped, searing hot onto his skin, again and again until he had a shining silver circle like a third eye in the centre of his forehead.

He neither moved nor cried out and gazed upward with an expression of bliss. Only his long tail, which thrashed uncontrollably, indicated his abundant pain.

. . .

Curver Thist, himself unworthy of hallowed ground, stood with the crowd and wondered what it must be like to feel such loyalty. His devotion to the Mag was simply a matter of self-preservation.

The disciple poured the remaining metal into a mould and plunged all into a pail of ice chips. She broke away the mould and handed the still warm disk to the North Priest who blessed it and put it into the Watcher's outstretched hands. She held it to her face and tilted it. When an image appeared, she showed the Mag. Pleased, he looked about, smiling. 'Who will be his second?' he asked. Sturgar were always marked in pairs. Several warriors stepped forward, eager for the honour.

CHAPTER SIXTEEN

Junas was glad to find the way-mark was a clump of trees alongside a shallow stream. She quenched her thirst and filled up the two waterskins. Then she climbed the tallest of the trees and looked out from every direction. Apart from some vegetation that followed the stream's path, the Flatlands stretched on every side empty of life as far as she could see. If she was alone, then she was safe. She climbed down and set about making a fire.

There were plenty of dry sticks and the crow feathers made good kindling. She stuffed as many as she could into the coin purse for later and cooked all six birds. The crow meat was dry and tough but at least she had plenty of water to wash it down. When she had finished eating Junas wrapped the remaining three birds in leaves, tying the bundles with grass. There was just enough light to see by as she put out the fire and made herself a sleeping platform high up in the tree.

The night was cold and she slept fitfully, not daring to risk another fire. In the morning, her shivering woke her. She ate one of the crows whilst sitting in the topmost branches. There was nothing to see and the turn was dawning as hot and windless as those before.

Junas picked a way-mark ahead and began to walk. Halfway across, she stopped and stood still, looking back. Once, as a small child, her mother had carried her this far. They had joined a spring hunting party and the Flatlands had been green and lush after the rains. It had looked a different place then, but it was the same place. Even as a child, she had always felt the way. Facing the direction she must travel she said goodbye to her family, saying each of their names with every step into the unknown.

The sun was past mid-turn when she reached the way-mark, a grey rock jutting like a jagged tooth from the earth. Junas sat down in the shade it provided, drank some water, and ate more crow. Then, deciding not to risk the sun's vengeance, lay down and slept.

When she awoke, the air was cooler and the horizon ahead more easily seen without the heat haze. What looked like a sky-pinnacle pierced the horizon line ahead. As she walked, she looked through the maps in her mind. None showed a pinnacle here. Leaving out such a definitive and ancient feature seemed strange.

Night had come when she stood beside it. Even in the starlight, it was easy to see that this was not the work of Mother God. Shoken hands had built it from many stones fused together with rock-dust paste. Junas stood and wondered what was next. Around her, all was flat, empty, and quiet. Climbing it might provide some answers. She bent down, rubbing her hands in the dust and as she did so, saw a hole.

This, like the pinnacle, was not born of the Mother. It was imperfectly round and edged with white pebbles. This was the fourth horizon. Was this the circle marked on the stone-map? Junas knelt and put her head in, sniffing and listening.

There was a faint smell of smoke. She put her knife between her teeth and crawled in.

The tunnel was long and soon dark. Smooth stones lined the entrance, but now she crawled on dry mud. Where she had felt no fear out on the endless plain, here her heart pounded and the darkness pressed against her, like death.

After a while, she put away her knife. Occasionally she lay down to rest and listen. Without any natural light, time muddled even though she tried to imagine where the moons would be on their journey over the sky. All she knew was that she could not give up.

Exhaustion claimed her and she slept dreaming that she would never escape. When she next awoke, there was a prick of light far ahead. She ate the last crow and crawled on.

Gradually the light grew until she could see the shape of the tunnel ahead, then her hands. At last, it ended and she was in a chamber, sparsely furnished and dimly lit. She stooped beneath the low ceiling.

'What's your name, child?'

Junas had not noticed the old woman sitting on a stool by the curved, mud wall.

'Junas,' she said.

'The first moon's true name,' said the old woman, putting aside the basket she was weaving and standing up. 'Come here so I can see you,' she added.

Junas went over to her and the old woman reached up, touching her face lightly with her fingertips. Then she examined each of her hands and Junas looked down at the old woman's pale unseeing eyes and deep-set wrinkles. The old woman nodded, then began measuring with her hand's span, from under Junas' chin to her waist then around her waist, across the top of her shoulders and the length of her arms. Her lips moved as she worked, counting each hand measurement. Junas stood completely still, too polite to ask questions. When she had finished she seemed happy. 'You are young and strong. Come, Pathfinder,' she said, leading the way. Junas followed her into another room half-filled with water from an underground stream. The walls seeped and trickles of moisture dripped and echoed from the low ceiling.

'Wash. I will bring you fresh clothes.'

Junas stripped and went down the steps into the cool, still water. It was deeper than she was tall and she ducked her head beneath the surface, relieved to free herself from the dust.

When she got out the old woman dried her and helped her into a simple cotton dress. Then she sat her down with some food. Junas ate ravenously while the old woman sat opposite weaving a basket with experienced hands.

'Now all you need is rest,' she said when Junas had swallowed the last mouthful. Putting aside her work, she got up and Junas followed her down a long, low tunnel to another room. Bright shafts of sunlight filtered through narrow cracks in the rock ceiling. Under an arch lay one of the Faar.

Automatically Junas began to sink to her knees, but the old woman caught her by the elbow. 'Go to her child. She is the reason you are here,' she said.

Junas did as she was bid and went over and knelt beside her. She had never been so close to one of them before. She felt tiny next to her.

The Faar spoke, 'I was Loncha. I am glad you have come at last, Junas. Sorry that the path you must take will be long and lonely. Do you accept the task willingly?'

'Yes.' Junas had never heard their language spoken by them. It sounded different, clearer and somehow of the earth like the sound of rain or thunder or wind. She looked into her eyes, bluer than any sky.

'What is it that you want me to do?'

The Faar laid down her head and stretched out her legs. She was unbelievably beautiful, the colours of her striped fur black, orange, every brown and cloud-white.

'Lay here with me, Pathfinder. Rest. On the new turn, you will know,' she said, her voice a low rumble.

Junas lay down. The Faar reached a great paw over her and pulled her near, tucking her close, and Junas could feel the soft thick fur next to her skin. She smelt warm and clean like sun-dried grass.

The Faar were sacred. They were not to be approached, spoken to and least of all, touched. Strange then that this felt so natural. Junas moved up closer, nestling her face into the fur and holding on. The great Faar was a mother, a raft on a stormy lake, a clear view to home. She purred slowly and the steady rhythm sent Junas to sleep.

Much later, when she woke, the light had changed. Having turned in her sleep, she was facing the room now, although she was encircled by the Faar's front leg. The shafts of light were moonlight. All colour had gone and as Junas lay there, she became aware there was a new stillness to the room. The only breathing she could hear was her own. She freed herself from the Faar's embrace and looked at her, disbelieving what she already knew. The bright blue eyes looked into the next life now. Junas stroked the broad head.

The old woman came in and knelt. She was crying and this made it easier for Junas to cry also. They sat together, stroking the Faar's beautiful head.

'I thought they lived forever,' said Junas at last.

'Nothing lives forever, child. Even gods die if they must.'

The old woman crawled along the length of the body, feeling her way, and pulled the back leg aside. There, nestling in the soft white belly fur, was an egg.

'This is why she died. Once they lay, they only have a short time left. We waited so long for you. From all the tribes, seven failed. It is a wonder she managed to last this long. Loncha was always stubborn. It was her deepest desire to know you before she died.'

'I didn't know they laid eggs.'

'Why would you? It has been a hundred and fifty years.'

The old woman carefully turned the egg, and pushed it well into the fur again. 'She is still warm, but not for much longer,' she said, getting up. Junas followed her to a small room. It was full of clutter. The blind woman could make more besides baskets.

'Do you realise what you must do?'

'Am I to take the egg somewhere?'

'Somewhere, yes. Take off your clothes.'

Junas did as she was bid and stood naked while the old woman fitted a harness around her, carefully adjusting it here and there until she was satisfied. She left and returned carrying the egg, which she eased into the harness. It fitted snugly so the egg sat over her stomach and her skin was in contact with it to provide warmth. The old woman had clothes tailored ready. When she was dressed, the old woman led her to a corner of the room. There was a long mirror hung on the wall, her reflection was barely visible. Junas found a piece of cloth and wiped away the thick dust.

She looked like she was halfway through pregnancy.

'Eat, while I mend your hair. It will be better if you pass as a young widow.'

Junas sat at the table and ate while the woman made the braids and hung them with widow's beads.

'I can't believe I am so hungry,' she said.

'That's because you have been asleep for two turns, child.'

'Where am I to take the egg?'

'Loncha told you.'

'No, she never said anything. I thought we would talk

when we woke.' Suddenly Junas felt overwhelmed. The old woman held her head, smoothing out her frown.

'While you slept she gave you the answers you needed. All you have to do is hold her image in your mind and ask.'

Junas thought about Loncha. No answer came. The old woman laughed. 'You will have to find a quiet time and make more of concentrating. Her wisdom will not come to you like a magic trick.'

'When will the egg hatch?'

'I don't know. No shoken living has seen such a thing. But it's a big egg and the bigger the egg then the longer it takes to make life. Turn it often. Keep it warm next to your skin and only set it aside for a short time. Don't let anyone else touch it. No one. Only you.'

The old woman was fitting a basket onto her back. It was heavy. 'I have put food and bedding and a few items you would carry if you were expecting a baby.'

Junas followed her from the room and into another. Many items were laid on a large table, including the things she had arrived with.

'Take what you think might be useful.'

Junas chose a good knife that had its own sheath and belt. There was also a proper slingshot and a bag of stones. She put the coin bag into her basket and took a long-handled stick from the wall.

The old woman picked up the gold necklace that had been on the dead girl and fastened it around her neck. 'A widow would have some jewellery,' she said and felt her way across the room, moving newly made baskets stacked against the wall. Behind was a narrow door that opened reluctantly.

'It's time to go, Junas Pathfinder,' she said, standing aside to let her pass.

She stepped through the doorway and turned to thank the old woman, but she had already closed the door. Alone in the dark Junas wished she was enveloped in the embrace of the Faar with the feeling that nothing bad could ever happen and she would soon return home to her family. From the other side of the door, she heard the old woman call out. 'Don't look back.'

CHAPTER SEVENTEEN

E tter lay in her tent listening to the night. Nearby a line of tethered horses shuffled as two soldiers on night watch passed with a war dog. A light breeze ruffled the canvas and the small brazier that warmed her tent crackled as logs shifted to ashes. There were sounds of soldiers murmuring and something else on the very edge of her hearing. She sat up, turning her head the better to hear. Faintly a voice raised in triumph, this answered by several others.

Etter threw aside her sleeping fur, re-positioned the eye patch that had been hanging around her neck and stepped out into the darkness. The camp was random, identical tents pitched in groups here and there. This was against regulation but she felt safer this way. Any observing would have little idea where more experienced soldiers were. They had camped on this plain for three turns. Her maps had it marked as Clisotian territory, yet of the Horse Lords, there was no sign. Their winter dwellings in nearby woods were deserted. This was a nuisance as she had planned to buy horses from them and knew Clisotian conscripts made good soldiers. Disappointed, Etter marked the map for a Freeland.

After the morrow, she planned to move on, following the Soster River to Thrane. They had gone as far north as she dared collecting taxes and conscripts, stopping as often as possible for army training. It was little good simply signing bodies to the Median army. They needed skill and she saw no point in arriving at Valkarah with a host of raw recruits that were little more than prisoners. The task was difficult. Most of the conscripts were reluctant, many tried to escape and those that could make it as soldiers were hampered by a lack of uniforms and weapons. She hoped the town would remedy this and had sent word for supplies. As she walked through the camp, she thought about Thrane. It used to be one of her favourite towns although a good many years had passed since her last visit. After the cold and the endless, empty road, she knew the town would lift everybody's spirits.

Etter walked beyond the camp toward the voices. Shouts and whoops were coming from a copse at the edge of the grassland. She jogged toward it, stopping now and then to listen. Some of the voices she knew. When near, she sank to her knees and crawled through the long grass.

In a coppice recently used to cut arrow shafts six men stood, at their centre a woman. She was almost naked; shreds of her clothing lay about her like lost hopes. She did not cry out or try to move away. The men pushed her from one to the other, jeering and laughing. The ring leader, whose voice Etter recognised, soon tired of the game and when she stumbled toward him, he caught her and threw her to the ground. She lay face down in the mud, silent and unmoving. With ceremony, he undid his breeches and pulled out his cock, turning slowly so his companions could admire his erection.

'Let us rejoice that although this useless woman will never make a soldier for the king's army or any other army for that matter, we can at least employ her cunt.' He knelt and pulled her onto her knees, ripping away the last of her clothing. 'See how compliant she is, lads,' he said, stroking her naked buttocks. 'She understands that being a morale booster will be her soldier's duty.' The other men laughed and argued amiably amongst themselves as to who would go next.

Etter took up a small horn that hung from her belt and blew it twice. The two short, shrill notes would bring a pair of the night watch. Drawing a short sword, she walked toward the men.

They stopped laughing.

Many commanders allowed themselves to fall below peak condition, believing their high rank would always win respect, but Etter trained every day. She was strong, taller than most and even as she was outnumbered, each feared to face her.

'Pick her up,' she said. One of the men, keen to appear a bystander, came forward and lifted the woman to her feet. She looked worse standing, gaunt, naked, and shivering, staring down at her booted feet. The man took off his cloak and draped it around her shoulders.

'Name and rank,' she said, approaching the ring leader, although she knew him well enough. He stood to attention. His cock less so.

'Jarrish, Master of Horse,' he said.

Two of the night's watch arrived on horseback. Etter re-sheathed her blade. 'Give your volte to Ban,' she said. One of the riders stepped his horse nearer, trying and failing to keep the grin from his face.

'What, you'd make him Master of Horse over me? He can barely ride,' he said, placing a protective hand over the dagger in his belt that marked his rank.

'I'd like to cut your little cock off,' said Etter, 'but sadly that's not in the code. Like rape.'

'She was willing. Think about it. Did you hear any cries from her?' said Jarrish, covering himself with haste. He glanced around at the others. None of them met his gaze.

'This woman hasn't spoken since she was conscripted. You think silence and weakness give you leave to do as you please?'

'I think trying to train feeble women into soldiers is a waste of my time,' he said.

'I agree. Now you're a foot soldier the problem is no longer yours.'

'Foot soldier!'

'Keep talking and you'll soon be a pacer.'

Jarrish could not contain his anger a moment longer and reached for his shortsword. Etter swung a punch at him so fast his blade was only a quarter drawn when her fist hit him like a war hammer on the temple. He fell to the ground unconscious. She had always been freakishly strong.

She took the volte from his belt. Newly-made and of a lesser quality than the old ones – the horse head hilt cast in base metal, the blade short and crudely engraved. A sign of an army growing too fast. Even so, it was well polished. She tossed it to Ban, and then looked at the other men, meeting each with her one, dark eye. They stood to attention. She knew them all by name. 'You will all join the foot march. Any trouble and you will be pacers.' Early in her career, she had decided having wrongdoers whipped was a waste of time. Most bore the scars like a badge of honour. Dropping rank had a much stronger effect.

The woman, silent and shivering, had put on her ragged clothes. At least she had that much sense. Etter took her by the arm and steered her away.

She would not condone rape or bullying for that matter. Yet there was some truth in what Jarrish had said. There were too many in the new army that would never make fighters. Able-bodied and of reasonable mind was the only criteria for a conscript. Half her army comprised unwanted women, feeble boys, and old men. Drilling and training would, in time, make soldiers of the young. But most she knew would never gain the strength to swing a sword or draw a bow. Few could even ride a horse with any skill. They already had fletchers and cooks aplenty. What the Trilands needed were soldiers.

Suddenly tired, Etter led the silent woman into her tent where she lay down next to the brazier. Etter poked the ashes until a spark came, added a log, and found a rough spun blanket for the woman before crawling back under her sleeping furs.

In the morning, she was still there. Etter looked upon her sleeping face, trying to remember the turn she had conscripted her. A season past and if memory served, she was a massacre survivor. Her ragged clothes were that of a noble and there was something about her name. Etter closed her eyes, seeing again the looped, educated writing. Lorimore, that was her name, her family name she could not recall. Etter believed everyone had a use. This woman could read and write and no doubt had some ability with numbers.

Etter threw off the furs, stepped over to the sleeping woman and nudged her with a booted toe.

'Lorimore,' she said softly. 'Lorimore, wake up.'

She awoke with a start, leaping up.

'You're to be my steward,' said Etter. 'Get dressed, I'll show you how best you can serve.'

Over the following turns, Etter set Lorimore to any writing task she could find, and was glad of the reprieve from the constant paperwork her rank evoked. The woman hardly spoke but she filled in ledgers and wrote letters and reports willingly in her beautiful handwriting. She also kept the tent tidy. When they broke camp, Etter found her a horse and was pleased to see she rode well.

Thrane was about seven turn's ride. This would be the biggest town they would pass through this side of Valkarah. It would be a good exercise to arrive in parade formation. Some of the old soldiers had ceremonial uniform; admittedly, many of the recruits had no uniform at all and most were unarmed. Even so, she believed it would benefit all to put on a show and the town of Thrane had not had a visit from the king's army for ten years according to her records. She hoped the spectacle would encourage volunteers from Thrane and instil pride in her recruits.

Halfway to Thrane, they stopped for a turn to practice. In recent towns, too poor to pay money, she had taken weapons in place of taxes. Recruits who were yet unarmed, she allowed to choose for themselves any weapon that they liked from the wagons. Afterwards, some remained unarmed. She had them make wooden spears, tipping the ends with arrowheads; they were crude yet better than nothing.

Etter inspected the near-empty wagons. There were a few remaining items taken for their metal, plough blades, cooking pans, and a rusty gate. The metal would be useful for horseshoes. The pacer sweeping out the cart handed her a crossbow. A small thing, more toy than weapon, light enough for a child to carry. Beautifully made, the metalwork was etched with a herd of running deer and the slim bolts decorated with hunting hounds and fletched with coloured feathers. She wound back the string, slid a bolt into the shaft, and loosed it. The bolt was small yet flew in a true line, hitting a nearby tent post with a satisfying thwack. At close range, the bolts could still kill.

That night she gave Lorimore the crossbow and showed

her how to carry it hooked on her belt and how it worked. Etter was unsure if she understood her instructions or if she would practice loading and aiming. Lorimore said nothing, the same vacant expression on her face. No wonder they called her Dead Woman.

Returning to her tent late one evening Etter was glad to see Lorimore hard at work, carefully copying scrawled notes about supplies and taxes neatly into ledgers. The crossbow was on the table in front of her next to an oil lamp. She doubted the silent woman would have the speed or sense to use it with any accuracy. Etter was glad to see she had the sense to keep it near as a deterrent.

Etter nearly fell over the dead body sprawled on the ground. It was Jarrish. He lay on his back with his legs buckled beneath him, the bolt that had killed him sticking out between his eyes. It was a good shot.

'Did he try to rape you again?'

Lorimore just carried on writing.

Etter stepped over the body and put a hand on her shoulder. 'Did he try to hurt you?'

Lorimore put down the quill. 'No. He was looking for you.' She spoke Median with a strong Kassnets accent.

'Lorimore, he wouldn't have harmed you again. I'd already punished him.' She tried to keep her voice calm although in truth she was annoyed. Jarrish had always been trouble but nothing she could not handle. Losing her Master of Horse was something she could have done without.

Lorimore shrugged and took up the quill again.

CHAPTER EIGHTEEN

Ath's temple in Lak-Mur was small, tucked between shabby flat-roofed buildings on the edge of the citadel. A queue of shoken curled back through the narrow streets from the carved wooden door. Sho doubted the neglected God had ever been more popular. Inside it was dim after the bright sunlight and cool. She edged her way through the crowd toward the huge statue at the centre. Yellow silk fabric draped the God. Ath's image was kneeling with outstretched arms as if to embrace the worshipper. The material touched the ground and provided a little privacy for the Healer beneath the canopy.

Jie stood outside the makeshift tent, alert for any danger; he brushed the ground with the fingertips of his remaining hand as she approached. Sho nodded and ducked inside. Orrld, untroubled by the intense heat, attended an elderly man. He stood with his eyes closed as if in prayer, clasping the old, misshapen hands within his own soft, webbed hands. Sho watched the old man's face gain an expression of pure relief. When Orrld opened his eyes and let go the old man flexed his fingers in disbelief. Speechless, he was ushered away by one of the blue-robed temple acolytes. Orrld washed his hands in a stone bowl of water, careful not to disturb the flower petals floating on the surface. He looked tired.

'It's the middle of the turn,' she said, her face blank. 'You should rest, at least until the cool of the evening.'

Another of the acolytes stepped forward, passing Orrld a cloth. 'It's true, Soorah, so many wait, you can never hope to attend them all. Even you,' she said.

Standing in the shadows of Ath's image was the Strick child Math, though he was no child now. Already taller than the Healer, he stood motionless in simple, pale blue robes, the cowl pulled low to hide his eyes. Once he used to hiss whenever she came near.

The acolytes led them through the temple and let them out of a side door into a narrow street, this shaded by coloured silks strung between the buildings creating a rainbow beneath.

Orrld knew better than to offer his healing touch; instead, he walked alongside her. *Why is she here?* Jie was further away than he normally would be. She was pushing him back. The street was empty and quiet and the air was still and heavy. The shoken of Lak-Mur slept on the hottest part of the turn.

'There is someone I know that I would like to take Jie to. He might be able to help him,' she said in a pleasant manner, pulling a smile onto the mask of her face. 'We could escort you to the palace first. Or you could come along, it's not too far.' Orrld wondered what Sho really wished him to do. Go back or come with them? He knew Jie would not leave his side. He was his constant bodyguard now, sleeping outside the king's door, waiting while he healed the sick. Jie and Math were as faithful as shadows.

'There is no more I can do to help Jie. I will come,' said Orrld.

Sho led them through winding back streets keeping to the shade as far as she was able until they came to a small square at the centre of which stood a circular watchtower.

The guard at the door stood aside when he saw them. Sho led the way up the spiralling tower steps and into the cluttered room above. The dwarf, standing on his workbench, made a low bow as they entered; the green monkey beside him did the same.

'This is Godwin, Blade-Master to the king,' said Sho. Orrld inclined his head and shoulders politely. 'The king's Healer, Orrld from the River Ekress,' said Sho, standing aside.

Godwin walked to the end of his workbench. 'Seems like we are both the king's men,' he said, meeting Orrld's eyes with a grin. Orrld took a step toward him to offer his healing touch. Sho caught his sleeve.

'You must be Jie,' said Godwin. Jie came near and pulled off the soft leather he kept around the stump of his wrist.

Sho watched Orrld as he stared in disbelief at the fine silver thread that trailed from Godwin's ankle. The green monkey sidled over to Orrld. Orrld squatted and held out his hands muttering enticingly in Ekressian. Soon she came close enough for him to pet. 'Oh, she's very pretty,' said Orrld.

'Thanks,' said Godwin, smiling but not looking up from examining Jie's arm.

Jie knelt before the dwarf bare-chested as he examined the stump where his hand had been and the arm that remained. 'This is good. Very good,' said Godwin, going back to his workbench and rummaging about in a drawer until he found a measuring tape. 'You've kept your muscles strong on this side.' He carefully measured every aspect of Jie's arm and torso and wrote his findings on a large piece of parchment on his workbench, checking them over and again until he was satisfied. 'I can't give you your sword hand back. But I can help. Come back in a few turns,' he said when he was finished.

All the while, the Strick boy, Math, waited nervously by the door, his face turned toward the wall.

'She seems to have taken a liking to you,' said Godwin amiably, ignoring the hooded figure by the door. The monkey was on Orrld's shoulder now, patting his face with her little black hands.

'My sister, Issolissi, had a pet like her. What's her name?'

'Mirril.'

Sho watched them play with the monkey. Godwin had taught her a few tricks and Orrld laughed joyfully as Mirril did backflips and handstands and stood as still as a stone until Godwin clicked his tongue and threw her a date.

'We should get back to the palace. The lord will be expecting us,' said Sho. As they made to leave Orrld pointed at the silver thread. 'Does that keep you here?' he asked.

'It does.'

'Why?'

It was Godwin's turn to laugh. 'The king binds those he needs close,' he said.

Sho returned to the watchtower in the cool of the night by way of an underground tunnel. Being small, she could easily stand inside. There were many such tunnels beneath the streets of Lak-Mur; they were clean and well-aired because of their regular use. Sentinel dogs carried messages to all parts of the city during peacetime and in times of trouble, war dogs began the attack from here. Sho walked softly, listening. She disliked dogs and never used the tunnels on the light side of the turn when they were busy. The well-trained sentinel dogs would trot past her, intent on receiving their reward on delivering their saddlebags. These dogs were not sent to attack her – this did not stop her wanting to kill every dog she ever saw. This night the tunnel was empty.

All dog-tunnels began and ended in army compounds except this one under the north watchtower. It had a metal grille over it. She gave it two taps with a blade and waited. The monkey arrived first, chittering with excitement to see her. Sho handed Mirril nuts while they waited for Godwin.

'I knew you'd come tonight,' said Godwin, setting down his candle and unlocking the grille. Sho jumped into the vault and followed him up the many steps to the roof where they could sit beneath the stars and talk unheard.

Godwin, who had been expecting her, was roasting slivers of meat on thin metal skewers over a small fire. It smelt delicious in the warm night air. Sho sat down on the rugs watching him season with dried herbs and salt. She had not realised how hungry she was until now.

'The king's companion, what's his name again?' he asked.

'Orrld,' she said in her perfect Ekressian.

Godwin pulled his earlobe and laughed.

'Just call him 'Orr', it's pretty much impossible to pronounce unless you speak River. Although he is often called Soorah, which is more respectful, I think. It means teacher, leader, wisdom.'

'I'm guessing *you* don't address him as such,' he said, passing her a skewer. Sho sighed. They ate together. The meat was delicious.

'I think I know what the problem is,' he said when they were nearly done.

'You sensed something?'

'I did. But not on the Ekressian. There was nothing. He

carries no weapons and has no more of the seeing metal on him and no ability with any weapon. As far as I can tell, he is completely and utterly harmless. You can rest easy.'

'And you like him…'

'How could anyone not like him? All that warmth and love pouring out of him. He's extraordinary. Can he do all that healing as they say?'

'He can. It's like some miracle. I've never seen anyone who can do what he can do.'

'He can heal the king?'

'Yes.'

'Then surely you can forgive him, Sho, with such a gift.'

'Now I know he's harmless…' her voice trailed off and Godwin watched her face in the firelight. Sho never minded him seeing her true expression.

'It must be hard to get used to. Him having a lover and a new confidant when you've been so close all these long years.'

Sho said nothing as she slid the last bit of meat from the skewer and chewed it.

'I'm not jealous if that's what you think…'

'I didn't say that…'

'I just want the lord safe. There is still something I don't understand about him.'

'You'd trust him if he accepted Crystal?'

'If he loves him like he says he does, why won't he?'

'A lot of shoken misunderstand why some of us are happy to be bonded,' he said, running a finger under the silver thread about his ankle. He got up and Sho could see his dark eyes glistening. 'I found something that might ease your burden,' he said.

She followed him down the stairs into his private workshop. The smell of molten metal hung in the air and she wondered what he had been making this turn as he lit an oil lamp. When the room was bright, he took a sugared almond from his pocket and showed the monkey, then pointed upwards. Mirril knew what was required of her. Climbing the wall shelving, she made her way to the highest shelf and followed her master's pointing finger until she found a long, narrow case; this she put between her teeth and returned the way she had come. Godwin took it from her, tossing her reward in the air. She caught it easily, and then sat on the corner of the workbench, noisily sucking off the sugar coating.

Godwin held the case under the lamp. Made from thin cushos steel it shimmered every shade of blue. 'Why not give him this?' he said, selecting a minute key from many that he had on a long chain around his neck. He lifted the lid and tilted the case under the lamplight so that the necklace within caught the light and cast it about the room.

Sho knelt and he placed the open case on her outstretched hands. 'I can't believe you have this…'

'Remember when Sneela saw it in that painting and decided she wanted it when they were first married?'

Sho recalled the time well enough. Sneela had searched every part of both treasuries here and at Valkarah looking for the jewels. Her crying and sulking were limitless. The king told her the piece was long lost. The new queen was used to getting her way.

'He brought it here. Although I always thought he should have made her wear it.'

'It would have saved him a lot of heartache, I think.'

'I always thought he'd give you the sun and rain.'

'I'm a soldier, not his lover,' she said, closing the box. She had never coveted jewels and wondered if the Healer would consider such an item ostentatious.

'You'd feel better though if he wore it. You'd trust him more than you do.'

'He might not want it.'

Godwin unthreaded the key and passed it to her. 'Everyone wants to belong to someone. It's shoken nature.'

She locked the case and tucked it inside her doublet.

He sat down on the floor and smiled. 'You left most of your linegold at the palace then.'

Sho shrugged. 'Seems little point in carrying it.'

'It's swapped its allegiance. The Strick boy, he's the linegold mover.'

'He must be handling it when I'm not there.'

'He'll be drawn to it, just like you were. See if you can get him to come along when I fit Jie with his new hand so I can instruct him.'

'The Healer treats Math like a son. I don't think he will want him to carry weapons. River shoken frown on any sort of violence.'

Godwin laughed, they both did. 'First-generation Strick with fight prescience... what's he going to do with him, teach him herbalism? Talk to the king. We'll dedicate your linegold to the Strick and I'll forge you some more.'

CHAPTER NINETEEN

Etter pulled her horse up. Her bannerman Gatten, holding the king's standard, a gold tiger on a blue field, flanked her on one side. On the other, her steward, the Kassnets woman, Lorimore. They watched the army... her army... ride past in formation. She was pleased with her achievement. All looked as smart as they were able, given the lack of equipment and supplies, and even if they could not fight yet, at least they marched neatly. It was a beginning.

By mid-turn, she hoped to reach Thrane. Then, after a few nights, on to Valkarah. Already she could feel the weather was warmer. Patches of snow clung beneath the hedges and the morning air was cold. At Valkarah, it would already be spring.

When the last of the company had gone by, she cantered her horse to the lead again. Ahead she could see a smallholding, a clutch of slate-roofed buildings and scrub fields. She expected the farmers to greet them. All was deserted. The next farm, this one bigger, the fields and barns visible long before the homestead, also abandoned.

She knew Thrane had a wall. Not such a fortress as

Valkarah yet better than nothing. Perhaps they had taken their families and beasts into the city until they were sure they had nothing to fear from the approaching army. When the city walls were in sight, she expected outriders to meet them. They saw not so much as a stray dog.

They knew something was wrong long before the smell, the unmistakable odour of rotting flesh growing more putrid with every step. In the still, cold air it hung, heavy as a corpse. When they reached the city gates, most were gagging and retching. Etter dismounted and led her nervous gelding through the empty streets.

At the city centre, the slain populace lay in an intricate pattern of circles, the naked bodies bloated and grotesque. Despite the cold, flies had found them, each body unrecognisable from rot and infestation.

Gatten spoke first. 'I thought the Sturgar– I thought they ate their victims,' he said behind the gloved fist he held in front of his nose and mouth.

'The hunting party would eat some. Many would be taken to the north, to Tarestone, for the Sturgar to feed on there,' said Lorimore.

Etter looked at Lorimore, surprised she had spoken and that she was completely calm as if nothing could shock her.

'Surely it's too far? The bodies would be rotten by the time they got so far north?' said Gatten.

'They salt the meat and transport them under the sea. Or sometimes they bring ice overland to pack the meat and keep it fresh,' she said, leading her horse away. Etter followed with the army behind her.

They camped on the outskirts of the city on what would have been pasture. Although they were downwind, the smell lingered as though lodged in their heads. She gave orders for setting up camp – where horses should graze and latrine ditches dug. From experience, she knew it was important to give clear leadership and keep the soldiers busy lest they should panic. As soon as her tent was pitched, she went inside. She needed time to think. There was no army procedure for this.

Some soldiers made it known that they wanted to ride on, afraid that the Sturgar were still near. Etter felt bound by a code of duty to honour the dead. After a battle the fallen would be identified and buried, their graves marked. This was a massacre on an unprecedented scale, all the victims unrecognisable.

She called the soldiers to her and sat astride her horse that they might better hear her words. Firstly, she reassured them that the enemy was long gone and then reminded them of their responsibility and asked for volunteers. Many came forward and together they sacked every dwelling for anything that would catch alight, and built a pyre over the corpses. By night-time, the city burned.

It took three turns to cremate the slaughtered and those who could not stomach the furnace she set about building a memorial. City stone was prised from path, building and wall and heaped in a great mound on high ground. So big, they could see it for two turns when they marched from the smoke and horror.

CHAPTER TWENTY

Posing as a pregnant widow afforded Junas a measure of sympathy wherever she went. Market store holders gave her handfuls of food and wished her well. A childless couple took her in who, no doubt, hoped Mother God would bless their kindness so that fertility would follow. Junas was grateful for a safe roof over her head while she decided what to do next.

She had walked for seven turns, the ground becoming ever flatter and more barren until she reached Coz, the last town this side of the desert. In reality, it was little more than a village gathered around an oasis, scratching out a meagre living from the trade trail across the sands into the west.

Junas knew she needed to cross the sands. Carrying the egg had brought a sharp focus to her mind as she had walked here. Just as the blind woman had said, she was able to understand what Loncha wanted her to do. She had only to close her eyes and imagine the Faar mother, how she looked, felt and the smell of her. Then words spoke in her head – it seemed as though she was with her, like a living dream.

When she was lonely, homesick or afraid she thought of her and the dream was a comfort.

Most who came to Coz were here because they wanted to join a crossing party. The childless couple assumed she wanted to cross to re-join her own family now that she was widowed. Junas said very little, knowing her silence was construed as grief. It felt wrong to trick them especially as they were so kind. Junas prayed to the Mother to bless them with new life.

Junas had considered crossing the sands alone. She could navigate well enough using the stars. Finding her way was not a problem. Having enough food to last such a journey was. That and loneliness. Junas missed her family, her little sister most of all. She thought of Arla a lot and measured out the turns wondering what she would likely be doing at any given time. At least when she was with others there was some distraction from this.

The sand drifters spent their whole lives on a journey. Most groups were like the one she joined, a large extended family. Junas counted forty-five adults and twelve children of various ages. There were seven travellers, like herself, paying for a safe desert crossing. The sand drifters called them dashen, which meant fainters. Hardly surprising, the sand was hard to walk on and reflected the heat in a way that soil never did.

Junas and the other dashen carried their own packs and water. Their burdens looked like nothing in comparison to those of the sand drifters. Even the smallest child had a bag twice their size strapped to their backs. Little wonder they grew to be so big and strong. Certainly, they were a race apart with golden skin and pale, amber eyes peering from under the blue hoods. She was fearful of them at first. Their language sounded as harsh as the cries of the great camels they led. After a few turns, she saw the kindness in them, the way they cared for one another and welcomed the stranger. Even the great camels, so huge and grumpy, were not so bad when she got to know them.

When the shadows lengthened across the dunes, the drifters would pitch communal tents. The women would cook and the men would unburden the great camels, brush and feed them and settle them to rest in a good place so they would be untroubled by sand winds and cold.

Each evening there was food and song and all sat about talking and laughing. Inside the tents were beautiful, lined with carpets and cushions woven from brightly dyed camel hair. Junas had always thought of the drifters as homeless. Now she understood. They took their homes and families with them and the desert was not the wilderness she had feared, but a place of beauty. The undulating dunes in the sun-shimmer and the long shadows in the evening. She liked to sit with the other women, helping them spin the camel hair onto wooden bobbins and watch the sun setting.

The walking pace was slow due to the sand and the heat. Junas estimated it would take two of the moon's cycles to reach the west. She had not realised there might be storms.

From one horizon to the next, this part of the desert was flat, the sand shallow over smooth rock, and endless – they had been crossing it for three turns. The sand drifters called this place the Knife.

Junas walked with the other dashen in the middle of the long line of great camels. They used the shadow of the beasts for some respite from the sun and still, the going was hard. Junas did not notice anything different until abruptly the line stopped. Then she could hear a humming as if a massive swarm of bees approached. The sand drifter at the head of the line led his camel about and those behind followed to form a circle. Everyone helped, some unloading the camels, others pitching a vast tent at the centre of the circle. The noise grew ever louder. A dark swirl appeared in the sky. Every breath it became bigger until it obscured the sun and the temperature plummeted as though it were night.

They huddled into the one tent. With supplies and the trading goods, it was cramped and confused. The drifters had weathered many a sand storm and soon organised the interior. Shoving the camel packs to the edge and securing the tent canvas beneath, they put out carpets to sit on and gave rugs for the sudden cold. They shared dried fruits, meats, and camel milk sweetened with honey.

The storm had come quickly without warning. Sand and dust lashed the outside of the tent. Inside only the dashen looked worried whilst the drifters welcomed the rest. Dice games ensued. Women chatted and knitted and the children played.

One of the dashen, a short man, possibly in middle years, if his voice was anything to judge by, stepped through the crowded tent and sat beside her. Over the past few turns, he had spoken a few pleasantries to her and she had noticed that he watched her.

'Is this your first sand devil?' he asked, sitting down.

Junas nodded.

'There is no need to worry. I've made this journey many times. There is little strength in this one. By morning it will have blown itself out,' he said. The tent shuddered from a gust of sand and Junas thought about the camels outside weathering the storm.

'You look like one of the Mithe.'

'I am,' she said – it was no use denying the obvious. Junas was typical of her race, tall and lean with deep black skin and dark eyes, her hair to her waist, each of the many braided strands beaded at the tips.

As he talked he unwound strips of cloth that covered his hands and then those about his face. This was not unusual.

Many shoken walked the sands thus, to protect themselves from dust and the sun's fire. His were in two layers, rough hessian on the outer and fine whisper silk next to his skin. Revealed, she understood why he took such care. His skin was translucent; blood-lines, muscle and where bones were near the surface – all visible. She tried not to stare, having never seen his like before.

'I wish my eyes could do that,' he said, smiling at her. Junas looked down to hide the extra eyelid that came unbidden when she was fearful.

'Mine get sore no matter how much I hide my head.' His eyes were rat pink. He took his time brushing away any particles from the cloths and neatly rolling up each length of fabric.

'There is a lot of dust in here,' she said, although her protective eyelids had only covered her eyes when he had joined her. He made her uneasy.

'When we get to the other side, where are you heading?' he asked.

'I'm going on to Hes. I have a sister there,' she lied.

'That's where I'm going.' His smile came too easily.

A bag of dried apricots – she took three. She was not hungry, only aware, having observed the four pregnant drifter women – how much they ate, how they stood and moved –and had begun to imitate them. She gave the bag to him and he passed it on.

'Do you have family there?' she asked.

'No, only trade. I hope to buy some gems.'

Junas searched through the map of Hes in her mind, looking for landmarks.

'My sister's man, he works in the opal mines,' she said.

'We could travel together if it pleases you,' he said.

'Some of my sister's people are coming to meet me, but thank you,' she said, not wanting him to think she was alone.

Junas lay down, covered herself with a blanket and pretended to sleep.

The sand devil raged on, oil lamps snuffed and people slept. There was no fire as the number of people kept the space warm. Junas was glad of this. The blind woman had told her that it would not matter how hot the egg became. Any heat she could stand, so, too, the egg. Cold was more of a problem. At night, in the women's tent, she slept as far away from others as possible so she could turn the egg, bringing the cold side to rest against the warmth of her body in the night's cold.

It was common practice for the Mithe to give a young child an egg to care for and hatch. Most got broken or never created life. Hers did; the little songbird that came forth was her constant companion for the rest of her childhood, sitting on her shoulder, pecking her braids and singing. Just as then, Junas felt an affinity for the egg and the miracle of life contained within.

After the noise of the storm, the silence woke her. She lay still, listening and when she opened her eyes, the see-through man was watching her. Junas looked away, got up, and stood holding the small of her back as she had seen the pregnant women do.

The tent was open and the sand drifters were attending to the great camels. Despite their grunting and moaning, they had come through the storm unscathed. Soon the tent was struck and the animals loaded. Judging by the sun, half the morning had passed. They ate as they walked; even the great camels had nose bags on. The drifters did not want to waste any more time.

The see-through man took up pace beside her, his head once again wrapped to protect him from the sun.

'My name is Quel,' he said.

'Junas.'

'Would you like me to carry something for you? It must be hard...'

'No. Thank you, I can manage,' she said it a little too harshly and strode on to walk in another camel's shadow.

Over the next few turns, Junas avoided him as best she could, seeking out the company of women. Yet wherever she went, she could feel his eyes upon her.

There was a change in direction. She felt it immediately when the camel line went off course and took note of the sun's position. At first, it was subtle; just a few paces then more until the whole group were heading in a different direction. Suddenly, he was there beside her again.

'I see you sense we have altered our course. A rare ability to notice such a thing. I don't think any of the other dashen realise,' he said. She could not see his face beneath the cloth about his head, even his eyes were obscured, but she could tell he was amused. Junas walked on, measuring out her stride with the long walking staff, ignoring him.

'There is an oasis just ahead. Sometimes it is dry. The camels only turn toward it when there is a chance of refreshment.'

Junas looked down at him and nodded politely, wishing he would go away. The great camels were moving quicker with more purpose. Junas lengthened her stride. Now Quel took two paces for each of hers.

Junas had maps of where the deserts were but nothing about them. They were just blank spaces in her mind. While Quel chatted about other times he had crossed the sands, she made careful note of the route they had taken from Coz and the new direction. Thus far, it was the only landmark, as she understood the dunes, no matter how large, were part of the ever-changing face of this wilderness. Later, she would check the stars to make a more accurate entry to her mind map.

Quel enjoyed the sound of his voice. She wondered if he

was just lonely and if he desired her. The thought repulsed her. He talked until, as the sun began to set, a few ragged palms were visible on the horizon.

The oasis was sparse, eight trees around a dip in the sand and some spindly plants. It was fully dark when the drifters had dug down to the water's level. The great camels drank deeply, then waterskins were replenished. Seeing the glint of the shallow water in the moon's light Junas was aware of the dust on her skin and in her hair and longed to wash. There was not enough water. It sank back into the ground as soon as the men ceased their digging.

That night they had a good fire from dried palm leaves and grasses. It burned brightly and smelled sweet unlike the usual smouldering cookfires made from dried camel dung. All gathered around, singing and talking.

When she was ready for sleep, Junas went to find the women's tent. When she got there, Quel stepped out of the shadows.

'I've been thinking, how unusual it is to see one of the Mithe beyond the shadow of the Sky-Pinnacle,' he said, smiling. 'You're young to be pregnant and widowed. The Mithe usually marry late. And I was in Hes a season past and I never saw your like there.'

Junas made to walk past him, into the tent. He blocked her way and drew a thin blade from his sleeve. Her second eyelid glided into place. He was not smiling now and the amiable tone in his voice was gone. 'You see, I don't think that's a child you carry. I think you're hiding something much more precious.'

Junas took a step back and put a protective arm over her bump.

'Don't worry,' he continued in a conspiratorial whisper, 'no one else has noticed how you move whatever it is you have hidden in there,' he pointed his blade at her belly, 'and the way you protect yourself. I'm fascinated to find out what it is you're carrying and where you think you're going.' He slid the knife back up his sleeve. 'Here's what we're going to do. I'll let you keep your secret. But when we reach the other side...: then you're going to show me. Make a fuss, and I'll make sure everyone knows your secret. Be good and I'll let you keep some of whatever it is. In the meantime, you're going to act like we're best friends.' He stood aside and let her pass.

CHAPTER TWENTY-ONE

When he awoke Llund lay still, feeling where each part of himself touched Orrld. The morning rain pattered on the balcony and the air was cooler for it. A silk sheet covered them, so fine and pale it felt as though it might float away of its own accord.

Llund wished he could hide that he was awake from Sho. He had tried keeping still and clearing his mind of all thought. Nothing worked, she always knew and already he could sense her coming closer. Before Orrld, she would have come into his room, if she had not already been there, as soon as she sensed he was awake. He had welcomed her constant presence then. Now she waited until he beckoned her.

Orrld moved in his sleep, rolling onto his back, and Llund raised himself on one elbow to look at him. Without expression, he was a plain-faced man. With his dark, expressive eyes closed there was nothing to bring his face out of the ordinary. Llund smiled – everything about Orrld was who he was, not how he looked. The way he laughed and what he said. His kindness toward everyone. The living love that flowed from him.

Sho was on the balcony now, out of view, standing in the rain. Llund kissed Orrld's shoulder and reluctantly got out of bed, pulled on a robe and went to her.

Half the balcony was under an awning. He sat beneath it to keep dry whilst she shaved him. This used to be their special time, as the light dawned and most of the world slept. Once they would have shared some private talk. He missed the intimacy they had lost. Every turn he strove for a way to return to how they once were.

The last turn he had spent in counsel with the Faar. Most of the talk had been about war. A little had been about Orrld and the Crystal Bearers. They had advised that Sho would never truly trust Orrld, not until he bore some Crystal. They had urged him to mark Orrld. Lashka had not. In her wisdom, she had said that the Healer would take the Crystal willingly sometime in the future. For now, they should wait until he was ready. Llund was glad she was on his side. After the assembly, when they were alone, she had told him he must strive to find a way for Sho to trust Orrld. For as long as she felt he was a threat, however small, she would find a way to kill him. Llund watched Sho's impassive face as she expertly slid the blade over his chin and knew Lashka was right.

'You went to the Blade-Master again then...' It was easy for him to know where she had been from the distance she was from him. Lak-Mur was the place of his childhood, every pathway well known.

'I did. I took Jie there. Godwin has an idea to replace his hand,' she said.

The king wiped his face with the cloth she gave him. 'And did he sense any other metal on Orr?' he asked. That was the real reason she had gone there.

Feeling his irritation, Sho knelt before him. Once they would have sat side by side like the childhood friends they had been.

'No, your Grace, he did not. The Blade-Master found no threat in Orrld.'

The rain was heavy now, pouring like a waterfall over the edge of the awning. Before he could consider what would have happened if the dwarf had sensed something wrong with Orrld, Sho spoke again. She was always good at diverting his attention.

'He did discover something of interest about the Strick child,' she said brightly. 'Math is a linegold mover.'

This was interesting and explained a lot. Not able to bear her kneeling in front of him any longer, he got up, went to the edge of the balcony, and held out his hand in the water's flow. It felt warm.

They had never spoken of her loss of ability. He had thought, as she grew strong again, the linegold would return to her.

'I'm surprised no one saw him with my linegold,' she said, coming to stand beside him.

'I'm not. He's Strick.' They both smiled then and she put her hand out, next to his in the rain. Such a tiny hand.

'Have the boy trained by Godwin and yourself. Dedicate your blades to him and I'll ask the Faar to send more metal. New linegold will make you stronger,' he said, enclosing her hand in his. For a moment, they were as they had always been. Then Orrld came out onto the balcony looking for his clogs. She backed away.

'The Blade-Master asked me to give you this.' She looked at Orrld who was tipping water from his clogs. 'He thought Orrld might like it. Now that Sneela has gone.' From her doublet, she took a thin metal case. He knew what it was and what she asked.

114

'No. Take it back. I have no need of such a device,' he said, trying to keep his anger under control.

When she had gone Orrld sat on the balustrade, leaning back, catching water in his mouth. Llund laughed and Orrld pulled him near, wrapping his legs around him, holding him fast. He liked that. Orrld shared the rain with a kiss. He liked that, too.

The royal rooms were carved from the mountainside and this balcony, being the highest, was not overlooked. It provided a view over the valley where, far down, a thin river coiled between lush trees. Orrld liked high places. More than that, he understood he needed some illusion of privacy.

Orrld kissed him until they were both soaked and they made love there, standing in the rain. Afterwards, they lay together, contented on the warm stones. The sun came out, turning the puddles to steam.

It was always like this. Many turns where Orrld, drained from healing, was too tired for sex. Then he would take him with such a passion, he was left breathless and spent. Llund, too shy to make the first move, waited longingly between times. It was always worth the wait.

The sun was soon too hot and they moved back to the bed. They had planned to spend this morning together and it was nice not to rush.

'So, are you going to tell me what's on your mind?' said Orrld, bringing over a bowl of fruit and setting it between them on the bed.

Llund smiled; there was nothing he could hide from him, Crystal Bearer or no. 'Sho was telling me you paid a visit to the dwarf.'

'He's going to make some sort of new hand for Jie,' said Orrld, peeling an orange. Llund watched his hands.

'But that's not the real reason she took me there. She still doesn't trust me. She never will unless I take Crystal, will she?'

Llund shook his head. 'You're still against it?'

Orrld reached over and smoothed his frown. 'You know I am,' he said, not unkindly.

'She needs some reassurance…'

'Do you need some reassurance? Do you doubt me?'

'No. I never have. Never will.'

'But…'

'I fear for your safety.'

'You think Sho will try to kill me?'

Llund got up and stood by the window. Sunlight flooded over him, lighting his fair hair. The question hung between them.

In the evening Orrld walked alone through the king's chambers. There were many rooms and most, he realised, had been re-furbished with him in mind. The walls were newly painted with River flowers, birds and fish. Woven grass mats covered the floors. Orrld loved the smell of them. They smelled of home. Sometimes, when he closed his eyes in the warm breeze that wafted through the shutters in the evening, he could imagine he was once again in the treehouses of Ekressia. Every detail of that place would rise around him with clarity so bright he felt that if he reached out his hand he would be able to touch once-familiar objects. Each turn he tried to remember with joy and not sadness. But it was hard to quell the pain of grief for a life lost.

On this night, the king had gone to an initiation of a new Crystal Bearer – a replacement for Isk the Archer. Because he bore no Crystal, he was forbidden to attend. In truth, he was glad to remain here, where no one needed his healing or counsel. It was relaxing to be alone, tie a length of silk cloth around his waist, and feel the warm air on his skin. Math was not far away. He had become like a Crystal Bearer, the way he kept himself concealed.

Wandering through the rooms, he found a sitting statue of Ath in front of a large window. Made from a single clear water-stone, twice the size of a man, the sunset made the God radiant. Orrld sat and tried to clear his mind. Tried to pray. Sleep claimed him.

Issolissi walked through his dreams – when he awoke he tried to remember what she wanted to tell him, for it always seemed that she needed to impart some advice or warning. The waking world blurred her message even as he lay with his eyes closed trying to piece together the fragments and make sense of them. Her presence was strong, almost as if she was in the room; he felt her love wash over him like warm River rain.

When he opened his eyes, it was not Issolissi who stood near, it was Sho.

The world was dark now. Sho held a candle, the flame shining a thousand times within Ath's image.

'I thought I'd find you here,' she said.

He felt wary; it was disconcerting to be alone with her. If she was here then the king must have gone to visit Lashka.

He got up and stretched his aching limbs. 'I came to pray but slept instead,' he said amiably.

'Sometimes the body's needs cannot be denied,' she said.

Sho placed the candle in Ath's webbed hand in such a way only one flame was reflected, large where the heart would be. It was a neat trick.

'Why do you seek me?' he asked.

Sho reached out and took one of his hands and placed it on the back of her neck, and stood quietly. Even when she had been seriously ill, she had never willingly accepted his touch. Whenever he had healed her, apart from the first time, she would repel the flow. This time she allowed the warmth to course into her and let him learn things about her that normally she denied.

When at last he took away his hand, he looked at her anew. Orrld understood she cared deeply for the king's life, as did all the Crystal Bearers that protected him. Now he had seen into the very depth of her and understood what she felt was far above caring, love or loyalty. Protecting the king was her whole self. Even her own life was nothing to her. And on the edge of this feeling, like a dark spot, was her mistrust of him.

'What can I say to prove to you how much I love him and that, like you, I would lay aside my own life that he might live?'

Sho sat on the floor and he opposite her. He wished he had put a robe on.

'There is nothing you can say that will help,' she said.

He reached over and took both her hands in his. 'Sho, I'm a Healer. Can you not sense the truth of me in my touch just as I can appreciate how you feel?'

Orrld looked at her dark eyes and wished he could do something to allay her fears.

'You know if you kill me it will break his heart?' he said.

Sho nodded, frowning. The mask of her usual blank expression lifted as she spoke. 'I cannot understand why you will not take a little Crystal. It would help us to protect you...'

'You know how I feel about it. I'm sorry, Sho, but I'll not be bonded to another. I wish there was some other way I could reassure you about my love for him.'

'There is one way,' she said, taking a slim metal case from inside her doublet. She set it on the floor between them and unlocked the lid with a small key. 'In times past the king's consorts were given this to wear.' She opened the case and the necklace within lit the darkened room with a thousand beads of coloured light. 'It's called the sun and the rain.'

Orrld looked at the jewel. It was beautiful but he knew there had to be something more to it.

'Is this a bond of a different kind then?'

'It is,' she said. 'Only those who truly love him may wear it with safety.'

'And those who don't love him truly?'

'Fall out of love, the necklace will strangle you.'

'Are you saying that every time we argue I'll be in danger of losing my life? That I must always agree with him? Sho, what he needs is someone who can give him a different view…'

'Bearing Crystal does not mean always agreeing with the lord. You've seen me argue with him…'

Orrld had seen how much effort it cost her.

Every turn the River called. Sometimes a whisper, sometimes a shout. He would have to go back sometime. This, more than anything, kept him from taking a bond. Deep within he knew he needed to remain free.

'I'm a Healer. I cannot always stay close…'

'You have my word, this will only take your life if you hate him; disagreeing will not be enough and it does not have a proximity bond. You may be as near or far as you please,' she said, putting one of her hands in his. 'In the past, lovers wore this as a mark of honour to show their heart's honesty. I swear it, on the life of my lord, unless you wish him harm it is safe.' Through her touch, he could feel her sincerity and more, her sheer need to trust him.

Orrld looked at her worried face, then at Ath's serene image and he longed for a better time where he could be trusted.

He reached out toward the necklace but she stayed his

hand. 'I must put it on you,' she said, taking it from the case. It shimmered, casting rainbows over the ceiling. Sho stood behind him where he knelt. 'Close your eyes and bring his face to mind,' she whispered, holding the necklace in front of his face. He could see why it was so named. Many clear beads hung randomly from the finest silver thread and they shone as raindrops lit by the sun with delicate prisms of coloured light. Often he had sat in the tree's canopy watching rain like this with his sister. When he closed his eyes, it was Issolissi's face he saw, so clear it was as if she knelt before him. Her face was rain-soaked, her dark hair slick and wet. Her eyes, so knowing and full of compassion, looked into his and he loved her.

The king found him and carried him back to bed. But he could hardly remember. Dreams filled his night. The River Ekress so vivid that, when he awoke, he felt disorientated. The king's voice, raised in anger, returned him to reality. Orrld got up.

Out in the wide hallway, Sho stood before the king. The Crystal Bearers waited in silence. Even as they spoke in Faar, he knew they were arguing about him.

'It was my choice,' he said. All turned toward him. Orrld touched the necklace. 'My choice. She did not force me or trick me. I understand the risks and I accept them freely.'

He walked over to them and placed a hand on the back of each of their necks, connecting them with his healing warmth.

CHAPTER TWENTY-TWO

W hen the king spent time with the Faar, he always went alone. Whoever or whatever they were, clearly they could protect him. Sten enjoyed the extra measure of freedom. It had been six years since he had last been at Lak-Mur. Then he had been in the grip of training to take the trials to become one of the lord's protectors. Soon after he had taken the Crystal burn, the king and the pack had left for Valkarah. Now he could take his ease and walk the streets of this beautiful city.

Sten had not realised how much he missed the heat. Valkarah was never truly hot for any length of time. Here rain fell warm from the sky and the air shimmered.

At the centre of Lak-Mur, at the highest point, stood Nenimar's Temple. Seamlessly carved from the red stone of the mountain, it was imposing and vast. From the lower parts of the citadel, it did indeed look as if the seven spires held up the sky... some believed the world. Sten watched what looked like a red flame winding, licking the temple walls. When first seen, he had thought the building afire. Now he knew the effect came from many pilgrims, dressed in red and waving lengths of silk, who walked around the temple hoping for good fortune.

Sten did not share their faith. These gods were not his and even his own beliefs had long deserted him.

All the important buildings were carved from the mountain rock. Lak-Mur Palace, like Valkarah, was massive, yet where Valkarah was built to impress, every room and hall gilded and ornate, Lak-Mur had an earthier feel. It had evolved to no specific design and the result was softer, more natural. The rooms were simply furnished and airy with fountains and pools refreshed from the frequent rains through sky-vents in the roof. He liked it.

Sten nodded to the guard on duty at the gates, wandered between the orange and lemon trees and went in through a side entrance. After the sunshine, it seemed dark and he waited a moment for his eyes to adjust.

A piano echoed through the empty hallways, the notes slow and faltering as the player tried out a melody. He knew it was Sho. Stepping quietly, to listen, he followed the sound.

He watched her from the doorway. He could just see the side of her face, which was blank. The music was not. There was a pathos beneath a slightly happier melody. There often was when she played for herself. He had not known she could play this instrument.

She beckoned him, a soft tug within his chest. She moved along the stool for him to sit. It looked too flimsy to take his considerable weight, so he knelt on the floor beside her. She smiled.

Unusually, her dark hair hung loose and she was wearing a silk robe, so fine he could see her skin beneath. He could see linegold blades on her forearms and thighs and he felt relieved for her. The Crystal tiger etched onto her back shone. He tried not to stare.

'Do you want to play?'

He shook his head. 'I don't think music is a skill I have.'

'Your shoken, the Lamash, they make music using rhythms, don't they?'

Sten was not sure the heavy drumbeats and harsh sounds of his tribe would lend themselves to this delicate instrument.

She took one of his hands. 'Press this key. Softly. That's it, now keep a steady beat,' she said. Then she began to play around him and he watched her slim fingers, so quick and agile. He sped up and slowed down and she made a melody around whatever he did until they were both laughing. Then he kissed her.

Kissing Sho usually left him confused and frustrated. Not this time. When their lips touched she sent him her love and it washed through him like fire. He pulled her onto his lap and kissed her differently, holding her head cupped in his hand, pinning her body close to his. Then he stood up. She wrapped her legs around his waist and he carried her into the next room where a large bed was sunk into the floor.

He made her wait, kissing and caressing her and one by one each linegold blade fell away and she was truly naked. Then he entered her and it was sweeter than anything he had ever known. Sten was surprised to see a different side of Sho in her arousal, which he had imagined would have been a guarded thing. This woman, who hid her facial expressions lest she give away any thought – sex was her undoing and he basked in her abandonment. Afterwards, she slept while he held her and for a moment, she was his and his alone.

Her rooms were without doors and set about a circular courtyard. Sten watched the evening rain splash on the red stones.

When she awoke, he expected her to leap up and leave. Instead, she stayed, languishing in the bed and he was grateful that the king was safe with the Faar.

Sho lay on her back sending her linegold blades spinning slowly in an arc above them. Like this, they were beautiful, like autumn leaves, catching the light.

'Hard to believe they're weapons,' he said.

She let them fall into her stomach and took his hand in hers, holding it so she could look at the scar across his palm. 'You don't believe it?' she said mischievously.

'I know it,' he said.

'Does it still hurt?'

'No. I think you just cured me,' he said.

'Then my work is done.'

He just lay there grinning. He felt absurdly happy and had no way to hide it. They were Crystal Bearers, one another's emotions plainly revealed. She smiled, too, and for a while they were content, two lovers taking joy in each other's company.

'It's returned then, your linegold,' he said, stating the obvious.

'In a way. These blades are new,' she said, picking them all up in one hand and spreading them like a fan. Now he could see they were different. Lighter in colour and where her old blades had been plain, these revealed a pattern if they were tilted in the light. One by one, Sho floated them so he could admire the fine engravings. Each of the eight had a pattern of flames and within the fire, when viewed carefully, every blade had a different animal.

'What happened to your old ones?' he asked.

'The Strick boy is a linegold mover. When he is ready I will dedicate them to him,' she said.

'And he has fight prescience. He is a lot like you then.'

Sho smiled at this and rolled onto her stomach. Sten stared at her back. He would have liked to admire the Crystal burn, for it was amazing. Somehow, he knew this would annoy her, so he rolled over next to her.

'What will you do about your outline?' she asked.

Sten held his forearm out, showing his Crystal burn. A fine, delicate tiger. An outline.

'I don't know. Sometimes I think I should have it finished,' he said.

'It would double your strength,' she said.

'Then I think, as I don't have any special ability, perhaps I am strong enough. Perhaps my ability is that, as an outliner, I can be parted from the lord. If I stay as I am I may be more useful.'

Sho offered no comment. Only nodded.

'What do you think I should do?'

'You must do whatever is in your heart,' she said.

'I thought I would ask the lord.'

'He'd tell you the same.'

CHAPTER TWENTY-THREE

Mag'Sood found the reflecting room overly hot. The tables, arranged in a series of circles, were tightly packed and crowded with hundreds of reflecting disks. So many, how could a single Watcher observe them all? Once again, he considered breaking with tradition and having more than one Watcher, perhaps even more than one reflecting room?

The Watcher cowed at his feet. Like this, he found her beautiful. The smoothness of her virgin back was easily glimpsed between the folds of her dress. He stepped away to alleviate his arousal. Moments ago, he had been so annoyed at her he thought he might hit her. A Watcher, sacred, blessed by Crotus, must never be touched, not even in anger. Super-stitions learnt in infancy were not easily put aside.

'Redeemer, I have failed you,' she whispered. 'I should have noticed sooner. Then perhaps the Curver would have been able to do something about it. There may be others marked who could be sent?'

'No. You are not to blame for the shoken's death,' he said, picking his way between the tables to the opening in the floor. By a chain, he lowered himself into the map room below.

It was cool and dim here, under Tarestone. The ancient map painted on the floor stretched out in every direction. Normally the very sight of his war efforts soothed him. Not this turn. He banged his fist on the floor. Several doors opened and warriors appeared in the flickering shadows.

'Fetch me the Curver,' he said.

Soon Curver Thist was before him. The guards pushed him through the door and left. The terrified Curver pressed himself against the wall trying not to tread on the map.

'The Watcher has just shown me the death of a young soldier in the shoken king's army. I thought the incident of no matter until I learnt that now we don't have a seeing eye in his entourage.' His voice was as loud as any Sturgar could manage in speech, every word a hiss of rage.

'There were others, Master. But shoken are unpredictable and weak. They died or were not chosen…'

Mag'Sood strode across the room and grabbed the Curver, jamming him onto the floor, kneeling on his back to keep him in place. The Curver wriggled and squealed as the Master felt beneath his clothes for his tail.

Light seeped around the edges of the shutters in the Curver's sleeping chamber, yet he could not sleep. He sat hunched among his bedding furs nursing the end of his tail. Pain coursed through it, where the Master had bitten it, right along his back and into his neck. He knew in time it would heal and the searing agony would cease. But his tail would never re-grow and he hated the Master for taking so much. Too much. Now it only reached just past his buttocks. An apology and a sign of his weakness. No female would want him now. Not that there had ever been many, despite his position of power. For the Sturgar, physical strength was prized above all else.

Last time he had been punished in this way he had made a promise to himself that if such a violation happened again he would avenge himself. Hard to achieve as a runt. Cunning had kept him alive thus far. He would find a way to show the Master his true worth.

CHAPTER TWENTY-FOUR

Ashmi, Lorimore's lost child, slid on her belly beneath the tables in the reflecting room. She pulled herself along using her elbows until she reached the table where the Watcher had been teaching her disciple. As usual, it had been in vain. No matter how many ways the Watcher showed her, the disciple was unable to make the reflecting disks obey her touch. Ashmi knew the real reason was that the Watcher did not want the disciple to know how they worked. Why else would she keep telling her untruths about the disks? Ashmi smiled.

With the light, they had gone, and she was alone. Very carefully, she got up and stood peering into the disk they had been observing. Images flitted over the surface. She picked the disk up and slowly brought it to her face. She tilted it to the left a tiny amount then held it still again. Intuitively she knew the images now showed what the marked one saw two turns ago. She tilted it again, this time the other way, returning the reflection to the present. Ashmi found no difficulty handling the disks and could not understand why the disciple was so stupid. The trick was easy.

This disk was not special. It showed the reflections of a shoken farmer. The mark on his face reflected what he saw as he walked behind a pair of plough horses. Nearly all the disks in the room, and there were many, were from shoken who had been marked without their knowledge. Ashmi set the disk back into its groove in the table and lowered herself onto the floor. Taking her time, so as not to jog any of the tables, she slid herself over the floor. A table by the door had some food remains on it. She stood up and reached a piece of dried seal meat. There was also a wrinkled apple. Ashmi tucked it into her sleeve, saving the sweetness until last. With the seal meat between her teeth, she sank to the floor, slid herself to the edge of the room, and waited, listening, feeling for any vibration of movement. When she was satisfied that all was still, she knelt up and folded back the shutter from the window. The bright light made her blink.

Unlike most of Tarestone, these windows had glass. Ashmi crawled in the space between the shutter and the windowpane and re-folded the shutter. It was safe here in her secret hidey-hole. The Greys never sought the light. If they never heard her, they would not look.

The windows were tall and the glass at the top was coloured and had pictures of people riding horses. A long time ago, she had broken a hole in the corner. The glass was brittle, so it had been easy to do but the sound it made had been terrifying. She had hidden in the space under the floor that turn, listening, expecting the Greys to come. They never did. Ashmi moved the dead reflecting disk she kept in front of the hole to stop the cold and put her hand through, taking up a handful of snow, then another, placing them in a pile on another dead disk. She stoppered the hole and moved her pile of snow so that what sun there was would change it into water.

Ashmi chewed the seal meat and now and again, when a puddle formed, she took up the disk and drank the snowmelt.

A weak sun shone through the window and created a little warmth. Ashmi had a small fur that the Watcher had given, which she kept there. When she had eaten, she pulled it over herself and slept.

Later, when she awoke she lay still and listened until she was sure no one was there. Then she came out of her sleeping place, closed the shutters and slid herself over the floor to the centre of the room. Here a round table contained the most important disks, the ones the Watcher looked at most. They were special; sometimes they were taken away.

Ashmi stood up and moved around the table, sliding her feet. Instinctively, she knew her shoken footfall had a different beat and if they heard it, they would take her. Just as she knew she needed to come into the light to stop from getting sick.

Two of the disks on the table always sat side by side. That was because when the Greys had the seeing metal they always had a friend. Ashmi touched the shining speck on her cheek and wished she had a friend. Not for the first time she wondered who was watching her reflections. Was there another room like this where other Greys watched and another room after that, on and on forever?

Ashmi rested her chin on the table in front of the two disks as the Watcher liked to do. These were warriors, she had glanced at them before – they were running at the head of a large group. There was not much to see as they mostly ran at night. She was just about to move away when something different caught her attention. They were crouched beside a cooking fire, talking to each other, each disk reflecting the other's face. Even the Greys could not make any sense of the wisps of sound the disks made. She wondered what it was they talked about. One of the warriors moved a little and now his face was visible in the fire's light. She knew the face. She had looked into those strange eyes before, with the black slit pupils edged with a fine red line.

Ashmi reached out, took the two disks, and knelt with them under the table holding one in each hand. They were marked differently from the shoken, their seeing metal a large glistening, silver mark in the middle of their foreheads. Perhaps because their marks were so much bigger, the reflections they made were bright and clear. Ashmi held the disks in front of her face and rocked slowly back and forth. She could not remember where she had seen the Devil and she could not remember why she hated him. But she did hate him.

The light was fading quickly. It was time to light the oil lamps ready for the Watcher and the disciple's return. She returned the disks to their grooves in the table. Six lamps hung on chains from the ceiling. Ashmi lowered each one and refilled the seal oil from a stone jug by the door. It was heavy. When done, she struck flints to light the stump of a candle and used it to light each wick. The lamps had dark blue glass and gave just enough illumination for the Greys to see without hurting their eyes. They called them softlights.

When all were lit and fastened back in place, Ashmi carried the smoking taper to the central table, fascinated to look into the face of the Devil again. She reached over and put the candle stump between them. They were eating now, the Devil and his friend. Ashmi watched. The candle was in the way, so she moved it back a little. Too much, the flame licked the other disk and when it did, the Devil flinched. Ashmi moved the candle flame and let it touch the image of the Devil's face. Now the friend grasped his seeing mark and Ashmi knew she had caused him pain.

She picked up the disk which she knew was the Devil's and held it over the flame and watched him writhe. The friend tried to help him. Other warriors gathered around, watching as he clawed at his face.

Ashmi was filled with glee.

CHAPTER TWENTY-FIVE

J unas would not usually have minded the journey across the sands – the Mithe had no beasts of burden, and she was well used to walking. She was careful to keep herself always with the women, yet wherever she went, the see-through man, Quel, watched her. Whenever she turned her head, he would be near and, even when she could not see him, she felt his eyes upon her like a cold shadow.

At night in the women's tent, she wondered how she could be rid of him. Completing her task would have a positive effect on the world – failure would be devastating. Deep within herself, she understood she would have to succeed at any cost, even if it meant taking another's life. Junas knew the value of what she carried and prayed to the Mother to save her from killing.

As they neared the edge of the desert, she thought about sneaking away and crossing the last part alone. Finding the way would be easy enough, it was only the threat of a sand storm that put her off, that and the fact that these good people would surely look for her and in her loss believe themselves cursed. She needed another solution.

The landscape changed when she judged that they must be three turn's walk from Hathenfont. The sand was shallow with protruding white rock and here and there were patches of dry soil where cacti grew, their columns taller than the great camels with spikes a stride long. But the smaller cacti that clung to the rock, although less impressive to look at, proved to have the greater interest. They bore edible fruit. The drifter children chased between the rocks picking the dark-purple berries, by turns eating and handing them to their families. A child ran beside her and showed her how to twist the fruit to break the thick leathery skin and reach the pink flesh inside. This was harder than it looked. When she managed it, a bright green beetle emerged. Junas caught it between finger and thumb, gesturing to the child whether it was good to eat or not. Immediately he pulled an agonised face and clutched his stomach and then his behind with accompanying noises. Junas laughed and flicked it away. Most of the fruits she was given had beetles, and she killed and hid them in her clothing.

That night when Quel manoeuvred himself to sit beside her at mealtime she did not leave as she normally did. She saw a thin smile at the edge of his lips when he unwound the strips of cloth he kept about his head to protect his translucent skin from the sun. He thought he'd won.

The drifters passed food from the centre, where the cooking fires were. Stacks of round, unleavened bread came first, upon which all else was piled. When a stack was given to her, she got up to hand it out. The sand-drifters considered bread passed by a pregnant woman lucky. When it came to Quel, she used her other hand, the one covered in juice from the beetles she had been squeezing in her pocket. Apart from a polite smile when she handed him the bread, she never looked at him again. So whether he ate it or not, or noticed a strange taste and cast it aside she had no way of knowing.

The following turn she resisted the urge to look for him among the throng of shoken getting ready to leave and went about her business helping the other women pack up the tent. As she rolled mats and tied cooking utensils together, she glanced where she could. There was no sign. Later, as she strode in a great camel's shadow, he was not there and she began to have hope. If he were sick, he would be at the back of the line with the old and infirm.

At midturn, when the sun liked to trick the eye and show phantom water, there was a city shimmering white on the horizon. At first, this, too, seemed like a vision. Every step closer made it real.

Feeling the firmer ground beneath their huge splayed feet, the great camels quickened their pace as the turn wore on. Now, as Hathenfont loomed ahead Junas lengthened her stride. When they went through the gateway, she was walking alongside the lead camel. No one noticed. Most of the children and the young had come to the front to be the first through. There was much excitement as the great camels broke into a strange gallop with the children running beside, whooping for joy. Ahead was a fountain fashioned from the white stone in the shape of a fanciful bird with wings outstretched and water cascading from its carved feathers. Any water would have been beautiful to the parched travellers. This was magical. The air was full of mist, rainbows, and the water-sound, amplified by the city walls, deafening.

She had planned to walk away from the camel train, to lose herself in the crowd and be gone. She had not expected this. Now all she could think of was water, how much she needed to drink, fill her waterskin and wash away the dust. Swept along by the crowd she found herself at the pool's edge next to a great camel. It plunged its whole head into the water and drank, then came up for air, sending a great arc of water into the air with a bellow of delight. Droplets clung to its long eyelashes and ran in rivulets through the thick fur. Then it drank again, from the surface this time, gulping and swallowing, and Junas realised that these beasts had not quenched their thirst for twelve turns.

All around shoken were washing. Most of the children were naked and Junas waded in to fill her waterskin from one of the spouts as the others were doing, presumably because this water was the cleanest. She stood with her mouth open, drinking her fill. It was surprisingly cold and, closing her eyes for a moment as the water washed her face, Junas was happy.

Pain around her neck startled her.

'There you are.' It was Quel. He had both hands gently about her throat as he smiled up at her. To any onlooker, it looked like affection. Unseen was something sharp pressing into her skin, just enough so she could feel the danger of it. He showed her a fine chain he held in his hand. 'One tug and the thorns will pierce you,' he said. Quel did not waste time washing or drinking. He led her from the fountain and away from the crowd. Junas prayed to Mother God for forgiveness – she had allowed herself to become distracted.

'Try to run and I'll pull. I promise you'll be dead in two blinks,' he said, steering her to the edge of the square and through an alley. Junas fancied she saw a smile beneath his head cloths. He was not sick.

They walked against the flow of people. The city was making toward the fountain and the newly arrived travellers. At first, the streets were wide, flanked by tall, ornate buildings, but soon these gave way to more modest dwellings and when they reached the outskirts the buildings were little more than shacks, crudely put together with oddments of stone and strips of wood and cloth. They looked barely able to provide shade let alone withstand a sandstorm. The sun was high and most shoken had taken shelter. Among the shacks there looked to be no discernible pathway, yet Quel knew where he was going and ducked beneath one of the small buildings, dragging Junas with him. Now she saw the buildings were nothing more than coverings for the holes beneath.

Quel pulled off his boots and tossed them aside among a pile of other footwear. Then he embraced her, wrapping his arms about her waist. Before she had a chance to protest, Quel leapt, taking her with him and they were sliding, encircled together, down a chute cut into the rock. It looped, ever downwards, spiralling first one way, then the other until, at last, they came to a halt on the level ground deep beneath the surface of the world.

'Welcome to the Ramshales,' said Quel, standing up. Junas lay where she was, terrified for the safety of the egg. She wanted to check it. Smooth her hand over its surface and reassure herself it was unharmed. All she could do was get up and act like a pregnant woman.

As Junas' eyes became accustomed to the dim light, she could see they were in another city. Roofless buildings made of leaf screens filled the cavernous space.

This was his world. Around them, many gathered. Where she had thought him one of a kind, now she knew him to be one of many. All had the strange translucent skin, pink eyes and milk-white hair and here, away from the sunlight, every shoken glowed with their own luminosity.

Quel addressed the onlookers in his language. Some pressed through the crowd to greet him. Most just stared at Junas.

'I have told them you are my guest, sort of,' he said, holding up the thin chain and walking onward.

Junas went to take it in her hand, but she saw the whole length was barbed. Even so, she stood where she was and the thorns pressed dangerously into the back of her neck.

He turned. 'If you want to wash and eat, you might as well follow. Even if you could get free, you don't know your way down here, Pathfinder.'

This was true. She had a mind map of Hathenfont and from what little she had seen, it was accurate enough. This place was missing both above and below. She glanced at the chute, and Quel laughed. 'No return there. They're impossible to climb. Every child tries and fails,' he said, walking on.

Reluctantly, Junas followed.

CHAPTER TWENTY-SIX

Godwin pushed away his plate of food and Mirril, the green monkey, helped herself. He watched her picking out the choice bits. She would eat it all, he knew, but she liked to eat her favourite first. There was a lesson – grab the best immediately and take no chance of losing it.

The evening was warmer than most. The rain, unusually, had not fallen and the air was thick and heavy. Sitting at the top of the watchtower offered no respite; he made his way down the stairs in search of coolness. Normally he stopped at his workroom on the ground floor. Even this low room was stuffy. He picked up his latest project – the replacement hands he had made for the Crystal Bearer, Jie. There were three. One was a three-fingered hand, another a short stabbing knife and the third was a device that could hold a short-sword. He hoped the amber-eyed soldier would find them useful. There was something about him with his restless countenance and his Crystal burn of a sleeping tiger. He had seen a burn like that before. Unusual, and somewhere on the edge of his memory, he knew what it meant.

Godwin lit a fresh lamp, pushed aside a lidded chest, and

opened a door in the floor. He descended the winding stairs and the silver thread that bound him fell before him like a bright snake.

He lit more lamps from the first until the underground forge was illuminated. Then in the cool, he sat down and opened the closejar that Sho had given him and tipped the two tiny pieces of the seeing metal into his palm.

He felt the metal with his fingertips. It was a strange material, many small and rare amounts melded together to create unusual characteristics. A little more would have made the task of separating each element easier. But he had enough to work with if he was careful.

Godwin folded a length of soft velvet and placed it on the halfway step for Mirril. She did not like it when he lit the forge but she was unhappy if she could not see him. She would settle there when she realised he was going to work here all night.

Unhooking a crucible from the wall, he set a small fire within it, thankful that he did not need to light the forge proper on such a hot night. These tiny grains would readily melt. When liquid he would decide what they consisted of. Once he had achieved that it was only a matter of trial to make more.

Mirril crept down the stairs and chattered crossly at him. Godwin ignored her and looked about at the jars and tins stacked on uneven shelves around the walls. They contained every metal, gem and stone known to shoken kind.

He looked at the two silvery pieces in his palm and knew their reproduction would be complicated. But then, he liked complicated.

CHAPTER TWENTY-SEVEN

Orrld put on his Healer's robes. These were fine silk, probably from the River, although he had never asked. They were a pale grey, the hem embroidered with delicate orchids. He loved the feel of the cool, fine fabric on his skin. He tied his sash, eyes closed in silent prayer, asking Ath's guidance.

There was a glint of gold light, then another. Orrld looked toward the balcony, expecting to see Sho playing with her linegold blades. Recently she had re-gained the ability. Orrld did not understand why and was pleased her old powers had returned. He stepped into the bright sunlight to speak with her. If she was near, the king was probably returning from his morning meeting. Perhaps they could breakfast together before they began the turn's work.

Sho was not there. It was Math who sat cross-legged in the shade, his arms folded across his chest, smiling up at him.

Orrld went over and placed one hand on the back of his neck, another atop his head, healing and greeting in one, as a father to a child.

In the touching there was nothing different. Math was the

same uncomplicated child he always was. But Orrld had seen the linegold glint too often not to know it. He knelt in front of the Strick boy. 'Show me,' he said softly. Math turned his face away at first, then slowly the blades appeared one after another, sliding under his sleeves, down his arms onto his upturned palms. Eight tiny blades, bright against the grey of his skin. They looked too fragile to be weapons.

Orrld was appalled. 'Did Sho give you these?'

Math shook his head, indicating with his hands a crown, the king. Orrld got up and went over to the edge of the balcony, and leaned over looking at the thin river so far below. Math came and stood beside him, stooping to see into his face. Orrld saw the confusion in his eyes.

Moments later the king returned, striding in to meet him, all smiles. Math backed away, swung himself onto the roof and was gone. Every turn that passed, he behaved more like a Crystal Bearer, guarding him from some unseen place.

Orrld pointed at the neatly stacked linegold Math had left on the balustrade and was suddenly filled with rage. 'Why didn't you ask me?' he said.

Llund took off his crown and placed it next to the line-gold and ran a hand through his hair. He was still smiling. 'It's a very rare ability...' he began.

'He's a child. He's barely two years old. And now you've given him a weapon!'

'He's not a child. He's Strick and almost fully grown. It's amazing he can do this and so soon,' Llund enthused.

Orrld could no longer hide his anger. 'You should have asked me first.' His voice was raised and the blood rushed to his face.

'Why?'

'Why? Because he's my son!'

Llund laughed then, shaking his head at the absurdity of such a statement. But when he saw the hurt on Orrld's face,

143

he stopped. Of course, it was true. Orrld had raised Math, healed him and nurtured him. The boy was not angry and violent like other Strick he had known. He was calm and quiet, peaceful even. Where he had always been amused by the way he followed Orrld around like a faithful dog, he realised now, he followed like a devoted son.

'Why must he be a killer just because of what he is?' said Orrld, trying to control his temper.

'Because he is what he is. Even you can't change that. He's practically a Sturgar with fight prescience and now we know he's a linegold carrier. You can't change what he is, Orr. What were you thinking? That you'd make a Healer of him?' He said it too harshly and then he was sorry. Orrld was crying.

Llund took him in his arms. 'I'm sorry, I'm sorry,' he murmured into his neck. 'I didn't think. It just seemed natural to give him the knives.'

Orrld broke free of the embrace and left.

Jie was waiting outside the door. He followed him down the stairs. Lak-Mur was shuttered against the sun even this early in the turn. When they came out onto the street, the sun was blinding. As usual, a crowd waited. Some had come to be healed; still more came filled with religious fervour. As his renown spread, the crowds had grown. At first, he had tried to avoid them. This soon proved impossible, because many roads led to Ath's Temple. Two mounted soldiers rode alongside them as they walked through the steaming streets. Orrld ignored the cries of devotion. It was ridiculous to be hailed as such when his kind was commonplace in Ekressia.

Ahead he could see the temple through the mist. Not far now. He would be glad to be within the cool walls and clear his mind. The crowd was particularly noisy this morning. Among the shouts, one cry stood out. It was not a shout of praise but one of anguish, a woman's voice piercing his heart.

Orrld stopped and turned about trying to find her. Jie was by his shoulder. 'What is it?'

'That… do you hear? I have to find her!'

'It's not safe, Soorah. Wait until we reach the temple. It's not far now.'

Orrld ignored him and began to go into the crowd. Jie caught him by the sleeve and called up to the guard. 'The woman who screams, bring her to the Healer,' he said.

The guard jumped from his horse and waded into the throng. Soon he brought the woman to the space where Orrld stood. She was young, distraught and carried in her arms a lifeless child. Orrld took the child from her. He could not understand her words as she tried to explain what had happened. It did not matter. It never did. Touch was all he needed. The babe had choked. It was a simple matter to slap the child's back so the nut he had swallowed came forth. The baby cried and all was well. The crowd, eager to witness the healing, pressed close. Even the horse guards were unable to keep them back. An old woman reached and grabbed his arm. Straight away Orrld's body responded, curing the fever that ailed her. Then many were reaching out, touching, grasping, and he was overwhelmed. He fell backwards and still the shoken clutched him. People were calling; Jie was shouting and drawing his sword. Orrld prayed to Ath there would be no violence. Then he was sinking and all was muffled, like voices on the riverbank heard from underwater. He was drifting away, letting the current take him to a quieter place.

Strong arms lifted him from harm.

Math strode through the crowd, hissing. Taller than any and bareheaded, the very sight of him made the shoken back away. Those few that feared he had come to harm the Healer and had stepped forward in the hope of protecting him soon shrank back when he approached. Math carried Orrld, slinging him over one shoulder and running. With his free hand, he unbound his tail, which he kept tied from sight lest it frighten the shoken. He knew he needed it for balance. When he reached the palace, he leapt, landing first on a narrow ledge almost half the height of the building. Delicately he picked his way between the stone deities perched there and then climbed to the roof. So swift, by the time the guards had realised what was happening, he had gone.

Two turns later Orrld opened his eyes and lay watching gold leaves rise and fall, swirling and intermingling in a delicate silent dance of complex patterns that caught the sun's light. When consciousness fully returned he realised what he saw was the linegold blades.

He sat up in bed. His movement stopped the linegold dance and the blades lay silently down upon the balustrade where they had been left. Getting up he went onto the balcony and Math was there just as he thought, standing in the shade. Before he touched him, he knew a change had come upon him. Math was not meekly covered, his head shrouded and his tail tucked away along with any of his grey skin. He was bareheaded and wore only a simple sleeveless tunic. Was he even bigger now?

Math came over and knelt so they could embrace and in the touching Orrld knew no weapon would make him a killer. Resorting to violence would never come easily, even if life meant that he would have to. In a troubled world, he knew this would surely happen.

Orrld went to the linegold, nodding to Math that he should take it up and the Strick boy smiled as the blades glided into his hand. Orrld saw a look of relief on his face and realised then how hard it had been to leave them untouched. The linegold was a part of him and yet he knew he would never use them for ill. Orrld knew Math would always be his protector.

There was more movement than usual, footfall in the hallways, sounds of the Pack talking. Lak-Mur was usually quiet. Beyond the palace walls, a crowd was humming a sad lament, the sound of it rippling through the air.

'Are we leaving?'

Math nodded.

CHAPTER TWENTY-EIGHT

Etter had experienced battle, been a part of the bloody aftermath of war, more death should not have disturbed her. Thrane was different. It was hard to put aside what she had seen. Visions of bloated, naked bodies remained in Etter's thoughts. Even as the figures were almost featureless, it was possible to tell man from woman, old from young, and the killing was uglier than war. The Sturgar had butchered the shoken, giving no chance to fight, just to demonstrate their superior strength. What troubled her more than anything was the complete ease of the massacre. No indications of a struggle. The shoken of Thrane slaughtered like unwitting cattle.

Many years ago, she had witnessed the result of a massacre on a remote northern village. She forgot the name of the place now. The bodies had been few and no more than windblown skeletons by the time she and her small command arrived. They had buried the remains and marched on. Back then, no one was sure if it was the work of the Sturgar. Now the slaying was becoming almost commonplace. Fools who believed the Sturgar were no threat to civilisation were beginning to understand the reality of genocide.

Etter reined in her horse at the top of an incline and looked around. This was a good vantage point, clear in every direction for a hundred paces. She raised her right hand and the army who followed behind stopped. It would lift morale to make camp early.

She sent out foraging parties to make use of the extra light and hoped they would be successful. Thrane should have replenished their supplies. With each step since then, they rationed food. The populace had been murdered and every beast, grain and crop taken. Even finding enough fuel to make the pyre had proved almost impossible. The Sturgar were a plague of locusts.

Etter lifted her eye patch and looked up. After many turns of rain, the sky was clearing. Tonight she would be able to take a reading from the stars and renew her sense of direction. The weather was warmer and the land was flattening, making the going easy, and providing much-needed grazing for the horses.

Before her tent was pitched, a foraging party returned with news of an abandoned farm with a field of root vegetables. Etter made sure all was dug up and loaded onto the supply wagons. The work took four turns. Everyone was glad to remain in one place. Here there was grass and clear, running water. It was a relief to wash and rest. Hunting parties managed to find deer and hare. They chopped wood and smoked meat to take with them. Arrow shafts and spears were cut from nearby woods and stones gathered from the river bed for slingshots. They made repairs to tents and clothes and the farrier did what he could, mending and replacing horseshoes, although metal was scarce. The sun shone and she was glad to see her little army was beginning to put aside the horror they had seen.

There was so much to oversee and organise, she had not noticed the change in Lorimore until it was almost too late.

Etter was a light sleeper. Any sound or change woke her. She had grown used to sharing her tent with the other woman. On waking, she noticed the absence of Lorimore's breathing. Imagining she had gone to relieve herself, Etter waited for her return. She did not come back.

Outside the tent, she kicked the young sentry awake. He leapt to attention, dropping his spear. 'How long ago did Lorimore leave?' she asked, handing him back the weapon she had caught. The boy had no idea. It would be no use asking him which way she had gone.

The bright turns gave brilliant, starry nights and the moons were clear in the cloudless sky. Etter looked at the ground. Lorimore's steps were visible in the dew. She followed them toward the stream. Lorimore had gone alone; it seemed unlikely that she would go there to meet another – she did not seek the friendship of others. She was not even sure if they were friends. Even so, Etter was concerned as she reached the water's edge, calling out her name. No answer came. The riverbank was formed of shingle stones and they left no trace of footfall. Etter walked upstream, looking to the ground, hoping for a clue. A hundred paces on she saw a body slumped against the bank. It was Lorimore, the shallow water lapping around her waist, arms floating strangely on the water surface, black ribbons from each wrist flowing in the current.

Etter waded to where she lay and lifted her out of the water. Lorimore was thin, brittle from lack of appetite and limp. Limp but not dead. Etter tore strips of dry cloth from her clothing and bound them tightly around Lorimore's wrists to stem the flow of blood. When it was done, Etter stood up with her in her arms.

A bright object glinted in the moonlight – the knife she

had used to slash her wrists. Etter kicked the cursed blade into the water.

For two turns, Lorimore lay in the tent, barely moving and saying nothing. Etter attended her and put all plans to march again aside. She did not care what the men were thinking. She already knew what they said about her and the Kassnets woman. The thought made her smile as she spooned broth into unwilling lips. In truth, affection from any female would be welcome. Her need to keep Lorimore alive was something more. If asked to explain why she kept the woman close, she would not have been able to put words to the strong feelings. Keeping Lorimore alive was more of a basic survival instinct. Something she had to do. For all their sakes. Letting Lorimore die was like letting all the shoken caught unawares in the conflict die.

On the third turn, as the light faded, rain began and the air was chill so she brought a small brazier inside the tent. Etter managed to get her to eat a little more and as the rain thrummed on the tent wall, Lorimore went back to sleep. Etter watched her for a moment then pulled out a small bundle that contained Lorimore's belongings.

There was no written code against looking through another soldier's items, yet it was forbidden. Even as she told herself Lorimore was not a real soldier, her skin prickled.

Slowly Etter began to remove the contents of the kit bag. Stuffed in the top was the dress she had been wearing when she was conscripted and a tatty pair of mud-caked shoes, some small-clothes and a hair comb carved from shell. Etter lay them out before her on the cow-hide that lined the ground of the tent. She picked off the dried mud from the dress hem and looked at the embroidery. Fine silver thread in a pattern of flowers. The clothes of a noblewoman.

Next inside the bag was a shawl, this of soft, pale pink wool wrapped around some books. The books were full of drawings. With one hand holding up her eye patch and the other turning the wispy pages she studied the pencil sketches in the firelight. All were pictures of people, mostly faces. Often the same shoken was drawn from several angles. Were the drawings Lorimore's? Etter was unsure. If they were, Etter resolved to make sure she would find a suitable place for her when they reached Valkarah. No wonder the poor woman was so troubled. The army was no life for an artist.

Fascinated, Etter turned over a page and was shocked to see drawings of Sturgar faces.

Etter knew that Lorimore's home town of Biscos had been massacred. But these drawings were not a glimpse of Sturgar faces half-remembered from that night – each portrait was rendered in fine detail. Lorimore, if indeed she was the artist, knew these faces intimately. She set one book aside, opened another, and was confronted with an even greater shock. On the first page was a woman's face drawn and redrawn many times, always with the same blank expression. Many years ago, Etter had seen this face in the flesh; it was unmistakably one of the king's protectors.

Outside the rain grew louder, waking Lorimore.

'I need you to tell me how you know this woman and what you know about the Sturgar. I need you to tell me everything that has happened to you,' said Etter.

Lorimore was silent.

Etter hoped she would speak freely. It would be difficult to have to hurt her to make her talk.

Then, gathering the blanket about her, Lorimore moved closer to the brazier and sat there, staring into the flames. Slowly and without emotion, she told her story, from the beginning when the Sturgar came, capturing her and her little girl Ashmi and taking them back to Tarestone on the northern Ice Wastes. She spoke about her rape and the appalling Strick baby that came forth. She told all she had learnt from the Watcher with the reflecting disks and how she had been forced to capture the woman, Sho.

To Etter it seemed she spoke to herself and she let her go on without interruption, understanding it had been too long since she had confided in anyone. She left nothing out. Dawn had arrived by the time she had finished.

'Do you still have the disk?' asked Etter.

Lorimore looked over, surprised to see another.

'The reflecting disk they gave you to see your child, do you still have it?'

Lorimore crawled to her kit bag and tipped everything out. She found the disk wrapped in a piece of soft leather and handed it over.

'It doesn't work now. It only works if the bearer of the seeing metal lives,' she said.

Etter examined the disk. It fitted in the palm of her hand and was silver like a mirror except the surface was blank. There were none of the moving images described – now this part of the story seemed fanciful.

CHAPTER TWENTY-NINE

Curver Thist leaned against the wall of the reflecting room. His legs ached from too much standing and he was bored and tired. Around the huge room, tall shutters covered the windows from which long, thin shafts of light lined the blackness. Outside it was always bright now and the dark lasted only a few short candles. This meant the Sturgar had to do their work beyond the night. All were tired and aggressive and would be until the world changed again and there was a more even balance of light and dark to every turn. The Curver had calculated this would not be until three moons' phases had passed.

At the centre, the Master knelt behind the Watcher, both looking at a disk. Now and again, they spoke – mostly they were silent. Every turn the Master viewed the images from the Shoken-Slayer and his paired warrior. The Curver wished to speak to the Master about a letter he had received and fingered a sliver of whisper silk recently rolled within the hollow wing of a messenger bird, waiting.

At least the Aulex was not here. He had seen her crossing the ice flow with her brood. Occasionally she took her cubs seal hunting. When the Aulex waited for the Master the Watcher's disciple hid away. Without the beast, she went about her business, quietly moving among the concentric lines of tables, wiping between the disks with a cloth of softling leather and dusting each disk with a bunch of feathers. Her movements were slow and careful but her eyes were quick as she glanced at the Master and then toward one of the shuttered windows. She never turned her head in the direction of her gaze and the Curver knew few would have noticed the flick of her eyes. He wondered what it was she wanted behind the window, a male perhaps? The Watcher was sworn to celibacy, her disciple was not. Sturgar numbers were so depleted all breeding was encouraged. The disciple set aside her cloths and began to repair one of the fireplaces near to where he stood. She had none of the Watcher's beauty – her face was flat and her skin, ravaged by some disease in infancy, pitted. Voluminous black robes concealed her figure. Even so, he could tell her limbs were thick and heavy. It was unlikely a male who waited beyond the window. More likely, she had food hidden there that she was looking forward to eating when they had all gone. He could definitely smell softling although the food on the table was seal meat.

The fire was burning brightly as she swept up the ashes. Ugly as he found her, he mused about whether he would turn her away in the unlikely event she should offer herself to him. She could always keep her clothes on, one cunt felt much like another, after all. Unless she was still a virgin. That thought made him harden.

At last, the Master got up, whispered a few words to the Watcher then went to the hatch in the floor and lowered himself, by a chain, into the map room below. The Curver knew better than to follow him there and left, cursing the time he had wasted.

Back in his chambers, his thoughts kept returning to the disciple. What was she hiding behind the shutters? It would be easy to go to her and demand she show him. But so much more interesting to find out for himself.

When Tarestone slept, the Curver crept through the empty hallways until he was above the reflecting room. This was unused space. As far as he knew, only he had a key. Once it had been a feasting hall. A long table stood in the centre surrounded by vetrolla bone chairs. Walls were draped with threadbare tapestries so dust-laden it was impossible to see what they depicted. Steel chains hung from the rafters; from these, just above the table, eight Sturgar skeletons were suspended, some from their wrists, others from their ankles. Many parts of Tarestone were in dire need of repair, this was one such place. Draughts moaned through the cracked shutters, turning the grinning skeletons about on their chains.

The Curver went to a fireplace on the far wall and pulled back a massive Aulex skin. Time past the fire basket must have tipped over; the wood floor was burnt through in places. He lay down and looked at the reflecting room beneath.

The view was not clear. Beams and rafters obscured much; the Curver had overcome this by fixing many shards from a large mirror he had smashed. The effect was satisfactory. Peering into the hole enabled him to observe all of the reflecting room without the need to move about and so risk making a noise.

Below he could see the Watcher and her disciple. The Watcher sat on a chair, the disciple kneeling at her feet. They were eating. The disciple handed her mistress choice bits of seal meat, putting each piece into her hands. Since he had last spied on them, the Watcher had become quite blind. This was the fate of all who looked upon the disks. He wondered how long it would be until she became useless.

When they were finished, the disciple led the Watcher away to her chambers to rest. The Curver stayed, expecting the disciple to return. No one came and he was just about to leave when the window shutter slowly opened. Light flooded into the room and he had trouble adjusting his eyes to the brightness. When he could see again, a child slid on its belly over the floor. Beside the food table, it stood up and the hood it was wearing fell back. What was revealed was such a shock he had to stop himself from hissing. An infant shoken with matted hair clothed in ragged seal skins was helping itself to the scraps. His mind spun as he tried to think where and how this child had come to be here. It turned its head and then he remembered. The artist they had sent forth in the hope that she would capture the shoken king's protector. As was often the way with shokens, they had used her young to manipulate her. After the artist had failed he had never given another thought to the child they held captive, assuming she had been killed and eaten.

The Curver sat up and watched the skeletons turning in the draught. Many schemes had taken place since then, yet the Curver had a good memory. Lorimore, that was the shoken and her child, Ashmi. How strange that she still lived and to what purpose.

He lay down again and watched her. She was quite at home, stuffing extra food inside her clothes. She sank to the floor and slid, using her elbows to pull herself along. The faint sound blended with the constant shushing the many reflective disks made. If he had not seen her, he would not have known she was there. Even if she had walked quietly, any Sturgar would have felt the vibration of her shoken footfall.

The Curver looked at a different mirror; Ashmi was at the centre of the room now beside the tables where the most important disks were. Carefully, she got up. Standing on her toes, she could just reach the top of the table. Then she did something extraordinary. She took one of the disks and looked at it, twitching it this way and that with tiny, almost imperceptible movements. When she had finished looking, she put it back and reached for another. The Curver realised she could manipulate the reflecting disks and the knowledge gave him an idea.

CHAPTER THIRTY

Quel led Junas to his dwelling. Like all the others it was roofless and made of little more than leaf screens and woven grass. Inside were baskets stacked one upon the other, these presumably containing his belongings. There was no furniture. They sat on the moss-covered ground.

He held the chain in one hand and with the other, he began to unwind the strips of cloth he used to protect his delicate skin from the sun. One of the leaf screens was lifted back and a bright woman entered carrying a pitcher. She helped remove the rest of his clothing. Various objects were hidden in the swaddling. Small things stolen from the dashen and the drifters. Coins, jewellery, a silver spoon, a thumb knife and some sugar crystals. She took them all with much delight and then poured water over him. As the dust of his travels washed away, his body took on a soft, golden, irides-cent glow. The woman left and returned with a bowl of water, which she set in front of Junas. Junas washed her hands and face while the woman watched. It was clear she was terrified of her. Quel laughed. 'This is my sister. She has never been above. That is why she has so much light.' He smiled and sat down again, perfectly comfortable in his nakedness. 'We are the Gorund,' he said, waving a hand to encompass their surroundings.

Another woman came with a basket of food. Slices of raw fish and some sort of root vegetable that had a strange taste all its own. They ate in silence and she wondered why he had not pressed her to find out what she carried. When the women had cleared away and they were alone Quel looked at her.

'What you carry must be very precious,' he said.

Junas said nothing.

'Did you steal it?'

Again, Junas was silent.

'I'd like you to show me,' he said, in a patient voice.

Junas thought about leaping up. If she was quick, she might yank the chain from his hand and run, although where she had no idea without any sort of map in her head.

Quel twitched the chain and the noose tightened until the barbs pricked her skin and she could feel blood trickle. He spoke quietly, 'Show me.'

As he squeezed the chain, she felt the thorns go a little deeper and she could think of no other way of surviving this moment than to show him. She took a step closer to slacken the chain and began to undo her garments, terrified that she had failed her task before she had hardly begun.

Somewhere a bell tolled. The deep sound echoed around the cave and before it had faded away, rang again, adding echoes to the first. Soon the air was alive with the sound and all began to move in the direction of the noise.

'It is time,' he said, leading her. He walked fast weaving in and out of the shacks until they met the stone wall of the cave rising into blackness. Junas tried to find a mark point, something that would give her a bearing. All the dwellings looked similar and without the sun or any landscape, she was lost. As they walked, others joined them. They followed the rock face for many paces until they came to a small tunnel into another cave. This one was smaller, the lower roof visible and encrusted with strange crystals that hung in sharp profusion, glinting in the light from the bodies below.

When they reached a place where a jagged jewel filled the space between ground and cave roof, a throng of a hundred or more surrounded them. So many bodies of light made the jewel shine.

This must be their sacred place, thought Junas, as a woman appeared in shimmering silver robes. She was uncommonly tall, her head almost touching the crystallised roof. She stepped, spider-like, in front of the gemstone on long, unsteady legs; in each hand a thin pole helped her balance. Stilts provided her height. The effect gave her authority. Even from the distance, Junas could see she was very young and this, more than anything that had happened, frightened her. Quel began to address her and the crowd added their ideas. Junas prayed to the Mother and wished she understood what they were saying. The young priestess listened and Junas watched her face for any clue as to her fate. The talking went on. Shoken came forward with their own opinions and they began to argue. One thing was certain; the priestess would make the final decision.

Junas wrapped her arms about the precious egg and sat on the ground hoping to appear a vulnerable pregnant woman. Judging from the looks that they gave her, they had little sympathy for her kind, pregnant or otherwise.

Around her the arguments ensued, it would not be long until they stripped her and discovered her secret. There was some hope they might not harm her and send her on her way to complete her journey. But she had no faith this would happen and she did not trust Quel to translate her story accurately if she tried to explain. He may have brought her back to his shoken to share with them what wealth he imagined she had hidden. But he was still a thief.

Junas looked about. This cave floor was rock, warm and smooth. She looked at those around her. All were barefoot. She remembered how Quel had removed his boots before they entered the Ramshales.

The priestess had begun to speak, her voice light and melodic. They only had eyes for her now and Junas pulled off her boots. She began to ease the barbed noose around her neck; it cut her fingers and as she worked the thorns out of her skin, her wounds bled afresh.

Quel turned around and took a step closer to her and the crowd moved back – whether to give them room or because they were afraid, she was uncertain. Whatever the reason, the time had come to make a decision. There were too many of them to fight, even as they seemed to be unarmed. She would have to flee. She pulled the noose over her head, cutting her face and hands and, leaping up, ran.

She ran the way they had come and the Gorund, fearing a stranger, shrank from her as she passed. The opening to this cave was easy enough to find, and once through the tunnel, she stayed by the wall and ran on. Nearly all the shoken must have been in the other cave because without their light it was dark. Junas kept her hand on the wall for guidance. She did not want to get lost in the centre where everything looked the same. The cave began to light again. They were returning.

Beneath her feet, the stone was flat and smooth. Junas stopped to listen. There were shouts and patches of light moving about in all directions. They were hunting her.

Junas looked up. Somewhere in the blackness, there had to be an opening to the world above. The nearest patch of light was a hundred paces away. She pulled off her coat and unstrapped the harness that held the egg. Her heart beat loudly as she fastened the egg to her back. There was no time to put on her coat, so she bundled it up and threw it. Somewhere in the darkness, it crashed into something and the Gorund set off toward it.

A million hands for a million years had smoothed the face of the wall. Junas was taller than the Gorund and when she reached up, the rock had a rougher surface. Junas felt for a handhold and began to climb, digging her fingers and toes into the crevasses, climbing with instinct.

In the darkness, it was not possible to tell which way would make the best climb so she concentrated on getting as high as possible. Soon they would follow. She needed to reach the top before they could catch her.

Junas climbed until her limbs ached and the weight of the egg grew heavy even though the feel of it was a part of her now. Time was hard to gauge. Below, the shouts of the Gorund had become distant and fear had given way to tiredness. She prayed to the Mother that soon she would reach the top and find freedom.

As she felt for the next handgrip, she gave thanks. Not the top but a ledge, wide enough to lie upon jutting from the vertical rock face. Tentatively she pulled on it and then, with one hand and foot safely anchored, gradually eased her weight on it, listening should the rock protest. Only when she was sure it was safe did she haul herself up. She lay on her stomach with closed eyes, relieved to rest and feel the egg, safe on her back.

The ledge was wide enough to lie on comfortably but not quite as long as she was tall, her feet hanging over the edge. Junas rested her chin on her hands. Far below tiny spots of light moved about. Still, they searched for her. Soon they would realise she was climbing. She expected them to aim lighted arrows at the rock face to find her. Then she recalled how Quel mistrusted fire. She had seen no fire here. The food had been raw. Perhaps they all disliked fire.

Junas turned the egg, held onto the edge of the rock, and slept.

She had no idea how long sleep had claimed her. Below, the Gorund were not dashing about in a frenzy. Many of the pools of light were still. Perhaps they slept. Did shoken who lived under the ground have a time for sleeping and waking?

From up here, she had a sense of how vast the cave was. The shoken were a million points of light in the blackness, like a night sky. The eye was naturally drawn toward the light, yet Junas knew escape was not possible below. She sat up, legs dangling over the edge and peered into the dark, looking for a way out. Even as she had climbed so high, above was only a void. No chink of light gave a sign of the cave roof, the dark so complete, she was blind.

Junas reached behind and turned the egg, closing her eyes and praying to Mother God to help her find a way. The rush of fear from escaping was replaced now by a feeling of being trapped and lost. All she had learnt, every map and pathfinding way, was of no use in the dark. In here, there was no light or sound to guide her.

Quel had known the way – how, she could not tell. The dwellings were all but identical and there was nothing that distinguished one part of the cave from another, yet somehow he had found a path.

Junas sat still and closed her eyes again for she was sure they did not use their eyes. And she had not seen them feeling their way with hands or feet. Was there a sound that she had not noticed? Junas turned her head this way and that, listening. Then she felt it. A soft breath of air over her face, so very faint, she thought it her imagination at first. Without her coat, much of her skin was bare. She concentrated her thoughts about how the air felt on her face, on the naked skin of her back around the egg, her shoulders and legs, the soles of her feet. The air came into the cave from one side, not from above. Junas began climbing sideways, stopping now and then to feel the air currents as they drifted over her skin.

CHAPTER THIRTY-ONE

In the morning, after the change of the watch, and if it had been a peaceful night, Etter felt most at ease. This turn dawned clear and fresh after the rain. She took a stroll through the camp as the light brightened then went back to her tent. Inside, Lorimore slept. She let her be, gathered up some clean garments and her wash things, and left quietly.

These past few turns Etter had busied herself with recruitment training. She needed time to think through all that she had learnt. After Lorimore had told her story, Etter had tried to decide how much was true. The more she thought, the more she came to realise that Lorimore had no reason to lie. The woman went about her duties, but far from being unburdened by the telling, Lorimore was an empty shell, a dry husk. No kindness made any impact on her demeanour. It was clear her death-wish was still upon her and Etter kept a vigilant watch lest she came to any harm.

Etter thought through the many things that Lorimore had told. One piece of information kept returning to her – the Sturgar planned to lay siege to Valkarah. By her reckoning, three moon cycles and her army would reach the city.

Considering how far they had come, this was not long. She knew that they should move on. Yet they remained. If any had asked her to account for her actions, she would have said the reason was the massacre at Thrane. They needed to make arrows, gather food and be ready should they meet the violence of the Sturgar. An argument that made perfect sense. Only she knew in her heart that if they met them, nobody would survive. Even an army twice the size, peopled by the good king's best would die against this foe, much less her ragged tribe of conscripted recruits, almost all untried in any battle let alone against the Sturgar. No, Etter remained because she feared the bloodbath that awaited them.

Beside the stream, it was quiet and mist hung over the water. Taking advantage of rare solitude Etter stripped and waded in, leaving her sword on the bank within reach. Despite the warmer weather, the water was so cold it made her bones ache. Checking once more that she was truly alone, Etter removed her eye patch and placed the well-worn triangle of leather next to her weapon and dunked her head under the surface, hoping the bitter chill would clear her mind. She floated there, looking up at the sky through the haze of the water. Despite the cold, it was peaceful and her thoughts drifted with unimportant matters, like when she had last washed all of her body. She rubbed her fingers through her hair loosening the grime. It was getting long – perhaps she should cut it. She stood up, shaking the water from her face with a mind to find her last slither of soap and make a proper job of getting clean.

Her wash things were not in a bag, it was more a fold of leather tied about with a frayed string. Inside she had a shard of polished metal that served as a mirror. She propped it up and began to cut her hair. The thumb knife was rusted and blunt. She had to saw back and forth to cut clumps of hair off. When the last had floated away, she rubbed the soap into the tufts on her scalp. Committed now to the business of washing, she began picking the grime from under her nails with the knife. The water's rush and the morning birdsong was loud and she was engrossed in the novelty of her task. It was only when instinct made her look up that she saw Lorimore standing there in the mist.

She reached for her eye patch too late. Lorimore had already seen the Sturgar eye she took such pains to conceal. Etter tried to smile. 'I can't change what I am,' she said, turning away. She soaped herself and rinsed, plunging her head under the water. It felt colder now. When she surfaced, Lorimore was still there. Only now, she was pointing the little crossbow toward her. It was nothing, a child's toy, yet a well-aimed bolt could kill at close range. She already knew Lorimore had a good aim.

'I'm still the same. I'm no different just because you know this about me,' she said, staying in the water. There was no need for Lorimore to see her other part of Sturgar inheritance. It was no more than a stump and she was unsure if that was how it had always been or if her tail was cut at birth. Even so, no shoken had such a thing. Etter stood in the waist-deep water and talked to Lorimore about incidentals – what they might eat later and whether it would rain, trying to soothe and reassure. It was unlikely that she would loose the bolt; the real concern was whether Lorimore would keep her secret. Some in the camp knew. Living in such proximity, how could they not. Etter had never willingly revealed her ancestry. Oftentimes she had considered showing the truth about herself. King's Law stated that any race, including the Strick, could join the army. Bitter experience had taught her most were not so free-minded as the lord.

Lorimore aimed the crossbow. The tiny bolt was faster than expected and Etter only just managed to dodge a lethal strike. The bolt hit her shoulder and Etter let fly the thumb knife that was still in her hand. It happened before she could think – a soldier's reaction. She knew she had killed her. Lorimore did not possess the strength and reflexes of the Strick. The thumb knife struck her in the temple, piercing her brain, killing her instantly.

Etter crouched beside her dead friend and cupped her face in her hand, brushed strands of straggly hair from her cheek and looked into her unseeing eyes. 'I'm sorry,' she said. 'I'm sorry I frightened you. I'm sorry I didn't manage to get you to safety.' She eased the knife free and tossed it into the water. The death-wound it left was nothing more than a nick and a trickle of dark blood. Shoken died too easily. It was their weakness.

The mist was beginning to fade. Etter picked up the eye patch and rinsed it in the water. Now she was clean, everything felt grubby and she wished she had had the foresight to wash a set of clothes for herself. The ones she put on were scarcely less dirty than those she had taken off.

Etter carried Lorimore's thin, light body. It was hard to believe such frailty had survived so much. At the camp, a pacer ran out to meet her. 'What happened, captain?' he asked.

'She tried to kill me,' said Etter.

He saw the bolt then, sticking from her shoulder and how her clothes were folded away to keep free of the injury. He took the body from her. 'Shall I feed her to the war dogs?' It was the fate of any traitor.

A small crowd had gathered around them. 'No, she was not in her right mind. It was misty. I believe she thought I was someone else. Build her a pyre, we have wood enough,' she said.

~

When the light faded, they lit the pyre and for a while, Etter stood and watched it burn. Her shoulder ached even though the wound was sewn and dressed with clean cotton. What was done was done, she knew this, yet she kept reliving the moment of Lorimore's death and wishing it had been different. If only she had not been holding the thumb knife, if only she had been able to talk to her a little longer. Then there was the worst thought of all – that she would have needed to kill her anyway to keep her secret safe.

Outside her tent was a lamp. Etter took it inside and tied the tent opening securely. Tomorrow they would have to move on, of that much she was sure. She had not realised until now how restless the army had become. They were without purpose and they needed to march.

Strewn on the ground were Lorimore's belongings. Sketchbooks, the reflecting disk and a pile of ragged clothes. Etter knelt beside them with a mind to stuff it all back into the kit bag. A fleeting movement over the surface of the reflecting disk stayed her hand. She thought it a trick of the lamplight. It was no trick. The disk was propped upright against one of the books. Without disturbing it Etter lay down on her stomach so she could more easily see.

She lay very still and watched other lives in other places. Time slipped past and it was not until morning began to lighten the tent walls that she pulled herself away. Etter stood up and stretched, rubbing her face in disbelief. At her feet, the disk continued showing what Lorimore's daughter looked at. Reluctantly she scooped the things into the bag, picking up the disk last. As soon as she moved it, the images disappeared and the surface was as clouds. Saying a silent prayer to Nenimar that she would be able to make it work again, she tucked it inside her doublet.

Etter put the shard of polished metal she used for a mirror into a seam of the tent wall and took off her eye patch. She examined her true face. Her Sturgar eye, the black slit expanded in the dim light and her shoken eye, dark brown. What she had seen on the reflecting disk was the horror of a Sturgar army as they systematically razed a small farming village to the ground. It was time to conceal that part of her that might be construed as allegiance to them. She looked about one last time. Uncovered, the Sturgar eye gave a sharp focus to her surroundings. In comparison, the shoken eye was a poor tool. Etter took up a needle and thread and sewed her eyelids together.

CHAPTER THIRTY-TWO

Orrld awoke from a good dream. As he lay with his eyes closed, he listened to the wind in the trees. If he did not look, it almost sounded like water. More and more his unconscious returned him to the River. In the dreams, reality blurred. Llund swam with him, the Pack and Math rowed boats and fished and talked in Ekressian to his now-dead family and Issolissi was ever close, her brown eyes laughing, her gentle healing touching the back of his neck.

At the beginning of the journey, Llund was sad. He managed to hide it from most. But the Pack knew, especially Sho who wore his sorrow on her face whenever she thought no one was looking. He grieved for the child he had longed for and lost and he missed the Faar. Orrld realised now how much he loved them. They were his true family and leaving them tore at his heart.

They had been travelling for twenty turns and Llund's mood began to lighten. The pace of the daily march slowed. Orrld understood, here between the two great cities of Lak-Mur and Valkarah, he could put aside the burden of kingship. Horses were a remedy for any of Llund's moods. He was always happier when he could spend the turn riding.

Outside the tent, the army was almost ready to leave to make the most of the early morning cool. They would stop before the sun became too hot and take up the journey again in the evening, riding until dark. There was no rush and a relaxed atmosphere prevailed. Sho would play her guitar around the campfire at night. They travelled through ancient woodland, the prime-oaks tall and vast. For the most part, it was uninhabited, which allowed the army to spread out, giving the king and the Pack a measure of privacy.

Orrld pulled on a robe and walked through the woods to a nearby stream to wash and pray. Math and Jie followed at a respectable distance. There was no sign of the king or any of the Pack. It was usual for him to take the prey birds hunting at dawn.

At the water's edge, Orrld stripped and waded in, welcoming the chill of the knee-deep stream. They had been following this for several turns. Every turn it became wider and deeper and they told him that soon it would be a river proper, deep enough to swim in, and they would follow it all the way to Valkarah. Orrld longed to swim.

He knelt and spoke quiet words from the scriptures, cupped water in his webbed hands and tipped it over himself, rocking back and forth with the rhythm of the prayer. Then he was still, listening to the lapping of the stream and the birdsong and waited for the peace of Ath to fill him. At his throat, he felt a sting and made to brush away the fly that had bitten him. His hand found a blade instead.

The blade was at the end of a long spear, and it moved with him as he stood. He dared not turn his head to look for Jie or Math and met the dark eyes of his attacker. The uniform marked him as a Kassnets soldier. There were many, emerging from the undergrowth and now he could hear the clash of steel and the cries of men.

Sho was uneasy about camping in the forest. She would have preferred a different route of an open plain that gave a good view of any approaching threat. But the lord wanted to show his lover the river. At least this way the journey would be longer and give the lord some respite. He always hated returning to Valkarah. She would be relieved. For the past few turns, her prescience pricked and she was jumping at every twig snap and bird sound.

Sho rode at the back of the hunting party, behind her a cohort of twenty foot soldiers. The forest was ancient, the trees well-spaced, the ground beneath quiet from leaves and moss. The king and Arrant, at the head of the line, halted and dismounted handing their mounts to the two new Crystal Bearers.

Sho stood on her horse's back, watching. The two young Crystal Bearers, excited by the newness of their office, made the horses nervous. Their faces were swollen and sore from a recent fight. Their injuries were not from the trials. Indeed, both had emerged relatively unscathed, despite the tough competition. They had fought Math and would have lost their lives if she had not intervened. She had not warned them about the Strick boy and when they met him in a hallway at Lak-Mur, they had attacked with spear and fist. Math had fought them off as easily as if they were children. Two Crystal Bearers, supposed to be the most adept fighters in the Trilands, defeated by an untried boy. Math had not even drawn his linegold. She was glad no one had seen. At least the fight had dampened their bravado. If they could not win against one of the king's party who had no

Crystal, how then could they pick a fight with any of the Pack?

Six years had passed since the lord had accepted new Crystal Bearers. All felt the strangeness of having new Pack members, none more so than her. The king, bored with the selection process, had accepted both rather than let this last pair fight. She could feel their animosity to one another growing stronger each turn. When they found who was stronger they would begin to find their place within the Pack and a new order would begin.

Nearby, Reem called the hawk back to his arm. She swooped among the branches, landed lightly and began pecking at the morsel of meat in his hand. When she had finished he flew her again but she returned without him calling her and settled to preening herself as if to say, no rabbits here.

Math concerned her. She found herself looking for him even though she knew he would be with the Healer. Without Crystal she could not control him – this, and the fact that in her heart she knew if they fought, she would lose. Size of the opponent had never been her concern, although true he was huge now, taller than Sten, broad and strong. Their shared abilities troubled her. Linegold and fight prescience had always set her apart. She wondered what else he might be capable of as he matured. Dark thoughts troubled her about the safety of the lord. If the Strick boy ever turned against them, could they beat him? If he had a Crystal burn, would Math become the king's first? From this, she was safe for the moment. Those who took the bond needed to train and she was sure the Healer would not give up his adopted son – yet.

Ahead the king had moved a little too far away for comfort. Sho stepped her horse on, past the outliners, and waited beneath the dipping branches of a prime-oak. She did not wait long. Soon the king returned, striding through the woods, laughing, Arrant at his side. The hunt was over; there was no need to be quiet now. The king and Arrant mounted and they rode for camp.

The foot soldiers, seeing no kill, began a song in praise of animals that escaped the hunt and the lord joined in with a smile. Such was tradition.

They took a quicker route back through the woods. As the soldiers turned into a clearing, a familiar dread filled her. She looked around trying to find the threat she so keenly felt. There was nothing. Sho rode close to the lord, so close her leg touched the red mare's flank. and at her bidding, the Pack encircled them.

The arrow came from high above and pierced the neck of the red mare with deadly accuracy. She tossed her head in shock and screamed, staggering on for four more strides in an attempt to keep her rider safe. Then she fell, slowly, sinking to her knees, only rolling over when the king was free. He held her handsome head in his lap, weeping while she died. Sho could hardly move, so great was the lord's pain within her.

From nowhere Kassnets soldiers rose from the ground where they had concealed themselves with sods of turf and plants. The trees were alive with archers. Their foot soldiers were outnumbered and, caught unawares, fell like scythed corn. She and the Pack tried to protect the king.

CHAPTER THIRTY-THREE

They had been captive five turns, each collared in iron from which a chain was fastened to a stake driven deep into the ground. They were in a line, the lord at the centre and she beside him. For that much, Sho was grateful. On capture, knives at the king's throat made her relinquish her linegold. The glassknife, sheathed like a skinning knife, was in her saddlebag. She wondered what had become of the cruel blade.

A circle of fifty men guarded them, standing, back to back, one facing outward and the other in, their watches short to keep them ever vigilant.

At first, they had stood in their chains, defiant, but hunger and thirst took their toll and when the king came to his knees, so did the others.

Sho was glad they were in the forest's shade and the ground was soft to sleep upon at least. She watched and thought. Her linegold was too far for her to summon and although she was armed, killing a few soldiers was pointless – a few deaths would not release their chains.

Sho resisted the urge to finger the iron collar; this was

not the first time she had been treated as a slave. Nothing would change the way it felt, only freedom.

Beside her, the outliners lay in a bloodied heap. The new Crystal Bearers, keen to assert themselves, had goaded the guards and been whipped into submission. She and the Pack had no trouble holding their silence. They would wait and pick the next fight with care. In the meantime, the bonds they shared sustained them. They gave each other feelings of hope and reassurance and the lord sent them love. The untested outliners had no such comfort – it was too soon. Sho wondered if they would learn the full extent of their bonds or die, without ever seeing Valkarah. She did not even know their names.

Sho looked along the line – every Crystal Bearer except Jie and Sten. Both lived. She sensed Jie was injured and then cured. The lord had felt it too and understood from the healing that Orrld also lived.

Arrant, on the other side of the king, also stood, although she knew it cost him dearly to do so. He looked strange without his longsword and she could feel his disappointment in himself. It was a shame he never learnt to use his gift of fire for harm.

Her body was different from the others. She could last many turns without food or sleep, her thirst was annoying, but she could survive. What bothered her most was the waiting for the violence that was surely coming. Live or die, she would rather fight than wait.

Somewhere beyond the wall of men, she heard something new and sure enough, they parted at a shouted command. All the Crystal Bearers stood as a party approached on horse-back. It was Saur with a small honour guard of six. A good number – more and it would look as if he was unable to fight, fewer and it would give the impression he was low ranking. Six would offer protection as well as kudos. He dismounted and walked toward them. She noticed he kept a safe distance despite their chains.

He stood before the king, who reclined, one arm propping up his head. The lord looked as if he was relaxing on a palanquin. She sent him her love and he returned it.

Saur surveyed them and reached out behind. Immediately a pacer ran forward and placed a waterskin in his outstretched hand. Saur drank, allowing the water to drip from the corners of his mouth and spill on the ground. When he was done, he wiped his mouth with the back of his hand and smiled.

'You look thirsty,' he spoke in Kassnets to the lord. There was a swagger in his step as he came closer, holding out the waterskin to the king. The king jumped up, as lithe as if he had indeed been resting. Saur stepped back at the sudden movement, his face twitching. Sho imagined the sweet pleasure she would experience if she threw a blade at Saur's throat.

The king took the waterskin and without drinking himself passed it to her, saying in the language they shared, 'Give it to the children.' There was no word for outliner in Faar. They were reluctant to drink. She told them it was the lord's command they drink and wash their injuries with the water. Saur walked away, his face twitching violently. Around them, Sho believed many of the Kassnets soldiers looked uneasy. It was one thing to talk about Kassnets rule, quite another to commit treason.

Nearby, they made a fire and butchered a carcass. It was the red mare. Her handsome was head placed before the king. When the meat was cooked, a terrified pacer served each a platter.

The intense hunger of the Pack was as nothing compared to the king's revulsion and grief. No one ate.

By nightfall, a slave wagon pulled by four oxen arrived. So

many spears pointed at the king there was no chance of escape when the Kassnets chained them within.

Sho was thankful they were together, no matter how cramped and dark. She knelt with her face pressed to a seam of light between the doors and prayed to Nenimar to save the lord.

Five turns later when the wagon came to a halt and the doors opened, all reeled from the light. Filthy, weak from hunger and crazed with thirst they crept meekly at the end of their chains.

Once her eyes adjusted to the light Sho looked about. She recognised this place although it was years since she had visited. A ruin of an old hunting lodge known as Midford Hall dating back to when this was Kassnets' territory.

The parts of the roof rebuilt with new timber looked strange next to the weathered stone walls. A ditch with sharpened wooden stakes surrounded the building, and lookout platforms in the tallest trees made a fortress of sorts.

None of this was makeshift. From the well-ordered army encampment to the iron collars about their necks all had been long in the planning.

Their guards stopped. Somebody approached. Sneela stepped out from a line of trees. In the clearing, the light caught her silver armour – a fitted breastplate and helm etched with windflowers. She strode ahead of her honour guard in boots and green satin breeches, a thin sword at her side. She had styled herself as the warrior princess Straganna. All she needed was a pair of white wolves and a talking dove. Sho thought she looked ridiculous, but her honour guards were happy to believe the fairy tale from the looks on their faces.

The soldiers that led the king and the line of Crystal Bearers bowed low. It took only a few prods and shoves from them to make the Pack and the king kneel. They were weak and feeble after so long without food or water. Even if she could contrive an escape, she knew none of them would have the strength to fight.

Sneela walked along the line, considering each in turn. Saur strutted beside her like a lapdog and both smiled at one another, pleased with what they had achieved.

She stopped before the king and took a step closer. Saur tugged her sleeve, pulling her out of harm's reach.

'Where is your companion, the Healer?' she asked in Kassnets.

Slowly, the king stood and looked down on them both. Even in his sorry state and un-crowned, he looked regal. His beard had grown and was as golden as his hair, which made him look like his ancestor, the Warrior King, Bok. The resemblance was not lost on the Kassnets soldiers. Some of them muttered the name.

'The Healer is dead,' said the king, hanging his head to make the lie real.

Sneela turned her back and stooped to speak quietly with Saur. Sho listened, hearing all.

'Two are missing. The one who lost his hand and the Lamash. They are the ones who usually guard the Riverman,' she said, looking over her shoulder at them. Sho slumped her shoulders and hung her head as if she, too, was weak from lack of sustenance. In truth the deprivation would have little effect on her, not for many more turns.

'They cannot be parted from the king. They won't be far away and when they sense that he is hurt, they will bring the Healer. He never could lie. The Healer lives,' she said.

A nod from Saur and they were led away.

They imprisoned them separately, in the cellars beneath

Midford Hall. The walls and ceiling were quarried long ago from the bedrock, the doors hurriedly made from unseasoned prime-oak already beginning to warp.

Sho tested her metal collar and the chain fastened to a ring in the floor – she poked her fingers around the new mortar. It had been well made and was as strong as the stone.

Around her she could sense the other Crystal Bearers in their cells, could feel their exhaustion and defeat. The lord, she knew, was on the other side of her wall. He was calm, resigned even. Sho thought about her linegold and the glassknife. She wished this last was still pressed against her back – longing for murder. A glassknife would aim true over great distances and return to her hand, it was undetectable except by the most discerning Blade-Master and it left no mark on the victim, although it carried the image of every soul the user killed upon its surface. It was the perfect murder weapon. No doubt Saur had discovered it among her things.

Sten and Jie had followed, keeping much distance between themselves and the Kassnets. She sent them her love and a small push, letting them know they should not come any closer.

Above, a circle of light shone between two stones, creating a line of brightness in the narrow cell. Whether a spyhole or a fault in the rock, she was glad for the comfort it gave her.

That night bread and water came through a hatch in the door. Sho ate and waited for approaching danger. She could hear music playing and voices lifted in song. The Kassnets were celebrating.

The line of light had disappeared and the darkness was complete when she heard footsteps approach. She knew the footfall from the first audible step – Saur.

Sho stood up as he entered, fight prescience prickling all

her senses. He was alone and annoyingly he was not carrying any of her weapons. He came in and set the lantern he carried on the floor and allowed the poorly made door to swing shut. Saur stood by the wall. He knew how far the chain reached. Sho knew he wanted to hurt her but was too afraid to come any closer. Sho folded her arms and looked at him. At his waist was a coiled whip. She wondered if he would dare to use it. Sho wished she had her linegold. It would be so easy to float a blade at his throat until he called the turnkey.

'I know that all of you are connected somehow,' he said, his face twitching. She could smell the wine that had given him the courage to see her alone. 'The queen wants you to bring the other Crystal Bearers here and the Healer.'

'The Healer is not connected to us,' she said, 'and they are far away. Too far for me to summon alone.'

'What do you mean, alone?'

'The lord and I together could bring them here,' she said.

The whip came quicker than she anticipated, missing her face and cracking in the air. Three more times he struck and she avoided the lash so easily she almost smiled.

'You lie,' he spat. His fury overcame him as he struck at her over and again until spent from the effort.

'Shall I cry out so the guard will think you've managed to hit me?' Sho folded her arms. Her words seemed to sober him. Saur coiled the whip and hung it back on his belt, then wiped his twitching face with his sleeve.

'I could order an array of archers here. Even you could not evade that many arrows,' he said.

'If you have me killed, the agony in your face will never go. It will just get worse until it drives you crazy.'

'You're a witch. I will not listen to your words.'

'You could kill me yourself, of course. That would work. I'm willing to fight, even here chained and without a weapon,' Sho smiled. They both knew he could never win. 'Set me free and help rescue the king. The Healer may have mended your skin. He cannot cure the poison the linegold leaves. Only I can do that. I promise the pain will stop if you do.'

Saur scrubbed his face with his hands as she spoke. His pain was deep, reflecting his hate.

Sho knelt. Meek, hands on her knees. 'Let me be with the lord. The small act of kindness will relieve some of your discomforts. What difference will it make? The king is no fighter, that's why he has us.'

In truth, Sho had no idea what caused the pain of linegold cuts. She only knew some suffered more than others and those that hurt the most hated her the most.

Saur walked out saying nothing more. The light had returned when she heard marching. Their steps were light and quick. Archers.

Over the long watches of the night, she had considered what she would do if Saur did intend to kill her. Behind her back, she wound the chain into her hand. If she must die this turn, at least Saur would die if he came to watch and he was stupid enough to get close.

Most of the array stopped at the top of the stairs and Saur and two archers came down. For a moment, hope filled her. Two archers gave her a good chance of survival. The footfall passed her door and on to the king's cell.

Sho felt the arrow pierce his shoulder, hot and sharp. The shock of the pain brought her to the ground and she shuddered, breathless, clutching an arrow she could not see, tearing her clothing to mop blood that was not there. Above, she knew she was being watched yet could not hide what the lord felt or her fear as she called out his true name over and over, the words in Faar ringing out of her, both a lament and cry for help.

Eventually, she absorbed the shock and sat down, leaning against the wall to help stem the blood flow and pressed her hands around the arrow shaft. Anything to stop the bleeding. He did the same, as she knew he would, their actions a mirror of each other.

While she had the strength, she cast about within herself, found Jie and pulled him to her, praying to Nenimar that he would bring the Healer. Only Orrld could save him now. Sten she pushed back hard enough to hurt him – there must be no doubt in his mind, he must return to Valkarah or find a way of getting a message to the Hush. Then she took all of the lord's pain to herself.

CHAPTER THIRTY-FOUR

J unas slept when she was tired, finding a ledge or sometimes a crevice to crawl in. How long it took her to become tired was hard to tell. Lack of food and water slowed her and she had no way of knowing how many turns had passed. Below was only blackness, she had climbed so far. Only the breeze, for it was a breeze now, kept her to her task – it was all she concentrated on, the feel of the air against her skin as she climbed.

Junas reached up, touched a ledge, and welcomed the chance to rest. As she felt the rough rock face with her fingertips, searching, reaching for the edge, moving along, first one way then the other, slowly the truth dawned that she had at last found the cave roof.

She climbed with her eyes closed. It felt less frightening somehow. Opening them, she saw shapes in the dark, faces strange and contorted, shafts of sunlight and running water. Junas knew it was just her mind, addled from lack of sustenance and proper rest.

She did not believe in the light when she first saw it, not until she put her hand in a narrow beam and then saw more, tiny daggers cutting into the blackness. She climbed toward the largest. It grew as she came near.

The fissure was narrow. Too narrow for her to fit with the egg strapped onto her back. She took it off and with a prayer to Mother God eased it ahead of her. Light and air filled her senses as she slid her shoulders onto the surface of the land and hauled herself out.

The light was the first moon, so bright after the darkness she could barely see. Junas lay low, one arm curled around the egg, watching, listening. After a time she came to understand that she was on empty waste ground. No shoken or animal and flat as far as she could see. In the distance was the cityscape of Hathenfont. The stones were still warm and her tiredness begged her to stay and sleep. She knew she needed food and got slowly to her feet. After such a climb, the very act of standing was strange.

The rock was smooth and plant free, the cracks that let in light and air to the Ramshales below varying in thickness. Junas crawled, feeling between the cracks for any cold-blooded creature that might chance to spend the night using the warmth of the stone for comfort until the sun returned. She caught a lizard, slow without the sun's heat. A tiny thing, barely a mouthful, the next was bigger – she had to break its neck before she ate it. Two more and she was sated.

They were easy to catch, and mindful that food would be hard sought she killed five more and tucked them away.

On the edge of the horizon, the second moon began to rise. The night was already half gone and she was keenly aware that the egg was uncovered. She needed more clothes. Or at the very least, something to cover it with.

Junas felt safer when alone. Yet she decided her only course was to return to the city. She had nothing. No money, no weapon or waterskin, even her feet were bare. Quel had taken every useful item.

After the long climb, it was good to walk again. The ground was flat, the cracked stone soon giving way to packed sand. The first dwellings were little more than shacks, the poor safer to rob than the rich. The homes were simply made of piled stone roughly mortared together. All was quiet as Junas crept along the narrow alleyways. She carried the egg at the front again. If anyone saw her in the shadows, her shape would look like a pregnant woman. Shoken saw what they thought they saw. That much she knew. Junas stooped, bending her knees, aware she was taller than these sand dwellers. Let any who saw her, pass her with no more than a glance.

A low arch opened onto a small, square yard surrounded on each side by the primitive buildings. Junas waited in the doorway, listening and watching, then crept in. Washing, draped over poles from the windows, crisscrossed the space. Junas reached up and pulled a length of fabric down, crept back under the arch and wrapped it about herself. She took another and covered her head. Now she looked like any woman here. She left and continued along the alley.

Junas had mind maps of Hathenfont. Like most maps, they were about and for the rich. Rarely was there any detail of the poorer quarters. She had seen enough city plans to understand that buildings often followed some kind of tradition. A pattern that in some distant past became the norm for a particular area. Sure enough, she came upon another cluster of houses built around a yard. This one had a well at the centre and waterskins filled ready for morning hanging inside to keep cool. She took the largest and left, quenching her terrible thirst as she walked.

Throughout the night, she went from one hovel to another taking only one or two items that she needed from each place. Now she had clothing, food, water, a skinning knife and a long walking staff. She found good leather and thong ties for her feet. Not as good as the boots she had lost, but better than nothing. As dawn broke, she walked through the rich quarter. These streets were wide and airy, cobbled smoothly and neatly swept. She passed a few shoken, presumably on their way to work, and night guards returning to their homes. She went unnoticed; in her new garb, she resembled any poor woman of Hathenfont.

Junas stopped by a gate, tall and gilded. Within was a verdant garden. She stared at the flowers and trees, never before having seen nature so tamed. Of a sudden, a dog flew snarling at the railings, making her stumble back, shocked and afraid. She was too tired to run away. The creature was on a long leash. She watched the dog trot, tail between its legs back to the end of its rope where it cowered, more afraid of her than she was of it. The street was empty. She sat down, took out a hunk of bread, and began to eat. Strange how the small folk left their belongings unguarded and their doors unlocked and the wealthy kept all they possessed under lock and key. The dog, curious, came closer. He was big, lanky and cruelly thin. His pale fur was patchy, bald places showed his mottled skin and he was badly scarred from a recent whipping. Junas threw him a hunk of bread. He snatched it up, swallowing it whole. Several more lumps brought him closer until he was almost near enough to touch. She sat quietly, not looking at him, and placed one of the lizards next to her. He would have to put his head through the railings to reach it. For a long while, he sat on his haunches, and then slowly slid himself on his belly until he was next to her. Carefully he took the morsel, carried it back two paces then ate it in two gulps. Junas looked at him and the dog looked back, straight into her eyes, like a shoken. Then he wagged his straggly tail, twice.

'I don't think you want to be a guard dog,' she said and reached through the gate with her walking staff. It was a stretch, but she managed to get hold of the rope and pull it toward her. When she had it, she took out the skinning knife and cut it. Now she had him and he understood. He braced himself, splaying his front legs and leaning back. Junas did not pull, only waited and spoke soothingly until at last the dog walked to her. He was so skinny he stepped through the railings easily and together they walked on.

By the time the sun was up, Hathenfont was far behind them. She held the rope and the dog trotted lightly beside her. The narrow road twisted through ancient cacti groves and was empty, save for a few farmers herding goats or driving laden mules into the city. When the cacti became dense she stepped off the road and found a hiding place where the ground dipped, putting down her burdens and resting a while, sharing her food with the dog who ate cautiously, watching her the while expecting to be beaten.

Through the night, she had stolen many things and had, in the long darkness of the cave, time to think. It was far better to travel alone. To do that safely, she would need to change the way she looked. She took out the skinning knife and cut off her hair. The dog sniffed each long braid as it fell, brown eyes questioning. She wrapped her head in a length of black cloth and pulled on the garb of a man, putting the egg on her back in a pack and covering herself in a long loose robe. Better to look like a boy travelling to the next town to trade than for shoken to wonder why a heavily pregnant woman was alone.

Junas scraped a hole and buried her hair after removing all the gold beads that had clasped the ends. Some were old, passed from one generation to the next, others new. She tied them in a square of cloth to sell when she got the chance. Thieving had not come easily; even if she had found some money, she would not have taken it. Better to sell the beads and buy a weapon and something to hunt with; both would be easier to purchase as a man than a pregnant woman.

Survival occupied most of her thinking. When thoughts of home and family pressed, she put them aside. Concentrating on the moment was the only way she could carry on or else sadness would consume her.

But now, as she walked on the dusty road with the skinny dog trotting lightly beside her, she thought about her brothers, how they walked, how they sat and spoke. It would take more than clothing to pass as a man.

CHAPTER THIRTY-FIVE

Math could hide, despite his size. Orrld thought perhaps the grey of his skin helped that and the stillness he could so easily impose upon himself. Orrld watched him standing among the trees. Only because he knew he was there could he see him. They were free because of him. The Strick boy had effortlessly killed the Kassnets soldiers. Killed them with his bare hands, splashing through the water, swiping aside their weapons, snapping their necks as if they were kindling twigs. One of the soldiers, crying out in terror at the sight of him, ran. Math had chased him, caught him up in three long strides, grasped his head one-handed and smashed it against a rock on the stream bank.

Orrld had knelt in the water, reaching out his hands to heal them, while Jie and Sten were dragging him away. He was numb.

For the first few turns, it was all they could do to avoid the soldiers. Jie and Sten knew how to cover their tracks and hide. Then, when the Kassnets army moved on, they followed at a distance. Now they were camped far enough away from where the king and the Pack were captive, yet near enough so that Jie and Sten felt comfortable.

All they could do was wait. Wait and worry. Once again, the horror of this life choked Orrld. That people should die and kill at the behest of others and that he was somehow a part of it felt like an unforgivable sin. When he closed his eyes, all he could see was Math, his adopted son, killing, and this seemed so wrong because when he touched him, cruelty was not his nature. Orrld wished those men had not had to die for his safety. Given the choice, he would have surrendered. But there was no choice in this life. Life just happened.

Sten came through the woods carrying four braces of pigeons; he sat down and passed one of the birds to Jie. Jie held the bird in the claw-blade that served as a hand. With his true hand, he began to pluck away the feathers. Jie had other devices he could attach that the dwarf Godwin had made. Hand-like claws with parts he could open and close by flexing the muscles in his arm. Mostly he chose to wear a weapon, a knife or a spike of some kind.

Orrld watched them working and envied their connection. Crystal Bearers had no need of small talk. They never asked where the other had been nor did they look for signs that told of mood for they felt each other's hearts. In the past, the way they knew the king, his state of mind and health, whether he was tired or sad or happy, had seemed impossibly invasive and he had resented it. Now he constantly inquired of the lord and wished, for the first time, that he had been marked with Crystal so he could share the closeness they had with Llund.

Jie had already dug a pit in which to light the fire to hide the flames. When it was dark, they roasted the birds and some root vegetables that Orrld had found. He was surprised what little knowledge they had of the edible plants around them. For them food always meant meat.

'When I went to fetch water this morning, I saw some deer,' said Sten.

'I think that ruin, it must have been a hunting lodge once,' said Jie. Both men sat facing outward from the campfire and spoke in whispers. Math had taken his food raw and climbed a nearby tree with it. With his clear night vision and superior hearing, he was the better lookout. Orrld had not touched him since the killing, dreading that this creature who he thought he knew was different now, had become what he looked like, despite all the love he had poured into him. Nor had he offered a healing hand to Sten or Jie. Inside himself, he felt weary and sad as if he had no more to give. Or was it because without Llund everything felt pointless?

After they had eaten, Jie began to extinguish the fire with the soil from the pit he had dug, slowly scooping it in with his knife-hand. He would make the ground good again and when they moved on tomorrow all would look as it did before. Orrld began to make himself a place to sleep, gathering some leaves into a pile when suddenly Jie cried out, his good hand clutching at his shoulder. Sten was at his side and the two men held each other. Orrld could see both felt the same injury although Jie, who bore much more Crystal than Sten, suffered greatly.

Orrld was at his side offering his healing, even as he knew it would be of little use. He understood what had happened. They did not need to tell him. The king was wounded.

Jie retched, bringing up the food he had just eaten. Orrld held his pale face between his hands, trying to soothe that which could not be soothed.

'We have to go to him,' said Jie. 'Sho calls me now.'

'And you?' asked Orrld, looking at Sten.

Sten shook his head.

Jie stood up, wiping his mouth with his good hand, his face pale.

'You're alright now?' said Orrld.

'I feel it. It's an arrow, I think. But Sho has taken the pain to herself,' he said.

Orrld looked up at Sten, who nodded. 'She can do that, carry his physical pain.'

Math was standing near, looking from one to the other.

'I must go with Jie, to the king; you must stay with Sten,' he said. Math knelt and Orrld took him into his arms, hugging him, pouring his healing into him. Math held Orrld around his waist and his long tail curled about them both. Math was shaking his head, no.

Sten put a hand on Math's shoulder. 'You and I, we will go for help now. There is nothing to be gained from waiting here or giving ourselves to them.'

Math stood up. Half-naked, grey skin rippling with muscle, head and shoulders taller than Sten now, he was a formidable sight.

Tears came, welling at the corners of those strange eyes and rolling down his face. Orrld had not known he could cry, sure he had heard that Sturgar did not. Math looked entirely Sturgar. Perhaps tears were the only shoken trait he had. Orrld prayed to Ath they also came with compassion.

If the Kassnets took him prisoner they would torture and goad him and this would release the monster within. 'You must help Sten, it is our only hope.' Even as he said it, he knew he would take no notice. Orrld reached up and wiped the tears and Math fell, the weight of him making the ground shake. Orrld knelt beside him, his webbed hands spread over his face.

'He should sleep for a turn. By then we will be far away but you will have to persuade him to stay with you. If he thinks it is just to keep him safe, he'll come after me anyway.'

'I don't know if anything I could say will make a difference,' said Sten.

Jie had gathered up a few things they might need. Waterskins, weapons, sleeping rolls. Orrld took his share and slung them over his shoulder. Sten and Jie shook hands. Orrld put his healing hands on the back of Sten's neck. 'Remember, he's still only a child,' he said, following Jie.

Sten called after them, 'Good luck.'

CHAPTER THIRTY-SIX

Saur had not foreseen the outcome of recent events, nor thought the child the queen carried was not the king's. Even if he had known, he doubted he would have made such a contingency plan as this. Looking out from the battlements, he could only admire what she had accomplished. The fact that he had not been privy to her plans rankled a little, but then perhaps she knew his heart better than he realised.

Every Kassnets young or old, whatever their status, believed they were the rightful rulers of the Trilands and that time and fate would eventually bring them power. How this might happen was the table talk of all. Yet the reality of this, capturing the king and his loyal guard? This felt more like treason than victory.

Mindful not to let her know the depth of his doubt he had carefully voiced his concerns about not having enough troops to counter an attack if the Median army marched from Valkarah. Each turn they remained here the threat grew. He had personally checked that every Median soldier was dead. Just one wounded man able to get a message to

Valkarah would be their death. Each turn they stayed brought danger closer and the three of the king's own, the two Crystal Bearers and the Healer who had avoided capture, were ever on Saur's mind. And the other thing – the Strick who guarded the Healer. He, too, was missing.

On the surface, the queen's plan was sound. When the Healer arrived, she would use him to control the king. She knew she needed more support from the common shoken and especially the Medians. Saur also realised she believed the Healer would cure her, take away the pain of the linegold and make her hair grow again. He dare not tell her that the Healer, even with his extraordinary powers, would only be able to soothe but not cure. The scars of the linegold ran deeper than flesh, some dark magic that connected with Sho's hate and she hated Sneela far more than him.

They arrived in the dark sooner than expected and Saur, recently roused from a troubled sleep, met them in the centre of the ruin that once was Midford Hall. White sculls of hunting trophies, horned and hollow-eyed, gazed down from the high walls. The roof was still missing and the smoke from the central fire drifted up to the stars in the still night.

The hall was full of high ranking soldiers; they parted as two figures walked slowly through. As they had hoped, the one-handed guard had brought the Healer.

Saur seated himself at the high table, his six honour guard stood either side of him. 'What's your name?' Pointedly he ignored the Healer and addressed the king's guard.

'The Soorah, you need to take him to the king.'

'I asked your name, soldier,' said Saur. Two of his guard loosened their swords; the king's man ignored the question. He was short, not much taller than himself. He met his gaze with fearless amber eyes. Saur could have his men torture him but knew it would make no difference. These were not as other men; they had no care for their existence. Saur looked up at the clear sky and sighed. He could feel his face twitching; it was uncontrollable now Sho was so close. Looking around at his men, he doubted they had any more respect for him to lose and he was weary of violence.

'Take him away,' he said and turned his attention to the Healer. The hem of his robes was heavy with mud, his face pinched from hunger and fear, yet it was more than his dishevelled appearance. Saur stared at him a moment asking himself why he looked so different. Then it came to him. Orrld was not smiling and without the open smile, he was plain, the thinness of his face magnifying his brown eyes. Saur looked away from the sadness in them.

At the back of the hall, the men parted again, this time a wider path and knelt upon one knee as the queen passed. Mostly she kept herself hidden away in the renovated parts of the building. When she did make an appearance, she always made an entrance. This was no different; she glided through the hall in a silver gown shimmering perfectly in the starlight. Her head was covered by a veil of wasp-silk so fine it floated in a cloud behind her as she walked, and when she stopped, it hung in the air before sinking and laying softly about her shoulders and upon the ground around her. Two handmaids stepped forward and took the fine fabric from the hem at her feet, flicking it backwards from her face. Whisper thin, it floated skyward framing her like wings, then softly, silently, fell behind. It was well-rehearsed.

Now her face was visible. Newly thin after the roundness of childbirth her features stood out, vulnerable and brittle. At that moment, every man in the room felt protective of her.

She smiled sweetly as she adjusted the diamond coronet that held the wasp-silk in place, covering her head, hiding her baldness.

'Much has been said about your abilities, Healer,' she said, soft and needy.

DJ BOWMAN-SMITH

The Healer hugged himself and looked down. It reminded him of the king, before he had the sword, before the new-found confidence.

'You must understand I mean you no harm,' she cooed. 'All are safe, only the Median king was injured in the skirmish. It was my wish you'd come... to heal him.'

Still looking down, the Healer, ever so slightly, nodded.

'I hope,' she said, speaking quietly so all leaned toward her, listening intently in the silent room, 'he and I can reach an accord. It would, after all, be so much better for the Trilands to avoid war.' She smiled mildly. 'It's important, don't you think, to put aside past violence and start afresh so that the common shoken feel safe in the knowledge that their sovereigns' are united against the threat of the Sturgar.' She glanced around the room, acknowledging him, Saur, and those gathered.

Saur came down from the high table and stood behind the queen. 'The Kassnets and Medians together are better able to unite all the shoken peoples against the coming threat,' she said. Once again, the Healer nodded.

'I would ask one small favour,' she said, her face meek. 'That you bless me with your healing touch before we reunite you with the Median king.' With that, she stepped closer and knelt before the Healer, head bowed. The wasp-silk fluttered as she moved. The Healer closed his eyes, took her head in his webbed hands and all held their breath. A cool breeze blew down from the emptiness above, catching hold of the wasp-silk – she was an angel framed in ethereal mists. They stayed thus for some time. The room waited in silence.

Suddenly, she stood up and stepped back. 'You hurt me,' she said. Smiling a different smile now she turned full circle, holding her head. 'Hurt!' she repeated, then with one hand pulled off the coronet and with the other the wasp-silk, revealing her head. She was hairless, her scalp interwoven with a thousand tiny cuts that suppurated pale yellow pus. She stepped away and screamed, 'Look what he did to me!' Then turning to Saur, 'I want him whipped. Whipped until he's dead!'

If she had entered the hall an angel, she left it a monster, her face twisted with malice as she ran out. Saur ran after her, grabbing her dress. She whirled around, slapping him in the face. It was nothing, a woman's slap, but the pain stabbed his face as if he bore an open wound, causing him to stumble backward. He was grateful they were in an ante-room away from the onlookers. Only her honour guard had followed. They were well used to witnessing the queen's temper; they stood against the walls, expressionless, mute, trying to be invisible.

Saur collected himself, ignoring his agony as best he could, and caught her wrists. She was furious but there was no time to wait until her fury had abated.

'Cousin, the king will surely die if we kill the Healer,' he said.

'Median king!' she screeched.

'If he dies, you will have less chance of winning over his shoken,' he said, although he believed there was no chance.

Sneela tried to yank herself free. 'Let him die! Let them all die. Look what he did to me!'

'We both know he did not do that. He just could not cure you, is all. Let me speak with him. Perhaps he was nervous,' he said, holding her fast and looking into her eyes, trying to find the proud girl he had once admired. Had she always been this cruel? 'We need to keep them alive. Bend them to our will. That was your plan and it was a good one,' he was speaking calmly, trying to reason with her. 'If you kill the Healer or let the king die, the Medians will always be against us, against you.,' he said. Then leaned in closer and spoke words only she could hear. 'Remember, they want him alive.'

She ripped her hands free, walked away and smoothed her dress. Saur hoped she was regaining her composure. Not for the first time he wished Braadarlia was here to calm her. She always knew how to handle her daughter.

Sneela came back and stood in front of him, 'Whose side are you on?' her face was so close he could feel her hot breath, 'Seems to me you act as though you believe he is the true ruler,' she said. A droplet of pus formed within a scalp sore and trickled down, over her forehead and along the side of her nose leaving a glistening trail. Saur sank to his knees and kissed the hem of her dress, as he used to do when she was beautiful. 'Madam, you are the true ruler. Salvation for all Kassnets and true hope for every shoken race. My only wish is that you are safe. I fear we have not enough men if the Median army marches from Valkarah.'

'I have already thought of that. Loyal Kassnets arrive any turn now.'

'We need the Median king as a hostage,' he whispered into her hem knowing that with a toss of her head he would join Medians in gaol. Perhaps now was not the time to make her see reason. 'In the morning I will see the Healer is made an example of for all to see,' he said.

'Have the executioner take his time. I want the Healer to have a slow death.'

'As you command,' he said, kissing the hem of her gown again.

Placated, she left, her honour guard falling into line behind her. Alone, he remained kneeling, rubbing his hands over his face, aware he had sidestepped execution himself.

Saur went back into the hall. It was empty now. Warm air came into the space from above, swirling leaves along the floor, pulling at the Kassnets flag, worrying the candles. He walked to the centre of the room and stood where the Healer had stood. At his feet, the diamond coronet pinned the wasp silk to the floor, it fluttered around the weight like a live thing wishing to be free. Saur picked up the coronet and the wasp silk flew, stretching and curling in the breeze, higher and higher it looped and turned, silver smoke in the first moon's light. Silent and ghostly it flew ever upward - an angel wing returning to heaven. He watched until it was only a white speck against the night sky.

CHAPTER THIRTY-SEVEN

B eneath the ruins of Midford Hall, the cellars and storerooms had become a makeshift gaol for the king and his guard. Saur descended the worn steps and walked with a purpose to find the turnkey.

'The cell of the River Man, if you please, Cott,' he said amiably, pleased he was a soldier he knew of. The tall man saluted, turned on his heel and marched along the corridor, the eight soldiers on prison duty standing to attention as they passed. Saur took up pace beside him. 'The queen has ordered his public execution in the morning. I would speak with him first. He may have some information about the Median army,' he said.

Outside the door, Cott took the keys from his belt, selected one and put it to the lock.

'Your son has the makings of a fine archer, I hear,' said Saur. A good memory for the little details was something he prided himself on. Cott smiled down at him, flattered.

'Thank you, Commander Saur. Bows 'n arrows were always his thing ever since he were a boy.'

'The best archers are those who begin young,' he said, and

then added in a low tone, 'You're a man I trust. I need a stake driven into the ground at the centre of the training field and a viewing platform erected for the queen and her entourage. Can I leave the details to you?'

Cott nodded.

'The prisoners, when were they last fed?' asked Saur.

'They've had nothing this turn, commander.'

'And are they quiet?'

'Hardly move at all now…' Because the king is dying, was what they both knew although neither would say.

'This needs to be ready by sun-up,' he said, looking back at the line of prison guards. 'Have you good men here?'

'They are all good men, commander.'

'Take four with you, and best post the others outside. I'll shout if I need help,' he said, 'and cut enough wood for a pyre. I don't want any disease spreading in this heat.'

Cott saluted proudly and handed over the keys, then marched off, calling out orders to his men.

Saur opened the door and went into the cell. The Healer sat on a rug with his legs crossed and his eyes closed, the strange webbed hands spread on his knees. He was very still, only his lips moving as he spoke softly. Saur listened to the River speech, so gentle and melodic. So calming. In front of him was a pail of water, on the top of which floated a single leaf. It moved over the surface hither and thither like a moth.

'Why didn't you heal her?' he asked.

Slowly, the Healer opened his eyes and stood. He walked to Saur and placed one hand on the back of his neck and the other over his brow. Saur felt warmth and relief from the agony in his face, and the feeling spread through his body, cleansing his exhaustion, curing his aches.

'Why?' was all Saur could say when he took his hands away.

'Occasionally, Ath's gift cannot be bidden,' he said, folding his arms across his chest.

Saur walked the length of the cell and back, eight paces. The remains of a meal lay by the wall and another blanket for the night's chill. It was clear the Ekressian had given his care to Median and Kassnets alike. Many he had helped had not forgotten his kindness. Saur remembered the crowds that gathered wherever he went at Lak-Mur. Shoken flocked to his side in the hope he could heal more than their bodies. The cry of Soorah was synonymous with saviour. Making a martyr of him would be disastrous for the queen's popularity.

'If I took you back to the queen, in her own chambers where no one is watching, then I'm sure you could help her. I understand you cannot cure the linegold's hurt, but you could ease her pain and in turn, I know she would let you live,' said Saur.

'I feel no sympathy for her; without that, I cannot help,' he said.

Saur felt his anger rise. 'In the morning you will be whipped to death if you don't do as she asks. You understand that?'

'I understand,' he said quietly.

'I don't think you do,' said Saur unravelling his whip and cracking it in the air. The Healer did not flinch. Furious, Saur struck out; unlike Sho, the Healer did not move and the bull-whip caught him a blow across his face. As soon as it was done, Saur was filled with remorse. He helped him from the ground and offered him his silk square to mop the bleeding welt. Even touching him brought the warmth of his healing pulsing up his arm. The Healer sat down, closed his eyes and returned to his prayers.

'Prayer cannot save you,' said Saur.

'I pray for the king. Take me to him, Saur,' he said.

'If I let you heal him, then will you cure the queen?'

The Healer shook his head. 'I told you. I cannot.'

'Cannot or will not? I've seen you heal bad people. I'm a bad man, you heal me!'

'You're not such a bad man. I've touched worse. You're just an ambitious man on the wrong side.' He was smiling now. How much more like himself he looked then.

Saur coiled the whip and returned it to his belt.

'When I touch her all I remember is the baby she killed. I'm unable to put her cruelty aside. But you should let me heal the lord before I die,' he said.

Saur remembered how the infant's body had bounced down the steps, his little hands grasping at the air and at the end the quiet and the shock. The tiny, blood-stained corpse haunted him, so broken even the Healer could not put right what she had done.

Saur rubbed his face, more from habit than discomfort. The lack of pain made him long for sleep, untroubled and free. Saur left him to his prayers.

The passage was empty as Saur made his way to Sho's cell and stood outside. Whether he had planned this all along, he was unsure. Certainly, a part of him, perhaps the greater part, had changed allegiance. He took a deep breath and went in.

She was sitting in the corner, her knees drawn to her chest. Her tired face grubby and her hair hanging in lank strands, she looked as vulnerable as a street child. He squatted down in front of her and tried to keep the disgust from his face – she smelt of urine. 'I will make a clear way for your escape,' he said, quietly.

'All of us?'

'Except for the Healer.'

Saur watched her face; she seemed distracted. He saw how she clutched at her shoulder in the same place as the king's wound and realised she felt his physical pain. How strange the Crystal Bearers were. More than that, she was weak now and he knew he could hurt her if he wanted to. Until recently, causing her pain was his dearest wish. Funny then that given the chance he had lost the desire.

'Why? Why would you set us free?' Her blank eyes searched his face.

Saur stood up. It was a good question, but he had no sure answer for it. In truth, there were many reasons. 'The Healer. I need your word that he will remain,' he said.

'So you can execute him tomorrow for Sneela's pleasure?'

'I will not let that happen,' he said, realising she had heard the conversation he had had with the Healer.

Sho tilted her head to one side as if doubting he had that much influence. She hoped he did not. It would be far easier if the Healer met his death in the morning than the Kassnets keep him captive and use him to bribe the king.

Sho stood up slowly, using the wall for balance. 'You have my word as a Crystal Bearer that the Healer will remain if you help us escape.'

'Alive. I want him alive and unharmed.'

She smiled briefly. 'Alive and unharmed,' she repeated, 'if you let him heal the king.' She wanted her blades back, but that was too much to ask.

'I will leave this door unlocked. I will send a signal and keep the guards occupied when the time is right,' he said.

Saur left before she had the chance to ask what the signal would be.

CHAPTER THIRTY-EIGHT

S ho felt the pain lift warmly as though Orrld himself had laid his hands upon her: the sensation as the arrow was pulled away and then after, flesh mending and renewing itself and the intense exhaustion that came after being healed. The king lay down on the stone floor and slept.

To hold another's pain was a hard task, it took all her concentration and dulled her senses. Now the lord was cured and peacefully sleeping Sho felt her instincts sharpen and her thoughts clear. It was enlivening. Squatting on the floor, she put her palms on the stone, feeling the vibrations of movement and speech. Only four guards remained and another, whose voice she knew well, Saur. He was talking and laughing and there was something else. He had left her linegold in a pouch on the floor. This was the signal and Sho smiled. No doubt, he had believed the advice of the Blade-Master, Godwin, that he could only cure the unseen agony of his wounds by becoming a linegold mover himself. Perhaps he had hope in the myth that carrying some could make the linegold swap allegiance and turn the carrier into a mover. She knew they would have only caused him more pain.

Sho knew each blade intimately and summoned the finest and thinnest of them. It slit the leather bag just enough to free itself and, unseen by the guards or Saur, floated to her, slipping beneath the door and onto her upturned palm. The very feel of the linegold, both hot and sharp, gave her a shiver of excitement. The other Crystal Bearers felt the change in her and, although weary from lack of food and water, roused themselves. The prison guards and Saur thought them spent and useless. They were the king's own and the Crystal that marked them set them above all others. It was the Crystal that gave them strength now.

Sho sent each her love as she unpicked the lock on the chains that bound her and then sent the linegold blade gliding beneath the door and into the next cell where Arrant waited. He stood perfectly still as she controlled the blade, unpicking the lock as deftly as if she were holding it in her hand. When it was done, silently and unseen the blade moved on until all the pack were free of their chains and every door need only be pulled open. Whether or not Orrld was chained, she had no idea. Even if she knew, it would be impossible to free him. Without the Crystal, she could not tell where he stood or sat or how he was in mind or body. She only knew he was there because he had healed the lord.

In the king's cell, the two lay sleeping, curled about each other like the lovers they were. Sho moved silently, each footfall softly made. Orrld bore no chains. No doubt, the Kassnets thought him harmless. Gently she took away the metal collar from the lord's neck and fastened it around Orrld's, clicking the lock shut. It was easy to do. He was too exhausted from healing and lack of food to wake, and the king, deep in the sleep he had been given, slept on. Sho untangled one from the other, lifting arms and legs until they were separate, then dragged the king to the door and summoned the rest of the Pack. They came quickly, lifting the king between them.

Saur was there, alone. He watched nervously as she summoned the rest of her blades. 'Follow this passage to its end. There is a way out concealed beneath the floor. The tunnel is narrow and long, and it will take you far enough to make good your escape,' he said.

'Will you not come with us?' said Arrant. She saw him hesitate.

'My blood is Kassnets. Better commander in this army than a soldier in yours,' he said, glancing over his shoulder. 'I have sent the guards on a fool's errand. They will return soon.'

The Crystal Bearers, carrying the sleeping king aloft, made their way along the passage.

CHAPTER THIRTY-NINE

Arrant led the way through the tunnel, a tiny flame just visible in the fingertips of his outstretched hand. Sho took up the rear, the newly returned linegold hot on her skin. She crept twenty paces behind to keep any fight as far from the king as possible. No one followed and the end of the tunnel came too soon. She would have liked longer beneath the ground to take them from danger.

They emerged into the quiet, starlit night. A sparse copse gave some cover on slightly higher ground. Beneath, they could see the half-derelict Midford Hall surrounded by the neat array of the Kassnets army camp. Sho went to the front of the line, hoping her prescience would help her lead them to a safer place. The second moon was low, the first long since chased away, and dawn was near. At first, they went slow. Each footfall well considered, every breath and movement made soft. The thin trees met an open plain, which spread flat and silver to the horizon. Londard and Kren, who carried the king, laid him down on the grass. She prayed to Nenimar that he would sleep. If he awoke, she knew they would have to return for the Healer and that would surely mean capture if not death.

Sho waited on the edge, looking, listening, feeling her senses. There was no time to check for watchmen, she knew the best chance, possibly the only chance they had, was distance. Sho ran out onto the open plain and the Pack followed.

It was fully light when they came under the cover of trees. Exhausted, they ran on, Sho leading them deep into the forest. As the gap between the Pack and herself widened, she knew they must stop and rest. This forest was ancient, the trees tall and thick trunked and the ground was soft with moss and leaves. With the king at their centre, the Crystal Bearers lay down and Sho climbed a great oak to keep watch while they slept.

The clear night became a bright turn. From her vantage, she could see far and wide, across the forest canopy and over the plain they had crossed. In the distance, thin curls of smoke rose in the sky from the Kassnets soldiers' cooking fires.

Sho was so still birds soon forgot she was there and when they landed near she flicked linegold, stabbing them. The songbirds were so light she could float both blade and bird back to herself. The first two she tore off the wings and after plucking away the feathers, ate them raw. In truth, she preferred her meat this way and when she could she ate it thus, out of sight of the others. The Pack needed fire to make flesh palatable, but it would be some time before that would be safe.

Sho summoned Yosh to her. It took him some time to climb the tree. Despite the sleep he was still exhausted from hunger and thirst. When he had settled himself on a nearby branch, she handed him three of the songbirds. They were tiny and he was twice her size. 'Eat these, you'll feel better. When the darkness comes we'll look for water,' she said.

Sho climbed down and gave un-plucked birds to Arrant to share out. The king was awake now. Weak from loss of blood and hunger he leaned back against the trunk of a prime-oak. His food she had plucked thoroughly, cut into slithers and laid them on a leaf. Sho knelt beside him and offered him slices of meat. He ate well and then slept again.

Arrant came over to sit beside her, his arms folded; he looked naked without the longsword.

'We need water, so I sent both of the outliners to search,' he spoke softly in Faar. Sho looked up. The sun was shimmering through the leaves, bright as any jewel. She saw no beauty in it.

'Which way should we go? Valkarah or Lak-Mur?' he asked. They were equidistant between the two. Both places had an army.

'I think the Kassnets expect us to run for Valkarah, or the city of Mesh on the river here,' said Sho. She drew in the air with a blade, causing the linegold to leave a thin trail of golden light. 'I think we should go west. Try to get to Donsidion. It's small, I know, but we should be able to avail ourselves of horses at least and weapons, maybe even some fighting men.' Sho was well aware she was the only one among them who was armed. 'And the outliners, we should send them here,' she drew a sweeping line around Mesh, 'tell them to get horses and supplies without saying they are the king's men.'

Arrant knew she was using the outliners as a decoy. 'The lord won't like it,' he said softly. They both knew the ordeal was sure to kill them. Even if they were not captured, being parted from the lord so soon after taking the Crystal would probably be fatal. They were only boys. Sho felt Arrant's sadness and ignored it. She felt his dislike of her also and ignored that, too. 'He need not know. Send them before he wakes. I will tell him they went hunting and never returned.'

'Why did you leave Jie and Orrld?'

'That was Saur's price. The Healer and one Crystal Bearer. I had no choice.'

'Why don't you sleep a little? We cannot move again until nightfall,' he said.

'The outliners, when you give them the orders, they must believe we head for Valkarah, this way, the shortest route,' she said. The new line she drew glowed the brightest.

Sho lay down beside the sleeping king, and the glowmap faded and was gone.

She slept until dusk. Nenimar had smiled upon them. Clouds had gathered – the night would be dark. The outliners returned carrying water in well-made bark pots. Arrant sent them forth. It was easier for them to take his orders, believing as they did, as they all did, that he was the king's First. This way they were saved one fight at least.

The water was good and all were grateful to heal their thirst. Londard had gathered various sticks and she sat in the fading light and sharpened each to a point. Even a crude weapon was better than nothing.

When it was full dark, they set off, picking their way through the woods. The fair weather was changing as Sho led. The faint shadow of the outliners pulled a little at the edges of her mind as they drifted away, and Sten, so far gone now he was more memory than a feeling. As she walked, she cast out her love to him and hoped he was safe. Surely they would have felt it if he had died? Even an outliner like him?

They walked all night and at dawn found some shelter in a shallow cave at the base of a hill. It was enough to protect them from the wind and rain. Arrant lit a fire with the wood they had collected and they cooked what meat they had killed along the way – squirrels mostly and wood pigeon.

After, when those of the Pack who were not on lookout slept, Sho sat by the mouth of the cave and watched the rainfall. It was a blessing: covering their tracks, hiding the fire's smoke and filling the water pots. She dropped her linegold into the fire to hone the blades, gave thanks and prayed for the lord's safety.

For three turns, they continued thus, travelling by dark, hunting and collecting fuel as they went and finding some place to hide in the morning. All the while, the king was silent. He walked at their centre, compliant in their protection and spoke not a word. Sho's heart was heavy with his sadness. So many losses, his child, his horse and his lover. It was far worse than carrying his physical pain – from that she could shield him, hold the hurt for him, but from melancholia, she could provide no respite.

Seven turns they walked. Over plains and through forests until the wilderness became farmland and they walked in the light to appear less suspicious. Arrant and Sho had decided it would be better to disguise their identity and the king had agreed, less for his safety than for the protection of the ordinary shoken. When the Kassnets came, as surely they must, better no one had seen them.

Sho walked into Donsidion late in the morning. She had been here once before, many years ago as a child. This was an ancient trading town and the streets and buildings built of solid stone had changed little. They had walked the river path that led here these last two turns and Sho had stolen clothes from trading barges for herself and the Pack. She wore a dress, long, plain, and dark blue. She had washed and braided her hair about her head, pretty as a maid.

Walking along the busy main street, she took her time, stopping to look in the shop windows, smiling at passers-by. She made a left turn into the Gold Quarter. Here the shop fronts were pillared with pink and white marble and the doors carved blackwood. Protected from horse-drawn traffic the pavement was clean and smooth. Sho picked a jeweller on the sunny side of the street. A little bell tinkled over the door as she entered. Inside, the shop glinted with rainbows and stars from the precious gems arranged in glass cases on every wall.

A man in middle years came through a dark doorway at the back of the shop. 'Can I help you?' he asked, brushing crumbs from his neat velvet doublet.

Sho smiled shyly and looked at the floor. 'I have something to sell,' she said.

He had already taken in the tatty hem of her faded dress.

'Try the market tomorrow,' he said.

Sho nodded at the floor and meekly turned away. He took pity on her then and stood behind the counter, hooking his thumbs in his doublet. Sho smiled up at him and came over. From a tatty purse at her waist, she took out an item wrapped in a piece of linen and placed it on the counter. 'My father has sent me to sell this,' she said, unfolding it. The jeweller looked at the linegold blade and reached out to pick it up. Sho moved the cloth back toward herself. 'My father said I'm not to let anyone touch it unless they have paid for it,' she said, turning her head so he could see the welt on her face inflicted by Saur's whip. 'He said he'd know if I disobeyed him.'

'Why did he not come to sell this himself?' he asked, folding his arms.

'He thought I'd get a better price,' she said, smiling again, 'and anyway, it's to be my dowry.'

He placed a magnifier in his eye and leaned forward to examine the fine engravings of running deer.

'My family have had it for three generations,' she said, guessing he thought she, a simple barge girl, had stolen it.

'Once it was in a belt,' she said, picking it up and holding it at her waist.

'It looks like some sort of knife to me,' he said.

'Oh, it's not sharp, and gold would make a poor blade. Too soft,' she said, running her fingers around the edge.

The jeweller shook his head, disbelieving it could be gold. Nevertheless, he lifted a small set of scales onto the counter. Linegold was light. Sho placed the blade onto the scale, pressing down, and then took her hand away but kept the linegold weighted so it showed a good tally. Too much and he would think it was fake. Using tiny lead weights, he balanced the scale and she saw a flicker of avarice in his face.

'It's not worth much. Just a curio. I don't think I could sell it.'

'But it could be melted down,' she said, picking it up before he could.

The jeweller looked disinterested, glanced toward the back of the shop as if he would rather return to his lunch. In a bored manner, he took from his pocket three nickel-coins and placed them on the counter in a line.

'My father told me he'd had it valued at Valkarah and it was worth at least ten clowsters,' she said, wrapping it in the linen strip and looking sad and hurt.

'Two, I'll give you two clowsters,' he said, shaking his head as if he thought himself to be mad.

'I'm going to ask another. I know it's gold, lots of shoken have told us.' Sho put the blade back in her purse and went to the door.

'Five then.'

'No,' she said it quietly, turning to face him so the sunlight bathed the whipped side of her face. 'There is a barge I want to buy so we can start a life of our own, and I need eight clowsters. Real ones.'

'Wait here,' he said, going to the back of the shop;

returning he put eight clowsters on the counter. Sho went to them and examined each, weighing them in her hand and studying the king's profile. When she was satisfied, she put the clowsters into her purse one at a time. The nickel coins were still where he had left them. Sho looked at them longingly. He pushed them toward her. 'Here,' he said, 'buy something to soothe your hurt.' He indicated her face.

Sho snatched up the coins and smiled. Took the slip of linen, wrapped the linegold in it, and handed it over as if she was giving him a gift.

'A pleasure doing business with you, my lady,' he said, making a bow.

Outside, the street was busy; Sho walked to the next shop and stood in the sunlight looking in the window. Her mind was on the linegold blade and she followed its progress in the jeweller's hand – it needed all her concentration to prevent it from cutting him to shreds. He carried it out to the back of his shop and put it down, possibly on a table. Relieved, she walked on and down a narrow alley to get to the back of the shop.

In contrast to the front, the back street was narrow and untidy. Wooden crates, old carts and furniture abandoned in weed-infested piles. Sho crouched beneath the window and waited until the jeweller left his lunch to attend a customer. Then she summoned the linegold blade. It cut through the linen wrapping, glided through the air and under the door, slipping up the sleeve of her dress obedient as a magician's rat.

CHAPTER FORTY

That night, far from the Gold Quarter on the outskirts of town they stayed at an inn. It was large, big enough to accommodate them all, although they arrived at different times. Sho stayed with the king, posing as man and wife, newly wedded, a part they had played many times. The rooms were cheap but clean, the food simple but hearty. They were glad to wash and put on fresh clothes.

Sho sat on the window ledge looking out on the street while the lord slept fitfully in the large bed. In the morning, the Pack would buy weapons, horses and provisions so they could be on their way. Now was the time to accentuate their diversity. Each member of the Pack emphasised his race with clothes and movement and speech, remembering an identity before they were Crystal Bearers.

A thin rain had begun and the cobbled street glistened in the lamplight. Sho smiled, wondering if the jeweller was still searching for his purchase. For the moment she felt safe, there was no niggling feeling of danger on the edge of her mind. She felt relieved and sent the king her love, which he returned. He was awake and watching her from the bed, and the warmth of his love flowed through her. She came over and sat on the edge of the bed.

'Do you think Orrld is dead?' he asked.

'I don't know,' she said.

'When you get back to Valkarah, send a troop to get his remains. I'll make sure they are put in a temple of Ath. He'd like that.'

Sho nodded and looked at her hands. He reached over and pulled her to him and she lay down beside him with her head on his shoulder. Often, before the Healer had come into their lives, they had lain thus, companionable, platonic and safe.

'I thought I was going to die,' he said. Sho knew – she had sensed his despair. He placed his hand on her head, feeling the smoothness of her hair. 'At that moment, when the arrow struck me, I had a realisation. That I truly was the last of my kind. After me, there is no one to continue. It never bothered me before. Perhaps I never really thought it through,' he said.

'When we get back we'll find a woman…'

He interrupted her, already having heard the argument so many times. 'Lashka has always told me I need to find a woman I like,' he said. They lay together listening to the patter of rain on the window. 'You're the only woman I like, Sho.'

She laughed. Then stopped, suddenly realising what he was suggesting.

'I don't think we're going to make it. They'll guess we took some obscure long route and instead of searching, they will send troops the fastest way and lie in wait around Valkarah. No doubt they already sent a rider to Castle Dreeb for reinforcements,' he said.

'Then we should go back to Lak-Mur,' she said, but they both knew that would be surrounded, too. 'I sent Sten to get help. He's resourceful… I have not felt his death.'

'He'll be weak by the time he gets that far. If he gets that far,' he said. 'When I die, you will not follow but live on with my child. Go back to the Faar.' He gently stroked her head.

Sho's mind reeled. She could not imagine living without the lord. Could not comprehend a life without him and the Pack. When he died all his bonded protectors died along with him. That was the natural way. This, this seemed an abomination.

He leaned on his side, propped on one elbow, gazing down on her. 'I have already asked too much of you and yet I must ask more,' he said.

'But what I am, lord...' she said, shaking her head, no.

'You know that has never bothered me,' he said. Sho looked into the impossible blue of his eyes. He kissed her then, cupping the back of her head with his hand, pulling her to him. She was a Crystal Bearer, bonded to him for life; whatever he wanted to do to her, to any of them, he could, but what she would have given freely all these long years now came with a price. His kiss was soft and warm and her yearning, so long suppressed, surged. Yet a part of her felt detached, knowing he had no physical desire for her and that this was only a means to an end. Where in her youth she had fantasised about having sex with him, the reality was different. He was shy, and she too embarrassed to put him at ease. She lifted her skirts for him and helped him find his way inside her. She had imagined the connection they shared through the Crystal would have enabled them to experience some sort of intimacy. He thrust and she moved with him until he came. Then he held her, his head buried in her neck and sent her his love over and over.

In the morning, Sho washed in a basin of cold water then stood naked in front of a narrow mirror. It was a long time since she had looked at herself and she was surprised how thin she had become. Backbone and ribs protruded beneath skin too tightly stretched over her tiny skeleton. Could this body produce a child when she hardly ever allowed herself to menstruate? The thought seemed preposterous. Her hair, recently washed, hung in a curtain down her back, black and glossy. She braided it with practised hands and fastened it into her nape. Now she could see the crystal burn that covered her back. For a long time, she looked at the tiger in the flames that marked her, hoping for an answer. None came. All she could do was wait. If pregnant, the lord would be delighted and if not, saddened to the point of grief. Either was a dark path.

Turning from the mirror, she stood over her linegold and let the blades float up from the floor and settle onto her skin. She put on a dress and settled a gentle expression on her face to act the good wife.

By midturn, they had acquired all they needed and left Donsidion, taking different directions and meeting together at a crossroads. They journeyed as a gang of traders with a string of mules loaded with provisions and items they might sell and kept to the road, making a steady pace as if they were on their way to the next trading town.

Spring rains continued and the twilight lingered. Sho pulled her hood over her head. The king rode at their centre and the Pack around him were silent. All would have felt their union in the night. There was no privacy for a Crystal Bearer. Each knew when the other slept or ate or defecated or pleasured themselves in the lonely watches of the night. Hunger, thirst, pain, despair, sexual cravings, fatigue and joy were part of the intimate knowledge they shared, willing or no, with one another. They knew about last night and how she felt now – trapped by the simple fact that she had been born woman. For the first time in their life together she resented him.

CHAPTER FORTY-ONE

Junas lay facing the fire. At her back, the dog pressed himself to her and she had the egg against herself. Always she slept with one arm around it. The embers glowed a little brighter in the occasional puff of breeze and Junas gave thanks to Mother God that they had made it through another turn safely. This night they had found soft open ground shielded by shrubs and low trees not far from the road they followed. She travelled alone. Using the byway was much easier than striking out across the open country. Roads led somewhere and made her look less suspicious. To see a young man walking from one place to another was normal. Towns and villages enabled her to trade for things they needed and most of all provided reassuring landmarks that told her the route was correct.

Behind her, the dog twitched in his sleep. The feeling was relaxing; she closed her eyes and slept.

Later she awoke of a sudden and lay listening in the quiet of the night. The dog also listened, head up, ears pricked toward the road. A cart trundled past, thick wheels snagging stones and the heavy plod of oxen. When the sound had died away, she placed more wood on the fire and watched it spark and come to a flame. As a matter of habit, she turned the egg and settled herself. Sleep would not return and she lay looking into the flames, with the dog resting his head on her shoulder. With one hand under the blankets caressing the smooth shell and another on the dog's head, it almost felt like family. She could feel tiny movements as the sacred creature within the egg moved. Only when everything else was still, often at night, she felt these reassuring vibrations of new life. A tremor, barely discernible through her fingertips, made her smile. Another came, this one stronger, which became a shudder. Junas threw aside the blanket. The egg rocked back and forth and she feared it would hatch too soon. Then it settled to a gentle tremor, leaving her feeling strangely elated.

In the morning, she felt a curious lightness in her heart as she set off. The dog trotted ahead, stopping now and then to wait for her to catch up. He had grown in height and stature, his coat lush and glossy, yellow like corn.

As the town came into view she called him to her side and slipped a rope over his broad head; that way shoken felt less intimidated by him, believing a slip-knot held him. In truth, it was a quick-release knot enabling her to set him free if she felt herself in danger. This had not happened yet, he was a natural deterrent.

Junas watched the skyline of the town as they approached, looking for landmarks from her memorised maps. Finding none she worried that they had taken a wrong turn and this was not the town of Anker that she sought.

Within the town walls many shoken burdened with goods were heading for the centre. Junas followed and found the morning market and seated herself near other food sellers. This turn, as on many others, she had herbs to sell, which she had picked on the wayside and dried in the sun. They grew profusely in these parts and she was surprised any would buy something that was so freely available, yet they did. As soon as she opened the sack and their aroma wafted in the morning air she was scooping handfuls into cotton squares for the buyers. Trade was good and she needed money – not for food, this was a fertile country, food easily hunted or found along the way. The money was for passage across the Opherion Sea. They should reach the coast in two more turns.

Sitting on the ground, her wares spread before her and the dog guarding the egg in its bag, Junas listened to the talk about her. There had been a recent fire; this explained the missing watchtowers. The town's people were keen to get them replaced. Everyone spoke about how best to begin rebuilding, and there was much speculation about the cause of the fire.

When she had sold all the herbs, she bought some bread and walked to the centre of Anker where the watchtowers had stood. The earth was black and a skeletons of the ruined buildings lay contorted on the ground. A temporary structure stood among the debris with a young boy sitting at the top – he looked toward the way she would go. Junas watched the workmen clearing away the mess for a moment and then went back to the market. This time she was a buyer, not a seller. She needed provisions for the sea passage and different clothes. Junas was aware she looked a stranger. Shoken stared openly at her and she wanted to go unnoticed. She needed to dress the way the men here dressed and she knew it would be colder where she was going and that was something she had never experienced.

In the evening, she left by the road and lengthened her stride. Behind, she could just make out the boy lookout silhouetted against an orange sky. It was unlikely the enemy they feared would approach by road.

The dog trotted ahead and she was glad to be gone from this place. All the townsfolk were uneasy.

Hearing a cart behind her she walked to the edge of the road to let it pass, calling the dog. The cart stopped alongside and a young man leaned down to speak. 'Need a ride? I could use some company if you don't mind the dead,' he said amiably in Median. His load was a single coffin, long and thin of polished wood with a lid engraved with flowers. 'Although, to be fair, this one's empty,' he added, smiling and tossing his head backwards.

Normally she shunned the company of others but a lift even part of the way would save time and food and, since last night when the egg had behaved so strangely, she felt a new urgency for her task. Within her soul, something had changed.

Curious to learn why the town felt wrong, Junas climbed in beside him and the dog sat at her feet. He flicked the reins and the horse trotted on.

'I saw you in the market. You're not from these parts,' he said, stating the obvious. Her clothes were long and brightly coloured, her head covered as if to shield it from great heat; the sun was not so cruel in these parts, it did not try to kill you at midturn and ordinary shoken went about their business bareheaded. She sat with her legs splayed. He stared at her black hands resting on her knees.

The dog put his head under the seat and sniffed at the coffin. She tapped her leg and he put his head on her lap. 'Big dog – what's he called?'

Junas had never considered that she ought to give him a name. In the beginning, she had imagined he would run off. She looked at the dog's brown eyes, so full of trust. 'Crom,' she said, without hesitation. In the language of the Mithe, it meant both home and friend.

Junas did not want to speak about herself, which was fine

as the young man was happy talking. All he needed was a few questions now and again to keep him talking. Junas marked all he said: the watchtowers were burnt deliberately; the townsfolk feared a Sturgar attack; a village two turns east was razed to the ground eight seasons past and ever since they had been diligent.

'Do you think they will come back, the Sturgar?'

He turned to look at her. 'My Master's the best coffin maker in Anker,' he said, pointing behind him with his thumb. 'All the noble families want to be buried in one of his. They order them long before they think they will be dead and have them on show, which if you ask me is unlucky.' He shrugged. 'That's going to be shipped to the family Krestallon. They're rich,' he said, glancing at her, 'but not as rich as some. This one I'm to leave with the captain, but others I travel with all the way and deliver them personally. The last one I took, the lid was laid with seventy millistones, seventy!'

Junas was not sure what millistones were but she tried to look impressed just the same. 'Of course, he tells them that he has carved every lid himself, only it's not true, I did that one.'

She looked behind her. 'It's very beautiful,' she said, and so it was, flowers and birds and tendrils entwining all in woods of different hues. Now she noticed that, though the lid was nailed down, each brass nail had been left a little proud as if to ease the removal of the lid later. Crom strained his neck sniffing toward it; she reached in her bag and gave him a hard crust to chew on.

'So, you see, I get around a lot, I hear a lot,' he nodded almost to himself and was silent for a while.

'What do you think then, about the Sturgar?' she asked.

'They're coming, and when they do, we're all going to die, watchtower, city guard, won't make any difference – if you're not on their side, best thing is to run.'

'Are there shoken on their side?'

'From what I've heard.' He said it like it did not matter.

They had been making a steady pace upward and now, just before the road went downhill, they could see a valley and the sea glistening in the last of the sun and the sea city of Morstanner just beginning to twinkle as lamps were lit. He slowed the horse to a walk as they descended the path. She admired the view.

'Looks better from a distance. Morstanner's not so pretty when you get close up,' he said. 'Anyway, that's enough about me, what brings you to the seaport?'

'Oh, I need to get a passage to Lom,' she said.

'You don't like talking about yourself, do you?' he said in a friendly way.

Junas shook her head and smiled, deciding acting shy was probably best.

He laughed then. 'That's fine, most of the time I'm carving away and chatting to corpses and they can't hear.'

'My dog does hear, but he doesn't say much.' They both laughed and then he talked on, about his family and carving and wanting to be good enough to make things that would not just end up rotting in the ground. When they reached the port, it was dark and they stopped outside an inn. A stable lad took the horse's head. 'Where are you staying?' he asked.

'I'm going to meet family now,' she said, hoping her face looked suitably excited. It must have. He did not question her. 'Thank you for the ride, they'll be glad I'm arriving sooner than expected,' she added.

'Anytime,' he said, although it was doubtful they would meet again.

Junas walked away, Crom trotting at her side. She made her way through the town toward the sea and looked down upon the quayside from a high road. In the moonlight, the sea was darkly moving, slow waves sucking and slapping at the massive creaking ships straining against their ropes to be free. Crom sniffed deeply of the new smells.

She had a detailed mind map of the sea city Morstanner. But how accurate this was she had no way of knowing. The learnt map was probably old and cities, even ancient ones, changed. Nothing stayed the same. Buildings were pulled down, roads re-made along a different path. Fires and famine took their toll and places altered accordingly. If she was lucky, a few monuments remained to counteract the modification and the imaginative flourishes from the map-maker. These well-remembered pictures were less than accurate and all she had to rely on. She walked through the dark, back streets, avoiding any that were busy until she came to a high wall – relieved that map and reality matched.

Junas put down her bags and bid Crom sit beside them. Climbing the wall was child's play. At the top, she could see the pleasure garden, safely gated shut for the night.

Junas went first with the bags, then with the egg, placing all together among tall, flowering plants. Distressed, Crom whined when she was out of sight. She had considered tying him up and leaving him this side, but she doubted he would be quiet and it was impossible to explain to an animal what you intended. She expected him to protest when she put him in the bag she used to carry the egg, yet he seemed to understand and allowed her to do it. Although the dog was big, she was strong and climbing second nature. In a moment, they were safely down and among the flowers.

They found a safe place under some ornamental trees where the ground was soft. It was too risky to light a fire but the night was warm and she had food enough for them both. The park was empty and still and she fell asleep to the rhythmic breath of the sea.

Loud birdsong awakened her. Taking advantage of the fact that it was still dark, she followed the scent of freshwater and found a small lake. Careful not to damage the plants that grew along its edge, she bathed. Crom came and swam too, and it would have been fun if she had not felt the need to hurry. Back beneath the trees, she cut what remained of her hair so that it was scalp-short. She dressed in the new clothes: britches and a rough wool high neck tunic in dark grey. A blanket that served as clothing and for sleeping, this was folded and cast over one shoulder and held in place with a belt. Beneath it she hid her skinning knife. On her feet, boots replaced sandals, well-worn but a good fit. Crom was dry now and she called him to her with a click of her tongue. In these parts, many who had large dogs made them carry packs. She was unsure if Crom would mind. He seemed not to care at all as she strapped the harness on him and filled the side panniers. Crom trotted beside her with his tail in the air, happy as ever, and she was glad to have less of a burden. The gates to the park opened with the dawn; she could hear voices in the distance. As they left, Junas walked by the lake to look at her reflection and was pleased; apart from her skin, she appeared as any boy from these parts.

The turn was bright and windy. At the waterside, the sea was different as if awoken; it churned and lashed at the ships, threw sudden waves onto the cobblestones and shone a dark malevolent blue. Sailors called to one another, seabirds shrieked and cargos of every kind were manhandled on and off the ships.

Junas walked the length of the dock, confused. Paying for passage was her only option and she hoped she had enough money. Working aboard was not an option – the egg needed her body warmth, she could not leave it. A crowd of shoken were standing in a ragged queue, looking no richer or poorer than she did, and all were laden with bags. Near her stood a huddle of boys and young men. Some tossed knives in the air and caught them, others wrestled one another. Junas leaned on her walking staff. Opposite she could see the boy she met last night supervising two men carrying the coffin up the gangplank. She doubted he would recognise her – she looked a different boy today. An old man walked past the posturing men; he stopped to ask one a few questions then he came to Junas. Crom curled his lip just a little when he approached, making the man stop a few paces away.

'Apart from the dog, what are your skills?' he asked. Junas was unsure what to say. The gang of men were looking over. The old man took a step closer and Crom growled a warning. One of the men bounded between them shouting at the dog. Junas, shocked and thinking he intended to harm Crom, struck out with her walking staff, striking a blow beneath his chin and sending him flying backwards. He hit the cobbles with a thud. She glanced at the gang, wondering if they intended to fight. They were laughing. The man got up, visibly shaking yet unharmed. A loud bark from Crom sent him back to his gang, who slapped him on the back and re-enacted the incident with comic cruelty.

'You carry a weapon?' asked the old man.

Junas pulled aside the blanket to reveal the skinning knife. The old man nodded. 'You'll do,' he said, walking off. Junas followed along the dockside to the biggest ship. She paused at the bottom of the gangplank, looking up. The ship was sleek and made of a pale wood that shone like gold in the sunlight. On the prow was a carving of a mythical creature, head and forelegs of a stag and a fishtail behind. Massive, leaping into the wind, its jewelled eyes on the horizon. Within the antlers a carved banner bore the name Greatship Ranghorn.

The old man came back the few paces he had taken on the gangplank and looked up at her.

'Where is the Ranghorn's destination?' she asked.

'Port Blannet,' he said, as though that were obvious.

Junas stayed where she was, a hand on the dog's head, thinking, searching through the maps in her mind, trying to find the place. She had to be certain that she was going in the right direction. Four maps and she found it. Much farther along the coast than she had hoped to get to, imagining she would only have enough money to reach Lom, the nearest port from here.

'That's a long way,' she said, more to herself than to the man.

'I'll pay your return passage and food for you and the beast. And your fee,' he said.

Above, sailors were climbing the masts, the Greatship Ranghorn making ready to go to sea. 'You will get your money when you deliver the cargo, unharmed.'

Junas stayed put. 'Where?'

'At Felm.'

That was inland from Blannet, about two turns' walk, perhaps three.

'You've been before? You know the way?'

'I know the way,' she said. From the deck came voices, half-song, half-chant as the men worked together hauling at ropes, bringing up the anchor, unfurling the sails.

He handed her a paper. 'The delivery details are here. You can read?'

'I can,' she said. Shoken ran up the gangway carrying the last supplies on their heads. 'Half now,' she said, not sure how much that would be. Crowds gathered on the dockside to watch the Greatship Ranghorn set sail. He considered her a moment then took out a coin purse and handed it to her. 'Seventy now. It's all I have.'

Junas pulled the strings and looked inside. They looked like clowsters. She was surprised, she had never seen king's gold before. 'Yes or no?' He was impatient now. Junas nodded and followed him up the gangway. At the top, he spoke to the sailor there, handed him a stack of common coins and signed a document. The sailor passed the quill to her. When she had dressed in the new clothes this morning she had invented a fresh name for herself, and wrote it in the space the sailor pointed to: Judd Koss. Setting it down made it real.

The man seemed troubled and not a little angry. He looked up at her as if about to issue a tirade of threats, then thought better of it, gave her a small silver key and hurried away. The sailor handed her another key, large and made from brass. He indicated a door behind him. 'Two decks down, cabin seventy-four. Any mess from your dog, Judd Koss, make sure you clean it up, and just so you know, most of the sea boys think a dog ill luck aboard. Keep the beast close if you don't want it drowned,' he said and began talking to the next shoken on the gangway.

Junas found the cabin in the narrow, lamp-lit passage and unlocked the door, curious to see what cargo she must guard. Inside, a girl stood, pressing herself against the back wall. Junas thought she had opened the wrong door until she saw the chain from the girl's wrist to a metal ring fixed in the deck.

The cargo was a slave.

CHAPTER FORTY-TWO

Knowledge of the forbidden shoken child gave Curver Thist new power. He had already learnt that the disciple was unable to manipulate the disks, he had known this for some time, and he was aware the Watcher's eyesight was diminishing fast. When he confronted them about their little captive, killing it had been their first suggestion, offering to share the meat with him, of course. They were surprised when they found out what she could do and how well.

Now the Curver came regularly to the Watcher's private chambers. Situated at the centre of Tarestone with no outside walls, her rooms were dim and warmed by a well-stoked fire.

The Watcher was compliant. They had reached an under-standing. He took a candle from his pocket and lit it from the fire. Light was no use to her now vision had almost turned to blackness. Setting the candle down on a table near where she stood, he looked at her face which was turned toward him. Both eyes were almost entirely white now except for a small black dot in their centre. He lit another candle from the first and put it alongside the other. Now the room was bright and he could look upon her – this his greatest pleasure.

When she slipped her robes from her shoulders and let them fall, it always made him hold his breath. The Watcher was perfect, her smooth skin silver in the candlelight, every curve of her body beautiful. He touched her – how could he not, when she was his to do with as he wished? He lightly trailed his fingertips across her unmarked virgin back, her tight nipples, sometimes encircling his hand around her long, slim tail, and sliding from root to tip. When the turn had been a bad one and especially if the Master had treated him with cruelty or contempt, he delved more deeply, feeling the inside of her mouth, her cunt and her anus. This turn had gone well and he was content to look into her unseeing eyes, trace the line of her brow and hold in his hands her perfect, impassive face. Hard and ready, he hissed for the disciple who set herself before him on all fours, lifting her robes in readiness. He fucked her slowly, never taking his eyes off the Watcher, imagining all the while he was the Mag and she was waiting her turn.

When he had finished he pushed the disciple away, he had no wish to look upon her. She was ugly and had been well used, her back raked with scars. He never added his mark.

Once he had regained his breath, he left. Staying would only tempt him and he did not want to spoil her purity. If the disciple became pregnant, so be it. He could even let it be known the young was his as she had not developed skill enough to work the reflective disks.

Sleep came easily after sex; it seemed to clear the mind. Perhaps that was why the Mag indulged so often. Curver Thist closed his eyes, the image of the Watcher vivid and the thought, the pleasing thought, that he had seen and touched what Mag'Sood most desired.

Lately, only the Curver had been privy to the information gleaned from the reflecting disks. Diligently he had spoken the news to the Mag'Sood, claiming the Watcher was sick and her disciple too devoted to leave her side. A moons' cycle had passed and the Curver, waiting in the throne room with the Master, prayed fervently to Wolash this had provided enough time to train the softling child. If not, they would all die.

Above, the Master reclined lazily over the Black Throne and filed his teeth; beside him the She-Aulex yawned, this repeated by several of the Primary Warriors who stood against the wall. He was unsure whose bite he feared most.

After an excruciating wait, the door opened and the disciple led in the Watcher. She helped her kneel and arranged the folds of her ceremonial gown about her before leaving. The soft, shimmering fabric reflected all light, the fires' glow and every torch on the round walls of the throne tower making of her a beacon. The Master came down the steps to be near enough to see any disks she wished to show him. There were no disks. Her delicate hands rested in her lap.

'Are you still sick?' he asked, seating himself on the bottom step of the dais. She turned her face to his.

'No, Master. I am not sick. What afflicts me has no cure. I have gone blind.'

Observing from where he stood against the wall, Curver Thist saw on the Master's face and felt in his countenance, something new – sympathy. Mag'Sood knelt before her and took her hands in his. A visible tremor overcame her at his touch, a mixture of fear and ecstasy. She was right to be afraid. The Curver remembered when her predecessor had spoken these words, the Master had been so angry he had throttled her before she could present her successor. Beauty was a great asset.

'Master,' she breathed, 'my disciple, has been constant in her efforts yet she has not been able to acquire skill enough to serve you.' It did not take the Curver's gift to see the Master's mood change and the death threat that this implied. Remaining calm and perfectly still, the Watcher waited for his permission to speak. A short low hiss and she began. 'One with great skill has been found. Only an infant, she will need my guidance – I still can feel the vibration of the disks even if I can no longer see the pictures. In time, when she reaches voice and maturity she will take the vows and become your faithful Watcher, as I have been. The honourable Curver has checked the scriptures, my lord, there is nothing to say an infant may not be a Watcher.' Knowing the Master was unlikely to care what the scriptures advised, he had not bothered. It was enough that the Watcher's piety was assured. He had also told her there was nothing to forbid a shoken, for it was one thing to trick the Master, another to lie to the god Crotus.

The disciple returned. Behind her, head bowed under a hood, in the purple robes of a novice, came the tiny shoken child. He had overseen her disguise and now congratulated himself. She wore a tail, cut from a dead infant of a similar size and they had made her eat kret, a blue lichen. Primary Warriors favoured this, despite its foul taste, or perhaps because of it, as it made the skin more silvered. Obtaining it had been difficult and expensive but the effect had been dramatic. Her extremities, hands, feet and her newly shaven head had a grey pallor. Also, and this most vital of all, it disguised her shoken smell. This tiny shoken had been easy to train. She slightly slid her feet as she walked in the Sturgar way. His biggest fear was that she would speak. Sturgar did not speak until they were fully grown but he knew shoken young made noise from birth. Strangely, this little softling never made a sound of any kind and he had beaten her often to make sure. Timidly she crept up to the Master, turned and with her back toward him, knelt, between the two. The disciple placed a reflecting disk on the Watcher's waiting palms.

The Watcher did not wait for permission to speak. 'Crotus, for your glory,' she began and the Primary Warriors knelt and whispered the response, 'Lead us to the fight.'

'We labour to bring the shoken under our rule so that they may serve the true God. Crotus, for your glory.'

'Lead us to the fight.'

'I have been the Watcher for Mag'Sood, Master and Redeemer of the Drith and Tethlic nations. I have watched, I have seen, and I have told. Now I am in darkness.' She held the disk toward the child who reached up, touching it with her fingertips.

'Crotus, for your glory,' she whispered.

'Lead us to the fight.'

'Bestow this novice child with a Watcher's skill and devotion. Crotus, for your glory.'

'Lead us to the fight,' intoned the warriors.

The novice took the disk and held the clouded surface near her face, keeping it still with tiny yet steady hands, feeling the delicate vibrations before making an almost imperceptible tilt to bring the image back. Then more movements, slowly, carefully, until the place in time she searched for was revealed and she held the disk up to show the Master.

The reflection was from the face of the warrior paired with the one they called the Shoken-Slayer. The disk needed no announcement. Mag'Sood had seen many a massacre wreaked on shoken settlements led by him. This was different. The Shoken-Slayer walked ahead, his Primary Warriors keeping step behind him, and the shoken were neither already dead nor fleeing in terror. They lined the walkways kneeling in supplication. The Master chattered his teeth with pleasure and placed a hand upon the novice's head. 'You have done well, little one,' he whispered gently.

The Curver gave thanks that they had shaved the shoken's head.

'You have served me faithfully, now you will nurture the novice,' he said to the Watcher, and then turned to the disciple. 'You will look at what she sees and tell both the Watcher and myself anything you learn.'

Inside himself, the Curver felt the familiar knot of annoyance that he had not been included and consoled himself by looking at the Watcher. When he visited her again he would make her put on the dress of silver. Suddenly the Master's mood changed to suspicion. 'Where did this infant come from?'

'The Curver will tell how we searched for an adept…' she said.

The Master did not give the Curver permission to speak. He loathed long detailed accounts.

'Is this your child, is this why you have lost your eyes so soon?' he hissed.

'No, Master,' she said meekly.

'Prove your fealty,' he said.

With dignity, the Watcher stood up, the folds of the silver gown rippling as she moved. 'I have been ever faithful to my vows,' she said.

Fearing that she was about to speak out against him, the Curver put his hands behind himself and took hold of his tail. Only complete subservience could save him.

The Master glared at him, suspicion turned to anger now and the Curver averted his gaze. She turned, nodding in the direction of the disciple, who, guessing her intent, came forward to help unfasten her. The dress fell, cascading as molten metal to the floor and she was revealed, naked, perfect and unmarked. Her smooth virgin back, the curve of her long tail, her gleaming flesh. Every male in the throne room was hard except the Curver. As the disciple dressed her mistress, she cast him a look of defiance. His humiliation was deep. She had been his treasure, a secret, a joy entirely his own and he had revered her. Now all had seen what he considered his.

Returning to his throne the Master looked down at the warriors, still kneeling to hide their erections; at the tiny novice, intently looking at the disk; at the disciple and the Watcher side by side; at the Curver and the She-Aulex, who revealed herself in black scales resting her head on his leg. Suddenly he burst forth laughing, the rarity a shock in itself, and waved them all away.

Mag'Sood looked at the place where the Watcher had stood, imagining what he would like to do to her. No longer was she truly Watcher, her virginhood no longer sacrosanct. But he had seen how the infant had run to her side and taken her hand. Young were so fragile. They needed the comfort of a female. No, he would leave her to nurture the novice; there were plenty to meet his needs.

Lazily the She-Aulex loped down the steps and wandered about the room, sniffing the air and the floor in all the places Sturgar had stood. She often did this when they were alone again. Often she had something to say so he waited as she examined the place where the Watcher and the infant had sat, breathing in their scent through her nose and mouth.

'Here... sho-ken...' said the She-Aulex, licking the floor. Mag'Sood waited. Her speech was poor and disjointed, so it was always best to listen to all she had to say and then decide what she meant.

'You think... sho-ken... will... be... loyal?' she said, looking up at him with her red eyes.

Mag'Sood thought she spoke of the kneeling masses seen on the reflecting disk; certainly, he had been aware of her, close and invisible when it was being shown.

'Yes, they know what will happen otherwise, and all creatures want to live,' he said.

The She-Aulex padded to the doorway. 'Better... for... eat,' she said and left.

CHAPTER FORTY-THREE

Sho lay on the open ground face down, arms and legs spread, head on one side, an ear pressed against the soil, listening with all her body. She was twenty paces from the Pack, so their movements did not distract her and had stayed completely still for most of the night.

Dawn was breaking; a few birds began to sing. Sho felt a tremor of movement, a barely discernible vibration that she had noticed briefly in the night. It was so slight she had questioned if it was, after all, just the movement of deer or farm animals. It was fully light when she got up and by then she was sure; riders approached – less than a turn's ride away. The pursuers had stopped to rest overnight and had taken up the chase again. Possibly as many as eighty mounted soldiers headed their way with uncanny accuracy. Sho stretched and brushed the mud from her clothes. She did not feel the stab of apprehension. Did the child she carried blunt her prescience? Hungry, she returned to camp where Kren stirred a pot of oats over a small fire. All she wanted to do was eat.

Arrant came through the trees smiling broadly, the rarity

making herself and the others stare. Hugging a blanket around his shoulders the king sat down by the fire and warmed his hands; he, too, was smiling. Both looked at Sho, clearly expecting her to share their good mood. On the contrary, she had come to tell them that horsemen galloped toward them and they should break camp quickly and move on. Then she realised what they felt. Sten. It was Sten who approached sending his love, again and again, a signal to them that he returned not as a prisoner but with hope.

Sho forced a smile on her face and took the bowl of oats that Kren offered her. 'I think he comes with eighty horse-men,' she said and they all talked about whom he might have enlisted. They decided to wait for his arrival. Some of the Pack took the opportunity to hunt. Others improved the camp, cutting firewood and gathering water. Sho climbed an ancient prime-oak, the tallest and most ancient tree in the vicinity and sat on the topmost branches keeping watch.

Below, in a clearing, she could see Reem watching over the horses and donkeys while they grazed. They were poor creatures compared to the well-bred beasts they had lost. Nevertheless, he did what he could for their welfare, brushing their tatty coats and picking out their hooves almost as if he believed a little hard work was all they needed to make them true-bloods. Putting aside thoughts of her black horse Swift and Secret Star, the king's gentle red mare, she worried instead about why she had not been aware of Sten.

Laying back on the wide branch Sho looked up at the dull sky and placed her hands on her stomach. Too soon to feel any quickening, that much she knew. Yet she felt different, separate somehow from the other Crystal Bearers, as she never had before. There was a distance, even from the king now as if a veil had settled between her and them. She still knew they were there, only now she was not so acutely aware of their every movement and mood. She would have minded less if, despite this, or perhaps because of it, she experienced a closeness, a bonding with the king's child growing in her womb. She did not.

Sten arrived with the darkness alongside a mass of Clisotian Defenders. As they neared, he leapt from the horse and ran the last twenty paces to embrace the lord. She felt his exhaustion from his separation only faintly, where once she would have felt it as her own.

The Clisotians formed a semi-circle in the clearing as smartly as any army. From behind, something bounded into view on all fours – Math. He stood up. Even bigger now, a monster, tail swishing, eyes narrowed in the sunlight as he surveyed the scene. As she felt the threat of him, he looked up to where she sat, watchful in the dark.

Demik, the Clisotian who had once guarded Orrld, stepped his horse from the circle and dismounted. His face with its broken nose was the same but his body was changed. His legs were crippled and he had to lean on a war dog to walk. Evidently, his injuries did not matter; ribbons blew in his horse's mane and the white parts of the gelding's coat were painted with the double-headed wolf – an incarnation of their god, Krixis, marking him chief. Sho looked at the front riders trying to find his woman, the Savant Indess.

The king greeted Demik as an equal and the Clisotian Defenders began dismounting.

Through the night, there was much talk. Sten had seen sections of Sneela's army twice. Mostly he and Math had travelled west, believing rightly that returning to Valkarah was too far. The Clisotians found them.

Talk around the fire turned to Sturgar raids. Many had seen the carnage. They discussed ideas for war. Most advocated that marching to the Ice Wastes to lay siege at Tarestone was the only way to prevail. Some believed all shoken should endeavour to build a wall to keep them in the north and as they spoke, they glanced at Math with open hate.

Later, Sho returned to her lookout in the tree and when most slept except those assigned to keep watch, it was Math who troubled her most. He wandered about the camp agitated that the Healer was not there and presumed dead. He went to each Crystal Bearer in turn and stood, trapped within his muteness, pointing in the direction of Midford Hall with a beseeching look on his face. Nothing anyone said could ease his discomfort. Without the Healer, he was a loose arrow and she hoped he would take Orrld's rescue upon himself and be gone by morning.

She was wrong. In the morning, he was still there glowering on the edge of the camp, tail swishing back and forth watching her. Sho ignored him and ate with the others. Sten, now recovered from the pain of separation from the king, noticed her detachment. When he came to sit near her, she moved away, unable to meet his gaze. How do you tell your lover that you carry another man's child, even if that man is the king? Accused of being the king's lover so many times throughout her life, it was almost amusing. Had the world seen the natural outcome the years would bring?

Demik and a group of Clisotians approached to present the king with a horse. Sho was glad of the distraction. A fine bay mare, her black mane and tail long and silky.

The king stood at the horse's head, made a low bow and then mounted in one easy leap in the manner of the Clisotians. The horse stood square and calm. Sho was relieved, although he was an adept horseman, that they had not gifted a skittish animal. Once again, Sho was aware of their need to protect him from any small injury, lest he should bleed to death. Orrld's gift had shielded him, and they had taken for granted the fact that he was safe from his affliction. Now the old burden weighed heavy.

The king took the good horse through her paces, cantering and trotting her in a circle and then the many pretty steps she was trained to make. All were pleased to see that the horse was not wasted on a poor rider. The king was happy, his smile filled the morning, and everyone, Crystal Bearers and Clisotians alike, rejoiced in his presence.

Bringing the horse to a halt the king faced the Clisotians, some on foot, most mounted. Then he pulled the Pack around him so they stood either side of the mare in a line. They ran to their places, herself included, the sensation of him directing them rare and strange.

'You, the noble Clisotian, have pledged your loyalty to me,' spoke the king, his voice rich and deep. 'Ever will I remember how you came in my time of need.'

The Clisotians growled their accord. 'Last night many spoke of returning me safely behind the walls of Valkarah.' Again the growl of approval. 'Yet I must ask of you something more. Too many of my brave soldiers lost their lives in the battle with the Kassnets and now lay upon the blood-stained earth, food for crows and wolves. I would ask that you return with me so they are not forgotten. Help me build a pyre and set the sky aglow in their honour.' At these last words, he made the Pack kneel as one and bow their heads. A loud cheer came from the Clisotians. As she knelt, perfectly still and compliant, in her heart she knew all the Crystal Bearers wished to return the king to Valkarah. None of them had been aware of the king's plan, as far as she knew. Now he had spoken, they had no chance to talk him out of it. More and more he kept his counsel. Once she would have known everything.

The king rode on and they were released from their kneeling. Sho stood up and watched him ride through the cheering Clisotians. His clothes were practically rags, he had no weapon or crown, yet he was a king because of his morality.

~

In the woods was a shallow stream, where Sho went to wash. When she arrived at the water's edge Math was already there, cupping water in his hand to drink, a gesture strangely reminiscent of Orrld. He stared at her openly. Without the Healer, he was dangerous. She had advised the lord to mark him with Crystal. Strick made good soldiers once their devotion was harnessed. At least then, they would have some control over him. The king refused, seeing Math as Orrld's protector.

Big as a Sturgar, linegold mover and possessor of fight prescience, every turn she sensed his growing superiority over her. In her heart, she knew if he had received a Crystal burn at Lak-Mur, he would be the king's First now despite his immaturity. She remembered when he was no bigger than a child how he used to hiss whenever she was near. He had feared her then.

Sho waited, the narrow stream between them, hoping he would leave. When he had finished drinking, he splashed water over himself a few times, his silent lips moving in prayer to Ath before standing up. Without Orrld's civilising influence, he was almost naked, grey flesh glistening, long tail switching back and forth over the water's surface. Math watched her calmly, head on one side, questioning. Despite his size, she knew in his mind he was very much a child and with a child's logic blamed her for Orrld's loss.

'There was nothing I could do, Math. The one who helped us escape would not let me bring the Healer. We had no choice, I had to save the king,' she said, trying to make him understand. But Math's loyalty did not rest with the king.

Math banged on his chest and pointed in the direction of Midford Hall, then cast his arm behind, waving imaginary others to follow. Then with palms up, beseeching her, why?

'You know we cannot leave the king, you know why,' she said, pulling back one sleeve to show her Crystal burn. He pointed again, then at himself.

'You could go, but Math, he's almost certainly dead and you will have given your life for nothing. There are not enough of us to go after him; even you cannot take on an army alone. The Kassnets will have moved on. No reason for them to stay. They will be on their way to Castle Dreeb,' she said, although she was unsure if that was true.

He took a pace toward her. She was scared of him and knew he felt it. 'When we get back to Valkarah we will send an army to take the king's revenge and you may ride with them if you wish. Or you could return to your kind,' she said.

He laughed then, a silent, head-shaking laugh. She had never seen him do that. What she felt from him was not mirth but irritation, as he pointed at her and then away. The gesture obvious – you go. He came closer. Sho stayed where she was. Running was pointless and he already knew her fear. He did not have protection from the Crystal. The Pack would feel her distress as if it was their own. She called to them, pulling them near. But the bond was weak. She was on the edge of their consciousness now like an outliner. Only if they were focused on her would they know she was in trouble.

Sho was alone.

Math leapt across the water and took her by the throat. Her linegold rose, his the same, the two sets of blades suspended in the air pressing one against the other. The one

Crystal Bearer who thought of her came crashing through the undergrowth. Sten stopped in disbelief.

Sho was powerless as Math held her around the neck with one massive hand. A flick of the wrist would end her life. Math glared at Sten, teeth bared, daring him to come closer.

Math bent down and sniffed her, just to make sure, and then gently with his free hand put one thumb over her eye – pressing, pressing until there was a tiny snap. He did the same to her other eye.

Immobile in his death-grip she felt the first flutter of life within her. Her linegold dropped from the air. She would die revealed and take the king's child with her. Oddly, the thought calmed her.

Math released her. Gasping for air, she plucked away that which had concealed her true eyes, washing out the broken fragments in the stream. When it was done, she stood up.

Sten had summoned the Pack. What weapons they had managed to acquire were aimed at Math. The king stood with a sword drawn and on every side were Clisotian Defenders, double knives ready. Sho's eyes wept, blurring her vision and what she could see was too bright – the shields had provided some respite for her delicate Sturgar eyes. Through the haze, she saw Math take back his linegold, the blades flashing as they twirled in the air to his hand. Then the king was speaking, asking all to lower their weapons, his voice a father's voice, safe and kindly as he came nearer, treading softly, re-sheathing his sword. He pulled Sho to his chest and held her there with one protec- tive arm. 'I know, I know,' he said.

Then more quietly still, just for Math to hear, 'Sho was a silent Strick child when I found her. Just like you, she was ill- treated because of the gifts she possessed. I rescued her and she became my protector long before she ever bore Crystal for me. But the Crystal makes her protect me above all else and there is nothing she or I can do about that. Orrld had healed me from terrible wounds and made me sleep that night. I promise you if I had been conscious, I would have tried to find a way to bring Orrld with us. I know you think I should send a rescue party but Orr is surely dead and we are too few to fight the Kassnets army, even with the Clisotians.' The king released Sho and she stood there between them feeling tiny and useless and acutely aware of all those watching. She wished she had killed the Strick boy before he had become so dangerous. When that thought came, Math hissed at her. The menace in it chilled her spine.

'It's not her fault. If anything, the fault is mine for bringing Orr with me,' said the king, hanging his head. 'He is my waking thought and my last. My life is empty without him.'

Sho knew only too well the crushing grief he suffered and blamed herself. Even Lashka's words were little comfort, that she should keep him safe above all even if that meant he was unhappy.

Yet the unhappiness was hard to bear.

Math, his anger spent now, went down on one knee and the king placed a hand on his head.

Rain began, heavy drops falling through the trees and pinging off Sho's linegold blades as they floated back to her. Math stood up slowly, turning his head. He had heard something. Sho could hear it, too. Soon the sound of galloping horses was loud enough for all to hear.

CHAPTER FORTY-FOUR

They made their way out of the forest and onto the clear ground, and the rain quickened. Here they saw a Kassnets army arrive. Under the pounding rain came a tide of horses, wave after wave galloping and halting on the spot one beside the other, line after line, an endless sea. The king mounted his gift horse to meet the approaching riders. Behind him and on every side rode the Defenders, spears raised. Sho ran at the horse's side, her world blurred by the rain and her newly revealed eyes.

They came to a halt in the middle of the clearing and still, the army came. A tide of green stretching back, on and on.

Sho stood with her eyes closed and let the rain drench her face. She felt no sense of impending danger. These were Kassnets but they did not come in anger. Her prescience and linegold remained but every turn the baby separated her from the Pack. From the king.

Looking up at Arrant who stood alongside her she could see he was smiling, so too the king. They were unaware of the dulling of her senses; she normally kept her face blank, and she often blocked one or two of them. To them, she felt no different. The Kassnets turned their horses to create a path and as they did, she finally experienced what the Pack was feeling. Jie was returning.

Saur rode down the centre, dismounted and knelt before the king. Sho could feel something familiar about him – the glassknife. He must have found it. She should have taken more care with its hiding. Sho considered killing him as he knelt in the rain. She could retrieve the knife from his body later. But this would only look like outright murder and difficult to justify. Saur began to speak, his words drowned in the storm. He stood up and with one fist on his heart spoke out, louder this time.

'We, the Kassnets army divisions of…' His weak voice had no resonance and the words were lost. A little man with a little voice.

Behind, two more riders approached. Jie and the Healer. Saur was still giving his speech, his mouth moving with a passion, every word an unintelligible squeak as he tried to speak over the deluge.

The king leapt from his gift-horse, and Saur, hungry for acknowledgement, bowed his head. The lord walked past him and embraced Jie, pressing his forehead to his. Even Sho's diminished senses could feel his love. To the Healer, he just smiled and nodded, mindful of the Healer's health – all touch drained him. Even in the downpour, it was plain that the Ekressian was exhausted.

Beneath the old trees, a branch shelter protected them from much of the rain and the king sat, his Crystal Bearers in a circle around him, and spoke with Demik the Clisotian chief. Orrld had gone to wash and pray in the stream and had taken Math with him. Saur stood on the edge of the circle, ignored.

When the king had heard what Demik had to say he beck-oned Saur into the circle. He came tentatively and glanced at

Sho as he knelt before the king. Even the king's happiness could not dampen her hate for him.

'My lord, I bring the Healer and your bodyguard, freed by my hand. I and my Kassnets army pledge allegiance to you,' he said.

The king was silent, distrustful. Arrant spoke. 'You have pledged your allegiance before, High Commander Saur.'

Saur did not know what to say or do. He remained kneeling and Sho wondered where the glassknife was. She could not sense it on him.

'My lord,' said Saur in a faltering voice, 'I wish to speak to you privately. I have information that is for your ears alone.'

'We are as one. Speak,' said Arrant. Saur looked again at Sho. She kept her eyes downcast and flicked a blade from one hand to the other.

'What I know is only for the king,' he said.

The king stood. Sho knew he was anxious to be with Orrld. 'I doubt you have any new information but I thank you for returning my shoken. In the morning, I will speak to the Kassnets army and ask for their allegiance. Those who do not wish to march with me may go.' With that, the king and the Pack walked away through the trees.

Saur watched them leave. Sho remained. He rubbed his face. She waited, not looking up, hiding her newly revealed eyes. She expected Saur to make threats. He must have looked at the faces of the dead that swarmed across the surface of the glassknife. Any fool could piece together her crime. 'We need to speak,' was all he said, and she could hear in his voice something different – a greater fear.

Sho looked down at the mud. The rain had eased to a steady patter and she longed to find a private place where she could tilt back her head and let the rain wash her eyes until every fragment of the shields she had endured for so many years was gone.

CHAPTER FORTY-FIVE

Throughout the camp, talk spread of the Healer's execution. Cruelly whipped while Sneela watched, it had taken him a whole turn to die. Yet here he was, unmarked and alive. In the evenings when he walked among the soldiers to administer healing, many kneeled and whispered revenant. Ever modest, he tried to stop them. His efforts were all in vain. When they were together, the king and Orrld, Sho noticed most eyes were on the Healer now.

As Sho knew he would, High Commander Saur sought her out. She watched him walk with difficulty up the steep incline to the higher ground where she sat. He was alone and she felt no animosity from him. Saur sat a little way from her and looked down on the camp as she did. Evening sun bathed the scene in gold light, lengthening the shadows of every horse and shoken.

'Sho, I need you to get me an audience with the king,' he said.

'So you can speak against me, why would I?'

'I have no wish to do that...' He looked at her. His face, twitching in agony, became monetarily still. She stared at him openly. He looked away rather than meet the vertical pupils of her Sturgar eyes. Saur reached inside his doublet, took out a leather pouch, and laid it on the grass between them. She watched his hand shake and sensed the glassknife, different somehow. She tried to summon it and could not.

'I've come to make my peace with you, Sho,' he said, pushing the pouch closer. 'There are worse dangers. I expect you had your reasons for killing those on the knife...'

'It was not always my knife. Not all the dead are mine.' A half-lie.

Sho picked up the pouch and looked inside. Shards of glass and dust glinted within. Shame.

'It's evil. I tried to destroy it. Even shattered it lusts for blood,' he said with a shudder. He tried not to think of the four men he had killed for no reason at all.

Sho tucked it inside her tunic and stared at him. To his credit, he did not look away this time, even though his face flinched. Not so long ago they had looked into each other's eyes as lovers – the thought amused her. What was more distasteful to him now – the fact that she was a bonded soldier or that she was Strick?

'Did you have another killed in place of the Healer?' she asked.

'It was the only way. I needed the soldiers to have a reason to leave Sneela other than rumours about the Sturgar,' he said. Saur tried not to think of the sacrificed man's face after they cut out his tongue and disfigured him, slicing off his fingers and dressing him in the Healer's robes. An innocent, his only crime that he was as tall and thin as the Ekressian.

'Those watching the execution, they must have been easily fooled,' she said.

'Shoken see what they want to see. It was a sorry business,' he said, still troubled by what he had done.

'Some lives are more valuable than others,' she said.

'Will you take me to the king?'

Sho took a linegold blade into her hand, slipping it in and out of her outstretched fingers like a magician with a coin. She shrugged. 'I could make you tell me what you know,' she said.

'You could. I only hope you begin to trust me. I've been a fool, Sho. I never realised Sneela was with *them*. I'd heard the rumours. But you know how shoken talk. I've known her all my life.'

'You've known a version of her all your life.'

'No, not really. She's always been cruel. I just never saw it before…'

'Shoken see what they want to see.'

He looked at her and she shrugged again, stood up and tossed her head for him to follow.

The king was inside a tent of Clisotian making, horse skins stretched over bent-wood arches. Many waited outside seeking an audience. They walked past them and went inside.

Saur, on bended knee, handed the lord a piece of parchment.

'It seems not so long ago you were our gaoler,' said the king after he had looked at the scroll and handed it to her. 'Why should I believe you? This could be a Kassnets trick,' he said.

'It's no trick, your grace; it was given to Sneela by the Sturgar.'

Sho smoothed the parchment on the horse skins that covered the ground, weighted the corners with linegold. She had expected to see a letter of some sort in Saur's ornate writing. This was a war-map, crudely drawn but accurate, depicting every town and village in Median and Kassnets territories. Many Kassnets settlements including Castle

Dreeb were marked with a bloody thumbprint. Some small northern towns were scrubbed over and others, Valkarah and many Median towns and villages, pierced by knifepoint.

Arrant sat down and looked at the map. 'How did you get this?' he asked.

'I watched one night and saw them come. They climbed the walls of Midford Hall into her chambers. I thought they had come to kill her until I realised how unafraid she was. She spoke to them. She *knew* them.' Saur smoothed one hand down his twitching face. 'A few moments and they were gone. It seemed like a dream. I could not believe it. I wondered if I had gone mad, after all.' He rubbed his face with both hands as if he was trying to wash away the twitching. 'As the turns went by I convinced myself it was a dream. Imagination. Then one night when she was in a dark sleep I went into her chambers and took it.'

'How long ago did the Sturgar come?' said Arrant.

'What does it matter?' said Saur.

'You will answer the lord,' said Sho. Just the sound of her voice was enough to get his face twitching anew.

'Two, maybe three moon paths. It's hard to say.'

The king, who had been studying the map, looked up. 'We must warn these towns marked by knifepoint. Bring me your best riders that they can be sent to the task.'

Saur bowed low before leaving.

In the morning, the sun was hazy and mist clung to the ground. Sho watched the Healer return from his ablutions and prayers at the stream; behind him, cloaked and hooded in the manner of a disciple, walked Math. She could tell Math knew she was there long before she stepped out.

'Sho!' he said, surprised, and held out his healing hands to her. Usually, she ignored or openly shunned the offer, but her eyes continually hurt, so she stepped closer and allowed him to place his hand on the back of her neck. He did so very gently as if she was a frightened child that might run away any moment. She felt warmth in a slow trickle at first and he touched her eyes, lightly, carefully and cupped her face in his hand, mending the welt where Saur had whipped her. Then the warmth came quicker, stronger and flowed through her body, and he prayed the Ekressian words too quick for her to understand. Then he was speaking in Median, words of forgiveness for leaving him behind. She was falling, mind and body, slipping away to oblivion.

She awoke in the king's embrace. He held her close and she could feel his love. Firelight patterned the walls of the Clisotian tent and they were alone.

'Orrld has told me you carry my son,' he spoke in Faar, the words soft and low, the emphasis in his tone a mark of thanks in this language. Sho nodded and said nothing, knowing he would feel her apprehension.

'Sho, I'm not expecting you to be a mother. Unless that's what you want.'

'It's probably best the child doesn't know I'm its mother,' she said, looking at him, knowing the pupils of her Sturgar eyes were dilated in the half-light. The point was not lost on him.

'Orrld says you must rest and eat more,' he said.

'What if the baby has some of my… characteristics?'

'You are the bravest…' he began.

'Had you forgotten what I am?' she said, crawling from his lap and sitting on the floor.

The king stopped speaking and looked into the fire. What was done was done.

'I need to keep you safe,' he said. Sho guessed what was coming. He had felt her separation from the Pack. From him.

They both knew she was not the First anymore. She wanted to ask if her connection would return. But she doubted he knew and speaking such thoughts aloud would only serve to underline her weakness. Without the bonds, she felt diminished even as her linegold abilities and fight prescience remained.

'You will return to Valkarah. Orrld will go with you.'

Sadness filled her but she did not bother trying to argue. Everything was different now. 'And Saur? Where has he gone?'

The king lowered his voice even more, even though so few spoke the language they shared. 'Saur has gone to warn an unfortified town some six turns' ride from here. It had the knife mark. There is no telling when the Sturgar plan to strike. We can only guess and hope he will be in time to take these shoken to the safety of Valkarah or help them fight.'

'How can you be sure he won't return to Castle Dreeb?' she said. 'Or use his army against us on the road to Valkarah?'

'He goes only with his honour guard. He was keen to prove he is on our side.'

'The only side Saur is on is his own.'

'I will take a thorat of the Kassnets army, the rest go with you.'

Because the Kassnets now follow Orrld, thought Sho, although she did not speak this aloud.

'Demik and the Clisotians come with me to bury our dead and thence to Lak-Mur.'

Sho nodded and got up, bowed formally and left. There was only one reason he returned to the red city. Inside she was empty even as the child within her quickened.

CHAPTER FORTY-SIX

Junas did not stand out as she queued on the squally deck for her share of food. Shoken of many races travelled aboard the Greatship Ranghorn and she, among others, were confined to these lower decks where the steps from their cramped cabins led. Above, on higher decks, wealthier passengers leaned on the rails in their fine clothes and gazed out to sea. Music played up there and when the wind was in a certain direction there came the smell of freshly cooked meat. Down here, food was a bowl of rice or beans, hard bread, and every few turns a piece of dried fruit. Tobacco smoke drifted down from a high-class passenger above. He looked relaxed, enjoying his pipe and the sea views. She doubted they had to suffer a curfew. At least they could go on deck. Many more below never had the luxury of light. When she walked the decks in the evening, she felt the vibrations of many more shoken below. A living grave.

There were two men also charged with guarding a high-class slave as she was. Each of the neck-chained slave women wore all-enveloping robes. The other travellers shunned the silent slaves and their keepers.

Food was ladled out once a turn, usually just before dark. Junas made sure she was early for the queue so that she was not away from the egg longer than necessary. Too big to carry without arousing suspicion, she left Crom guarding it. Somehow, the dog seemed to understand he also needed to keep the egg warm and would lie down next to the bag, pressing himself close. Aware that the sailors and most of the other passengers believed dogs to be ill luck she only brought him on deck at night before the bell rang for the curfew.

The moons had thinned and grown fat twice since the start of the sea voyage. All, except a sorry few, had become accustomed to the ship's motion. The routines aboard had become their life. Rules were strictly enforced. Passengers were kept to their rightful decks and the gangways between were always guarded. The Greatship Ranghorn was their whole world now.

Junas kept her gaze within the confines of the touchable world as she waited in line with the slave girl beside her. She did not like to look upon the endless waters stretching to meet the dome of the sky. Not because she could not swim. She feared the blankness of the ocean. On her mind maps, they were unfilled spaces. Yet she had expected there to be something. The empty expanse filled her with dread and made her long for land. Samundarah had no expanse of water in any form. They collected water in huge stone drums on the years a little rain fell; mostly it came from deep holes underground, some of them thousands of years old. She was relieved this was the only sea she needed to cross.

The bosun sidled up to her, as he did every turn. 'Seventeen blackcoins and a quarter,' he said into her ear, 'for a go with the rinda,' he added as if she had forgotten. Each turn he upped his bid. Junas looked him steadily in the eye as she always did. She was slightly taller. 'The girl is not for hire,' she said, so used to making her voice deep she spoke easily.

Standing square, she stared back at him until he looked away and loped off. Junas knew that propositioning the passengers was against the rules. She noticed how he was careful not to let any of the officers see as they patrolled the upper decks. She had expected more trouble but discipline on board was strict, the intricate hierarchy among the crew apparent in the level of punishment metered out by every sailor to any below their own rank. Yet Junas was wary knowing that within any confined space violence was never far away.

After they received their ration, they returned to the cabin and did not stay to eat on deck as others did.

Junas had divided the cabin in half with a length of cloth. The need for this was twofold, to provide privacy so she could make water without being seen to be, in fact, a woman and to hide Crom, of whom the slave girl was terrified.

Junas locked the door and they went to their separate spaces to eat. She shared her food with Crom. The slave girl never spoke. She did not even know her name and so they ate in silence. A small lantern hung from a hook on the low ceiling. The oil was cheap and the flame dim but any light gave relief from the unnatural darkness within the cabin. Junas knew nothing about ships yet she was aware that in here they were beneath the water's surface. She tried not to think about this and kept her mind clear. But, much like the dog, she longed to be moving and hated the endless sitting about waiting for the journey to end. Junas gave the last of her food to Crom and lay down beside the egg. Every turn the weather became colder and she worried that her body would not be enough to keep it warm. She also worried about the slave girl. The Mithe believed that to enslave another was wrong. Setting her free would be easy enough, she was not concerned about collecting the rest of her fee. What concerned her was the girl's welfare. Alone and unprotected it was doubtful she would be able to survive and Junas did not want the burden of a travelling companion.

Musing thus, Junas slipped the bag containing the egg onto her back, took Crom by the leash and left, locking the slave girl within. The sea was calm and the ship rocked gently to the rhythm of the waves as she made her way along the narrow gangway to the stairs. As usual, she waited before climbing up to the deck. Noise from this last cabin always bothered her, something rolling back and forth. When the sea was rough, she could hear it from her quarters. Junas had no experience of travelling on water but she had noticed how they tied everything down against the constant movement of the vessel. Strange then, that within this cabin something rolled freely about. Junas had kept a watch on this door for many turns now. She had not seen anyone enter or leave or seen a glow of light around the door. When the ship moved gently on softly undulating seas the steady bang and slide of this loose object was more irritating than on rough nights when the creaking and groaning of the ship muffled the sound.

Junas tried the handle. It was unlocked. Junas went back to her cabin, fetched a lamp, then she opened the door and went in.

Inside, tied to the deck, was the wooden coffin. Crom sniffed about eagerly, wagging his tail. She remembered the interest he took in the coffin before. The ship leaned and the rolling object travelled the length of the coffin and hit the end with a thud.

Junas had no fear of coffins or the dead. She eased her skinning knife under the lid to free the wood tacks. With a creak, they gave way, and she was able to reach inside and catch the item as it rolled toward her waiting hand.

Junas had pondered what the object might be, a lucky charm to appease the dead? Tools inadvertently left by the woodworker? What she held was so familiar she was shocked; here was a map scroll.

A map for the newly dead to help them find their way in the afterlife, bound in leather and waxed for protection from the wet. The Mithe also provided their dead with a drawn pathway showing the journey they had taken in life and the way into the next world and what they would likely do there. Reverently she replaced it and left.

Over the next few turns, Junas thought about the map scroll. Why would a map for the dead be in an empty coffin? Perhaps it was a message and not a map. The map scroll knocked persistently on the sides of the coffin, calling to her. Curiosity won. One night, when she was sure the slave girl slept, she brought the scroll to their cabin.

She pared off the thick wax seal with her knife and tipped out the contents. A large scroll on fine, silk paper. This was not a path for the dead; the map showed a living city. Junas held it up in the dim lamplight. Beautifully drawn with skill and detail, it showed a plethora of small dwellings and alleyways that surrounded a low fort – the name written in Median in thin spidery writing: Mortling Hold. The simple buildings showed entrances and the shoken who lived within, these depicted as simple stick figures. How many men, women, children, old and young, and warrior. No other profession was of interest. Only the warrior.

The cartographer's mark in the north corner was a bird's eye, which indicated the map was drawn at the setting, and the title: Halflands. Junas had never seen any maps of the Ice Wastes, much less a city. The Mithe believed no one lived there or too few to warrant map making. If the map were real, and why draw it otherwise, then the Ice Wastes were far more populated than the Mithe realised. Junas looked again at the groups of shoken standing beside their dwellings and saw then what she had not noticed at first. Some of them had tails and others not. She doubted shoken and Sturgar were living in harmony. The population must be Strick.

Junas spent the night memorising the long scroll. This was hard to do at first. Ordinary maps were a journey and this was how she learnt them. The map of the ramshackle dwellings in the |Halflands lacked an obvious route. In the end, she imagined herself at the centre of the fort, Mortling Hold, and then walked a spiral ever outwards. This enabled her to build an accurate picture of these places without too much loss of detail. Junas was so absorbed in her work she did not notice the slave girl was standing watching her until she saw Crom look up.

'So, you are a Pathfinder,' she said. Her voice was sweet and quiet as she knelt beside her. 'I had wondered why you did not use me or sell me. After I realised that you're a woman, I thought you were waiting for a good price. Then I began to understand that shepherding me is not your reason for this crossing. The reason you cross the Opherion Sea is in that bag.'

Junas allowed the scroll in her hand to roll up.

'Did you draw these maps?' she asked.

'No, I don't make maps, but I can remember them,' she said in her true voice.

The slave girl slipped off the hood and veil she always wore. Junas had not seen her face before, although she had noticed her blue eyes and pale skin. Her hair was light, the colour of sun-bleached grass and hung in two long braids either side of her beautiful face.

'There was once one like yourself who had been taken into slavery. He always knew the way. Pathfinder, they called him. I spoke to him once. He said he was one of the Mithe. He told me about where he came from and how the ground has great spikes of rock sticking from it,' she said.

Junas felt sad to hear her home spoken of and Crom left

his place by the egg and put his head in her lap. 'My shoken, we think it wrong to enslave another,' said Junas. 'I just needed a safe passage. When we get off this ship I will set you free.'

The slave girl laughed. 'Set me free! What do you think I will be able to do with my freedom exactly?'

Her reaction shocked Junas. The girl stopped laughing and pulled down a corner of her dress to show the slave brands on her shoulders. 'I was born into slavery. I've been used since I was fourteen. What do you think I'm going to do? Find a nice husband and start a family?'

'There must be some way. Some way you could be free?' said Junas.

'I have no trade or skill. No family to protect me. And do you know what they do to slaves that try to escape, Judd Koss?'

Junas shook her head.

She spoke quietly, 'They skin them alive.' The girl stood up. 'You need to take me to my new master, Judd Koss. The slavers are everywhere and they'll kill you, too, or worse. With your skin, you'll be easy to find. Most are fair on Opherion.'

'Not all of the Trilands believe in slavery. I can take you to a place where you will be safe. Across the Opherion Sea the Median king rules and he banned slavery long ago,' she said.

The girl scoffed, 'Trust me, there are always slavers. The Boy King is far away and I don't think he's going to send his royal army to rescue a rinda like me!' She went back behind the makeshift curtain. 'I'll take my chances with my new master and keep my life, thanks.'

Junas rolled the map tighter and placed it back in the cylinder, fixing the lid as tightly as possible. She had no means of replacing the wax seal and decided that chipping off all the wax made the whole look less broken. 'How did you know I am a woman?' she asked.

'Your hands. They give you away. You should wear gloves. And this bit,' she said, stepping out from behind the curtain and pointing at her neck, 'men always have a lump here.'

Junas put a hand on her neck. 'Thank you,' she said. 'I had not thought of that. I'll tie something about my throat. Easy enough in this cold.'

'Apart from that, you're pretty convincing.'

'I have brothers. I try to move about as I remember them,' said Junas.

'My name is Ibby,' said the slave girl.

'Ibby,' Junas repeated, but she did not feel like sharing her real name with her and the slave girl did not ask.

Junas picked up the map scroll and returned them to the coffin. The cabin was stocked with other goods and she placed a bolt of cloth over the scroll to stop the noise.

Peace only lasted a night. For whatever reason, the scroll was freed to carry on beating out a rhythm on the coffin sides and when Junas tried the cabin door, it was locked.

Time passed slowly and boredom gnawed away at everyone's sanity. Passengers and crew were jumpy and fights broke out regularly. Every turn Junas looked at the horizon hoping to see a glimpse of land. At night, when she heard the curfew bell and listened to the sound of doors being bolted she closed her eyes and thought of Samundarah on a clear turn viewed from the top of the sky-pinnacle. The waking dream was the only way she could suppress her sense of panic.

As they crossed the Opherion Sea, the world became colder. Wind and rain battered the Greatship Ranghorn and Junas knew the clothes she had bought for this colder climate were far from adequate and she envied Crom who had steadily grown thick fur, golden and glossy. It made him appear twice as large and at night, she would push her hands into his pelt to keep them warm while she and Ibby talked in the darkness. Junas was glad of the company and told about her family and her little sister Arla, all greatly missed. Ibby spoke of the houses she had lived in, four in all. In the last, they kept her to amuse the oldest son in a rich family. They had sold her when he joined the army. Junas could hear in her voice her feelings for him.

One night she awoke. The egg was between her and Crom under a rough spun blanket she had managed to buy from one of the sailors. She lay and listened to the sounds of the ship and the girl softly sleeping on the other side of the curtain. All was strangely still and quiet and there was something more; she had lost the sense of travelling in the right direction that she so keenly felt. The ship was drifting aimlessly. Junas put the egg on her back, wrapped the blanket around her and went with Crom to investigate.

At the end of the passage she expected to find the door to the deck locked; it was well past the curfew. The door stood open and Junas stepped cautiously out.

The darkness was not without light. Stars glittered between dark shapes of cloud and the first moon admired her reflection on the sea. The Greatship Ranghorn rocked on the waves, and the sails, at half-mast, flapped uselessly. It was strangely quiet without the sea spray hitting the decks and the creak of the masts as they strained against the wind-filled sails. There was nobody about. Even just before the curfew when she walked Crom she could hear the sound of the sailors calling to one another in the rigging. Troubled, Junas hid among some crates of cargo lashed to the deck. She crouched low, wrapping the dog close to her with the blanket for warmth, and waited.

Beneath her, she could feel the vibration of sound and half-heard voices raised in anger. Idle talk of passengers and crew had sometimes spoken of pirates. This was often given as the reason for the curfew – to keep them safe. She had thought this nonsense. Now she was unsure. She put her ear to the deck, trying to hear what was happening. But the sound of the sea and the thick timbers muffled any sounds. The dog knew danger was close. His hackles bristled and now and again, he muttered a soft growl. Junas hugged him close, kept his head covered and waited.

The sea licked at the drifting ship and Junas tried not to think how deep and cold it was and what lurked beneath the undulating surface. When she was a child, they used to pretend they were swimming in sand. Thoughts of enough water to immerse a whole body were fantastical and strange; and the maps she knew with rivers and lakes and seas seemed incredible, that there was so much water in the world. They said all creatures could swim. She hoped Crom could swim well enough for them both.

Junas shrank back into the shadows. In the moonlight, a monster climbed over the side. Huge, water sliding from grease-smeared skin, it swung onto the deck with the effortless movements of the very strong.

Even as the creature had its back to her, Junas dared not move. She watched as it stood there, facing into the wind, tail sliding back and forth on the wet deck. One word fell into her mind – Sturgar. She had never seen an image of one, only heard description. Junas wanted to turn her head to see if there were more but she could not stop looking. His bare ribs had gaping gashes between them and as he stood, these gill-lines closed and he took a few deep breaths. He looked up to the empty rigging and made the sound of a sea bird, long and shrill. The night bosun came carrying an unlit lamp. He approached the Sturgar with bent knees, bowed head, and handed him something. It was the map scroll. The Sturgar tied it to the straps on his chest.

Then the thing came out of the sea.

It rose up and up, a mountain shedding water, silver in the moon's light. Until the Greatship Ranghorn was an insignificant speck at its side.

From where she crouched, Junas could see Sturgar climbing over it, opening a hatch door which they roped to the side of the ship. Suddenly the deck was swarming with Sturgar, their huge slick bodies outsized in the confines of the Ranghorn and their strange vessel looming like a beast opening its maw.

Crom, normally so brave, pressed up against her, shaking. Her fear seeped into him as she watched. The crew drove the shoken up from the lower decks and the Sturgar sent them into their vessel. Fights broke out and some shoken tried to throw themselves overboard. The Sturgar handled them as easily as shepherds manoeuvring a flock of reluctant sheep. None escaped.

Junas knew if they found her, she would have no chance. The egg would have no chance and she prayed to Mother God for protection.

The process was quick and when the last pitiful shoken was loaded, the Sturgar swarmed off, climbing onto their craft on all fours, tails raised like monkeys.

The sailors called out as they climbed the masts and hoisted the sails. In a moment, the Greatship Ranghorn was moving again with purpose.

Junas remained where she was, too frightened to move. The morning was near when she crawled from their hiding place and returned to the cabin. Ibby was safe within, unaware of what had occurred in the night.

~

The Greatship Ranghorn took up its course again and the sailors carried on as before. She realised that they had always known the fate of the passengers from the lower decks and they did not care.

Whenever they passed the cabin where the coffin was, Crom sniffed enthusiastically at the locked door and scrabbled at it with his paws. There was probably food in there, she thought. The big dog was always hungry and underneath his thick coat, he was thin, despite the lack of exercise. They were both thin.

The wind was fair and the Greatship Ranghorn docked at Port Blannet in three turns.

Junas stood on the deck with the egg strapped to her back; Crom with his packs stood on one side and Ibby on the other, both leashed. They watched the wealthy threading down the gangway. Around them, the sailors queued for a share of what had been locked in the coffin cabin. Each enthusiastically received a small leather pouch. Crom adored the smell of whatever it was and she had to keep a tight grip on him.

'We should leave Blannet as soon as we can,' said the slave girl. 'Dark-berry always causes fights.'

Junas had watched the coastline since early dawn as they sailed into port. Her mind maps were old with many new buildings built since they were drawn. But the landscape and some key features remained. Junas knew the way. She led them from the crowded dockside through the city. When they got to the outskirts, it was almost dark. Junas found an inn for the night. In the morning, she planned to take a carriage to Felm and deliver Ibby to her new masters. The urgency to be on her way was strong. It was strange to sleep without the rocking of the Greatship. But sleep she did and in the morning she awoke alone. Ibby had gone, taking the egg and Crom with her.

CHAPTER FORTY-SEVEN

Arrant rode at the king's right hand now where Sho would normally be and felt the weight of being the First. Sten had gone with Sho at the king's request. To lead the group and protect Sho and the lord's child that grew in her belly. It was strange not feeling Sho within himself, the sense of her ever on the edge of his thoughts, how she felt, where she was. After the king, she was the strongest presence within his mind. Anger and hunger, fatigue and joy, all gone. To carry someone for a lifetime, so closely they became like another self and then to lose them was peculiar. What remained was a kind of grief. Grief that lacked the certainty of death. When Sho had the babe would she become herself again, or was she lost to this life now? He could not imagine her as a mother.

Arrant sat tall in the saddle, composed, one hand resting on his borrowed longsword, and looked ahead. The appearance was not how he felt inside. Often, he had imagined himself First of the Lord's Crystal Bearers, proud and strong. When Sho had ruled, he often thought how he would do things differently, secretly believing himself stronger and wiser. Now inadequacies plagued him. He lacked the amount of Crystal needed to truly control the Pack, he was not a linegold carrier nor did he have fight prescience and no amount of Crystal could change that, and the powers he did have were weak. The flames he could conjure were useful for lighting the way or starting a cooking fire – nothing more.

Approaching the battleground, he wished he could sense danger the way that Sho did. There were too many trees giving cover to real or imagined foes and the fight they had lost here rose up to haunt him. He remembered too well how Sho, with her gift of prescience, had warned them and been ignored.

Arrant looked about him at the rest of the Pack, and riding close, the Defenders and a few Kassnets soldiers, all grim-faced and quiet. Each readying themselves to face the horror that awaited them. The freshly killed were ugly enough, but the time since the slaughter, when animal, crow and rot had done their work, would make this aftermath a recurring night terror for all.

They rode to the edge of the clearing where most of the carnage had taken place. Soft grasses and early summer flowers blew in the breeze and the ground was flat. There were no mounds of rotting corpses and the sky above was empty of circling crows.

Arrant picked some volunteers to dismount and walk across the clearing. Others rode through the nearby woodland.

'Do you think the Kassnets returned to honour the dead?' said the king, almost to himself.

They waited, the horses tossing their heads, restless. Soldiers returned in twos and threes. They found nothing. No bodies, funeral pyre, or burial mound. Arrant began to worry that this was not the correct place. But the Clisotians, who were better trackers than he was, pointed out the marks of war upon the land and they found a few objects that showed that shoken had fought and died here.

They rode on, through the ancient woodland. Arrant watched the faces of the Kassnets soldiers and wondered if they had been involved with the killing. Sho would not have trusted them.

Ahead, light poured into a circular clearing. Twelve tree stumps protruded from the ground. Midford Hall was nearby. Presumably, they cut the wood for fuel and repairs. Strange they had felled a circle of trees.

At the edge of the clearing, they reined in their agitated horses and stared at clean shoken bones arranged in a spiral – sculls at the centre, all the small bones of hands and feet and spine around them and long bones of legs, arms and ribs pressed into the ground in an elaborate pattern. All shone white in the sunlight.

The king turned in his saddle to the Kassnets soldiers who rode at his left. 'Did Sneela do this?' he asked. None replied and he asked the question again, this time in Kassnets. Arrant could see some of the Kassnets were looking at one man who rode at the back. He had been on the battlefield where the others had not. Tears trickled down his face as he glanced behind him, considering if it was worth trying to run, and his hands shook as he held the reins, making his horse dance about uneasily. One of the Clisotians swung from his mount, held the beast's head calmly, and indicated to the soldier that he should dismount. The soldier knelt before the king and laid his weapon down upon the forest floor.

Arrant waited. It used to be that he always spoke for the king. The lord would indicate what he wanted saying with a few words in Faar. More and more the king put aside his shyness and spoke for himself as he did so now.

'Do you know what happened here?'

The soldier trembled.

'You may speak freely and without fear. I understand you are a soldier. Following orders. Nevertheless, I want truth spoken. I will know if you lie,' he said.

All watched and listened. Quietly the soldier began, 'I didn't know what they did. None of us did.' He wrung his hands together. 'The queen...' he shook his head and glanced up at Arrant, knowing he had already spoken wrong and that if he was going to die, it would be from this man's sword. It was some moments before he began again. 'The Divergent, she's got the Sturgar in her power. They come in the night and commune with her. Just one or two at first. Then there were more. Many more. She chose some of us, we didn't know why. She gave us privileges and rank. We were proud. I swear, my lord, if we had truly known what she asked... we would not...' He wiped his mouth with the back of his hand. 'The Divergent planned the attack with them and we were told how it would come about. How the creatures would wait underground and how they were able to do so for many turns. Our thorat would bring down the king's party while the monsters killed the Median army. But it was after... after the fighting was done when the ugliness started.'

The soldier looked at the display of bones and then turned his face away. It was obvious the images in his mind had not departed. Arrant wondered if the man would vomit. 'They did that,' he said, 'they did that, after, with the bodies. They made us help. We thought we were going to honour the dead and we were bringing them from the battleground to a funeral pyre.' The man dry retched a few times and then got himself together, the words flowing now as if he spoke his conscience to Nenimar. 'They had us strip the bodies and string them up by their ankles.' He looked up. Arrant followed his gaze and noticed that lines of rope still hung between the trees. 'They slit their throats and bled them like animals and then they ate them. Divided the meat fairly amongst themselves. And us. They made us eat, too.'

The man was rocking now, like a demented child. 'She, the Divergent, she bowed down to them. By then they had begun to lay out the bones. She ate flesh. She ate willingly and spoke with them in a whisper like she was one of them.'

The king dismounted. 'How many Sturgar?' he asked.

The man startled as if he had forgotten they were there.

'How many?' the king repeated.

'Fifty, your grace.'

'Fifty Sturgar. And were any of them injured or killed?'

'Not that I could see, your grace.'

'And were they armed?'

'They had a weapon the like I'd not seen before. A pair of hooked blades either end of a short spear shaft,' he said, holding one imagined and indicating the two-handed nature of wielding it.

'A vetrolla spar,' said the king and walked past the kneeling soldier and around the circle of bones. Arrant walked with him, a few paces behind. They both knew the numbers. Three hundred experienced Median soldiers slaughtered by fifty Sturgar. Just fifty.

'Make sure that man is not harmed or takes his own life in his remorse. There is more I would learn from him,' said the king quietly in Faar. He was right. There were so many questions. Where were the soldiers' weapons, their clothes, and the horses?

'We will make a pyre,' spoke the king, his voice easily carrying for all to hear even as he did not seem to raise it. 'Then we will find saplings and plant them in the ashes so the forest can heal from the wound that has been made here. This place will not become a reminder of their foul ritual.'

Demik dismounted and his war-dog, Thrix, came alongside so he could lean with one hand on her back as he walked beside the king around the edge of the clearing.

'I have seen other places where they have marked the ground with their killing,' said Demik.

'Is it meant to frighten us?' said the king.

'I think it is to honour their gods,' said Demik.

The work took two turns and the king laboured alongside the Clisotians, digging the fire pit and piling in the bones, gathering wood from the forest floor for the pyre, and planting the young trees. Arrant worked beside him and saw how his humble simplicity bonded shoken to him.

The Clisotians found one weapon on some open grass where the horses had been set to graze. Demik led the king there.

'We'd bring it to you, my lord, if one of us could pick it up. But it seems strangely heavy,' he said, as they walked with him. A small crowd had gathered where the sword lay and they parted to let them through. Arrant recognised the tatty scabbard and the blackwood hilt. The king stooped and picked it up, smiling broadly. He drew the ancient sword and held it aloft for all to see and cried out, 'Behold N'gar, sword of my ancestors!' The longsword shone gold in the sunlight and the glassknife tip swarmed with faces of dead Sturgar. Around them, the Clisotians went down on one knee. Arrant did the same, as did the rest of the Pack. He was everyman and he was king.

As they walked away, the king drew him close so they were shoulder to shoulder. 'I'm sorry your father's sword was not found,' he said, the words in Faar little more than a mutter. 'When we return to Lak-Mur, visit the Blade-Master, Godwin. Have him make you a new weapon. By the time the rest is done it will be finished. If you are willing?' he finished, stopping and putting his hands on his shoulders. Arrant looked into the bright blue of the king's eyes and felt the love he sent him through their bond and nodded, knowing the question he was being asked.

'I pledge my life to preserve your life...' he spoke the first words of the oath every Crystal Bearer said before they took the Crystal burn and they walked on.

When the ashes from the pyre were cool, they sprinkled them around the saplings and the lord had water carried from a stream and poured onto them that they might grow more readily and he spoke words of honour for horse and man as it was done. Every face looked on the king with love and Arrant knew this was good. The Sturgar had grown bold. War was close and they would need the loyalty of every shoken race soon. What he had done here would be carried word of mouth and his honour would spread.

Riding at the king's right hand as they returned to Lak-Mur he thought of Pannitouli. What would she counsel at such a time? He longed for her calming touch to ease the fear he felt about receiving the Crystal that would make him First among the Crystal Bearers.

CHAPTER FORTY-EIGHT

The Clisotians, who had protected them, took their leave long before they reached the gates of Lak-Mur. The king, understanding their mistrust of city walls, asked no more of them and thanked Demik for the fine horses. Their return to the citadel was different from the last. Where before they had come triumphant and expectant this time they made their way through the streets at nightfall, unnoticed and alone.

As soon as they reached the Long Credola, the king went to seek counsel with the Faar.

Despite his exhaustion, Arrant could not sleep and watched the city from the roof garden. The king's melancholy weighed upon him and he knew that when he took more Crystal the lord's countenance would become the greater part of himself. Secretly he hoped that the Faar would advise against it. Surely they would say there could not be two Firsts – after all, Sho was not dead and she would regain her connection as soon as the baby was born. When they returned to Valkarah, would she fight him for the title, and if she did, could he win?

'These are troubled times,' spoke a voice in Faar, soft and low.

Arrant had not heard anyone approach and swung about, his hand upon his sword. Lashka stood before him, the white stripes of her coat standing out in the moons' light. She came closer, padding silently on the wood floor. It must have been fifty years since he last came face to face with any of the Faar. He had forgotten how big they were. Big and a little terrifying. He had never known them to walk about freely. She stepped past him and stood looking over the parapet at the sleeping city.

'Llund has told me all that has happened,' she said.

Arrant stared at her. It seemed so strange to hear the lord called by his name. She looked up at the moths that flew in circles about the lamps that hung from the trellis overhead.

'War comes now. The shoken races are picking sides,' she said, turning her great head and looking at him with eyes as blue as the king. 'He wants to know if you take the Crystal freely.'

'I do. I take it freely,' he replied.

'And yet you are uncertain,' she said, taking a step closer. He could feel her breath, warm upon his face now. 'Now that it is time, you feel you are less than Sho.' She spoke his mind as if she could read his thoughts. 'Your heart is true, Arrant Longsword. Sho Tar and you are different. Either of you makes a good protector for the king and a leader for the Pack.'

'And when Sho has the baby, will her powers return?'

Lashka moved away and walked about the roof garden, sniffing at the flowers in their pots. In the centre was a shallow pool. She waded in and lay down in the water. The question amused Lashka although he was not sure how he knew this. Was it the look in her eye or the way she shook the water from her fur as she got out of the pool?

'Who knows what childbirth will bring or take? But I think what you want to know, Longsword, is if they do, will she try to kill you?' She made a low noise in the back of her throat as she walked away. Was that a laugh? At the door she turned her head toward him. 'I don't know that either,' she twitched her ears, 'it is something you will have to work out when the time comes. If the time comes.' She shook herself thoroughly this time and thousands of droplets flew into the air and flashed in the lamplight.

'Why don't you ask me what you have asked yourself for most of your life?' she said.

Like a child caught lying, he was ashamed. For no matter how calm he had remained and how he had always told himself that he never challenged her because the lord forbade it, within his deepest self the doubt was always there. Could he win, was he rightfully the king's First?

He asked nothing. Just went and stood beside her and she tossed her head. Some questions were best left unanswered.

He followed her through the Long Credola, down stairways and along tunnels underground until they came to a room he only half-recognised. He'd been a young man of thirty when he had taken the Crystal on his right arm for the Boy King. He remembered how sure of himself he had felt that turn. Sure and unafraid. Prior knowledge scared him and he tried not to anticipate the pain he would have to endure. That, and the fear of death.

The roof was low. He could have reached up and placed his palms flat on the smooth, grey stone. The space was cavernous, stretching far beyond the lamplight. Every movement echoed, returning like a whisper. Shadows of chains hung down in the distance. Once they forced shoken to take the Crystal against their will, and the Packs of men that protected the king were large. Arrant gave thanks that his lord was kind and just.

'Are you ready?' asked Lashka.

Arrant looked about him sensing others although he could see no one. Unbuckling his sword belt, he laid the weapon down and undressed. His clothes were tatty like the weapon. He took from his doublet pocket an oval stone that he always carried. 'If I don't make it, will you see that Panni-touli gets this back?' he said, placing it in front of her. Lashka drew back her lips and he could see her fine white teeth. Was she smiling? Then she breathed upon the stone so that it lit up and glowed with a soft, yellow light.

'You have much to light you in the darkness, Longsword,' she said, her voice a thrumming purr in his head. 'Do you remember the words?'

'I do,' he said, kneeling before her.

'Then it is time. Close your eyes and speak your prayer, shoken.'

As he recited his Crystal Bearer's oath, he tried to concentrate upon the meaning and the rhythm of the words even as he could feel movement all about him on his naked skin. Halfway through he vomited in anticipation of the pain he knew was to come and had to breathe deeply before he began again. Lashka intoned the last verses with him and her voice was soothing and then he was floating or sinking, it was hard to tell and hands were holding him, pulling him, squashing him flat, pressing his face into the stone that was soft now. When he opened his eyes to see there was only darkness and his breath shallow, too small to speak and when the pain began he cried out, but no sound came.

The pain was fire and needles sharp as evil, unrelenting, piercing the skin on his back and pouring into him a thin liquid, which permeated his body like hot ants crawling. When he believed it would kill him, it stopped, just long enough for him to gather his courage before it began again. He had planned how this moment would be, the taking of the

Crystal, how he would endure with silent bravery and focus his heart and mind upon the lord. Agony was all he knew and survival his only thought.

When he awoke, he was in a different place and the king was close beside him. He opened his eyes and saw this was not true; the lord was twenty paces away, leaning on the balcony watching the evening rain. But he felt close both physically and mentally, as if he stood beside him. Where before the connection to the lord had been strong, now it was altered.

The king's mind was open to him. All his feelings and thoughts. He missed Sho, called constantly to her through the Crystal bonds and received no reply. She had gone, the bond broken and he could not reconcile himself to the fact. At that moment, Arrant knew he could never take her place and the thought saddened him. He was the First but he was second in the king's heart and always would be. As the sadness of this fact consumed him the king came to him, pulled him into his arms from where he lay and held him fast, and as he touched him, Arrant felt love and a deep understanding, unconditional and complete.

'I need you both,' said the king, holding him at arm's length so he could see his face. Arrant looked into the blue of the lord's eyes and understood the threat of the Sturgar and how great a burden this was for the lord, and that winning this war was their purpose above all else.

The king released him and then Arrant was aware of the other Crystal Bearers, each more sharply than he had known them before, not just their physical positions in relation to the king and a vague impression of their state of mind and body – this was a more complete impression. He knew who was hungry, tired or bored, whether they were alert or half-asleep. He was shocked at how much he knew and wished he could somehow lessen the invasive penetration of the Crystal.

'When Sho took on this role there were few of us, and each new member of the Pack joined with time between. So I understand it is a lot for you to assimilate so many at once,' said the king.

Arrant felt like an infant learning to walk.

'Four more have taken Crystal this turn,' said the king, standing. Arrant understood he wished to be there when they woke, just as he had been for all of them. 'Try not to worry; I'll be safe with the Faar. Go and see Godwin,' he called as he left.

When he had gone, Arrant got up and went to the wash-room. The rain had stopped and the air was warm and humid and Arrant was glad of the cool washing water left for him. He stood dripping between a pair of mirrors looking at his newly marked skin.

This mark was smaller than Sho's, covering just the top of his shoulders. Hers, he had only seen it briefly, covered all of her back. He could not imagine the pain it must have cost or the burden all that extra Crystal must make. Of course, he knew of the rumours that they had tried to kill her. Tried and failed. The result was a shoken with so much Crystal the lord became sick when they parted. Even now, although the bonds were broken somehow, the king fretted over her absence. The sooner they returned to Valkarah, the better.

He had longed for this moment, when he would stand and admire the Crystal burn that marked him as the king's First, had imagined basking in the glow of pride and strutting, bare-chested, so no one was in any doubt as to his rank. Instead, inadequacies beset him. He dressed in the new clothes laid out for him. Pannitouli's glow stone was on top of the pile – he tucked it into his doublet and set off for the Blade-Master.

CHAPTER FORTY-NINE

Curver Thist was restless. Sleep eluded him. He could not settle. He got up from where he lay by the fire, and after checking that the Strick slave Podder slept in his wall niche in the corridor, he left. He had a mind to walk the ramparts and look out over the Ice Wastes. When he saw the heavy snowfall, he wandered through the castle instead. From the keys he carried at his waist, he unlocked the doors into the disused, middle part of Tarestone to the abandoned feasting hall. Sturgar skeletons that hung from the ceiling grinned and spun slowly in the draught of his passing. Curver Thist knelt and slid back the Aulex skin to reveal his spy hole.

Below, the reflecting room was bright. The shoken child opened the shutters on the light side of the turn while the Sturgar slept. The glare made him squint as he looked upon the mirrors positioned in the rafters between the two floors. At first, he could not find her – she was so little. Then he saw her, kneeling on a stool so she was the right height for the tables. Like the previous Watcher, she was very still as she concentrated on the disk. Alone, she had taken off her hood and her head, although shaved every turn by the disciple and grey due to the kret they made her eat, was still a shoken head. Very much so. If, for some reason, the Master pulled back the hood, he doubted she would survive. Against religious practice, Curver Thist searched for another with the ability to manipulate reflecting disks. He had tried Sturgar and Strick alike, all to no avail. If the softling child died, he would have trouble managing the dark-berry plantations and more. This little shoken, so much more easily managed than her predecessor, had become in a short time his greatest asset. For now, for the first time, he had proper control over the reflecting room.

As he mused thus, she got down and walked soundlessly with the slight sliding of the feet in the way of the Sturgar. Light from the open shutters lit her face. She was smiling. He wondered whose disk made her so happy.

Ashmi went to the fireside and he thought she intended to sit there for the warmth. She took the fire-tongs and held the disk in the flames then took it out and looked at it. Whatever she saw pleased her. The little shoken rocked back and forth and although no sound came from her mouth, he could tell she was laughing.

The Curver had seen enough. He made haste and when he got to the reflecting room, she was still there meting out her torture. She fell to her knees when he strode in, hiding the disk behind her. He knelt and grabbed her.

'Show me the disk,' he hissed.

She was shaking. Terrified, she brought it in front of her face. Too hot to touch, she held it in the tongs for him to see. The image was clear. Truly, she was an adept. The disk was the Shoken-Slayer's paired Warrior. He looked on, his reflecting metal showing his leader's writhing agony. The Curver smiled and the child smiled back.

He had not known the wearers of the seeing metal could

be so easily hurt. He wondered what other information was lost when the Mag killed the blind hag who had been the Watcher's predecessor.

'Put the disk back now,' he said. She blew on it until it cooled enough to touch. Then carried it over to its slot on the central table. The Curver made a note of its position.

'Which others do you like to hurt?' he asked.

She shook her head then pointed at the Shoken-Slayer's disk.

'Just him?'

She nodded.

'Sure?'

She pointed again and nodded.

'Why him?'

She shrugged. Ashmi had no recollection of why she hated that face in particular. She only knew that hurting him made her happy. She looked at Master Curver hoping his face had a speck of metal. He would be nice to hurt.

The Curver looked at her. She was a little older now. Shoken young grew slowly. But she had grown into her face and looked like her mother with her slightly defiant, round-eyed gaze.

Now that the Watcher could no longer see, the Master never came to the reflecting room. He reported on the reflecting disks every turn. When the news was interesting, the Mag asked to see the reflection with his own eyes. So far, he had been able to put him off by saying the infant was ill or sleeping or with her mother. The Curver feared he suspected a trick. Certainly, the Curver felt his growing impatience – Mag'Sood always did like to see the disks for himself.

He went to the fire, sat down on the pile of seal furs, and stirred up the embers with the tongs. 'Come here,' he whispered. She came willingly and knelt gracefully, laid her tiny hands in her lap, and kept very still. How like the Watcher.

He looked at the curve of her naked head. It was passable when covered. But her stub nose and chubby shoken cheeks could never be disguised.

'You will not hurt any who wear the seeing metal ever again. What you did was wrong and against the will of Crotus,' he said, hoping that she had adopted the Watcher's religious fervour along with her mannerisms. The child looked at her hands and he sensed her remorse. That was good. 'I will not tell anyone what you have done,' he said. 'Your secret is safe with me.'

He felt her relief.

'But you must be punished or Crotus will be displeased.'

He felt her acceptance.

He grasped the back of her head and pushed her face into the fire, melting her shoken features in the flames.

CHAPTER FIFTY

Junas had never fully realised that when parted from the egg she felt its whereabouts. On the Greatship Ranghorn, she used to leave the egg occasionally to go on deck and the sense she had of it she attributed to her concern. Now stolen, Junas felt as if the egg was pulling her. Filled with panic she gathered the few belongings the slave Ibby had not taken and left the inn at a run.

She ran along an open road that led in the opposite direction to Felm where Ibby was supposed to go. She had chosen freedom after all. By midturn Junas knew she was near and hoped she could bargain with the girl – she could have everything, the money, the dog, but she must let her keep the egg. The egg was all that mattered. She prayed to Mother God that it was unbroken.

Junas slowed to a walk and caught her breath. The slave girl must have stopped to rest. Junas crept into the undergrowth and drew her skinning knife. She came upon them quickly in a small clearing. Crom leapt to the end of his rope as soon as she came near, wagging his tail and grinning. Junas expected Ibby to wake. As she came near she realised she was not asleep but dead – sprawled on the ground, her pretty face in the dust.

The bag the egg was in was open. Junas picked it up, relieved beyond measure. She smoothed her hands over its surface checking for damage. It was intact and one side was quite warm where Crom had lain against it just as she had taught him.

'Good dog,' she repeated over and again as she placed the egg in a patch of sun and turned it. 'So, she had made friends with you all along,' she said, undoing his collar. He was stupid enough to go with a stranger but smart enough to keep the egg warm.

The blind woman had warned her not to let anyone touch it. She had not realised the reason until now.

Junas undressed and strapped the egg onto herself, and dressed again, this time as a woman. A pregnant woman. Then she dragged the girl's body, pulling her hair, spreading her legs and tearing her bodice. She hit her face with a rock and left her.

Junas had no need of the road now and stepped out across the open country, which was safer and quicker. When she was sure that they were alone, she ran, her strides long and easy and Crom lolloped beside her. Now they were on Thanra she felt a new urgency coupled with a sense of direction that had nothing to do with being a Pathfinder.

CHAPTER FIFTY-ONE

S ho walked across the Keep courtyard toward the waiting Legates. Her fine silk dress billowed in the afternoon breeze. Summer heat and her advanced pregnancy made her warm. Sten walked behind, a self-appointed bodyguard. She was aware of his physical presence although she felt nothing through the Crystal bond now. Not from any of them.

She stopped a few paces in front of the kneeling Legates, summoning her linegold onto the front of her bare arms lest they thought her pregnancy made her less dangerous.

'What is it, Crowhurst?' she said.

They stood up and Sho watched them cautiously; the way they looked at Sten, weighing up the threat of him, wondering if six would be enough to best him. More of them came each turn. Her skin prickled. Her Crystal bond was dead but her fight prescience was stronger than ever.

'My lady, the Revenant has let more safety seekers in…'

'He's not a revenant, he's just a man,' she said.

He met her eyes and looked away. 'Yes, my lady…'

'Which gate?'

'South Gate. The safety seekers wait at all the gates now.'

'And has anyone seen him?'

'I've only heard a rumour. The Kassnets guard him closely.'

'Anything else?'

'In the king's absence the War Council and we, the Legates, have decided to move the safety seekers back. We advocate a new wall – further back so they can be controlled.'

'No… There will be no hunger wall. The king would not wish it,' she said.

'My lady, the city is breaking. We have barely enough food to feed ourselves. These shoken have no skills, they are uncivilised. They steal and rape. Make hovels for themselves in any space they can find. Kill good horses for meat. Something needs to be done before Valkarah is ruined.'

'Even so, they are still the king's subjects. Moving them would cause unnecessary violence.'

'They must be relocated if only to stop the spread of disease. Violence is all they understand. They must be moved. There is no place for them here. We all know that the threat of the Sturgar is minimal. The savages will not dare…'

'They will come,' she said and thought, if they do we will all be dead anyway.

Legate Crowhurst looked upwards and then to the others. Shook his big, bald head slightly as if trying to summon his patience and smiled down at her.

'You may believe whatever you wish. But the immediate threat to everyone's safety is the fighting in the streets. The murderers at our door. We need to take action soon or these beggars will destroy the king's imperial city.'

'The biggest threat to peace would be to start a fight between the Kassnets and the Median troops,' she said. Those Kassnets who had left Sneela had become staunch followers of the Healer and many sported a blue butterfly, the unofficial symbol of the Revenant, on their uniforms instead of the Kassnets wasp.

Another Legate stepped forward and whispered into Crowhurst's ear. She heard the words easily. 'Tell the Strick bitch that we will inform the king of her reluctance on his return.'

Crowhurst spoke in sweet tones as if addressing a small child. 'The king will not be pleased when he learns that you refused to hear our counsel.'

'I've heard the Legate every turn in the king's absence,' she said.

The whisperer leaned in again.

'Sir, if you have something to say, speak it aloud so we all may hear. Or shut up.'

I can hear you anyway.

'Median Commander Soanes agrees with us that something should be done,' said the whisperer, speaking directly to her.

Sho ignored him and looked to Crowhurst for an introduction. The bolder they got the less well-mannered they became.

'May I present Outan, chairman of commerce,' said Crowhurst, his pate reddening. Outan made a shallow bow but he kept his eyes on her. He was a new addition and she disliked him.

Sho was unsure whether her heightened fight prescience came when she lost the feeling of the Crystal or whether the child within her had a greater sense of danger than she ever had. Since stepping out onto the cobbles, she could feel the agitation of her unborn. The babe was moving so much she was surprised that no one was looking at her belly.

'Commander Soanes has spoken of his concerns. I told

him no barriers yet I learn that a wall is being built…' she said.

'What gives you the authority to make these decisions?' said Outan, sure of himself.

'We've been over this. I am the First of the king's body-guard. Until he returns, my word is his word. There will be no killing by the Median army of any Kassnets soldier or safety seeker within or without these city walls. You may close the gates to them and bar them from entering but you will not instigate violence,' she said.

Outan stepped closer. 'It seems to me,' he said, looking back at his associates and then at her with a sneer, 'that the king is not returning and something needs to be done about you. A woman in your… *state*… can not make decisions about the future of this city.' He looked back at the other Legates. Those who knew her were fearful. This urged him on. He was not afraid of a little pregnant woman. Someone needed to make a stand and he was that someone. This was his moment.

Sho imagined the flow of her linegold sinking into the flaccid flesh of his neck.

Sten stepped in front of her before Legate Outan could touch her. 'The king arrives in two turns,' said Sten.

The Legates muttered among themselves. This changed everything.

'Why haven't we been informed?' said Crowhurst, pushing Outan aside.

'You are being informed,' said Sho.

'Two turns. We must make arrangements for the king's arrival…' said Crowhurst, his thoughts turning to palace etiquette.

'No arrangements. The king wishes to arrive unan-nounced and without ceremony. You will keep this information to yourselves. Those are my orders,' she said, walking away.

Lillan opened the keep door as they arrived. 'Do you feel this?' she asked. Sten sat down heavily on the stairs, sicker than ever. Lillan unbuckled the shoulder straps on his breastplate and heaved it off. Without the armour, he looked thin. They had not seen or heard from the Healer for many turns and only he was able to alleviate Sten's discomfort.

'Something. I feel something but honestly, I'm not sure if it's more what I wish than actual truth,' he said.

Once she would have been the first to sense the king's approach. She felt nothing, only emptiness where he had been and the child within her did not fill the gap left by the Crystal.

'You should try to rest. See how you feel on the new turn,' she said. At least the separation no longer made her sick. That was something, she supposed.

Sten tapped lightly on the door at dawn. She slept in the king's bed as her need for sleep was great now and there was no bed in her rooms. Sho got up and slid the door bolt. One look at Sten's face told her the lord was coming.

'How long?'

'Soon. Very soon.' He stood at the window looking out at the Ten Cond Meadow. Sho followed his gaze. 'Is this the way he comes? Not through the city?'

'This direction... only not somehow. He is in a great rush,' he said.

'Is he afraid?'

Sten looked at his Crystal bearing arm. He was just an outliner, his bond so much lighter than the others. 'It's hard to tell. Yes, I think so.'

'I know the way he comes,' she said. He followed her down the stairs. Still a soldier at heart, Sho always slept in her clothes.

Beneath the keep was an underground room. In the middle was a mausoleum stone. Isk the Lepitoan Archer was the last shoken they had laid there. Here the Crystal Bearers stored their death effects. Body slates of various lengths were propped against the walls and hung with black burial bags. Sho moved a long slate to one side. Beneath it, dust-covered and smaller than all, was her own. Superstition forbade her to touch it and Sten lifted it away. There was no bag. She had never made one and the thought occurred that she might die in childbirth. A death she had never anticipated. Would they take her to Nenimar's Temple and lay her to rest with the others even though she had lost the bond?

'Sho?' said Sten softly.

'Sorry. Yes, here,' she said, tracing her hand over the stone-painted wood to find the catch. The door creaked and slid down into the ground to reveal a tunnel.

'The lord approaches fast,' said Sten.

'And the others?'

'Hard to know. Arrant…'

Soon they could hear their coming and a torch-flame, a speck at first in the far distance, grew steadily brighter.

'Where does this tunnel begin?'

'There are many,' she said. If she had been able to feel them, she would have known where they had begun their underground journey.

A new outliner walked ahead of the Pack to light their way. One by one, the Pack emerged, soaked. Sho could smell the river on them. Apart from the king, all were unarmed, the weapons too heavy to swim with underwater. Finding the opening on the river bed had been an ordeal. She did not need Crystal to tell her that... their faces showed they were relieved to be alive.

The king pressed his forehead to Sten's and gripped his Crystal-bearing arm, restoring the bond. He went back to the tunnel, crouched down in the opening and placed his hands on the stone. 'We lost two children,' he said. There was no word for outliner in Faar.

They ascended the steps into the keep. Sho, separate from the Pack as never before, realised they all knew what was happening, and she did not. A bystander, she watched the king embrace Jie as he walked in with the Healer. Then he took the Healer in his arms and kissed him full on the mouth. Held his face in his hands for a moment before turning to her and placing a hand on her belly proprietarily. Inside her, the baby leapt.

All the feeling between them was gone. She was an ordinary woman now. An ordinary woman carrying his heir.

'They're coming,' he said. 'Arm yourselves quickly. We need to get to Valkarah.'

'I'll go and see what horses I can find,' said Reem, taking a shortsword from the wall.

The two outliners went with him. At the edge of the group, Math stood against the wall, silent and still, watching and listening.

CHAPTER FIFTY-TWO

The king marched through Valkarah with his Pack close behind. 'Toll the bells!' he cried as they made their way to the Audience Hall. By the time they arrived, the room was crowded. Soldiers, servants, palace guards, Legates, guests, Adernist monks, anyone in the vicinity who had heard the words, 'The king has returned,' came to look with awe upon the king they thought was lost.

Reem led a horse across the marble floor and the king leapt into the saddle. Always more comfortable on horseback he took up the reins and circled to face the crowd. Wet from the River Goot, ragged and bloodstained from a recent fight, the king sat astride the shabby brown gelding and held aloft N'gar, the ancient linegold sword. The room became silent.

'A Sturgar army approaches from the east. There may be more that we do not know of coming from other directions.'

Nobody moved. Nobody spoke.

'They are armed and number five thousand. If they wait to attack at nightfall, we have a turn to prepare. I don't think they will wait.' The king looked at their upturned faces, re-sheathed his sword and wished he had a better plan.

'Find the bell ringers. Have everyone who is able take up arms. Tell the War Council to meet me in the watchtower.'

Suddenly all the shoken were shouting out questions. He turned the little horse on his hocks and trotted through an archway and into one of the siege tunnels that spiralled around Valkarah Palace.

The watchtower was long out of use, the great oak door locked and the key lost. Sho walked through the throng and began to unpick the lock with two linegold blades. She still had some uses.

When the door swung open, the king trotted in and the Pack ran behind. Sten lifted Sho and carried her up the curving hoofpath. He never found her heavy. The linegold liked him because she did.

From the top, they could see the city far below; busy shoken in the overcrowded streets oblivious to the encroaching threat. The king rode once around the tower, dismounted and leaned on the ramparts, looking across the plain to the horizon. There was nothing to see. Chief Legate Crowhurst had followed them. Two seasons ruling Valkarah in the king's absence made him bold.

'Where is the army?' he said, forcing out a derisive little laugh.

Clogs clicked. Orrld arrived, panting. Math ducked beneath the lintel. He wore the blue robes of an acolyte like many in the city who venerated the lesser God Ath and named Orrld Revenant. Jie followed them in, small and menacing with his knife-hand.

Math looked across the arable land to the east. 'What do you see?' asked the king softly.

Math faced him, pulling off his hood and revealing his grey, smooth head and the red-lined slit black pupils of his eyes. He pointed at himself and then to the horizon, marking the extent of the encroaching Sturgar.

'What? This thing can see the invisible?' said Crowhurst, expecting assent from those gathered. Everyone was still. None of the other Legates had the audacity to contradict the king.

'The safety seekers,' said the Healer from the other side of the watchtower. The Median army were herding the unwanted shoken out of the city gates. A crude enclosure of wooden stakes encircled the mass out on the open plain.

'You!' said Crowhurst. 'This man has instigated defiance against the Median army. Every turn he breaches the safety of the city and lets in the rabble. Thousands of them... He has disobeyed the advice of the Legates.'

'These shoken have the right to live,' said Orrld.

Crowhurst puffed himself up. He had more to say.

'You forget your manners, Chief Legate,' said Arrant.

'These are ordinary shoken families. They need the safety of the walls. They need your protection, lord,' said the Healer, coming over and placing his soothing touch on the king's arm.

'Yes...' said the king, looking at Legate Crowhurst for the first time.

'There are too many. Too many. Outside every gate now and don't tell me they can fight. Peasants can't fight. Women, children, old and sick can't fight,' said Crowhurst, taking a step away from Arrant.

'You will instruct the gatekeepers to let them in. Everyone needs to come in now...' said the king, looking at Math observing the horizon. Math counted and scratched a tally into the white stone of Valkarah with a linegold blade. Nobody but he could see that far even with an oculus and they waited until he had completed his reckoning.

'Why doesn't this thing speak?' said Crowhurst.

Arrant gripped the Legate by the shoulder and moved him back to a respectable distance.

'How many are these marks worth?' asked the king, running his finger over the many lines when Math had finished. Math opened and shut his hands, ten times; each mark was one hundred.

The king made a total. 'Seven thousand?'

Math nodded.

'How long?'

Math pointed at the sky and moved his finger, following the path the sun would make, and then indicated the moons rising.

A single bell rang out a mournful, persistent note. In the streets, the shoken stopped. Most expected more bells to join the peal and they waited for a ringing melody that signalled good news. The warning clanged deep and constant, a call to arms; a call to hide. On the seventh peal, the shoken ran.

The king turned to Crowhurst. 'You! Instruct the gate-keepers to let in my people. Get the rest of the Legate and bring them here. Go!' Chief Legate Crowhurst looked at the far horizon and then at the Strick monster. He wanted to ask why they thought they could trust this creature but thought better of that with the threat of the king's Pack. He made a low bow and hurried down the winding hoofpath, passing the War Council as they ran up to meet the king.

At the centre of the watchtower was a room of sorts. Open on all sides, yet roofed. In the middle was a large table with a crude stone model and map of Valkarah. The War Council and the Pack crowded around and listened as Arrant and the king made plans for the oncoming siege.

Sho had her first contraction.

The shock of the pain almost made her cry out. She leaned back on a pillar to steady herself and behind her back, pressed the flat of her hands onto the cool white stone of Valkarah and said a silent prayer to Nenimar.

For the first time in her life, Sho doubted the male God

she prayed to, looked around at the men, and wished for a woman's wisdom. As the next contraction arose and peaked Sho could not deny her pain and cried out. The men stopped their talking and all looked at her as though they had never seen her before. This then was the weakness of women, this all-consuming agony. Another involuntary scream and as her waters broke, spilling on the floor, she knew she had lost control of her body.

All the men were staring. Orrld came to her and she welcomed his touch.

'Take her to safety,' said the king.

CHAPTER FIFTY-THREE

Orrld could ease her pain but he could not make it stop. Sho paced the circular tower room. Green silk drapes still hung on the walls and the large round bed was dressed in white noss fur. How strange that she should give birth here in the king and queen's royal bed-chamber. How strange that she should give birth at all.

Childbirth was a lengthy process. In between contractions, Sho leaned on the window ledges and watched the siege of Valkarah. The Sturgar army easily breached the outer wall. She could see them climbing over the ramparts like a swarm of grey ants. She doubted any of the soldiers survived unless they fled. At dusk, the grey army amassed just beyond the inner, city wall and waited out of the archers' range.

Chief Legate Crowhurst had completed his traitor's work. He returned to his dwelling, sent his last messenger bird and instructed his household to pack. He left before noon by the south gate.

The lost king's return was a nuisance. Without him, the transition would have been simple and without bloodshed. The king would make a stand based on false ideals and thousands would die for his pride. A city under siege was no place for a Legate of his calibre. The town of Blannet, on the warm central coast, would welcome a man of experience.

The Sturgar army, ravenous after their long run from Tarestone, were glad of the caged shoken and gave thanks to Crotus for the gift of real meat.

The screams of the safety seekers as they were eaten alive carried on the summer winds and echoed off the palace walls long into the night. Orrld cried for them.

At dawn, Sho watched the king ride out to rally the troops. Someone had found him another crown. Unlike the plain gold band he used to wear, this one was jewelled and opulent and seemed at odds with the commonplace horse and his scruffy clothes. She could not hear his speech but she heard the cheers of armies and men. Emboldened by his words Kassnets and Median soldiers and any citizen who could wield a weapon waited for the advance of the Sturgar.

They came at dark. Despite lookouts on wall and watchtower, no one saw the stealthy approach of Sturgar warriors who climbed and slunk and entered the castle in ones and twos and hid – waiting for a signal that no shoken ear could hear.

For the shoken, those who would fight and those who could not, it was gruesome suspense. There was much talk and some advocated going out to meet the battle on the level ground. The king, unaware his castle was already penetrated, forbade this.

Sho's body was doing what came naturally and she had no

control over what was happening to her. Somewhere, deep in her woman's soul, she knew the birth would be soon. The pains were regular and very strong now and even the Healer could not quell them. And as the baby separated from her, there was something else... a reconnection of the Crystal. Faintly, feeling crept back. She thought it was her imagination but as each contraction brought the baby nearer to life, Sho knew that her Crystal bond had returned. Like recognising someone from their shadow, it was not whole and she doubted the Pack or the king knew her again. Not yet. But they would.

Orrld could not bear to look out on the fight below and had drawn the drapes. The room was in a green twilight, which was easy on her Strick eyes. Smoky air wafted in the windows. Somewhere Valkarah burned. Sho lay on the circular bed and looked at Orrld. 'You look tired,' she said.

'It won't be long now. I'm fine,' he said, smiling his Healer's smile, full of sympathy and self-deprecation. Sho wanted him gone. She needed to get to the king and knew Orrld would send her to sleep for the sake of the child. Another contraction occupied her and when it was over, he wiped the sweat from her face on the silk sheets.

'Is Math outside the door?' she asked. She knew he was.

'Yes, he's there,' said Orrld.

'I have nothing for the baby. None of what I got ready,' she said.

'It's all right, we'll make do,' said Orrld.

Sho tried to look sad. Like a mother worried for her child.

'Could you ask him to go back to the keep?'

'It's not safe,' he said, soothing her brow.

'I need some food. So do you,' she said. This was true; she knew how hungry the Healer got. 'Ask Math,' she said, knowing Orrld would not leave the king's heir unguarded.

Orrld nodded thoughtfully. 'You're right, we do need

some food. It's been nearly two turns since we ate. I'll go down the stairs, see if I can find one of the palace guards,' he said, after her next contraction. Sho clutched his webbed hand as he got up. Held it close to her chest and spoke softly, an Ekressian prayer of thanks. 'The life of the River flows through you. I thank Ath for the blessing of your touch.' Sho looked into his brown eyes. He was a kind man. He would do the right thing.

Orrld went quietly out the door and she heard him tell Math to stay there. Math hissed. He never liked to let the Healer out of his sight.

Sho got up with difficulty, staggered to the door, and turned the key. On the other side, Math hissed again.

Orrld was not gone long. 'Sho! Let me in! You need my help. SHO!'

Sho did not reply. Her pain was all her own now. She knelt on all fours on the bed and, making strange guttural cries, gave birth.

Now the baby was not in her body she felt the king and knew he was afraid. Trapped somehow. She sent him her love and he returned it. Soon he was calling out to her. They all were.

Math was beating against the door and the wood was beginning to split. Sho gave one last push and the afterbirth flopped onto the bed. The baby cried.

Sho got up. So much blood and mess. Birthing had not made her a mother. There was never a moment when she thought it would. The screaming helpless babe was a stranger. All Sho knew was the return of her Crystal bond. So strong, childbirth made no difference.

Sho pulled the window drapes and looked out. Sturgar walked through streets littered with dead shoken. The siege was nearly done. In her hand, she clutched the key.

Ignoring her baby's cries, Sho spoke to Math, her voice

quiet. She doubted Orrld would be able to hear her words, yet she spoke in Faar anyway. Math and she had the ability to collect language without effort. She knew he would have listened and learned. The Strick child was no fool and had been careful not to show his understanding when the king spoke in his own voice. 'Try to get back to the keep if you can. There are tunnels beneath that lead in all directions. You need to get them out of the city. Head for the mountains. The king will go there. Good luck.' Sho tossed the key over to the door and climbed out of the window onto the roof.

CHAPTER FIFTY-FOUR

Math knelt the better to sweep his tail under the door and slide the key into his hand. Beside him, his father had slumped to the floor unconscious. Too much healing and too little food. He had seen this happen often when they overused him.

Math lifted him inside, laid him on the bed and locked the door again. Fire and the enemy were close. He would have to be quick if he were going to save them.

The tiny girl was still attached to her cord and the part of the mother that came after. Math had seen his father at the birthing bed often enough to know she needed to be separated from this. He summoned a linegold blade and then thought better. He did not want to cause her any harm and he had seen how the linegold carried on hurting long after the wounds had healed. Math bit through the cord and placed one of his father's webbed hands on her to heal the wound and stop her crying. Math knew the healing always flowed. His father seemed unable to stop it, even when he was exhausted or sleeping. Once she was calm, he wiped her clean and wrapped her in strips of silk torn from the bedding. She watched him with jewel blue eyes, and Math felt the same feeling he felt for Orrld. What the shoken called love.

Math remembered his birth. How his shoken mother hated him when she saw him and the hunger and the cold after she tried to kill him. At least Sho had not tried to kill her. If she had wanted to it would have been easy; shoken babies were helpless, their minds only half there. This little one was mostly shoken. He hoped she would not remember that she was an infantabhor.

He laid her in the crook of his arm while he peered between the drapes and listened out of the tower windows. Below, in the palace grounds, shoken ran from the fire. The Sturgar killed any who showed aggression and herded the rest into groups. The fight was over. In the city Sturgar were walking about, casually gathering up any bodies. Laughing, eating, looting. Their songs of victory drifted in the warm air of the summer evening.

His pacing had sent the child to sleep. He had seen that, too. He laid her on the bed and took off the long, hooded robes he wore to disguise himself.

The Sturgar looked exactly like himself, only most of them were bigger. If he had not known he had come out of a shoken woman, he would have believed himself one of them.

They cried out to one another in the high sounds that shoken could not hear. He knew what the music meant. Sturgar song was instinctive.

Outside the room, he could hear such a song. Two came up the spiral stairway. They could smell blood. Math met them calling softly, a sound that meant, 'over here'. He had never cried the sounds before and when they replied, he had a surge of gratitude to be understood after so much silence.

They hissed a greeting when they saw him, which he returned. They were not expecting his eyes or the linegold.

Before they reached the top of the stairs they were both dead, their throats cut. Math took the clothes from the smaller of the two. Some soft leather breeches and boots. In the summer heat, they wore nothing on the top half of their bodies, only a strap for carrying their weapon. Math put the strap over his shoulder and picked up one of the vetrolla spars. He wielded the double-bladed spear this way and that. A good weapon that fitted his hands and had an easy balance. He slotted it in place.

Now he could pass as one of them, he slung his father over his shoulder, picked up the baby in one hand, stepped out onto the balcony, and leapt easily onto a nearby roof. From here, he could see the palace burning. Smoke curled from the windows and seeped between the rooftop tiles. Unseen shoken were running and screaming in the chaos. Math walked down the roof and stepped onto the branches of the great oak, just as he had seen Sho do. He was too big to walk through the branches of the tree as she did. He went as far as he could and jumped down. Ahead was the keep.

A group of Sturgar, also carrying bodies, walked toward him. Math returned their greeting song. There were too many for him to fight. His only chance was to pass as one of them. As they approached, they began to laugh and he feared that he was found out. He laughed back as they did, pretending to share the joke. They bent their knees and lowered themselves in supplication as he passed. Math walked on toward the keep, not sure what had happened.

The keep door was smashed and in the hall lay Lillan's corpse. He could not hear anything; it was empty. Math put his father and the baby on the kitchen floor and pressed a lump of stale bread into his hand, patting his face and hissing, wake up!

Orrld ate, drank water, gathered up the baby, and tucked her into his robes.

Math stuffed anything edible into a bag, filled two water-skins and pulled his father to his feet.

Math remembered. He would come to realise this was a particular trait of his Strick mind and was both a curse and a gift. At the end of the hall, he pulled back the tapestry that covered the door to the underground room.

When the king was sick and believed himself dying, he had told Math how to escape. While he had waited at the birth he had thought of little else than the words the king had spoken when he had given him his name. Sho had told him to go to the mountains but the king had already given him instructions. Keep the Healer safe, he had said. He would not take his father back into the fight where he would give his last healing to war wounded.

He found the tunnel opening behind the body slates. He closed it behind them as best he could and led his father by the sleeve through the dark, clicking his tongue to hear the sound bounce off the stone to make a picture of the way.

The way was long. Sometimes when the tunnel was not far from the surface they could hear the world above, screams and the sinister crackle as the palace burned. Math heard the victory song of the Sturgar and he wondered where the good king was and if he had survived.

When his father became weak he carried him, sleeping in his arms. After a night travelling he saw a prick of light in the distance and at last, the tunnel came to an opening on the surface, concealed within a low cave.

Just as the king had told, he could smell an aroma of an unknown spice. So faint that when the morning breeze fluttered through the cave it was gone, only to return when the air was still again. Math found the source; a bag hidden inside a large hollowed-out rock.

The baby cried softly, turning her face to one side and looking for food that was not there. Orrld laid the child in the dust. 'I don't know how we're going to feed her,' he said, stroking a finger across her face and sending her back to sleep.

Math had seen how shoken children could only feed on milk to begin with, and although her mother was Strick, she seemed to have only one Sturgar characteristic.

Orrld dressed in the rough spun peasant clothes from inside the hollow rock, breeches and boots and tunic. There was money in common coin and gold clowsters. Dried food, waterskins, blankets, knives and a small tin with flints and horsehair kindling, which his father was pleased to find and tucked into his tunic. There was nothing for a baby or for himself to wear.

'I think you have grown a bit since the king was ill,' said Orrld. The clothes left for him were for a child. Math put his father's robes and the blue sash that marked him as a healer into the rock and replaced it. If any of them came here, they would know they escaped. 'I wish there was something we could leave of hers. So that they know we have her and she is safe,' he said.

Math spat in his hand, took some dirt from the floor and made a paste and used it to print the baby's foot onto a stone and put it inside one of his father's clogs.

The cave was in the side of a hillock. In the distance, smoke hung in a cloud in the still summer air. They were near the outer city wall. From here, he could see the shelters the safety seekers had made, believing the walls could protect them even from the outside. Math ran his tail through his hands and thought whether to leave in the light or dark. Sturgar, like him, could see better in the dark and were more likely to be active on the dark side of the turn. He had no clothes to wear, and looking like one of them had proved useful. For the moment.

CHAPTER FIFTY-FIVE

S oft as a wisp of cloud that fades in the heat of the sun, Sho could feel where the king had been as he fled. Stronger was the sense of where he was.

Sho ran across the roof tiles, hot from the sun above and hot from the fire that burnt below. In the distance were storm clouds, dark as the smoke pouring from the palace.

A few Sturgar were on the roof to escape the smoke inside. To them, she was just another blood-stained, crazy shoken. Enough were dead for meat and victory. She presented no threat. They paid her no heed as she ran past toward the fire.

Sho climbed down the side of a turret. The Pack had tried to go through the siege tunnels to reach the far side of the palace, probably with the hope of escaping across the Ten Cond Meadow. The fires had cut them off, again and again, making them switchback. Now they were trapped. She could feel the king's fear mingled with the rest of the Pack.

Sho jumped onto another roof and ran, flames licking her bare feet. The fire was loud as it devoured the rafters, sending the thick orange pantiles crashing down. She made it to the edge and climbed again, entering a window. She stood there, blood running down her legs and pooling at her feet. Too much blood.

Inside, the long gallery had begun to burn. Flames curled around the statues, along the floor rugs and sank red fangs into the tapestries and paintings on the walls. Waves of intense heat made her step back. She always could put her hand in fire. This required more courage. Sho looked about as if Valkarah was going to present a different path – one she did not know. The king was not calling her now, his fear replaced with the calm of defeat.

The door at the end of the long gallery was the only way to reach him. Sho ran into the blaze with a prayer to Nenimar that he would spare her flesh from the flames. Hair and clothes burnt away, and the linegold blades she carried on her skin glowed red as when forged by the Blade-Master at Lak-Mur.

The fire was halfway down the gallery eating the priceless artworks like a ravenous war dog. The nearer it got to the end, the faster it came. Sho knew she must be quick for she realised when the door opened the fire would leap on the gush of air, hungry for the warmed wood panels and carvings in the Hunting Hall just beyond. It was a risk she must take. To save him she needed to get in there and take them through one of the secret ways that honeycombed the palace. Fire chased her as if it felt cheated by her unnatural abilities and wanted to prove her wrong. Sho ran ahead of the flames. As she opened the smaller door, set within the large doors at the end of the gallery, the fire curled up behind her and pounced. Drinking the new air it licked her naked back – her Crystal matched the colour of fire now. Sho tried to close the door behind her but the beast was too strong. The fire bounded in.

With her Crystal bond, she pulled the Pack to her. 'We

need to get this table over the door,' she yelled over the fire's growl. The Pack and some of the shoken trapped with them dragged the long banqueting table and pushed it flat against the door. Others smothered flames with tapestries pulled from the walls. For a moment, they were safe.

Sho walked to where the table had been and found a flag-stone with a faded crest. 'This is the way...' she said and Jie hooked his knife-hand under the rim and the others lifted it free. Sho jumped down and the king followed.

Then they were running for their lives into a dark, narrow tunnel made from grey stone – part of the old castle that had stood on this site before the elaborate palace was built on top. Behind them, the ordinary shoken followed, their panic a different sort of fire.

The passage opened into some unused rooms on the east side of the palace. The fire had not reached this far and royalty and common shoken alike ran through rooms where furniture and artefacts were draped in dust covers, down staircases until at last they were outside gulping the clean air.

The king turned to the shoken. Some of them were sitting, exhausted, coughing and gasping – clutching each other in relief. They felt safe. Sho did not. 'My lord, we must make haste,' she cried. They could have run on and the shoken would not have noticed. The king drew his sword and held it high. 'People of Valkarah! We must go on to greater safety. Follow me,' he cried. The shoken heard their king and roused the last of their energy.

It was said after, that if Nenimar, hungry for war, had brought the fire it was Ath that sent the rain at the end of the turn. As they ran, the storm broke with a fierceness to match the fires that consumed Valkarah. The mob followed the king and his Pack through the palace grounds to the East Gate. Seven tribes of Clisotians parted to let them in and closed their ranks around them.

Sho stood, naked, her skin glowing and her Crystal bonds dancing with tiny flames. The Faar-Tiger leaping through fire on her back felt deeply etched and the image lit her mind's eye. Sho knelt before her king in the benediction of the cool rain. All around there was movement – horses, shoken, war dogs. The king and the Pack became still with her.

This had been the purpose of her life. This fire-walk. Sho struggled to her feet and allowed the king to steady her. With one hand she held his and in the other a bright linegold blade.

Sho died.

The king caught her as life and body fell. He held her in his arms while each blade cooled and dropped away and her Crystal burns went out.

The pain of the ripping as the bond broke was deep. The Pack cried and clutched themselves in their agony. When it was over, she left an emptiness filled with fear; their great protector had gone.

The Clisotians provided horses and they rode from Valkarah in the downpour. Arrant watched the king holding Sho's tiny body, his face a quiet mask of grief. The newly made Crystal burn on Arrant's back tingled. All these years he had believed that if he had needed to, in a fight, he could have killed Sho. Told himself he was a better man because he chose the peaceful solution to keep the lord happy. Sho, limp in the lord's arms, her skin charred, hair and clothes all burnt away and her Crystal seeping from fire's heat. In death, he saw what she truly was – a fire-walker. All these years and he had not known what she could do or what she could endure. Now he knew that he would never be able to replace her. He was unworthy. Even dead, the king would love her more than him.

By nightfall, the Clisotians stopped on the Meddant Stretch. In the middle of the open grasslands was a place where ancient shoken had made a circle of stones to worship the moons. The king laid Sho on the rain-soaked altar-stone and they built a pyre around her tiny, childlike form.

The king stood at her head but he could not speak the prayer for the dead. Arrant spoke for him as he used to do, in simpler times. Arrant clenched his right fist and opened his hand. A bright flame leapt in his palm. He allowed it to grow tall and made a fireball which he held in his two hands, letting it swirl then tossing it to a corner of the pyre, where it hovered in the air like a sun. He made three more, taking his time until four burned, spitting in the rain.

As the Pack watched the fireballs descend and ignite the pyre, they saw for the first time Arrant's ability. As the flames burnt through Sho's corpse, releasing her Crystal, each endured the pain of the second ripping.

When Sho's body was ash, the king took a vial and collected the liquid Crystal from the grooves in the altar-stone.

CHAPTER FIFTY-SIX

I ndess sat close to the brazier inside her tent. The older she got the more the damp seeped into her bones. Staying warm helped and the firelight kept back the wraiths that harried her. They lingered in the shadows where she could ignore them.

She knew the king would come. He would ask for answers that she probably did not have, and she doubted that he realised the reason the Clisotian Defenders were ready to protect him was that she managed to persuade Demik of the need of this king. Demik was a seven tribe chief now, as she had foreseen. He listened to her yet sometimes it was hard to explain why she felt they, the Clisotians, should ally themselves to anyone when in the past their nation always considered themselves separate from other shoken. She had no explanation, only that, for the good of all common shoken, the Median king must be saved.

Indess began unthreading the rune-stones she wore about her neck. They replaced the ones she had lost. She read them often and although given freely or made for her, they still felt like strangers in her hands.

The king came quietly into her tent. She watched his grief-stricken face as he settled himself opposite her. Felt the nearness of his protectors as they kept a close guard. Rain pattered on the horsehide tent. She waited for him to speak.

The last rune dropped from its thread into her palm and she cupped the set in her two hands. She had seen this moment so many times in recent years. Sho's death and her funeral pyre on the pagan altar. Like any shoken, the king came seeking answers from the newly dead. Those without the sight did not understand that fresh dead were too busy asking their own questions to be bothered with the living. Most times they could not be reached. She doubted Sho Tar would be any different.

'The questions you ask are not always what the spirits want to answer. The dead are often busy with their own journey. Especially those who have just passed,' she said.

The king stared into the fire. In the orange glow, huge tigers prowled. 'I only wish to find a way to protect the Trilands,' he said.

Indess took the question to her heart and threw the runes. They hung in the air and sank slowly down. Indess expected to see spirits connected to Sho. But she was dead and had played her part. The shade that stood before her was the Ekressian woman, Issolissi. Since Indess had last seen her she had grown into a powerful soul watcher. Many stood in the light and warmth that shone from her. The devil that lurked at the edges of her sight shrank back.

Issolissi set a vision before her.

When it was over Indess closed her eyes to give herself time to make sense of what she had seen. The king was patient. He waited until she was ready. 'Your protectors would benefit from what I have seen,' she said, calling for Demik.

The king nodded and they came in and crowded around

watching as Indess drew a crude war map into the ash she
had tipped onto the ground. She showed them where hordes
of Sturgar waited and where an allied army rode to meet
them, this led by a female Strick. Indess marked out a safe
path to the mountains. 'You cannot fight them, my lord,' she
said. 'Not yet.'

'Let the people rest and at dawn, we will move on as the
savant advises,' said the king, looking at their faces, seeking
approval. They agreed this was as good a plan as any especially if the savant was right and another army met them at
the foot of the Meddants.

When they left the king remained. He took out the vial of
Sho's Crystal. The amber fluid glowed. 'All my life she has
protected me. Even in death, she gives sound advice,' he said.

Indess did not contradict him. He needed to believe Sho
had reached across the divide to give him a battle plan. She
picked up the runes and began rethreading them. A question
hung between them. 'What is it you would ask for yourself?'

'My son...?'

'Your child lives. The Soorah keeps him safe,' she said.

Indess felt his surge of gratitude and relief as he left. She
knew the child that Sho had carried was female. Just as she
knew the fire-walk would take Sho's life. But whether her
baby had lived or died and who looked after her was only
conjecture. Sometimes it was wiser to tell shoken what they
needed to hear so that they could carry on. For the peace of
the Trilands depended on this king and only him. Of that
much, she was sure.

CHAPTER FIFTY-SEVEN

Curver Thist looked up at Mag'Sood seated on the Black Throne as he walked in ahead of the Watcher. A lesser Sturgar would be dwarfed by such a seat. Mag'Sood occupied the space physically and emotionally. His confidence filled the room with awe and fear, making the Primary Warriors tremble when he flicked his gaze over them. Beside him, the She-Aulex lay with her head on his knee, her scales black as the reparda rock.

The Curver stood aside and the Watcher knelt on the bottom step of the dais. She kept very still as the disciple arranged the folds of her little gown and placed a disk in her tiny hands.

Mag'Sood joined her and the Curver was surprised that the Master was suddenly sad. He missed the beautiful female who had watched for so long. With surprising gentleness, the Mag pulled off the child's hood. Perhaps he hoped to find beauty. She kept her eyes downcast as he looked at her melted face and did not stop her when she replaced the hood. The Curver had a story ready but the Master was seldom interested in details.

The child raised the disk.

Mag'Sood saw the siege of Valkarah. The slaughter of the shoken, the burning of the palace. The Curver had already viewed the disk many times and seen how the Shoken-Slayer was revered.

'This is not what I ordered,' whispered Mag'Sood, waving the Watcher away. The disciple led her from the room in a calm, unhurried manner.

The She-Aulex got down from the Black Throne and stretched.

'Did you plan this?' he whispered. The Curver shrank low.

'No, Master. The Shoken-Slayer took the city of his own accord.'

Mag'Sood waved his Primary Warriors away. This was wise. The Curver sensed some of them had a strong allegiance to the Shoken-Slayer. If not for the protection of the She-Aulex, Mag'Sood would have been disposed of long since. No matter how much the Shoken-Slayer professed devotion to the self-made God, it was only a matter of time until the red-eyed warrior sat upon the Black Throne. If he did not kill the Mag himself, one of his devotees would.

Mag'Sood went to the fire, and two of the brood revealed themselves briefly as they got up to make way for him. The Curver breathed out slowly. This close the smell was very bad.

Mag'Sood sat down and gestured that he should do the same. The Curver remained where he was.

'Sit down, Master Curver, I'm not going to hurt you,' he whispered with a fleeting smile. His pointed teeth were blackened from the dark-berry.

The Curver knelt carefully. His back fluttered with the nearness of the Aulex behind.

'It is good that we speak alone,' he whispered, tossing

another log onto the fire. Flames leapt up but the room was never warm. 'Not so long ago you suggested my followers should take the shoken cities along the Plessic Coast...' He hissed softly: *speak*.

'Yes, Master, I thought it would open a trade route to Ekressia,' he whispered.

'You said we were not ready to take Valkarah.'

'I was wrong, Master. I am not a warrior.'

'No. I must not forget this,' he whispered.

The Curver felt the Master's countenance to be neutral. He was safe. For the moment. The dark-berry made him volatile. He must proceed with caution if he wanted to live. In the last three turns, the She-Aulex had killed two Tethlic warriors for no apparent reason that he could see.

'How goes the trade?'

From a pocket inside his cloak, the Curver brought out a softling leather pouch. No doubt, with his heightened addiction, the Master could smell the freshly dried berries.

'I think it goes well, Master. These are from a recent crop but I am no judge of their potency,' he whispered, holding out the bag.

The Master reached out his hand. His fingers were black up to the first knuckle now and the Curver could sense desire as strong as lust when he dropped the bag into his hand.

'You will leave war to those who know how to fight. From now on you will only concentrate on trade,' said the Master, waving him away.

The Curver got up, bowed low and left the Mag to his pleasure.

Back in his chambers, the Curver handed his cloak to Podder. His rooms were warm at least. He sat at his desk brooding while the Strick slave attended his duties: covering the birds' cages with lengths of cloth to quieten them;

turning the haunch of seal meat roasting on the fire; stirring a large pinch of rishlan-colvar into a cup of broth.

'Followers,' thought the Curver with disdain as he sipped the hot broth and wondered, not for the first time, if Mag'-Sood truly believed himself a God. Power was corrupting. He had seen it often enough. This was not the first Mag he had served. He doubted he could persuade the Shoken-Slayer to accept him as his Curver. When they interred Mag'Sood the Redeemer in the ice tomb he would definitely be alongside him. He shivered.

Mag'Sood never took his advice. He hardly let him speak. True, he had learnt how to let the Mag believe most of the ideas were his own. Being the power behind the Black Throne three times had taught him the best way to survive was never to take credit for any achievement. Now another Mag loomed on the horizon. Sturgar were choosing sides, even if they did not realise they were doing so and in some part of his conceited mind, Mag'Sood felt it, too. The last time the Shoken-Slayer had knelt before the Master, unarmed, unguarded and with total fealty, he had stood close and felt the Shoken-Slayer's true mood. It was not devotion. It was derision.

When the light side of the turn came, he went to his place above the reflecting room and waited until the disciple had taken the little Watcher to her chambers. He had given instructions that they attend her at all times to guard against her shoken fallibility and protect her gift. The disciple had agreed readily. They were all a part of the deception.

The reflecting room was silent when Curver Thist crept in through a side door. The disks glimmered in the threads of light around the closed shutters and in the stillness, the room murmured with watched lives.

Unlike her predecessor, she never left any of the disks with their images showing. He saw how she twitched them to blurredness as she put them down. The little shoken was no fool. She knew she had a rare skill. Nevertheless, when he picked up the Shoken-Slayer's disk he tried to find an image. Held his hands as steady as he was able, tried to feel through his fingertips the vibrations he had heard spoken of. All he felt was smooth, unmoving metal.

Gripping the disk in the fire tongs, he held it in the flames until the metal turned white, then allowed it to cool. He did this several times and hoped he had done enough when he returned it to its place on the table.

A turn later and the disciple guided the Watcher to kneel at the foot of the Black Throne so Mag'Sood the Redeemer could witness the warrior that the Sturgar nations revered, almost above all others, die in agony from no cause that any could see.

Standing near, the Curver noted the moods of those nearby. The Primary Warriors that were sorry. The indifference of the disciple. The delight of the Watcher. The Master's remorse. This last was the most telling; Mag'Sood did not recognise his return to power. But then, they never did.

Later, when the light came again and the nation slept, the Curver watched the She-Aulex and her brood leave the castle, so confident in their favoured position they did not bother to effect a disguise. Every few turns they left the Master's side and set off across the ice. Whether to hunt or visit the rest of their kind, he was unsure. Inside Tarestone, the cubs mostly kept themselves hidden. Outside, trotting behind their mother with glistening black scales, he saw they were almost fully grown.

The She-Aulex and her brood would not be gone long. The Curver put on his cloak and padded through the castle.

With the protection of the Aulex, Mag'Sood believed he did not need personal guards. The Primary Warriors were free to go to their ice dens. Warriors always patrolled the ramparts and the perimeter of the settlement but inside Tarestone, on the light side of the turn, the castle was empty.

The Curver listened outside the Master's chambers. All was quiet. He breathed deeply. The Aulex had a complex smell that changed the longer they were in a place. Disgusting as it was, he had made himself learn it. The lingering smell was old. They had gone. He always worried that an Aulex from outside remained to guard him. There never was. But he always checked.

Mag'Sood did not bar or lock his doors, believing that he was still a formidable warrior. This was always the failing of a weakening Mag; they held onto the idea of their former selves.

Cautiously the Curver pushed open the stone door, in his hand a tiny scroll from a messenger bird. His excuse for coming.

The Mag was sprawled in front of the fire, half-naked with open eyes that only saw whatever he imagined in his state of drug-induced bliss. The Curver stood over his prone body and smiled. Most of the Mag's once impressive torso had small V-shaped scars as though pierced by a shower of arrows. The marks left after administering the dark berry dust. More interesting to the Curver was what hung around his neck. A tiny glass vial with liquid Crystal that shone with gold light. He reached down and stroked it with a finger. One tug and the fine chain would snap and that which bonded the Aulex to the Master would bond them to him. But even with the Aulex on his side, he knew it would take more than the vanishing creatures to sway the hearts and minds of the Sturgar.

In the beginning, Mag'Sood was perfect. Strong, powerful and self-assured. Once the Master had believed bringing the shoken to heel was the way to rule the Trilands. Now they were just slaughtering them. Burning their cities. Killing their livestock. A fear-inducing scheme which had served them well. Now shoken were more than ready to bow down. If they had waited and captured the shoken king as planned, he would have yielded to save his people.

The king had fled and as long as he was out there, mustering his army, the war would go on for years.

Curver Thist sat on his haunches next to the Master and picked up a dark-berry spilt on the floor and crushed it between finger and thumb. He looked at his Mag – it was easy to find the new wound as blood seeped around the edges. The Curver pulled back the skin and sprinkled the dust onto the flayed flesh. Mag'Sood's teeth chattered with pleasure as he writhed with ecstasy. Then he was still again, locked in his vision.

The dark-berry owned the Mag now. Every turn, he diminished a little more. Even the females, disliking his ruined flesh, had ceased to visit. That was something else he must remedy. In their collective memory, the Sturgar remembered his magnificence and many believed he was a God. He could kill the Mag now and take the crystal. But he, the Curver, was a runt and far from what the Sturgar imagined a leader to be. Getting the nation to call him Master would take all his cunning.

He would use a trick learned from Mag'Sood; religion was the best way to control the masses.

CHAPTER FIFTY-EIGHT

Junas pulled off her boots and examined her bleeding feet in the fading light. Crom stretched out beside her. The constant running did not bother the dog overmuch. He was happy, happier than when cooped up on the Greatship Ranghorn. Junas could walk the whole turn but the sense of urgency she felt made her run as fast as she was physically capable. Her boots were cheap and ill-fitting. She had thrown most of her belongings away. All she carried now was some coin, two knives, a blanket, food and the waterskins. She bought food from any farm they passed. There was no time to hunt even though there were many rabbits on the plain. The nearer they got to Valkarah, most of the farms were deserted. The ground was fertile and she helped herself to anything edible as they hurried by.

Eating while she walked or ran was possible, she wished sleep was so easy. Fatigue clung to her and even the dog fell asleep the moment they stopped. Junas found a dip in the ground that was dry enough after the rains. She knelt beside the dog and cut away some clumps of Crom's thick fur with her thumb knife. He did not seem to mind. She stuffed it into her boots, pulled them back on, and lay down beside him. She thanked Mother God for the good dog as she turned the egg that she kept strapped on and fell asleep.

The egg woke her. Vibrating.

Crom was sitting up staring into the blackness, hackles raised. Junas put a protective arm over the egg and drew her skinning knife. Something approached on soft feet. She heard a quiet growl, deep and reassuring. The words purring out of the darkness filled her heart with joy. Crom saw the change in her and wagged his tail.

The Faar emerged in the twilight, her stripes every shade of bronze, her eyes sky-blue. 'I am Lashka,' she said, bending her head so that Crom could sniff her. 'We must hurry, Junas Pathfinder,' she purred and turned for them to follow.

Dawn was breaking as they ran over the scorched earth. In the distance, a cloud of smoke hung over the palace of Valkarah. Parts of the city still burned. Junas had many questions but the Faar ran too fast for speech. All she could do was follow.

They came to a deserted shantytown roughly built from found stone and mud against the outer wall. The Faar slowed, sniffed the ground, came to stand before one of the dwellings, and called softly.

The door opened and a Sturgar stepped out. Junas drew her skinning knife. The Faar mother made reassuring noises at the back of her throat, pushed past him and went in.

Inside, a thin man sat on the floor and cradled a tiny baby with webbed hands.

Junas had no time to speak. The egg was cracking. She released it from the harness and held it gently. The Faar mother spoke to the Sturgar and he left and returned with an armful of bracken which he spread on the floor of the hut. She laid herself down in the nest he had made and Junas put the egg beside her.

'Bring me Llund's child,' she said. Orrld could not speak Faar and Junas said the words for him in Median. He took the baby over and she laid on her side revealing her teats. Orrld latched the baby on, smiling with relief. She would live now. Math had tried to find an animal to suckle her. He had run across the country looking for a goat or horse or cow but the Sturgar left nothing alive.

The egg split and a Faar cub crawled out and with the instinct of the new-born, fastened onto a teat beside the child.

In the many turns that followed, this became a familiar sight, the baby gripping her Faar mother's fur in her tiny fists with the stripy Faar cub beside her, purring contentedly.

Math and Junas took turns hunting food. When the infants were strong enough, they moved on. Math would run ahead and find a place for them to hide and come back for them. Slowly they left the fertile Meddant plain and passed through Kassen. By the time they got to the Plessic Coast, the infants were weaned and it was autumn. They hid in the white stone quarry. Like all the places they passed through it was deserted. The Sturgar were locusts, killing everything in their path. Those shoken who had survived had fled to the mountains.

The nights were growing longer and colder. The Faar cub and the shoken child curled up together in blissful sleep, while nearby the Healer also slept. Math had gone hunting with the dog, Crom. The Faar mother got up and padded over the rocks to where Junas kept watch.

'You must dress like a woman now and pose as the Healer's wife,' she purred. 'Get a passage across the sea and take them to Elat. That continent has a river, take a boat to the green land of Ardem. The river is wider there. Not so broad as the Ekress, yet the Healer will be happy.'

'You're leaving?' said Junas, looking into the bright blue of the Faar mother's eyes.

Lashka bowed her head and sighed. 'I must take our cub to his own kind so he may learn what he needs to know. And the Healer will teach the little one and give her a good heart.'

'What about the king? Won't he try to find us?'

'He will try and fail. When the war is almost won, he will find her. Until he comes, her identity must be secret. Many would like her dead or hostage. Tell the Strick child to teach her Faar.'

'He can't speak.'

'When he is full grown he will speak.'

'Will I not teach her?'

'No, Pathfinder. When you have guided them to Elat, you must go on. Parting will be hard and you will tell yourself that they are not safe without you and you need to stay with them. But as soon as you see the river you must take your leave,' she said, pressing her head gently onto Junas's chest.

Junas could not bear the thought of parting, even though she knew they could not all remain together, and stay safe.

'Where must I go?' she said, resting her head on top of the Faar mother's and breathing in the warm, safe smell of her fur.

'You have done your duty, Pathfinder. The Faar and the shoken ask no more of you. You may return to your homeland.'

Junas closed her eyes and thought of Samandarah. The thin sky-pinnacles piercing the blue sky. The parched earth and her family. Her little sister Arla would be half-grown by now. Too big to pick up, and she tried to imagine her child's face changed to a woman's. In the language of the Faar, there was a difference in the words spoken and the tone. The tone was asking. She could choose one or the other, tone or words. There was a reason they said you had to listen twice.

'What is it that you want, Lashka?'

'The Trevelyan Halflands.'

'Yes. I have maps of the settlement the Strick have built there.' Junas had told the Faar mother about the maps she had seen on the Greatship Ranghorn.

'You must teach Math these maps before you leave and any others that you think could be useful.'

'Why? I could stay and be their guide.'

'It is better if you return to your shoken child,' purred Lashka.

CHAPTER FIFTY-NINE

Curver Thist waited for a still night to visit the ice tombs. Ordinary Sturgar looked up as he walked along the raised ice-path in the light snow flurry. Some of them bowed but most took no notice when they saw him. Even though he was the Curver, in the eyes of the nation, he was a runt, and runts never commanded respect. He rarely left the castle and the intense cold was ever a shock. Only the privileged could walk here. Let them think whatever they liked, he *was* the Curver, and he did not have to jostle with the crowds below.

These raised paths snaked all over the territory now; Mag'Sood liked to be seen walking with the Aulex. He had to admit, it was a good strategy. The Sturgar nation responded to the sight of Mag'Sood and the She-Aulex with adulation.

The Curver stopped and looked out over the ice-dens that stretched far across the south side of Tarestone. Millions of them glowing gently in the dark from the cooking fires within. Outside young played, many almost naked. Born in the cold they did not react to it. He had known warmth in his youth and his blood yearned for heat. He shivered and took the north path. Soon he was alone; the north side was always empty. Pulling his cloak tighter, he descended the steps and walked over the smooth, polished ice toward a pair of tall, tapered pillars. In between, more frozen steps led deep within the ice crust. In the still air, his breath hung in a cloud of ice crystals.

Along the lantern-lit tomb tunnel stood Sturgar Mags and other males of note. The Curver walked without looking or stopping until he came to a fresh block of clear ice. Inside, preserved for eternity, stood the Shoken-Slayer.

Out of curiosity, he had once watched an interment. Observed the priests as they fitted a body into a carved icebox and poured in the purified water. Witnessed the pains they took to position the body before the water hardened, skilfully moving limbs and facial expression with long balac rods. The Shoken-Slayer looked as terrifying in death as he had in life and Curver Thist needed to stop himself from crouching. As all the corpses, he was naked and like every Mag or revered warrior, he had an erect penis. The Shoken-Slayer was a magnificent example of Sturgar virility in every way.

The frozen dead had open eyes. Over time, the eyes lost their expression but new bodies looked alive. The Curver stared. The red-lined pupils and the silver mark of the seeing metal on his forehead would continue to make the Shoken-Slayer a legend. A safe legend now, he thought.

Footsteps echoed through the tunnel. A priest approached. The Curver adopted a reverential stance; knees bent, hands on his hearts. The South Priest approached with the measured, intermittent step of his calling. Behind followed a child acolyte with a red glass lantern.

'Crotus blessed us with this warrior,' said the South Priest, taking the lantern.

'Indeed he did. Strange that one so strong should be taken without a fight...'

The Priest sent the acolyte scuttling away with a hiss.

'When we cleansed his body we could not find any sign of sickness. We looked for a hidden wound that might have festered. We found nothing.'

'Do you think...' the Curver looked about, checking they were alone. 'Do you think he was poisoned?'

'We searched for the signs. He was an imbiber of the dark berry...'

The Curver looked again at the Shoken-Slayer.

'There is little sign of his penchant for the berry. He did not cut the flesh, only drank the dust.'

The Curver knew that many warriors did this now. It was a kinder way and the signs that appeared on the body's extremities took longer to show. He could not see any blackening at the ends of fingertips and even the huge, erect penis was without blemish. He wondered what they did to stiffen them. He was sure even these virile Mags and warriors had not all died with an erection.

The South Priest was the keeper of the scriptures and dedicated to their constant study. Of all the four, he found him the most pious and unwavering in his belief. In the other three, he sensed doubts.

'I heard a rumour,' said the Curver in a low whisper.

They walked deeper into the unlit tombs. Here the bodies were ancient and their ice blocks clouded. In olden times, they did not know how to purify the water to make the ice clear. Many of the corpses had raised hands that pointed upward. He often wondered why. Some spiritual connection with the living, perhaps?

'What have you heard?'

'Oh, it was nothing, Eminence,' said the Curver, feigning modesty.

'Speak your truth…' said the South Priest, holding the light higher and casting a red glow over them both. The Curver bowed his head. 'It was only a rumour. I hear many things.' He paused. 'I heard that the Shoken-Slayer sought the Black Throne.'

The Priest did not look surprised and adjusted the heavy silver casing around his neck that contained his tail – cut off in dedication to Crotus. The Curver tried not to stare.

'I heard rumours that he was not as loyal to our Redeemer Mag'Sood as he professed,' he said.

The Priest made a low hiss.

'Do you think Crotus took him for his wrongdoing?' said the Curver.

'The death he suffered was painful and prolonged and although he writhed in agony no one could find the cause of his suffering.'

'Crotus,' whispered the Curver with affected reverence.

The South Priest muttered an ancient and unintelligible prayer. When he had finished the Curver said, 'Only a true God walks with the Aulex.'

'Yes. Yes,' breathed the South Priest with a beatific smile. 'The sacred Aulex can only be controlled by a God.'

The Curver felt the Priest's religious passion and wished he shared such unwavering faith.

CHAPTER SIXTY

Orrld feared the sea. The thought of the suffocating saltwater made him hide in the cloying cramped cabin below deck. Motion sickness and the sadness he felt now Lashka had left for Lak-Mur with Menneth the cub overwhelmed him. Math and Junas cared for the baby. His relief to touch dry land was short-lived. Junas and the dog, Crom, left soon after they arrived on Elat. Orrld cried until they disappeared over the horizon. He thought there was no more room for grief in his heart yet there was and he knew he cried for so much more than just this parting. His melancholy lasted for many turns and the baby, missing her Faar mother and brother and sensing his sadness, cried more.

At least the weather was warmer on Elat and they journeyed through a forest which Orrld liked. Math knew the way. Junas had taught him – scratching maps on the ground with sticks whenever she could. When he had re-drawn the map that Junas had shown him he would spend time making pictures of horses and prey birds, so beautiful it seemed a shame they were made from dust.

Orrld did not care where they were going. If not for the

baby, he would have died, or so he felt. Here on this strange land, they saw hardly any other shoken. He assumed there must be villages and towns hereabouts but Math, for safety, kept them well away. Before, Junas, posing as the boy Judd Koss, had gone into any towns they passed to buy supplies and came back with news. They learnt how the good king had led the remains of his army, Clisotians and common shoken alike, into the Meddant Mountains. How Valkarah had burnt for three turns and the Sturgar had danced in the flames. News of the king. No news of Llund.

Now they knew nothing and the silence was worse than the rumours.

From where he lay by the fire, Orrld watched Math holding the baby. Something in her Strick blood made her naturally more wakeful on the dark side of the turn. She was a big baby now, healthy and happy with a head of fair curls and bright blue eyes, the image of her father in almost every way.

Math was fully grown. A hulk of taut grey muscle. The linegold blades he carried on his skin glinted on his back where Math had moved them out of her reach.

At night, he often watched them. When they thought he slept, Math spoke. It was their secret. He had a quiet, deep shoken voice and he said her name over and again, 'Atini, Atini...' She laughed and coiled her skinny tail around his arm.

JOIN ME

Connecting with my readers is one of the best things about being a writer - I'd love you to pop over to my website and join my mailing list for author news and a free novella:

Dead Gift
www.djbowmansmith.com

CAN YOU HELP?

Thanks for reading Flame Treader - if you enjoyed it please could you leave a review as this really helps a great deal -

Thank You!

ALSO BY DJ BOWMAN-SMITH

The Crystal Bound Series in order:

King's Assassin

Blood Compass

Flame Treader

Legend of the Sleepers

Discover them all at:

www.djbowmansmith.com

ABOUT THE AUTHOR

DJ Bowman-Smith writes dark fantasy books for adults. She also writes for magazines and for children as Tiger Molly. She lives in Hampshire, England with her husband, an imaginary dog and a real cat.

ACKNOWLEDGMENTS

Special thanks as always go to my husband Paul for his unfailing support and encouragement. To my daughters Katie and Jenny for putting up with a mother who writes strange things. And my editor, Amanda Rutter for saving my writing from many mistakes.

Made in the USA
Middletown, DE
28 November 2022

16258189R00210